11Q

DESERT STAR

ALSO BY MICHAEL CONNELLY

FICTION

The Black Echo

The Black Ice

The Concrete Blonde

The Last Coyote

The Poet

Trunk Music

Blood Work

Angels Flight

Void Moon

A Darkness More Than Night

City of Bones

Chasing the Dime

Lost Light

The Narrows

The Closers

The Lincoln Lawyer

Echo Park

The Overlook

The Brass Verdict

The Scarecrow

Nine Dragons

The Reversal

The Fifth Witness

The Drop

The Black Box

The Gods of Guilt

The Burning Room

The Crossing

The Wrong Side of Goodbye

The Late Show

Two Kinds of Truth

Dark Sacred Night

The Night Fire

Fair Warning

The Law of Innocence

The Dark Hours

NONFICTION

Crime Beat

E-BOOKS

Suicide Run

Angle of Investigation

Mulholland Drive

The Safe Man

Switchblade

DESERT STAR

MICHAEL CONNELLY

Little, Brown and Company

New York   Boston   London

Copyright © 2022 by Hieronymus, Inc.

Little, Brown and Company
Hachette Book Group
1290 Avenue of the Americas, New York, NY 10104
littlebrown.com

First Edition: November 2022

Little, Brown and Company is a division of Hachette Book Group, Inc. The Little, Brown name and logo are trademarks of Hachette Book Group, Inc.

The Hachette Speakers Bureau provides a wide range of authors for speaking events. To find out more, go to hachettespeakersbureau.com or call (866) 376-6591.

ISBN 9780316485654 (hardcover) / 9780316505420 (signed edition) / 9780316505222 (B&N signed edition) / 9780316505321 (B&N Black Friday signed edition) / 9780316474627 (large print) / 9780316509879 (international edition)
LCCN 2022943383

10 9 8 7 6 5 4 3 2 1

FRI

Printed in Canada

In memory of Philip Spitzer,
who believed in Harry Bosch

PART 1

THE LIBRARY OF LOST SOULS

1

BOSCH HAD THE pills lined up on the table ready to go. He was pouring water from the bottle into the glass when the doorbell rang. He sat at the table, thinking he would let it go. His daughter had a key and never knocked, and he wasn't expecting anyone. It had to be a solicitor or a neighbor, and he didn't know any of his neighbors anymore. The neighborhood seemed to change over every few years, and after more than three decades of it, he had stopped meeting and greeting newcomers. He actually enjoyed being the cranky old ex-cop in the neighborhood whom people were afraid to approach.

But then the second ring was accompanied by a voice calling his name. It was a voice he recognized.

"Harry, I know you're in there. Your car's out front."

He opened the drawer under the tabletop. It contained plastic utensils, napkins, and chopsticks from takeout bags. With his hand he swept the pills into the drawer and closed it. He then got up and went to the door.

Renée Ballard stood on the front step. Bosch had not seen her in almost a year. She looked thinner than he remembered.

He could see where her blazer had bunched over the sidearm on her hip.

"Harry," she said.

"You cut your hair," he said.

"A while ago, yeah."

"What are you doing up here, Renée?"

She frowned as though she had expected a warmer reception. But Bosch didn't know why she would have after the way things had ended last year.

"Finbar," she said.

"What?" he said.

"You know what. Finbar McShane."

"What about him?"

"He's still out there. Somewhere. You want to try to make a case with me, or do you want to just stand on your anger?"

"What are you talking about?"

"If you let me in, I can tell you."

Bosch hesitated but then stepped back and held up an arm, grudgingly signaling her to enter.

Ballard walked in and stood near the table where Bosch had just been sitting.

"No music?" Ballard asked.

"Not today," Bosch said. "So, McShane?"

She nodded, understanding that she had to get to the point.

"They put me in charge of cold cases, Harry."

"Last I heard, the Open-Unsolved Unit was canceled. Disbanded because it wasn't as important as putting uniforms on the street."

"That's true, but things change. The department is under pressure to work cold cases. You know who Jake Pearlman is, right?"

"City councilman."

"He's actually your councilman. His kid sister was murdered way back. It was never solved. He got elected and found out the unit was quietly disbanded and there was nobody looking at cold cases."

"And so?"

"And so I got wind of it and went to the captain with a proposal. I move over from RHD and reconstitute the Open-Unsolved Unit—work cold cases."

"By yourself?"

"No, that's why I'm here. The tenth floor agreed: one sworn officer—me—and the rest of the unit composed of reserves and volunteers and contract players. I didn't come up with the idea. Other departments have been using the same model for a few years and they're clearing cases. It's a good model. In fact, it was your work for San Fernando that made me think of it."

"And so you want me on this…squad, or whatever you're calling it. I can't be a reserve. I wouldn't pass the physical. Run a mile in under ten minutes? Forget it."

"Right, so you'd volunteer or we'd make a contract. I pulled all the murder books on the Gallagher case. Six books for four murders—more stuff than you took with you, I'm sure. You could go back to work—*officially*—on McShane."

Bosch thought about that for a few moments. McShane had wiped out the whole Gallagher family in 2013 and buried them in the desert. But Bosch had never been able to prove it. And then he retired. He hadn't solved every case he'd been assigned in almost thirty years working murders. No homicide detective ever did. But this was a whole family. It was the one case he hated most to leave on the table.

"You know I didn't leave on good terms," he said. "I walked out before they could throw me out. Then I sued them. They'll never let me back in the door."

"If you want it, it's a done deal," Ballard said. "I already cleared it before I came here. It's a different captain now and different people. I have to be honest, Harry, not a lot of people there know about you. You been gone, what, five years? Six? It's a different department."

"They remember me up on ten, I bet."

The tenth floor of the Police Administration Building was where the Office of the Chief of Police and most of the department's commanders were located.

"Well, guess what, we don't even work out of the PAB," Ballard said. "We're out in Westchester at the new homicide archive. Takes a lot of the politics and prying eyes out of it."

That intrigued Bosch.

"Six books," he said, musing out loud.

"Stacked on an empty desk with your name on it," Ballard said.

Bosch had taken copies of many documents from the case with him when he retired. The chrono and all the reports he thought were most important. He had worked the case intermittently since his retirement but had to acknowledge he had gotten nowhere with it, and Finbar McShane was still out there somewhere and living free. Bosch had never found any solid evidence against him but he knew in his gut and in his soul that he was the one. He was guilty. Ballard's offer was tempting.

"So I come back and work the Gallagher Family case?" he said.

"Well, you work it, yeah," Ballard said. "But I need you to work other cases, too."

"There's always a catch."

"I need to show results. Show them how wrong they were to disband the unit. The Gallagher case is going to take some work—six books to review, no DNA or fingerprint evidence that is known. It's a shoe-leather case, and I'm fine with that, but I need to clear some cases to justify the unit and keep it going so you can work a six-book case. Will that be a problem?"

Bosch didn't answer at first. He thought about how a year earlier, Ballard had pulled the rug out on him. She had quit the department in frustration with the politics and bureaucracy, the misogyny, everything, and they had agreed to make a partnership and go private together. Then she told him she was going back, lured by a promise from the chief of police to allow her to pick her spot. She chose the Robbery-Homicide Division downtown and that was the end of the planned partnership.

"You know, I had started looking for offices," he said. "There was a nice two-room suite in a building behind the Hollywood Athletic Club."

"Harry, look," Ballard said. "I've apologized for how I handled that but you get part of the blame."

"Me? That's bullshit."

"No, you were the one who first told me you can better effect change in an organization from the inside than from the outside. And that's what I decided. So blame me if it makes you happy, but I actually did what you told me to do."

Bosch shook his head. He didn't remember telling her that but he knew it was what he felt. It was what he had told his daughter when she was considering joining the department in the wake of all the recent protests and cop hate.

"Okay, fine," he said. "I'll do it. Do I get a badge?"

"No badge, no gun," Ballard said. "But you do get that desk with the six books. When can you start?"

Bosch flashed for a moment on the pills he had lined up on the table a few minutes before.

"Whenever you want me to," he said.

"Good," Ballard said. "See you Monday, then. They'll have a pass for you at the front desk and then we'll get you an ID card. They'll have to take your photo and prints."

"Is that desk near a window?"

Bosch smiled when he said it. Ballard didn't.

"Don't press your luck," Ballard said.

2

BALLARD WAS AT her desk, writing a DNA budget proposal, when her phone buzzed. It was the officer at the front.

"I got a guy here, says he was supposed to have a pass waiting. Heron—Her—I can't say it. Last name is Bosch."

"Sorry, I forgot to set that up. Give him a visitor pass and send him back. He's going to be working here, so we'll have to make him an ID later. And it's Hieronymus. Rhymes with *anonymous*."

"Okay, sending him back."

Ballard put the phone down and got up to receive Bosch at the front door of the archive, knowing that he would be annoyed with the front-desk snafu. When she got there and opened the door, Bosch was standing six feet back, looking above her head at the wall over the door. She smiled.

"What do you think?" she said. "I had them paint that."

She stepped out into the hallway so she could turn and look up at the words above the door.

OPEN-UNSOLVED UNIT
Everybody Counts or Nobody Counts

Bosch shook his head. *Everybody counts or nobody counts* was the philosophy he always brought to homicide work, but it was also his personal philosophy. It wasn't a slogan and especially not one he liked seeing painted on a wall. It was something you felt and knew inside. Not something advertised, not something that could even be taught.

"Come on, we need something," Ballard said. "A motto. A code. I want some esprit de corps in this unit. We are going to kick ass."

Bosch didn't respond.

"Let's just go in and get you settled," Ballard said.

She led the way around a reception counter that fronted the rows of library shelving containing the murder books organized by year and case number. They moved down the aisle to the left of the shelves to the official work area of the reconstituted Open-Unsolved Unit. This was a collection of seven workstations connected by shared partition walls, three on each side and one at the end.

Two of the stations were occupied, the heads of the investigators just cresting the top of the privacy partitions. Ballard stopped at the cubicle at the end of the pod.

"I'm here," she said. "And I've got you set up right here."

She pointed to a cubicle that shared a partial wall with hers, and Bosch moved around to it. Ballard stepped all the way into hers and folded her arms on the partition so she could look down at his desk. She had already stacked murder books in two separate piles, one big and one small, on the work surface.

"The big pile is Gallagher—I'm sure you recognize that."

"And this?"

Bosch was opening the top binder in the smaller two-book pile.

"That's the catch," Ballard said. "It's Sarah Pearlman. I want you to start with a review of that."

"The councilman's sister," Bosch said. "You didn't already look at this?"

"I did, and it looks pretty hopeless. But I want your take on it—before I go back to the councilman with the bad news."

Bosch nodded.

"I'll take a look," he said.

"Before you dive in, let me introduce you to Lilia and Thomas," Ballard said.

Ballard stepped down to the end of the pod configuration. The last two workstations were occupied by a man and a woman who looked like they were mid to late fifties. Ballard was closest to the man and put her hand on his shoulder as she introduced him. Both gave off professional vibes. The man's suit jacket was draped over the back of his chair. He wore a tie pulled tight at the collar. He had dark hair and a mustache and wore half glasses for the desk work. The woman had dark hair and was dark complected. She was dressed like Ballard always dressed, in a woman's suit with a white blouse. She had an American flag pin on her lapel and Bosch wondered if that was to deflect questions about whether she was a foreigner.

"This is Thomas Laffont, who just joined us last week," Ballard said. "He's FBI-retired and I've paired him with Lilia Aghzafi, who did twenty years with Vegas Metro before wanting to see the ocean and retiring out here. Tom and Lilia are reviewing cases to find candidates for genetic genealogy follow-up, which you may have heard is all the rage in cold case circles."

Bosch shook hands and nodded to the two investigators.

"This is Harry Bosch," Ballard said. "Retired LAPD. He won't toot his own horn, so I will. He was one of the founding members of the old cold case unit and basically has more years in homicide than anybody in the entire police department."

Ballard then watched Bosch clumsily handle the how-ya-doin's and small talk. He was not good at hiding his long-held distrust of the FBI. She finally rescued him and took him back to his workstation, telling Aghzafi and Laffont that she had more to go through with the "rookie" member of the squad.

Back at the other end of the pod, they moved into their workstations and Ballard once again stood and leaned over the privacy wall so she could see him while they spoke.

"Wow," she said. "I just noticed you got rid of the porn-stache. Was that since we talked?"

She was sure it was. She would have noticed its absence up at his house. Bosch's face reddened as his eyes darted to the other end of the pod to see if Aghzafi and Laffont had heard the comment. He then rubbed his upper lip with a thumb and forefinger as if to make sure he no longer had a mustache.

"It was turning white," he said.

No other explanation was offered. But Ballard knew it had been turning white since before she had even met Bosch.

"I'm sure Maddie's happy about that," she said.

"She hasn't seen it," he said.

"Well, how is she doing?"

"As far as I know, fine. Working a lot."

"I heard she was assigned to Hollywood Division out of the academy. Lucky girl."

"Yeah, she's over there on mid-watch. So, this genealogy stuff, how's that work?"

It was clear to Ballard that Bosch was uncomfortable with the personal questions and was grasping at anything to change the subject.

"You're not going to have to worry about it," she said. "It's good and valid, but it's science, so it's expensive. It's the one place I have to pick our shots. We got a grant from the Ahmanson Foundation, which donated this whole place, but a full genetic rundown costs about eighteen grand if we go outside the department. So we have to pick and choose wisely. I have Tom and Lilia on that, and another investigator you'll probably meet tomorrow. We have carte blanche on regular DNA analysis because it's all in-house now. With those, we just have to get in line and wait. I also get one move-to-the-front-of-the-line card I can play each month. The chief gave me that. He also gave us a lab tech specifically assigned to work with our unit's cases."

"Nice of him."

"Yeah, but let's get back to your orientation. What I'm requiring of our reserves and volunteers is that they give me at least one day a week. Most of them are doing more than that but I stagger them so that we have at least one body in here Monday to Thursday. I'm here full-time and I have Tom and Lilia come on Monday, Paul Masser and Colleen Hatteras on Tuesday, Lou Rawls on Wednesday, and now you...I would say Thursday, but I know you'll be here much more than that. Most of these guys are as well."

"Lou Rawls—really?"

"No. And he's not even Black. His name is Ted Rawls, and after he'd spent ten years as a cop, it would have been impossible not to come out of that with the obvious nickname. So some people still call him Lou and he seems to like it."

Bosch nodded.

"You should know, though," Ballard said, leaning forward and lowering her voice so it just barely made it over the privacy wall. "Rawls wasn't my pick."

Bosch rolled his chair in closer to his desk to hear better and complete the confidentiality huddle.

"What do you mean?" he asked.

"We have more applications than we have seats in the pod," Ballard said. "The chief gave me the go-ahead to pick who I want and that's what I've done, but Lou Rawls was a Pearlman pick."

"The councilman."

"He's very proprietary about this, he and his chief of staff. It's about his sister but it's also about politics. He's got higher aspirations than city council, and the success of this unit can help. So he put Rawls in and I had to take him."

"I've never heard of him and I think I would have with a name like that. He's not LAPD, right?"

"No, he's retired Santa Monica, but that was fifteen years ago, so he doesn't bring a lot to the table. A lot of hand-holding required, and the thing of it is, he's a direct pipeline to Pearlman and Hastings."

"Hastings?"

"Nelson Hastings, Pearlman's chief of staff. The three of them are like best buds or something. Rawls quit Santa Monica PD after ten years to go into business. So to him this is just a side gig."

"What's the business? Is he a PI?"

"No, it's a business business. He owns a bunch of those mail-drop places. Like UPS, FedEx, box-and-packaging stores.

Apparently he's got them all over the city and does pretty well. He drives a fancy car and has a house in Santa Monica in the college streets. And my guess is he's one of Pearlman's main campaign supporters."

Bosch nodded. He got the picture. A quid pro quo. Ballard leaned back and sat down after realizing that their whispering had been noticed by Laffont and Aghzafi. She could still see Bosch's eyes over the partition. She continued in a regular tone.

"You'll meet Paul and Colleen tomorrow," she said. "They're solid. Masser is a retired deputy D.A. who worked in Major Crimes, so he's helpful on the search warrants and legal questions and strategies. It's good to have him in-house instead of needing to call the D.A.'s Office every time we have a question."

"I think I remember him," Bosch said. "And Hatteras?"

"No law enforcement experience. She's our in-house geneal-ogist and what they call a 'citizen sleuth.'"

"An amateur. For real?"

"For real. She's a great internet researcher, and that's where it's at with the genetic stuff. IGG—you know what that is, don't you?"

"Uh…"

"Investigative genetic genealogy. You upload your suspect's DNA to GEDmatch, which accesses a number of databases, and you sit back and wait for a hit. You must know about this. It was trending big time in cold case investigations until the privacy police arrived, and now it's a limited resource but still worth pursuing."

"How they caught the Golden State Killer, right?"

"Exactly. You put in the DNA, and if you're lucky, you get connections to relatives. A fourth cousin here, a brother nobody knew about there. Then it becomes social engineering. Making contact online, building a family tree with the hope that one branch leads to your guy."

"And you have a private citizen doing this."

"She's an expert, Harry. Just give her a chance. I like her and I think she's going to work out for us."

She could see full skepticism in Bosch's eyes as he looked away from her.

"What?"

"Is this all going to end up in a podcast? Or are we going to make cases?"

Ballard shook her head. She knew he would act this way.

"You'll see, Harry," Ballard said. "You don't have to work with her but I'm betting you will want to eventually. That's how sure I am. Okay?"

"Okay," Bosch said. "I'm not trying to cause trouble. I'm just happy to be here. You're the boss and I never question the boss."

"Yeah, right. That'll be the day."

Bosch looked around the room and the pod.

"So, I'm the last guy in," he said.

"But the first I wanted," Ballard said. "I just needed to have everything in place before I visited you."

"And you had to make sure I was cleared."

"Well, that, too."

Bosch nodded.

"So, where's somebody get a cup of coffee around here?" he asked.

"There's a kitchen with coffee and a fridge," Ballard said. "You go out through—"

"I'll take him," Laffont said. "I need a jolt myself."

"Thanks, Tom," Ballard said.

Laffont stood up and asked if anyone else wanted coffee. Ballard and Aghzafi declined, and Bosch followed Laffont to the front of the archive room.

Ballard watched them go, hoping Bosch would play nice with the former FBI agent and not cause a clash on his first day on the job.

3

BOSCH WAS USED to being alone in his house when he went through old files and murder books and tried to think of case moves not thought of before. It was largely silent work. He now had to get used to working in a squad room again and relearn the skill of tuning out conversations around him so he could focus on the job at hand.

While Ballard worked the phones and the political demands of her job on the other side of a useless privacy wall, he opened the first of three murder books containing the records of the so-far-unsuccessful Sarah Pearlman investigation.

He started with the binder marked VOLUME 1 and immediately went to the table of contents. All crime scene and forensic photos were listed as located in the third volume. He moved to that binder. He wanted to start with the photos, knowing nothing about the case but seeing what the investigators saw on the morning of June 11, 1994, when Sarah's mutilated body was found in her bed at her family's home on Maravilla Drive in the Hollywood Hills.

The third murder book contained several clear plastic sleeves clipped to its rings, each holding two 5 x 7 color photos front and back. The pictures were standard harshly lit color photos in which blood looked purple-black, white skin was turned alabaster, and the victim was robbed of her humanity. Sarah Pearlman was just sixteen when her life was brutally ended by a rapist who had choked and stabbed her. In the first photos, Sarah's body was splayed on the bed with a flannel nightgown pulled up over the exposed torso to cover her face. Bosch initially took the positioning of the nightgown as an effort by the killer to keep the victim from seeing his features. But as he flipped through the photo sleeves, it became clear that the nightgown was pulled up after she had been attacked and killed. Bosch now recognized it as an action of regret. The killer covered his victim's face so he would no longer have to see it.

There were multiple stab wounds to the chest and neck of the victim, and blood had soaked the sheets and comforter and coagulated around the body. It was also clear from bruising around the neck that the victim had been choked at some point during the ordeal. Counting the years of war and police work, Bosch had been looking at the unnatural cause of death for more than half a century. To say he got used to seeing the depravity and cruelty that humans inflict upon each other would be wrong, but he had long ago stopped thinking of these explosions of violence as aberrations. He had lost much of his faith in the goodness of people. To him the violence wasn't the departure from the norm. It was the norm.

He knew this was a pessimistic view of the world, but fifty years of toiling in the fields of blood had left him without much hope. He knew that the dark engine of murder would never run low on fuel. Not in his lifetime. Not in anyone's.

He continued to flip through the photos, to imprint them

permanently on his mind. He knew this was the way for him. It was the way to enrage him, to inextricably bind him to a victim he had seen only in photos. It would ignite the fire he needed.

After the crime scene photos came forensic photos, individual shots of evidence and possible pieces of evidence. These included shots of blood spatter on the wall above the headboard and the ceiling over the victim, photos of her torn underwear discarded on the floor, an orthodontic retainer found in the folds of the bed's comforter.

There were several photos of fingerprints that had been identified by latent techs, dusted and then taped. Bosch knew that these would likely match the victim, since she had inhabited the bedroom. Notations made on these by the original investigators bore this out. But one photo of what appeared to be the bottom half of a palm print had UNK marked on it. *Unknown.* Its location was a windowsill and its positioning on the sill indicated that it was left by someone climbing in through the window.

In 1994 the partial palm print would have been useless unless directly compared to a suspect's. Bosch was working homicides then and knew there were no palm-print databases at the time. Even now, almost three decades later, there were few palm prints on file or in databases for comparison.

Bosch looked over the partition at Ballard. She had just hung up from a call with a local businessman known for building hundreds of apartments in downtown. She had been asking him to join the cause and financially support the work of the Open-Unsolved Unit.

"How'd that go?" he asked.

"I'll find out," Ballard said. "We'll see if he strokes out a check. The Police Foundation gave me a list of previous donors. I try to call two or three a day."

"Did you know you'd be doing that when you signed up for this?"

"Not really. But I don't mind. I kind of like guilting people into giving us money. You'd be surprised how many knew somebody who was a victim of an unsolved crime."

"I don't think I would be."

"Yeah, I guess probably not. How's Pearlman looking?"

"Still on the photos."

"I knew you'd start there. It was a bad one."

"Yeah."

"Any initial impressions?"

"Not yet. I want to look again. But the palm print—the partial. I take it you ran it through present-day databases?"

"Yep. First thing. Got nothing."

Bosch nodded. It wasn't a surprise.

"And ViCAP?"

"Nada—no matches."

ViCAP was an FBI program that included a database of violent crimes and serial offenders. But it was widely known for not being a complete database. Many law enforcement agencies did not require detectives to enter cases because of the time it took to fill out the ViCAP surveys.

"Looking at the photos, it's hard to believe this was a one-time thing."

"Agreed. Besides ViCAP, I put calls out to cold case squads from San Diego to San Francisco. No hits, no similars. I even called your old pal Rick Jackson. He's working cold cases for

San Mateo County. He called around for me up there, but no dice."

Jackson was a retired LAPD homicide detective of Bosch's era.

"How's Rick doing?" Bosch asked.

"Sounds like he's closing cases right and left," Ballard said. "What I hope we start doing down here."

"Don't worry. We will."

"So, listen. On Mondays I go to the PAB to meet with the captain and update him on the work, the budget, and all of that. I'll probably be downtown till I go home for the day. Are you good? Tom and Lilia can help if you need anything."

"I'm good. What are the rules about taking stuff home?"

"You can't take the books out of here. Sort of defeats the purpose of having all the unsolveds in the same place, you know?"

"Got it. Is there a copier?"

"Don't copy files, Harry. I don't want to get into a thing with the captain about that."

Bosch nodded.

"Okay?" Ballard said. "I really mean it."

"Got it," Bosch said.

"Okay, then, happy hunting. Think you'll be back tomorrow? No pressure."

"I think I'll be back."

"Good, I'll see you then."

"Right."

Bosch watched Ballard head out, then glanced to the end of the pod to check on Laffont and Aghzafi. He could see only the tops of their heads over the privacy walls. He went back to work, paging through the crime scene photos again so the images would be permanently seared into memory. Once he was through with the photos, he pulled volume 1 back over and started his review at the beginning.

The original investigators on the case were Dexter Kilmartin and Philip Rossler. Bosch knew the names but not the men. They were assigned to the Robbery-Homicide Division, which handled the major cases citywide. He turned to the chronological log they had kept. It showed that detectives from the Hollywood Division homicide unit initially responded to the case on the morning of June 11, but it was quickly turned over to the RHD heavies because, as a sex crime against a sixteen-year-old minor in the Hollywood Hills, it was bound to draw significant media attention.

Bosch was working Hollywood Homicide at the time but was not on the initial callout because it was not his and his partner Jerry Edgar's turn on the rotation. But he had vague memories of the case and its quick acquisition by RHD. Little did they know that the case would hold media interest for just one day. The next night, the ex-wife of football great and not-so-great actor O. J. Simpson would be found murdered along with an acquaintance in Brentwood, and that would suck all media attention away from the Pearlman case as well as everything else in the city. The Brentwood murders would garner intense media scrutiny for the next year and beyond, and there would be none left for Sarah Pearlman.

Except for Kilmartin and Rossler. The chrono showed that they made all the right moves, in Bosch's estimation. Most important, they held back from making an early determination about whether this was a stranger murder. The fact that the killer had entered through an unlocked or open window in the victim's bedroom suggested that the intruder was likely unknown to the victim, but it did not dissuade the detectives from conducting a full field investigation. They pursued an extensive background check on the victim and questioned numerous friends and family members. Sarah attended a private all-girls school in Hancock Park. Though school was out for the summer, the investigators spent several days locating and interviewing classmates, friends, and faculty in a full-scale attempt to draw a picture of the young girl's world and social life. The week before the murder, Sarah had started a summer job as a greeter at a restaurant on Melrose Avenue called Tommy Tang's. She had worked at the popular Thai restaurant the summer before and was already known and liked by several employees. They were questioned, and the detectives went so far as to study the restaurant's credit-card receipts for the days Sarah had worked. They traced and questioned several customers, but none rose to the level of suspect.

The investigation also included the victim's parents. Sarah's father was a lawyer who specialized in large real-estate transactions. The detectives interviewed many in his practice and business dealings, including clients who might have been unhappy with his work, as well as some of those on the other side of his more difficult negotiations. No one emerged as a suspect.

Finally, there was Sarah's ex-boyfriend. Four months before her death, she had broken up with a short-term boyfriend named Bryan Richmond, whom she had met at an annual social between her school and an all-boys school also in Hancock Park. He was extensively questioned and investigated but ultimately cleared. He had moved on from the relationship and had been dating someone new.

At the time of the murder, Sarah's parents were on a golfing vacation in Carmel, playing the courses at and around Pebble Beach. Sarah was staying at home with her brother, Jake, two years older. On the Friday night of the murder, Sarah had worked at the restaurant and then returned home at about 10 p.m. to the house on Maravilla. She was licensed and had use of her mother's car while she was gone. Jake Pearlman was out with his girlfriend and didn't return home till midnight. His mother's car was in the garage and his sister's bedroom door was closed. He chose not to disturb her because he could see no light on beneath the door and assumed she was asleep.

In the morning, Sarah's mother called home to check on her children. Jake told her he had not seen Sarah yet. As it was approaching 11 a.m., she told Jake to go to his sister's room and wake her so she could talk on the phone. That was when he discovered that Sarah had been brutally murdered in her own bed, and the family's nightmare began.

Bosch took no notes as he reviewed the many interview summaries in volume 1. The original investigation was thorough and seemed complete. Bosch saw nothing overlooked or needing follow-up. When he had previously worked in the Open-Unsolved Unit, it had not been unusual for him to review a case and see the poor or even lazy quality of a murder investigation. Such was not the case with Sarah Pearlman. It appeared to Bosch that Kilmartin and Rossler had taken the case to heart and had left no stone unturned. And what made this even more impressive to Bosch was the fact that at the time of their investigation, the victim was not related to a powerful politician. That would come many years later.

Two hours into his review, he moved on to volume 2, the

second murder book, and found the binder to be stocked by update summaries at thirty days, ninety days, six months, and then annually for five years before the case was officially classified as cold and inactive. No suspect or even person of interest ever emerged, and no determination of whether Sarah knew her killer was ever made.

The back of the volume 2 binder was where ancillary records of inquiries by the victim's family and others were kept over the years. These showed that Sarah Pearlman's parents made numerous calls asking for updates until these stopped seven years earlier. The inquiries were then taken up by Councilman Jake Pearlman or came from his chief of staff, Nelson Hastings. Bosch took this transition to mean that Sarah Pearlman's parents had died without ever seeing justice for their daughter.

Bosch finished his review by going back to the photos in volume 3 and slowly paging through the plastic sleeves, once more looking for anything in Sarah's bedroom that would possibly stand out as a missed lead or piece of evidence.

He finally came to the forensic shots and the final sleeve, which contained a photo of the print card on which a latent tech had taped the partial palm print. He was staring at it when he felt a peripheral presence and looked up to see that Tom Laffont had stepped over from his workstation.

"All good?" he asked.

"Uh, yeah, good," Bosch said. "Just reviewing this."

Bosch felt awkward with Laffont studying him.

"She's got you on the big one, huh?" Laffont said.

"What do you mean?" Bosch asked.

"The councilman's sister. I get the feeling if we don't solve it, we won't be around for very long."

"You think?"

"Well, Ballard sure spends a lot of time on the phone with him. You know, giving him the blow-by-blow of what we're doing here. The conversations always seem to come back to the little sister. So she's under pressure, no doubt."

Bosch just nodded.

"You find anything we need to do?" Laffont pressed. "Would love to close that one."

"Not yet," Bosch said. "Still looking."

"Well, good luck. You're going to need it."

"What did you do with the Bureau? Were you in the L.A. field office?"

"Started in San Diego, did stints in Sacramento and Oakland before finishing down here. Was on the Major Crimes squad. I punched out at twenty. Got kind of sick of chasing bank robbers."

"I think I get that."

"Lilia and I are done for the day. Welcome, and I'll see you next time."

"Next time."

Bosch watched Laffont and Aghzafi gather their things and head out. He waited a beat, then got up to look for a copy machine.

On his way to the archive room exit, Bosch stopped and looked down one of the aisles. Shelves on each side were lined with murder books. Some new blue and some faded, a few of the cases contained in white binders. He stepped into the aisle and walked slowly past the books, running the fingers of his left hand along the plastic bindings as he passed. Each one the story of a murder left unsolved. This was hallowed ground to Bosch.

The library of lost souls. Too many for him and Ballard and the others to ever solve. Too many to ever soothe the pain.

When he reached the end of the aisle, he made the turn and walked down the next row. The shelves were similarly stacked with cases. A skylight window above brought the afternoon sun down, throwing natural light on unnatural death. Bosch paused for a moment and stood still. There was only silence in the library of lost souls.

4

BALLARD PICKED PINTO up at the daycare on Hillhurst and walked him on a leash back to her apartment. He was a ten-pound Chihuahua mix but he managed to pull hard against the leash, his body clock telling him dinner was at the end of the walk.

As she got to the steps leading to the front door of her building, Ballard got a call and saw Bosch's name on the caller ID.

"Harry?"

She could hear music in the background. Jazz. She assumed he was home.

"Hey. Where are you at?" he asked.

"About to walk in the door at my place," Ballard said. "What is that? Sounds nice."

"Clifford Brown with Strings."

"So, did you finish your review?"

"Did. Went through it a couple times."

"And?"

"And the original team did a good job. Actually, a really good job. I saw no flaws."

Ballard had not really expected Bosch to break the case or

even find a flaw in the original investigation. She had reviewed the files herself and had found no strings to tug or stone left unturned.

"Well, it was worth the shot," she said. "I'll set up a call with the councilman and let him know that we—"

"I'm looking at the photo of the palm print," Bosch said. "The partial."

"What do you mean you're looking at it? I thought you were home."

"I am home."

"So you made copies when I told you not to. That's a great first day, Harry. Already you—"

"Do you want to hear what I'm thinking, or do you want to fire me for breaking the rules?"

She was silent for a moment before letting his infraction go.

"Fine. What are you thinking?"

"This is just a photo. Is the actual print card still around, or was it digitized and destroyed?"

"They don't destroy print cards, because all digital matches are followed up with a visual confirmation using the actual print before it can go to court. It's current protocol. Why do you want the original card?"

"Because when they picked up the print with the tape, I don't know, maybe they got—"

"Some DNA."

"Yeah."

"Holy shit, Harry, that might actually work. I wonder if that's been done before."

"One way to find out."

"I'll talk to the lab first thing tomorrow."

"You should pull the print—make sure it's still there after twenty-eight years—protocol or not."

"I will and then I'll take it to the lab. This is good, Harry. I should have thought of it, but that's why I have you. It gives me hope, and that will give Councilman Pearlman hope."

"I don't think I would tell him about this until you find out if it's got a shot, you know."

"You're right. Let's see where it goes first. It's not really Pearlman I talk to over there, anyway. His chief of staff is constantly up my ass about results."

Bosch realized that Laffont had been wrong about who she spent time with on the phone. It was Hastings, not Pearlman.

"Yeah, Hastings," he said. "I saw his name in the murder book. Maybe this will shut him up."

"Harry, thank you," Ballard said. "This is why I brought you on the team. And you already came through."

"Not yet. Let's see what the lab says."

"Well, I think you can move on to the Gallagher case if you want now."

"Okay. I'll start on it."

"Let me guess, you already copied the files you didn't already have?"

"Not yet."

"Then I'll see you tomorrow at Ahmanson?"

"See you tomorrow."

Ballard hung up, then punched in the combo on the gate and entered her building.

After feeding the dog and changing into sweats, Ballard called in a pickup order of cacio e pepe pasta to Little Dom's down the street. She had a half hour before pickup, so she opened her laptop on the kitchen table and went to work, trying to find a case where DNA had been extracted from fingerprints.

A basic search turned up nothing and she grew frustrated. She grabbed her phone off the counter and called the cell phone of Darcy Troy, the DNA tech assigned to handle cases from the Open-Unsolved Unit.

"Hey, girl."

"Darcy, how's it going?"

"Can't complain unless you're going to hit me up with something."

"I just have a question for the moment."

"Shoot."

"Have you ever heard of DNA being pulled off a fingerprint or a palm print?"

"I've heard it talked about at the forensic conferences, but are you talking about case law sanctioning it?"

"No, more like whether you can get DNA from prints."

"Fingerprints are made from the oils on your fingers. It's still bodily fluid."

"Palm prints, too?"

"Sure. And if you get people with sweaty palms, then you probably stand a better chance."

"Sweaty like from being about to commit a crime like rape and murder?"

"There you go."

"How would you like to be the first at the LAPD to try it?"

"I could use the change of pace. Whaddaya got?"

"I'm not sure I've got anything yet. But one of my guys is looking at a case from '94—home invasion, rape, and murder—and they pulled half a palm print off the windowsill on the suspected entry point."

"How was it collected?"

"Dusted with gray powder and taped to a white card."

"Shit, that doesn't make it easy. The powder would have absorbed the oil, and the tape they used won't help. But I could take a look."

"First thing tomorrow I'm going to latents to pull it."

"If it's still there, you mean."

"Should be. It's an open case. No RDO."

The department issued records disposal orders to the evidence units only when a case was solved and considered completed.

"Well, if you find it, bring it to me. I won't even count it as your jump-the-line pass for this month. Just because this is something new."

"That sounds like a deal I can't refuse. I'm going to go now before you change your mind."

Both women laughed.

"See you tomorrow, Darcy."

Ballard disconnected and checked the time. She had to go pick up her food. She grabbed the leash and hooked it to Pinto's collar, then headed out. Little Dom's was two blocks away. The restaurant people there knew her well from in-person and take-out orders on a weekly basis. It had been her go-to place since she moved into the neighborhood. Her food was ready and waiting and still hot. And there was even a dog biscuit for Pinto.

5

BOSCH LEFT HIS home before dawn because he wanted to get to his destination while the sun was still low in the sky. He got up to the 210 freeway and headed east in very light traffic until he reached the 15 and turned northeast, joining the cars headed toward Las Vegas. But short of the Nevada border he jogged directly north on Death Valley Road and into the Mojave Desert. The road cut across a barren land of brush and sand, the low-lying salt pan off in the distance, glowing white in the morning sun like snow.

At the Old Spanish Trail to Tecopa he pulled off the road by an Inyo County Sheriff's Department call box and cell tower powered by a sun panel. He put on a Dodgers cap and got out in the sun. It was 7 a.m. and already 79 degrees according to his phone. He walked past the call box and about thirty feet into the brush. He found the spot easily. The lone mesquite tree was still there, partially shading the four columns of rocks piled one on top of another to create a sculpture of sorts marking where the grave had been found. Three of the rock columns had crumbled over time, knocked down by desert winds or earthquakes.

To Bosch it was another place of hallowed ground. It was where an entire family had ended. A father, mother, daughter, and son murdered and then buried in the rock and sand, never to be found had it not been for a Cal State geological expedition studying the nearby salt pan for evidence of climate change.

Bosch noticed that a profusion of flowers had sprouted around the rocks and the trunk of the mesquite tree. Each flower had a yellow button center surrounded by white petals. They were low to the ground and probably pulling water as well as shade from the mesquite, which Bosch knew could send roots eighty feet down through the rock and sand and salt to find water. They were built to stand tall in the harshest of environments.

Bosch didn't plan to stay long. But he knew that this had to be the starting point to the work he was beginning. Before going once more into the abyss, he had to find his grounding in the case. The emotional core. And he knew without a doubt that he was standing at it. The media and everybody else called it the Gallagher case. Bosch never did. He could not diminish it that way. To him it was the Gallagher Family case. An entire family had been murdered. Taken from their home in the night. Found here by happenstance a year later.

Squatting down amid the flowers, Bosch started to rebuild the rock columns, carefully stacking them again in solid balance. He was wearing old jeans and work boots. He was careful not to catch a finger beneath the heavier rocks as he restacked them. He knew that nature would eventually undo his work here but he felt the need to rebuild the rock garden as he began to rebuild the case.

He was almost finished when he heard a vehicle on the road

behind him and the crush of sand and stone as it pulled off the paved road and came to a stop. Bosch glanced over his shoulder and saw the markings on the white SUV: INYO COUNTY SHERIFF'S DEPARTMENT.

A lone man in uniform made his way across the scrub to get to Bosch.

"Harry," he said. "This is a surprise."

"Beto," Bosch said. "I could say the same. You just happened to be passing by in the middle of nowhere?"

"No, couple years ago we put a camera on the sun panel by the street. I get alerts. I saw a car pull over and then I saw it was you. Been a long time, brother."

"Long time is right."

Beto Orestes was the Inyo County investigator who first responded to the call about bodies being found in the desert eight years before. The grim discovery led to a unique partnership between Orestes and Bosch and their departments. The crimes committed against the Gallagher family were Los Angeles–based but the bodies were found in Inyo County. While the LAPD took the lead on the case, the crime scene investigation was headed by Orestes and run by his department. An ancillary investigation went into why this spot in the desert was chosen and whether it was completely random or possibly a decision that could help identify and link a suspect. It didn't lead to a conclusion but it was thorough, and Orestes had impressed Bosch with his commitment to the case.

As the weeks and then months went by, Inyo County's involvement grew less and less. Orestes' superiors viewed it as an L.A. case inconveniently located in their jurisdiction. Orestes was handed other investigations and responsibilities. Meantime,

Bosch was also taken off full-time status on the investigation and given other unsolved cases to pursue until he retired. As the two departments pulled back, and the Open-Unsolved unit was disbanded, the Gallagher Family case fell through the cracks between them.

"I called to check on you about a year ago and they told me you were retired," Orestes said. "Now I find you in the rock garden we made all those years ago."

"I'm back on it, Beto," Bosch said. "I thought I should start here."

"They take you back?"

"On a voluntary basis."

"Well, anything I can do, you know how to get me."

"I do."

Bosch stood up and dusted off his pants. He was done here. Orestes reached down and picked one of the flowers.

"Hard to believe something so beautiful can exist in this place," he said. "And people say there is no God. You ask me, there's God right there."

He turned the stem between his fingers, and the flower turned like a pinwheel.

"You know what that is?" Bosch asked.

"Sure," Orestes said. "This one's called the desert star."

Bosch nodded. He wasn't convinced that it was God on earth, but he liked that.

They started back toward their vehicles.

"What about McShane?" Orestes asked. "He poke his head up somewhere?"

"Not as far as I know," Bosch said. "But I haven't started to look again. I will today."

"What's 'on a voluntary basis' actually mean, Harry?"

"The cold case unit is run by one sworn officer, and the rest are part-timers and volunteers."

"You know, you always struck me as the kind of guy who would do it even if they didn't pay you."

"Yeah, well, I guess so."

They got to the road and Orestes studied Bosch's old Cherokee.

"That thing going to make it?" he asked. "I got five gallons of water if you want to top off the radiator."

"No, I'll be fine," Bosch said. "The engine's solid but the AC not so much. That's why I came out early."

"So, let me know how it goes, yeah?"

"I will."

Orestes started toward his SUV and threw a line over his shoulder.

"I'd sure like to see this one cleared before I'm done," he said.

"Me, too," Bosch said. "Me, too."

6

BALLARD ENTERED THE homicide archive, expecting to find Bosch at his workstation reviewing the Gallagher books. She was excited to update him on her trip to Piper Tech and then to the DNA lab that morning. But there was no Bosch.

Paul Masser, Lou Rawls, and Colleen Hatteras were at their stations and she greeted them. Rawls was in a day before his assigned day. Ballard took this as a sign that he had caught a break on one of the cases he was working or he was just eager to meet the newest team member, Harry Bosch. She decided that it was likely the latter, as his case work moved at a glacial pace with breaks being elusive. In fact, he was the the first official member of the team but had yet to close a case—even a gimme, like a direct DNA case match.

"I thought we were going to meet the new guy you mentioned in the email Sunday," Masser said.

"We are," Ballard said. "Or at least we were. Not sure where he is, but he did say he'd be in. So why don't we start with updates on cases and then we'll see where we're at with him."

Ballard spent the next hour listening as her volunteer crew spoke about their cases and efforts. She was more than their supervisor. As the only full-time sworn officer on the squad, she was not only in charge of the team but also was each member's individual partner when it came to making decisions that one day might be questioned in court or reviewed by an appeals panel. When cases eventually made their way into the court system, it was likely that she would become the lead investigator and witness for the prosecution.

Lou Rawls went first and fastest, simply reporting that he was still reviewing the cases in the stack Ballard had given him three weeks before and preparing requests for DNA analysis. It was the exact same report he had given the previous week. Since Rawls was the only one on the squad whom Ballard was forced to take on, she felt no hesitation in expressing disappointment in the slow pace of his work.

"Come on, we gotta get these in," she said at the end of his report. "We all know the lab is backed up. We need to get cases in the pipeline. The department and the city council are not going to wait around forever. This is a results-based unit. Saying we're waiting on lab results is a lot better than saying we're working on it."

"Well, if we made some progress on Sarah Pearlman, I think we'd all feel less pressure," Rawls countered.

"We *are* making progress," Ballard said. "We'll talk about that later when Bosch is here. Anything else, Lou?"

"No, that's it from me," Rawls said.

He sounded annoyed that Ballard had called him out on his report.

"Okay, who wants to go next?" Ballard said, moving on.

"Just a quick one from me," Masser said. "I have an appointment this afternoon with Vickie Blodget at the D.A. As you all know, she's the cold case liaison, and I'll be asking her to sign off on the Robbins and Selwyn cases. Hopefully you'll have those in your next report to management and council."

The cases Masser mentioned were DNA cases that led to suspects who were guilty but would never be prosecuted because of extenuating circumstances, such as the suspect being deceased or already serving a life sentence for other crimes. The cases could not be officially classified as solved or closed without the review and approval of the District Attorney's Office and their designated reviewer. With Vickie Blodget as their go-to, this had become a rubber-stamp process, but it was still a protocol that had to be followed. These cases would be classified as "cleared other" because of the lack of prosecution involved.

The DNA match in the Robbins case led to a man who had died in prison in Colorado, where he had been serving a life sentence for another murder. The Selwyn case was also a DNA match but the suspect was still alive. He was seventy-three years old and on death row at San Quentin. He was never going to see freedom. Though Ballard had gone up to San Quentin to interview him and get a confession, the killer denied his involvement. Since his DNA had been found inside the body of his thirteen-year-old victim, Ballard was undeterred. She had no doubt he was the killer, and she was asking the D.A. to file charges but defer the prosecution. It was the most efficient way to proceed, given that the killer would never get off death row—at least not alive. This decision was agreed to by the family of the victim, who were not interested in rehashing the horrible death of their loved one forty-one years later.

"As soon as Blodget signs off, I want the families informed," Ballard said. "Will you handle that, Paul?"

"Gladly," Masser said. "I have the contacts in the files."

Even though on the face of it, the perpetrators of these crimes had escaped true justice, Ballard had found that those calls to the victims' loved ones were still very much needed. To give final answers to the mystery and pain that had in many cases accompanied a family for decades was the noble calling of the unit. Ballard had told the people on her team that this was their mandate and duty and not to be taken lightly.

"Okay," Ballard said, again moving on. "Colleen, where are we with Cortez?"

"Still working social," Hatteras said. "Growing the tree. Getting close."

Ballard nodded. Hatteras was working a genealogy case—a 1986 rape and murder with DNA extracted from swabs in the rape kit for which no match was found in the state and national databases. The next step was submitting the evidence to genealogy databases and attempting to identify relatives of the original DNA depositor. Hatteras called this process "watering the tree" and so far this had led to a young woman living in Las Vegas who Hatteras believed might be a distant relative of the killer. Before reaching out directly to the woman, Hatteras was now engaged in the social media sleuthing that would help grow the family tree, leading her from branch to branch and eventually to the identity of a suspect.

"When do you expect to make direct contact with the descendant?" Ballard asked.

"By the end of the week," Hatteras said. "You get me a ticket to Vegas and I'll go connect the dots."

"When you're ready, I'll put in the request," Ballard said.

She then started to end the meeting.

"Okay, everybody, good work," she said. "Keep at it and remember to give me your hours. Even though you're not getting paid for your work, we need to track hours for the bosses. They love knowing how much they're getting for free."

"So that's it?" Rawls said. "We have to wait for the new guy to come in to get the download on this new lead the lab's got on Pearlman?"

The question revealed that Rawls had already heard from Nelson Hastings, Councilman Pearlman's chief of staff, whom Ballard had updated during her drive in from downtown. On the call, she had only told Hastings there was a new lead on the Pearlman case but couldn't discuss it until she had results from the lab. She was tempted now to give a response that would lay out Rawls as a direct and unauthorized conduit to the councilman's office. But she decided to hold back on that confrontation and wait for a better time.

"Well, it's a wait-and-see situation," she said. "But thanks to some out-of-the-box thinking by our newest team member, we have a pretty solid genetic lead. This morning down at the Piper Tech print archives, I pulled a card containing the partial palm print believed since day one to have been left by the suspect. I took it to the lab, and they pulled back the tape, swabbed the print, and got DNA. Not a lot but enough to send through the databases. Hopefully we get lucky."

"Wow," Masser said. "Be great if it hits."

Ballard's attention was drawn past Masser to the aisle next to the case shelves. Harry Bosch was walking toward the pod. He was wearing dusty blue jeans, lace-up work boots, and a denim shirt with perspiration stains under the arms.

"And speak of the devil," Ballard said.

7

BOSCH APPROACHED THE cold case pod with the eyes of four people, three of whom he didn't know, cast upon him.

"Harry," Ballard said. "I was just updating the team on Pearlman. They got DNA off the palm print and we put a rush on matching. We should know yea or nay on a match by the end of the week."

"That's good," Bosch said.

He held up a hand to the strangers in the pod he had not yet met.

"Hey, everybody," he said.

"Oh, yes," Ballard said. "This is Harry Bosch."

As Bosch moved to his workstation, Ballard went around the pod, introducing Masser, Rawls, and Hatteras. Masser and Rawls nodded to him, while Hatteras stood and extended her hand over the privacy partition to shake his. She held it after the shake for an awkward two seconds like she was trying to get some sort of read off him, then released it. This prompted Rawls to stand and extend a hand.

"That was smart thinking on the palm print," he said.

"Oh, I bet somebody here would have thought of it," Bosch said.

"The councilman will be impressed," Rawls said.

"Well," Ballard said, "let's not get ahead of ourselves till we see where the matching goes."

Bosch remembered that Rawls was the one Ballard hadn't chosen for the team. He quietly sat down at his station, and Rawls and Hatteras did the same as Ballard continued.

"So, we were sort of having a team meeting, Harry," she said. "What I like to do is talk about the cases we're all working, because we all come from different places and departments and agencies, and I think it's good to put everything on the table. You never know where a good idea might come from. Like you with the palm print."

"Okay," Bosch said.

He felt uncomfortable with all eyes still on him. It felt like he was about to get called on in class and hadn't done the homework.

"So," Ballard said, "I know you haven't started yet on the Gallagher case, but why don't you give a general summary of the earlier investigation and your thoughts on where you might want to go with it."

"Uh, okay," Bosch said hesitantly. "I guess, first of all, I don't call it the Gallagher case. I call it the Gallagher Family case because it's a quadruple killing, a whole family: mother, father, nine-year-old daughter, and thirteen-year-old son."

"How awful," Hatteras said.

"Yeah, it gets pretty bad," Bosch said. "It takes a certain kind of killer to take out a whole family like that."

Bosch paused for a moment to see if there were any other comments, then continued.

"The Gallaghers lived in the Valley—sort of on the border

between Sherman Oaks and Van Nuys. And it was thought at first that their disappearance was voluntary. None of the neighbors saw them go, but once it was established that they were gone, it was thought that they just up and left because of business and financial issues. You know, pulled up stakes and just split."

"A family business?" Masser asked.

"Not really," Bosch said. "Mr. Gallagher—Stephen Gallagher—was an industrial contractor. He had a couple of pretty big warehouses and an equipment yard up on San Fernando Road in Sylmar, and he rented out cranes and hydraulic lifts and all kinds of equipment used in heavy construction. One of the warehouses was just for scaffolding and that sort of stuff."

"And then they were found dead," Hatteras said. "I remember this now. Out in the desert. And that's where you've been this morning."

Bosch looked at her for a moment and then nodded.

"Yeah, a year later they were found. A geologist from Cal State Northridge and his students were up there in the Mojave on some kind of climate change study and they found the boy's body. What was left of it. The grave had been disturbed by animals. Coyotes or whatever. That led to all four being discovered and eventually identified as the Gallaghers. They used dental records—the boy, Stephen Jr., had braces."

"So wouldn't it be a San Bernardino County case?" Masser asked.

"Actually, the location was Inyo County and it was a joint investigation," Bosch said. "I was on the first Open-Unsolved Unit back then, and we got the case because it was believed that after a year, the trail was cold. I was the lead. I worked it pretty hard but never broke it open. Then I retired and the case basically went on a shelf…

"But now I'm back and on it again. And, yes, I went up there this morning."

Bosch looked at Ballard to see if he had said enough.

"Why did you go up there?" she asked.

He knew that she already knew the answer. He didn't like being put on the spot like this—discussing or justifying his moves.

"I just thought it was the place to start," he said. "To try to get momentum going again. While I was there, the investigator I worked with from the Inyo County Sheriff's Department showed up. There's been nothing happening on it from their end either."

"Can you tell us about Finbar McShane?" Ballard asked. "The more the group knows, the more we might be in a position to have ideas."

"Stephen Gallagher was born in Ireland," Bosch said. "Dublin. He met an American woman visiting from L.A.—Jennifer Clarke—and they came back here and eventually married and he started his business. So then at some point he hired another Irish guy, named Finbar McShane. He was from Belfast in Northern Ireland and it was never established if they knew each other previously. McShane wasn't a partner but he was running the business with Stephen. After the Gallaghers disappear, McShane keeps the business going and piece by piece he starts selling off the equipment. To make this short, a year later the bodies that were never supposed to be found are discovered. And guess what? McShane is gone and the warehouses and the equipment yard are empty. It was a classic bust-out operation."

"What's that mean?" Hatteras asked. "A 'bust-out'?"

"It's like a scheme," Bosch said. "A con in which you hollow out a business by ordering products and selling them and basically selling everything until there's nothing left and it collapses, leaving all your suppliers unpaid and on the hook for the losses."

"You ever watch *The Sopranos*?" Rawls asked. "Great show. They did it all the time."

"So McShane is your suspect," Masser said, attempting to get back to Bosch's story. "Any estimate on how much selling all the equipment brought in?"

"We were able to track the sales," Bosch said. "It was just over eight hundred thousand."

"Four lives for eight hundred K," Rawls said.

"If he did it," Hatteras said.

"Tell them about the letter," Ballard said.

"We got a letter addressed to the LAPD, supposedly from him," Bosch said. "He claimed he was innocent and that he left because he didn't want to be falsely accused."

"Postmark?" Hatteras asked.

"It was local," Bosch said. "We put flags on his passport. If he left the country and got back to Belfast or anywhere else, then he did it without his passport."

"I think he's still here," Hatteras said. "I can feel it."

Bosch looked at her, then turned his eyes to Ballard.

"Talk about the evidence," Ballard said. "How were they killed?"

"They were executed," Bosch said. "With a nail gun from one of Gallagher's warehouses. It was in the grave with them. And there was evidence that the grave had been dug with an excavator."

"What the heck is an excavator?" Masser asked.

"It's got two wheels and it can be towed on the back of a pickup," Bosch said. "I've got a picture here somewhere I can show you. The point is, the grave wasn't dug with a shovel. It was too precise, and it was clear that some solid rock had been split by something with more force than a shovel or a pickax. The grave was close enough to the paved road up there that he could have backed in there with the excavator and used it to get in and out pretty quickly. And one of the first machines McShane sold after the family disappeared was an excavator. We can prove that."

Bosch pulled open one of the murder books on his desk and started leafing through it, looking for the photo of the excavator. He spoke as he searched.

"We were able to trace that sale, and the buyer let us examine the excavator. There was still a piece of rock lodged in one of the tire treads that matched the creosote at the gravesite."

"All four were in one grave?" Rawls asked.

"Yes," Bosch said. "It would have been the fastest way to do it. The hole was about six by four and then four feet deep. The parents were dropped in first, then the children on top of them. Along with the nail gun."

He found a brochure from Shamrock Industrial Rentals that showed the excavator in question. He handed it over the partition to Masser.

"But that was the only link we ever made to McShane, and it wasn't enough for an arrest warrant," Bosch said.

"You went to the D.A. with this?" Masser asked. "I would have been tempted to file."

"I did, and I guess I wish I'd come to you," Bosch said. "The filing deputy I brought it to said he wanted more. McShane selling the excavator was not proof he used it to bury the family. There were holes in the linkage. The equipment yard was unguarded at night. Someone could have used Stephen Gallagher's keys to open the yard and take the excavator for the night."

"That's a hell of a stretch," Masser said.

"I felt the same," Bosch said. "But I didn't get to make the call. I was told to get more evidence...and I didn't. So plan B was to find McShane, stick him in a room, and get him to cop-out. But that never happened and he's still in the wind. That's where it stands."

Finished with his summary, Bosch waited for more questions and suggestions from the others. There was only silence until finally Hatteras asked, "Do you still have the original letter McShane wrote expressing his innocence?" she asked.

"We do," Bosch said. "It's handwritten on letterhead from the company."

"I meant, do you have it there, or is it in evidence archives?" Hatteras said. "I'd like to see the original."

"It's here," Bosch said.

He opened the thickest murder book because he knew it contained the plastic sleeves holding the photos from the case. The letter was sealed in one of the sleeves. He opened the binder's rings, slipped out the sleeve with the McShane letter, and handed it to Hatteras.

She looked at it for a moment, holding the sleeve at the edges with two hands.

"Can I take it out?" she asked.

"Why?" Bosch asked. "It's evidence."

"I want to hold it," Hatteras said.

"It was processed back then, right?" Ballard said.

"Yes," Bosch said. "No prints, but the signature was matched to McShane's. He sent it."

"I mean, she can take it out," Ballard said. "It's been processed."

"I guess," Bosch said. "Whatever."

He watched Hatteras open the sleeve and slip the document out. She then held it the same way with two hands, no gloves. But she wasn't reading it. Bosch saw that her eyes were closed.

Bosch turned to Ballard, a puzzled look on his face. Before either could speak, Hatteras did.

"I think he's telling the truth," she said.

"What?" Bosch asked.

"McShane," Hatteras said. "I think he was telling the truth when he wrote that he was innocent but couldn't prove it."

"What are you talking about?" Bosch said. "You weren't even read—"

It hit Bosch then. But Ballard spoke before he could.

"Harry, let's sidebar this for the moment," she said. "I think it would be best if everybody went back to their own cases now, and I'll finish showing Harry around the facility."

Masser returned the brochure to Bosch, followed by Hatteras handing him the McShane letter, back in its protective sleeve.

Ballard stood up.

"Let's start with our interview room," she said.

Ballard started walking toward the aisle that led to the archive room entrance. Bosch put the brochure and letter sleeve back on the binder rings, snapped them closed, and then followed her.

8

BALLARD STEPPED INTO the interview room, bracing for what she knew would be coming from Bosch but acting like everything was routine and normal. Bosch closed the door after following her in.

"You put a psychic on the team?" he said. "Are you kidding me? You brought me in to work with a psychic? Are we going to hold séances to talk to the dead and ask them who killed the Gallagher family?"

"Harry, settle down," Ballard said. "I knew you would lose your shit about Hatteras. I didn't expect it to come out so fast. And for the record, she calls herself an 'empath,' not a psychic, okay?"

Bosch shook his head.

"Whatever," he said. "It's still kooky shit. You know you can never use her in court. She'll get torn apart and it will shred the case. I don't want her anywhere near Gallagher. She'll taint it with this mumbo jumbo."

Ballard didn't respond at first. She waited for Bosch to settle and be quiet. She then pulled out one of the chairs at the interview table and sat.

"Sit down, Harry."

Bosch reluctantly did as he was told.

"Look, I didn't know anything about this empath stuff till after she was on the team," Ballard said. "It's not why she's in the unit and it's not what she does here. I told you, she's on the genealogical work. And her people-reading skills—the so-called empathy—help with all the social engineering that is a necessary part of that work."

"Like I said, I don't want her near Gallagher and McShane. Because I'm going to find McShane and nothing is going to taint the case when I do."

"Fine. I won't let her near it."

"Good."

"So, can you cool off now?"

"I'm cool, I'm cool."

"Good. You just steer clear of Colleen and I'll make sure she steers clear of you. But you have to remember that, like you, these people are volunteers. They're giving their time and talents to this, and Colleen does good work. I don't want to lose her."

"I get it. She does her thing and I do mine."

"Thank you, Harry. Let's go back."

Ballard got up. Bosch didn't.

"Wait," he said. "Tell me about the palm print. It sounds like you told the whole team already."

"I did, because it's the best break on the case we've gotten," Ballard said. "Darcy Troy—our DNA tech—swabbed it and said there was enough for a full analysis. She's pretty stoked. I think she just wants to be first to pull DNA off a print, so she's put it to the front of the line. We'll know something soon, but there isn't much to say until she gets back to me. And when I hear from her, you'll be the first to know."

"Okay."

"So how are you going to attack the Gallagher Family case?"

"Dig into the books, go through property and evidence, see if anything pops all these years later. Gallagher had four other employees besides McShane. I'll probably interview them again. And now that I have some authority, I'll see if I can find McShane. He had family in Belfast, not that they'd give him up. But maybe he's surfaced. You never know what will fall when you shake a tree after a few years."

"Let me know how I can help. I'm not just the administrator here. I want to work cases. Especially this kind. Otherwise, I'll just be babysitting the others."

"Good to know."

"I mean it."

"Got it."

"Good."

They returned to the pod and each silently sat down at their respective workstations. Bosch took the stack of murder books from the Gallagher Family case and spread them out in front of him so he could see the labels on the front covers. He knew that volume 1 contained the investigative chronology, which would be the bible of the case, a multipage listing of the moves he had made during the original investigation—each entry noted by date and time with an addendum reference to any larger report written in follow-up.

He knew he would be working with the chrono now, getting his footing in the case again while also looking for any step that he had missed the first time or interpretation of the facts that bore rethinking. But what he first wanted was the 8 x 10 photo of Emma Gallagher in a plastic sleeve at the front of the book. He had put it there many years before so it would be unavoidable every time he and whoever might follow him on the case opened the first murder book to check the chrono.

He slipped the photo of the nine-year-old girl out of the sleeve. It was a school photo. She wore a green plaid jumper that announced Catholic school, and a smile that showed a second tooth just beginning to fill a gap in the bottom row. The photo made him sad. He had attended her autopsy and knew that the tooth never got the chance to come all the way in.

He pinned the photo with a tack on the half wall that separated his cubicle from the work space of Colleen Hatteras. As he leaned forward to do it, she looked over the partition.

"Detective Harry?" she asked.

"Don't call me that," Bosch said. "Just Harry is fine."

"Harry, then. I just wanted to say, I didn't want to upset you with what I said."

"Don't worry, you didn't. Everything's fine."

"Well, then I just want to add that I don't think you'll find Finbar McShane. I don't think he's alive."

Bosch looked at her for a long moment before responding.

"Why do you think that?" he asked.

"I can't explain it," Hatteras said. "I just get these feelings. Most of the time they're true. Do you know for a fact he's still alive?"

Bosch cut his eyes over the wall to Ballard's station. She was sitting and looking at her computer screen, but Bosch could tell she was listening. He looked back at Hatteras.

"For a fact, no," Bosch said. "The last confirmation that he was alive was three years after the murders."

"What was it?" Hatteras asked.

"Stephen Gallagher had an office manager, his first and longest-serving employee, named Sheila Walsh. Her home out in Chatsworth got broken into three years after the murders. Somebody rifled through her home office files and desk. They moved a paperweight and left fingerprints."

"Finbar McShane."

Bosch nodded.

"I was retired from the LAPD by then and was working cold cases for San Fernando," he said. "But I got word about the burglary from my old partner Lucy Soto. It was being handled by Devonshire Division detectives. Sheila Walsh told them that she had no idea what McShane might have been looking for. She didn't think anything of real value had been taken from her office."

"Weird," Hatteras said.

"Yeah. So he was alive then. Whether he is now is just a guess."

"I trust my instincts. I don't think you'll find him alive."

"What are you getting now?"

"What do you mean?"

"Behind you is the library of lost souls. Six thousand unsolved murders. Aren't they talking to you, sending messages?"

Before Hatteras could muster a response, Ballard broke in.

"Harry," she said.

That was all she said, his name in a tone that sounded like a mother warning a child to stop whatever it was he was doing.

Bosch looked at her and then back at Hatteras.

"I have work to do," he said.

He then hunched down over his desk and out of her eyeline as well as Ballard's. He opened volume 1 of the murder books and looked at the table of contents. Witness interviews and statements were in volume 3. He went there and found the summaries he had written after three separate interviews with Sheila Walsh.

Sheila Walsh was the first employee Stephen Gallagher hired when he started his equipment rental company in 2002, and she had been with the company through its expansion over the next several years. She had become a key part of the investigation in terms of telling Bosch how the business operated, opening its books, and tracing equipment that had been sold off by McShane.

There were three other employees at Shamrock but Walsh was the most important to the investigation. The other three were men who worked in the warehouse and equipment yard. Walsh was an insider, working in the same suite of offices as Gallagher and McShane.

Bosch reread the summaries of the Walsh interviews and wrote her name, birth date, and address down on a page in a pocket notebook. He then looked over the partition at Ballard.

"Do I have access to the DMV?" he asked.

"Uh, no," she said. "Only sworn officers. What do you need?"

Bosch tore the page out of the notebook and handed it over the partition to Ballard.

"Can you run her?" he asked. "I want to see if she's still at that address."

"Yeah, hold on," Ballard said.

Bosch heard her fingers on her keyboard as she pulled up the DMV database and ran Sheila Walsh's name and birth date.

"Her current license has the same address," she reported.

"Thanks," Bosch said.

He got up and leaned over the partition.

"You going to go see her?" she asked.

"Yeah," Bosch said. "Thought I'd start there."

"You okay going alone?"

"Of course. But I have a question. Back in the day, I sent a lot of stuff we collected at the family's house and at the office to property. Do I have the authority to have it sent out here, or do you need to do that?"

"Probably me. But it will be faster if we tell them to pull it and then you or I go pick it up. Depends on how soon you want it. Picking up, you can probably get it tomorrow. Delivery out here may take up to a week."

"I'll pick it up—if I'm allowed. I still don't have any credentials."

"I have the case number. I'll order it and tell them you'll be by in the morning to pick it up. Just show them your retired ID. That will work for now. You need to go to the front office here and make an appointment to give photo and prints. Then you'll get an ID."

"Okay. Thanks. Another question: Do I have access to the locker room here? I want to clean up, change my shirt."

"You still carry backup clothes in your car?"

"I did today. I knew I was going out to the desert."

"You have access to the locker room and showers. I can't promise they'll have a free locker for you."

"Well, they're police cadets in there, right? I don't carry a gun, and who's going to steal my wallet?"

The primary use of the Ahmanson Center was as a second

academy for the training of police recruits. Most field training remained at the original academy at Elysian Fields. The Ahmanson was for classroom training—and retraining in some cases. The murder book archive occupied only a small part of the campus.

"You could leave your wallet here and come back for it after you clean up," Ballard said.

"I'll be fine," Bosch said.

"Then, happy hunting."

"You, too."

Bosch headed for the door, walking along the endcaps of the murder-book shelves. Taped to the end of each row was a 3 x 5 card showing the range of files by case number, which always began with the year the crime took place. It was a Dewey decimal system of the dead.

Bosch ran a hand along the endcaps as he walked. He didn't believe in ghosts or the dead reaching out from the dark beyond. But he felt a reverence and empathy as he passed by on his way out.

9

BALLARD WAS JUST finishing the case summary that she had compiled as part of a request to the Ahmanson Foundation for grant money for a genealogical case Tom Laffont had put together and would work with Hatteras.

"Colleen, Tom's not here, so I'm sending you this grant app," she said without taking her eyes off her screen. "Read the case summary and make sure I have it right."

"Send it, I'll read it," Hatteras said.

"I want to get it in today. Maybe get a quick answer so you and Tom can go to work."

"I'm ready. Send it."

Just as Ballard closed the document, her desk phone buzzed. She saw on the ID screen that it was Darcy Troy from the DNA lab. She answered the phone while opening an email and sending the grant document to Hatteras.

"Darcy, whaddaya got for me?"

"Well, good and bad news on Sarah Pearlman."

"Tell me."

"The good news is we got a hit off the DNA from the palm print. The bad news is it's a case-to-case hit."

A case-to-case hit meant the DNA profile from the palm print was matched to the profile from another open case, one where the donor/suspect was unknown. Case-to-case hits were what led to genealogical investigations. This was disappointing in the moment for Ballard because she was looking for a street case, an investigation that took her out into the city and knocking on doors, looking for an identified individual whose DNA was in the law enforcement data banks. That was what Bosch was chasing now with McShane and she wanted the same for herself. It's what true detectives lived for.

She grabbed a pen off the desk and got ready to write on a legal pad.

"Well, it's better than nothing," she said. "What's the name and case number?"

Troy recited the case number first. It was a homicide from 2005, which meant there were eleven years between the Sarah Pearlman murder and the linked case. The victim's name was Laura Wilson and she was twenty-four years old at the time of her murder.

"Anything else on your end?" Ballard asked.

"Well, it's unusual on the science side," Troy said. "As far as how they even came up with the DNA on the 2005 case."

"Yeah? Tell me."

"You know the old saying, right? *Secretions, not excretions.* We extract DNA from bodily fluids—blood, sweat, and semen primarily. But not from bodily waste, because the enzymes destroy DNA."

"No shit, no piss."

"Yes, normally, but in this case, it was apparently extracted from urine. You'll have to get the full details when you pull the book, but according to the few notes I have here, urine was swabbed at the crime scene because the hope was they would find swimmers. If the guy raped the victim before he used the toilet, then there might still be sperm in the urethra and that would come out in the urine. But they found no swimmers. But what they did find was blood."

"Blood in the urine."

"Correct. The extraction was handled quickly and they didn't get a full profile, but they got enough to put on CODIS. They got no hits then but we just connected it with our case."

CODIS was the national database containing millions of DNA samples collected by law enforcement across the country.

"How did they know the urine with the blood in it came from the killer?" Ballard asked.

"I wasn't here then, so I don't know the answer to that," Troy said. "It's not in the notes we have here. But hopefully it's in the murder book."

"Okay. You said it was not a full profile. Are you saying it's not a full match to the Pearlman case?"

"No, it's a match for sure. But as far as going into court with it, I will have to run the numbers, and that will take me some time. But it basically means fewer zeroes. We are not talking about this being a one in thirteen quadrillion match. Something less, but still encompassing the human population of the last hundred years."

Ballard knew that Troy had the tendency to get lost in the wonder of the numbers. But she had handled enough DNA cases to be able to interpret what she was saying.

"So you'll be able to testify that this DNA is unique."

"Well, to be exact, I can testify that no other person on this planet in the last hundred years has had this DNA."

"Got it. That's all I need. Now we just have to find the guy. I'm going to go look for the book now. Thanks for the quickie, Darcy."

"Glad to help. Let me know how it goes."

"I will."

Ballard put the phone down and got up.

"Good news?" Hatteras asked.

"Think so," Ballard said. "Might be another case for you. Did you read that grant app?"

"Read it and sent it back to you. Good to go."

"Okay, thanks. I'll send it out in a few."

Ballard headed down the aisle that ran along the endcaps, looking for the 2005 row. She found it and turned the wheel to move the shelves and open the row. She ticked a fingernail along the spines of the murder books until she found case 05-0243 and slid it out. The Laura Wilson case was contained in one overstuffed binder, which Ballard knew she would immediately reinstall in two binders to make flipping through the documents easier. She double-checked that there was not a second binder misplaced nearby during the shelving and saw that none of the other binders on the shelf carried the same case number.

She stepped out of the row and cranked it closed again, thinking all the while about how Bosch called the archives the "library of lost souls." If that was true, she had one of those lost souls in her hand.

Back at her workstation, Ballard emailed the grant app first, then opened the thick binder she had brought from the archives. Because the origin of the DNA in the case was so unusual, she went straight to the forensics section to see how it came to be that DNA was extracted from urine.

A summary statement from the lead investigator told the story. The victim was murdered in her home, where she lived alone. The crime scene investigators noticed that the toilet seat in the bathroom off the bedroom was up, indicating that a man had used it. While checking the toilet seat and flush handle for fingerprints, a criminalist noticed urine droplets on the rim of the bowl. These drops were reddish brown in color, indicating the possibility of blood cells in the urine. The droplets were collected on swabs, and DNA extraction was conducted the same day because of the fear of possible DNA decay. A partial profile was established and then entered into the CODIS database, drawing no matches.

The summary went on to state that further analysis and medical consultation by investigators determined that the urine had come from someone who had kidney or bladder disease, causing hematuria, the medical term for blood in the urine.

Ballard was excited by what she had read and eager to see whether the investigators used the confirmation of kidney disease as an angle of investigation. Had they looked for a suspect among men being treated for kidney disease? She opened the bottom drawer of her desk and pulled out two empty binders. She removed all the documents and plastic sleeves from the original murder book, split the stack, and slipped each half onto the rings of a new binder. She then got up and went to the kitchen to get coffee before she settled in to read the case's investigative chronology.

Laura Wilson was a young African American woman trying to make it as an actress and living alone in an apartment paid for by her parents back in Chicago. She had moved out to L.A. two years before her death and was in the midst of a promise to herself and her supporters to make it and become self-supporting within five years or to turn around and go home. She was taking acting lessons and routinely auditioning for small parts in films and television shows. She had also joined an acting troupe that worked out of a twenty-seat theater in Burbank. Her apartment was on Tamarind Avenue near the Scientology Celebrity Center on Franklin. Wilson had joined the organization and was taking classes, also paid for by her parents, in hopes that she would make connections that would help her in the entertainment business.

She had been found murdered on Saturday morning, November 5, 2005, by a friend she was supposed to go with to a Scientology seminar. The friend found the door to her apartment ajar, entered, and found the victim dead in her bed. Cause of death was determined to be manual strangulation—a silk scarf was knotted around her neck. The body was mutilated postmortem.

"What is that?"

Ballard had been so immersed in her reading that she had not noticed that Rawls had come around the pod and was looking over her shoulder.

"The DNA we got on the Pearlman case was linked to this one from '05," she said.

"Wow, interesting," Rawls said.

Ballard closed the binder and swiveled her chair so she could look up at him.

"What's up, Lou?" she asked.

"I'm taking off," Rawls said. "I gotta put out a fire at my store in Encino. Angry customer says we lost a package containing a priceless antiquity."

"That's gotta hurt. You coming back later this week?"

"Not sure. I'll let you know."

"Okay. I'll see you when I see you."

Rawls walked off and Ballard immediately turned back to the binder, her mind already deeply embedded in the murder of Laura Wilson.

10

BOSCH RECOGNIZED SHEILA WALSH'S house from
the last time he had knocked on the door years before. She
answered quickly but clearly didn't remember him. He was
older and grayer and maybe his eyes weren't as sharp as that last
time, but after a long moment, she was able to place him, if not
remember his name. She smiled.

"Detective," she said. "This is a surprise."

"Mrs. Walsh," Bosch said. "I was hoping you'd remember me."

"Don't be silly, of course I do. And it's Sheila. Has there been
a break in the case?"

"Can I come in so we can talk?"

"Yes, yes. Come in, please."

Walsh stepped back and let Bosch enter. She looked the same
as Bosch remembered her. Now pushing sixty, she had more
wrinkles at the corners of her eyes, but she was still an attractive
woman who looked like she ate about one meal a week. Her
thin body, narrow shoulders, and big hair had not changed
at all, confirming Bosch's suspicions back in the day that it
was a wig.

"Can I get you a coffee or a water or something?" she asked.

"No, I'm fine," Bosch said. "But we can sit in the kitchen if you want. I remember that was where we sat before."

"Sure, let's go back."

She led him through a dining room—which was clearly being used as an office—to a kitchen that had a small round breakfast table with four chairs.

"Have a seat," Walsh said. "Has Finbar McShane finally turned up?"

"Uh, no," Bosch said. "In fact, that was going to be my first question to you. Have you heard any word about him recently? Anything at all?"

"Oh, no. If I had, I would have called you. But I thought you told me you were retiring the last time I saw you."

"I was. I did. But now I'm back working cold cases and so...I'm looking into the Gallagher Family case again. And trying to find McShane."

"Ah, I see. Well, if you ask me, he's back in Belfast or somewhere over there."

"Yeah, that's the consensus, but I'm not so sure."

Bosch looked past her and through a sliding door to the backyard. There was a deck and a small in-ground pool back there. A vegetable garden in long wooden planters had screened canopies over them to keep deer and coyotes and other animals out. The house was in Chatsworth, in the northwest corner of the Valley, and the wildlife came down out of the nearby hills at night. Beyond the planters he could see the rock outcroppings of Stony Point Park in the distance.

"I get stuck thinking about the break-in you had three years after the murders," Bosch said. "It puzzles me. What was he looking for here?"

"Well, that's a mystery that will last until you find him," Walsh said. "Because I'm just as baffled as you are. I didn't have anything of his. I didn't know anything about the case beyond what I told the police."

Bosch reached into the inside pocket of the sport coat he had put on after showering in the locker room at Ahmanson. He pulled out a document, unfolded it, and looked it over before speaking.

"This is the incident report," he said. "Written before the fingerprints were identified as McShane's. Says the burglar ate food out of the refrigerator, took a box of old record albums, then lifted money and an iPhone out of your purse."

"That's right," Walsh said.

"Rifled through the desk in the home office and moved the paperweight—a glass Waterford globe—and looked through your mail."

"Right, but not a desk. I use my dining room table as a desk. And I had the paperweight on my pile of to-do stuff. Bills and mail. At the time, I was learning to be an online travel agent. You know, after Shamrock was gone, I had to do something. So I had documents and cruise brochures in the stack, too. Stuff I needed for online training."

"Why would McShane be interested in that?"

"I don't know. I didn't know then and I don't know now. But he would not have known what was in that pile until he checked it, right?"

Bosch nodded and looked back at the incident report. It was a question among many that had nagged him about the case. What was McShane looking for?

"It's the only place his prints were found," he said. "There were his, your son's, and yours. That's it."

"I remember that," Walsh said. "I remember I also had that theory I told the officers about back then."

"Which was?"

"You know, the paperweight was Waterford glass. It's made in Ireland. He was from Ireland. Maybe he picked it up because of that."

Bosch nodded as he thought about that theory.

"Right, that's in the report," he said. "But Waterford is in Ireland and McShane was from Northern Ireland. And if he knew it was Waterford or it had some kind of nostalgic value to him, why didn't he take it?"

"Well…I don't know," Walsh said. "Maybe only he knows."

"Maybe….So, how's your son doing?"

"He's good. He moved out to Santa Clarita, works at a golf course up there."

"Good. Is he an instructor or—"

"No, he doesn't even play golf. Thinks it's too boring. But he likes the outdoors. He's a greenskeeper at Sand Canyon. It's a good job. Early to work and he gets off before the traffic builds up."

Bosch nodded and decided to end the small talk.

"Mrs. Walsh, I appreciate your time, especially with me showing up out of the blue," he said. "But I would really like to go back to the year of the murders and pick your brain again about what was happening with the business and in the office between Stephen Gallagher and Finbar McShane. Do you mind? Can you give me a few more minutes?"

"If you think it will help," Walsh said. "But my memory of it is probably not what it was back then."

"That's okay. It's sort of funny, because sometimes after a

good chunk of time goes by, people remember some things they didn't mention before and forget some of the things they said. So it helps to sift through everything again. I think that family, especially those two kids, deserves it."

"Of course they do. That's why I'm willing to help. I think about those kids all the time. Horrible."

"Thank you. I want to go back to the period before the murders, when it seemed that there was a strain in the relationship between Gallagher and McShane. I remember you told me that there had been arguments between them."

"Yes, there were. But it was always behind closed doors. You know, I could hear raised voices but not always what exactly was being said. Like that."

"How frequent were the arguments?"

"Well, for a while it seemed like every day."

"But the company—according to the books we looked at—was doing well, right? Before the Gallaghers disappeared, I mean."

"It was. We were busy all the time. I know that one of the things Fin wanted was to hire more people and, you know, expand. Maybe open another yard and fill it with equipment. He said more inventory would mean more business."

"But Stephen didn't want to expand."

"No, he was very conservative. He built the company from nothing. So he was cautious, and Fin always wanted to do more. They argued, but Stephen owned the business and had final say. Who would have thought it would lead to what happened? Those poor, poor kids. I mean, if it was a business dispute, why did they have to be killed like that?"

They were going over well-trod ground, but Bosch needed

to walk the case again to get his footing. He questioned Walsh for another half hour, and she never complained or tried to cut it short. She also provided nothing new in terms of significant case information. But her story of the final days of Shamrock Industrial Rentals had not changed in the years since Bosch had last heard it, and there was a significance to that.

He finished the interview with questions about the months after the disappearance of the Gallagher family when she and McShane attempted to keep the business afloat while they ostensibly waited for the family and the business owner to return. She once again said she had not known that McShane was running ads on Craigslist and selling off equipment rather than renting it out. That is, until he, too, disappeared, leaving the company with a virtually empty warehouse and equipment yard.

"He tricked me like he tricked everybody," she said. "We were used to having the scaffolding and the cranes and all the equipment gone for long periods of time because they were used in long-term projects. I had no idea the stuff was never coming back because he sold it."

"What do you remember about the day McShane disappeared?" Bosch asked.

"It was more like days. He didn't show up one day and then he called and said he was sick. He said he'd probably be out a couple days."

"But he wasn't."

"No, a couple days went by and he was still a no-show, and I had a customer come in who was having an issue with a JLG lift he said Fin sold him. He said Fin gave him a warranty and he wanted it fixed. That's when I found out he was selling stuff.

I called his number and the line was dead. Disconnected. I got suspicious, checked the bank accounts, and found they were empty. He took everything and disappeared."

"You called the police."

"I called the missing persons guy that I had called when the family disappeared and he said he would look into it. And then those bodies were found up there in the desert and you took over the case. Did you ever find out where he transferred the money to?"

Bosch shook his head. He didn't like being the one answering questions, but this one he answered.

"It was converted to cryptocurrency," he said. "Bitcoin was pretty new back then but we couldn't trace it after that. It was gone."

"Too bad," Walsh said.

"Yeah, too bad. So, I'm going to leave you alone now. Thank you for your time. If you have a piece of paper, I'll leave you my cell number in case you think of anything else. I don't have business cards."

"Sure."

"Sometimes a conversation like this can spark new memories."

Walsh got up from the table and opened a drawer below the kitchen counter. She took out a pad and pen and Bosch gave her the number.

"You think you'll catch him this time?" she asked.

"I don't know," Bosch said. "I'm hoping we do. It's why I came back."

"'The arc of the moral universe is long but it bends toward justice.'"

"MLK, right? Let's hope he was right."

Bosch left the house and Walsh closed the door. Bosch paused on the front step. Back when Bosch was a young detective going through two packs of smokes a day while working in the Homicide Special unit downtown, he had a routine he'd follow when he left someone's home after an interview. You never knew how an unanticipated visit from a police detective would affect a witness or suspect. He would stand just outside the front door and take out his cigarettes. He would then light up a smoke with a lighter that was always slow to spark. And he would turn slightly as if to block the wind, but he was really turning an ear toward the door. He would listen in hopes of hearing words spoken inside after his departure. On more than one occasion he picked up tense, sometimes angry voices. One time he even heard someone inside say, "He knows we did it!"

It had now been decades since his last smoke. Instead of a pack of cigarettes, he pulled out his phone while standing on the porch outside Sheila Walsh's home. He checked to see if any messages had come in while he had been conducting the interview. There was only one and it was a text from Ballard:

> I have news. Call me when you're
> clear.

He turned slightly to see if there was anything to hear. He heard Walsh's voice. It was a one-sided conversation indicating that she had made a phone call.

"That detective who was on the Gallagher case was just here," she said. "He just showed up out of the blue…"

He heard nothing else as the voice trailed off and Walsh

apparently walked deeper into the house and away from the front door.

Bosch stepped off the porch and headed to his car. He smiled as he remembered the case in which he had heard the confession from the front stoop. Now he wondered whom Sheila Walsh had called and whether it could be Finbar McShane.

11

BALLARD GOT TO Birds before Bosch. He was coming all the way from the far corner of the San Fernando Valley and it would take a while, even in reverse rush-hour traffic. She ordered a beer but held off on a food order. She was going through the chrono from the Laura Wilson murder book that she had copied before leaving. She knew she was breaking the no-copying rule, but she felt it was her rule to break.

This was her third read-through of the forty-five-page case chronology. Now that the Wilson murder had been connected to the Pearlman case, Ballard needed to know it like it was her own. The place to get that knowledge was the chrono, which was a meticulously detailed account of the original investigators' work. Though their investigation did not lead to an arrest and prosecution, the path they took would be very informative.

As a young would-be actress, Laura Wilson had myriad inter-actions with people across the city as she went to one cattle-call audition after another at studios and production facilities from Culver City to Hollywood to Burbank. It was her job to build a social network in the entertainment industry that could alert her to possible jobs in her chosen profession. In addition to that pattern, she was a frequent visitor to Scientology facilities and events in Hollywood. She was also attending a twelve-student acting class twice a week, and once a month her acting troupe put on shows at its theater in Burbank. These activities added to her many personal interactions, any one of which could have been with her killer.

As expected, the chrono detailed the investigators' efforts to get some kind of handle on the young woman's life. The detectives broke her interactions into groups they dubbed Hollywood, Scientology, and Other. Two former boyfriends, one in L.A. and one back in Chicago, were questioned and cleared by alibis. The investigators spent weeks and then months on the interviews, running records checks, and leaning hard on acquaintances who had criminal records. Still, no person of interest ever emerged and the case eventually went cold.

The last inputs to the chrono were annual due diligence entries that simply stated that the case remained open pending new information.

Ballard clipped the pages of the chrono back together and left it on the table. She was sure Bosch would want to take it with him to read when he got home. She was pulling her phone to call him and see how far out he still was, when she received a call from Nelson Hastings.

"Hello, Detective," he said. "I hear there is a major break in the Sarah Pearlman case. Is there anything I can share with the councilman?"

"Who told you that?" Ballard asked.

She knew it had been Rawls but she wanted to see how Hastings would answer. It would go into what Ballard called the matrix of trust. Details, actions, reactions, and statements of those she came into contact with combined to establish how much or how little trust she would invest in them. She was still gathering information on Hastings and his boss, the councilman.

"I just happened to be talking to Ted Rawls on my drive home today, and he mentioned it," Hastings said. "I was surprised that he knew but I had not been informed. I thought you agreed to keep me apprised on the case."

"Well, I think it's premature to call it a major break and that's why I haven't 'apprised' you," Ballard said. "We have connected Sarah's killing to another murder that happened eleven years later. But the newer case remains open and unsolved, so it's hard for me to consider it a break. We just have two victims now instead of one."

"How was the connection made?"

"DNA."

"I didn't think there was DNA in Sarah's case."

"There wasn't until yesterday, but we found it and it led to this new case."

"What is that victim's name?"

"Laura Wilson. She was older than Sarah by a few years. But there are case similarities. She was also sexually assaulted and murdered in her bed."

"I see."

"But that's all we really have at the moment, so I would relax, Mr. Hastings. If something develops from this that Councilman Pearlman needs to know, I will call you first thing."

"Thank you, Detective."

Hastings disconnected and Ballard looked up to see Bosch

entering the restaurant. She caught his eye with a wave and he came over and slid into the corner booth.

"How was your interview?" Ballard asked.

"Nothing really new," Bosch said. "But it was a good place to restart. She called somebody right after I left, so that's curious."

"This that trick you told me about, standing on the front step and eavesdropping?"

"It works sometimes. So what's up?"

"Well, thanks to you and the DNA we pulled off the palm print, we now have a hit on another case."

"Where? When?"

"Here in '05. In fact, right around the corner on Tamarind."

"I just parked on Tamarind."

"I'm going to walk over after we leave to check the place out. Here is the chrono. You can take it with you if you want to read it tonight."

"I thought no copies left Ahmanson."

Ballard smiled.

"No copies leave with you. I'm the boss. I can make copies."

"Got it. A double standard—you'll go far in the LAPD."

"That's not as funny as you think it is."

"Okay, so what else do you know about the case?"

Ballard started reviewing what she considered the important points gained from her read-through of the Wilson murder book.

"The bottom line is, if there wasn't a genetic link between these cases, I wouldn't have connected them," she said. "One victim is white, one Black; one in her teens, one in her twenties; one strangled, one stabbed. One murdered in her house, where

79

she lived with her parents and brother; the other killed in an apartment, where she lived alone."

"But both were sexually assaulted and killed in their beds," Bosch said. "Did you look at the crime scene? Did he cover the second victim's face?"

"No, he didn't. I guess eleven years after killing Sarah Pearlman, he was no longer ashamed of what he had done."

Bosch nodded. A waiter came to the table and they both ordered rotisserie chicken plates and Bosch said he'd drink what Ballard was drinking. After the waiter took the order to the kitchen, Bosch spoke.

"Eleven years between cases," he said. "That's not likely."

"I know," Ballard said. "There's got to be others out there."

"These two were the mistakes."

"Where he left DNA."

"The other thing is: two cases eleven years apart and both in L.A."

"Both in Hollywood."

"He's not a traveler."

"He's still here."

Bosch nodded.

"Most likely," he said.

After eating, they left the restaurant and walked down to Tamarind Avenue. They turned right and walked up the street, which was lined on both sides by two-story postwar apartment buildings with names like the Capri and the Royale. Ballard located Laura Wilson's apartment building—the Warwick— halfway up the block on the east side.

She and Bosch stood side by side and looked silently at the facade of the structure. It was a Streamline Moderne design and painted in shades of aqua and cream. It looked aerodynamic and safe. There was no hint of the violence that had occurred there so many years before.

Ballard pointed up at the windows on the left side of the second floor.

"Her place was second floor at the front," she said. "That corner."

Bosch just nodded.

"I'm going to put everybody on the team on this tomorrow," Ballard said. "We need to get this guy."

Bosch nodded again.

"You okay putting McShane on hold for a bit?" Ballard asked.

"No," Bosch said. "But I'll do it."

12

FROM HIS POD, Bosch watched Ballard rally the team into focusing on the Sarah Pearlman and Laura Wilson cases. She had told him the night before at Birds that she planned to call in everyone but Rawls because she didn't want him leaking everything they were doing to Nelson Hastings. Instead, she would text Rawls and tell him to take the day off if he still needed time to put out the fire at his business. Based on what she knew of his work ethic as an investigator, Ballard predicted the response from Rawls would be a thumbs-up emoji and he would not show up. So far she had been right.

Ballard gave assignments to each investigator in the pod, hoping that with many fresh eyes, they would break new ground in terms of finding the nexus where the two victims crossed paths with the same killer. The two young women were separated by age, race, financial status, and experience but somewhere in their lives there was a connection. Ballard put Bosch on crime scene review, while others on the team were assigned to review statements from family, friends, and witnesses. Tom Laffont would handle the medical lead. It did not seem that the original detectives had pursued the potential angle of investigation that the blood in the urine gave them. Blood in the urine was an indication of possible kidney or bladder disease that was either being treated or would reach a point that it needed to be treated.

"It also means our suspect might be dead," Laffont cautioned.

"That may be the case," Ballard said. "But we still need to identify him and clear these cases. I don't have to remind you all that Councilman Pearlman is our patron saint on the city council. If we can get answers as to what happened to his sister, we're going to be able to keep this unit alive for years to come."

While Bosch didn't like the political machinations inherent in the case, he wholly understood a family's need for answers. It had taken him more than thirty years to get answers about his own mother's killing when he was a boy. The answers did not provide closure but there was a resolution to his efforts. In that regard he fully understood what Jake Pearlman was looking for and needed. The fact that he was wielding his political power to get it was understandable. If he'd had that kind of juice, Bosch would have done the same in his mother's case. Instead, he had used the power of his badge.

Ballard had come in early and made individual packages of copies pertaining to each investigator's assignment. She handed them out at the end of the meeting, including giving Harry an inch-thick printout containing copies of the forensic reports and crime scene photos from the Wilson case.

Before starting in on the assignment, Bosch wanted to do something that had nagged at him since interviewing Sheila Walsh. He had been awake most of the night with thoughts that he had blown the Gallagher Family case by missing something about the break-in at her home.

Once Ballard was sitting down again at her station, Bosch got up and came around to the end of the pod.

"I need to run a name for criminal history," he said. "Can you do it?"

"On the Wilson case?" she asked. "Already?"

"No, on Gallagher."

"Harry, I want you working on Wilson and Pearlman. I thought we agreed on this last night, and I just finished telling everybody how important it is to us."

"I'm going to start on it today, but I stayed up all night thinking about this, so I just want to put it in motion and see what I've got to come back to after Wilson. Okay?"

"What's the name?"

Bosch was holding the fingerprints report from the Sheila Walsh break-in. Ballard opened up the portal to the National Crime Information Center database and he read the name he wanted checked for a criminal record.

"Jonathan Boatman, DOB July 1, '87."

Ballard typed it in and waited while the database was searched for matches.

"Who is he?" she asked.

"Sheila Walsh's son," Bosch said. "Probably a son from an early marriage and she changed her name when she divorced or remarried."

"And you never ran him before?"

"I did back in the day and he was clean. It's in the murder book. But right now I want to see if he stayed clean."

"And what makes you think he didn't?"

"Because yesterday was the first time I got a look at the incident report on that burglary at Sheila Walsh's house. McShane's prints were found, and it was assumed that he was the one who broke in. I was retired by then and Devonshire handled it. I heard about it from Lucy Soto and even I took it as a sign that McShane was alive and still local. I changed my mind yesterday."

"Why?"

"The incident report. It says food was taken from the refrigerator, a purse was emptied, a cell phone and a collection of old record albums were stolen. It was amateur hour. Like the work of a hype making a quick hit: getting food and cash and something he could sell for a fix."

"The albums. I remember there were shops all over Hollywood that would buy vinyl. Amoeba and few others."

"The son's prints were found but dismissed because the mother—Sheila Walsh—said he was a regular visitor to the house."

"I see where you're going with this. Drug addicts usually rip off their families before they get into serious crime, because they know the family won't prosecute. At least at first."

"Right."

"So if the son committed the burglary, McShane's prints being there take on a whole new meaning."

"That's what I was thinking. Plus, the call she made after I left yesterday. I was hoping it might be McShane, but her son might make better sense."

"But why would she report the burglary if she thought her son might have done it?"

"Maybe she didn't realize it was him till later. A lot of people in that position don't want to believe their son or their daughter would do such a thing."

The search results started printing out on Ballard's screen.

"Boatman's got a history now," Ballard said.

Bosch put a hand on her desk for support as he leaned down to read the screen. Jonathan Boatman had a record for drug possession, DUI, loitering, and disorderly conduct. All the arrests came after the murders of the Gallagher family, when Bosch would have routinely run his name, as well as after the burglary. Since then, Boatman had gone down the path of addiction and crime. The drug possession charge led to a plea agreement in which he escaped jail time by entering a six-month drug rehab program at County-USC Medical Center. The NCIC report came complete with mug shots from the arrests, and in them it was clear that Jonathan Boatman had been on a downward spiral. His face grew thin across the array of photos to the point of gauntness. The last shot showed skin blotches and a festering sore on his lower lip and, most telling of all, a dead-eyed look that showed no reaction to the fact that he was being sucked into the criminal justice system.

"Looking at the mug shots. I'm guessing meth," Ballard said.

"Yeah," Bosch said, pointing at the screen. "All the arrests came after the break-in. Maybe if I was still working the case back then, I would have picked up on it."

"But you weren't. You were retired. So don't beat yourself up about it. Maybe it leads to something now."

"Maybe."

But Bosch still felt like he had somehow dropped the ball and let the Gallagher family down. If he had stuck with the case instead of retiring, he would have seen that the burglary and McShane were not linked and there was another reason for his prints to be on the glass paperweight.

As if reading his thoughts, Ballard tried to give Bosch further absolution.

"Just remember," she said. "Sheila Walsh didn't see it for what it was and called the police. So you're not alone."

"She's a mother," Bosch said. "I'm a cop. Was a cop."

"I'm telling you not to—"

"Can you just send that report to me? Including mug shots."

"Harry, come on. This is exactly why we review cases. To see with new eyes. To see what was not seen before. So take the win here. You have a whole new angle to work."

"Will you send it to me?"

"Yes, I'm sending. But don't go running off on this. I need you on Pearlman and Wilson. I mean it."

"Don't worry, you'll have my take on the crime scene and forensics by the end of the day."

Bosch went back to his station to await her email. Once he had the NCIC report pulled up on his screen, he sent it to the printer. He noted that Boatman's last arrest was two years before. He might have cleaned up since then and kept himself right—with the law, at least. The fact that he reportedly had a job as a greenskeeper was a strong indication of recovery.

He looked at the booking photos that were part of the package and committed Boatman's face to memory. He then googled an address for the Sand Canyon Country Club and entered it in his phone's GPS app.

Bosch closed his laptop and got up to go to the printer and then his car.

"Harry, are you leaving?" Ballard asked as he crossed behind her.

"Printer," Bosch said. "Then I'm going to take a drive."

"A drive? Where?"

"Don't worry, I'll be back."

He could feel Ballard staring at him as he kept going.

While buckling up in the Cherokee a few minutes later, he got a text from Ballard. She was upset.

> You undercut my authority when you walk away like that. Please don't do it again.

Bosch felt both contrite and annoyed. He was trying to solve the murder of a family, and to him that took precedence over everything else in the world. He texted her back but restrained himself from saying anything that would inflame the situation any further.

> Sorry about that. You know how I get on a case. Won't happen again.

He waited to see if there was a reply. When there wasn't, he started the car and headed for the parking lot exit.

A few minutes later, Bosch was on the northbound 405 in moderate midmorning traffic. The freeway was elevated here and he had a good view of the towers of Century City coming up on his right and the Santa Monica Mountains dead ahead. His GPS app told him it was going to be fifty-eight minutes before he arrived at the Sand Canyon Country Club. He turned KJazz on the radio and caught the Shelly Berg Trio's take on "Blackbird," the old Beatles song.

He turned it up. It was good driving music.

13

BALLARD TOLD HERSELF not to be annoyed with Bosch. She knew that putting him on a team did not make him a team player. That was not in his DNA. She got up and went to his workstation. The package from the Wilson case that she had put together for him was sitting on the desk. He had said she'd have his review by the end of the day, but not if he did not have the records with him to review. She picked up the stack and went back to her station. She would do the work on it if Bosch wouldn't.

In the breakout of team assignments on the case, Ballard had given herself the digital media associated with Laura Wilson. Data from the victim's laptop and cell phone had been downloaded by the original investigators onto thumb drives that were slipped into the pocket on the inside cover of the murder book. Ballard had gone through the material on each drive earlier and had planned for a deeper dive. But she decided to put that digital work aside and to first review the materials she had given Bosch.

Since she had already studied the forensic reports and crime scene photos at length after connecting the Wilson and Pearlman cases, she decided to approach this new review differently. Whether in person at a crime scene or when looking at photos, the investigator always focuses on the center—the body. These photos were as horrible to look at as those of Sarah Pearlman. A young woman's body violated in many ways. A still life of stolen hopes and dreams. Ballard decided to put these aside and work her way from the outside in.

The crime scene photographer had been thorough and had taken dozens of "environmental" shots depicting the victim's entire home—inside and out—at the time of the murder. These included shots of the contents of closets and cabinets and drawers and of photos framed and hung on the walls. All of this allowed the case investigators ready access to the entire environment of the killing location. It also allowed them to better understand the victim by seeing how she had set up her home. It gave them an idea of the things that were important to her in life.

Though Wilson's apartment had only one bedroom, there was ample storage space for clothes and other belongings. Ballard moved slowly through the photos, enlarging areas that caught her interest as she went. The clothes in the walk-in closet indicated that either Wilson dedicated a large amount of her income to what she wore or money for her wardrobe was part of the support that came from her parents or other acquaintances. Nothing in any of the records showed that she'd had a current boyfriend. She had been on two fledgling social media apps at the time—Myspace and Facebook—but Ballard's earlier review of those did not show Wilson as a Hollywood party girl. She seemed to be quite serious about her five-year plan, and the rich assortment of clothes and shoes in her apartment were most likely part of that. Some taped auditions on her computer showed that she often tried out for young but sophisticated roles in movies and TV. In each of these she had dressed the part, and now Ballard was looking at the walk-in closet where Laura had put together those outfits. There was something depressing about it—that this young woman had had a plan, that she worked hard at it, prepared herself for it, stood in front of the mirror on the closet door and made sure she looked just right for a part, and that all her ambition was taken away in a horrible night of violence. Ballard made a vow to herself that she would never put this case back on the shelf. That no matter what happened, she would work this case as long as she was working cases.

The emotion of the moment hit her and made her go to the murder book to find the contacts page. The next of kin were listed as parents Philip and Juanita Wilson in Chicago. In short descriptions, Philip was listed as a fourteenth-ward committee member and Juanita was listed as a schoolteacher. Ballard knew she would be opening old wounds by calling, but she also knew parents never got past the death of a child at any age. Ballard wanted them to know the case was not on a shelf anymore and was being worked.

She called the number, and it was still good after seventeen years. An old woman's voice answered. If Laura Wilson were still alive, she would be over forty, putting her parents at least in their sixties and probably older.

"Mrs. Wilson?"

"Yes, is this LAPD?"

Ballard realized that her desk phone probably carried a generic LAPD ID.

"Yes, ma'am, my name is Renée Ballard. I'm a detective with the LAPD. I'm in charge of the Open-Unsolved Unit."

"Did you catch him? The man who killed my baby?"

"No, ma'am, not yet. I'm calling to tell you we have reopened the investigation and are pursuing new leads. I just wanted you to know."

"What new leads?"

"I can't really get into that right now, Mrs. Wilson. But if something happens and we make an arrest, I will be calling you and your husband to let you know first. For right now, I just wanted to introduce my—"

"My husband is dead. He got Covid and died two years ago. Right when it all started."

"I'm so sorry to hear that."

"He's with Laura now. At the end he couldn't breathe. He died like her, not being able to breathe."

Ballard wasn't sure how to exit the call. She thought she would be giving the parents of Laura Wilson hope, but she realized that she was just a reminder of the family's ongoing trauma.

"I can tell you one thing, Mrs. Wilson, and this is just between you and me for right now. We have connected Laura's case to another case and we are hoping that investigating them together will help lead us to the man who did this."

"What other case? You mean a murder?"

"Yes, a case that happened before. The DNA matches."

"You mean, before Laura was killed by this man, he killed someone else? Another girl? Did you put out a warning?"

"The connection was only made through DNA, and aspects of the crime were different enough that no connection was made back when these crimes happened. Do you have something to write my name down with? I will give you my direct cell number in case you have questions or anything else comes up."

It was a clumsy transition, but Ballard hoped it would bring the call to an end. Juanita Wilson wrote down her name and cell number. Ballard ended the call with an invitation to Wilson to call anytime if she had questions or thought of something that might be helpful to the renewed investigation.

After Ballard finally put the phone back into its cradle, Colleen Hatteras poked her head up over the privacy wall.

"The mother?" she asked.

"Yes," Ballard said.

She was annoyed that Hatteras had heard the conversation.

"The father is dead?" Hatteras asked.

"Yes," Ballard said. "He never saw justice for his daughter."

"Covid?"

"Yeah."

Ballard looked up at her, wondering if that was an educated guess or an empathic feeling. She decided not to ask.

"How are you doing with the witness statements?" she asked instead.

Hatteras had been given the statements made by Laura Wilson's professional and social acquaintances to determine if any were inconsistent or needed to be followed up. Such follow-ups would be a long shot, since the murder occurred so long ago and the people interviewed might now have little recall of that time period.

"Nothing is popping up so far," Hatteras said. "But I have more to go."

"Okay," Ballard said. "Let me know."

"Did you order the evidence from property?"

"I did. I said so during the briefing. It should get here today or tomorrow. Why?"

"Can I see the property list?"

"Sure."

Ballard easily found it in the murder book, unsnapped the rings, and handed the sheet over the privacy wall to Hatteras.

"What are you looking for?" Ballard asked.

Hatteras didn't answer until she had scanned the list of property and evidence stored back in 2005.

"I just wanted to see what was there," Hatteras said. "They kept her nightgown and the bedclothes."

"Right," Ballard said. "It would have been evidence presented in court if a case had ever been made."

"Sometimes I can get a communication from this sort of evidence."

"What do you mean by 'a communication'?"

"I don't know, like a feeling. A message."

"Colleen, I don't think we're going to go down that path. I have to safeguard our investigations so that they can't be successfully challenged in court. You understand? I think if we go the psychic route—and please don't take this personally— we will run into credibility issues."

"I know. I understand. It's just a thought, something to consider if we hit a wall with the investigation."

"Okay, I'll keep it in mind. But you said sometimes you get a communication from evidence like this. When have you done that before?"

"Well, I haven't officially done it before. But sometimes families have called me because they've heard about my gift. It was how I got into the whole genealogy field. From families wanting answers."

Ballard just nodded. She wished Hatteras had mentioned this during the interview process.

"I'm going to get back on this now, Colleen," she said.

"Sure," Hatteras said. "Me, too."

Hatteras dropped out of sight behind the wall and Ballard tried to put aside the growing realization that she had chosen wrong in bringing her onto the team. She went back to reviewing the crime scene photographs. Laura Wilson's bedroom walk-in closet had a built-in bureau next to the shoe racks. The photographer had opened each of the six drawers and photographed the contents without disturbing them. The first four drawers from the bottom were crammed with folded clothing, underwear, and socks. The two smaller side-by-side drawers that occupied the top tier of the bureau were filled mostly with jewelry, hair bands, and other accoutrements. One of these drawers also seemed to be the junk drawer. There were receipts, matchbooks, postcards, loose change, earbuds, phone chargers, Halloween candy, and other things.

But one thing in this drawer caught Ballard's eye in a big way. It was a round white pin-on button with orange letters that said "JAKE!" Attached to its bottom edge were two short lengths of red-white-and-blue-striped ribbon.

This gave Ballard pause and she moved quickly to the computer to open Google and run the name Jake Pearlman. While the councilman was not an internationally known politician, he did rate a Wikipedia page that listed his pathway to power in Los Angeles. The page documented his first bid for election to the city council in 2005. He had run for the Hollywood seat left

vacant when a councilman resigned following a federal indict-
ment for campaign contribution violations. Jake Pearlman lost
the election but remained active in politics, and more than a
decade later, he won that same Hollywood seat on the council.

Ballard had not known about Pearlman's early run for elected
office but recognized the campaign button because the councilman had used its simple style in his more recent elections.

Ballard leaned back in her chair and thought about this. The
2005 election came on November 8, just three days after Laura
Wilson was murdered. Somewhere in that campaign season she
had picked up or been given a button that ended up in her junk
drawer. What, if anything, did this mean? Was it coincidence
that she ended up with a button supporting a candidate whose
sister had been murdered eleven years earlier by the man who
would also kill Wilson?

She had to consider that this was no coincidence and that the
connection meant something to the case. She needed to pursue
this and get more information.

And she had to talk to Harry Bosch.

14

BOSCH WAS NOT a golfer. It was a sport that required more money than he could afford while growing up, and as an adult, he had always been too busy with his job to engage in five-hour outings on a golf course. Added to that, it still took more money than he could spare, and he had issues with calling any endeavor that involved drinking and smoking a sport. All that aside, he knew enough about it to know that it was likely that the greenskeepers worked early, doing much of their job on the course before the golfers came with their electric carts, clubs, and cigars.

He got to the Sand Canyon Country Club shortly before eleven and quickly found the hidden compound where the machinery involved in grooming the course was kept and the greenskeepers had a long break table under the spreading branches of an old sand pine. Bosch was not dressed for golf, so the workers knew right away that he had not wandered into their presence looking for a lost ball. He picked out Boatman's face from the many turned toward him and waved a hello.

"Jonathan, I was wondering if I could talk to you for a few minutes," he said.

"Uh, talk to me about what?" Boatman said. "Who are you?"

"Harry Bosch. I talked to your mother yesterday and I thought she was going to tell you I was planning to come by today."

"My mother? She didn't tell me shit. I'm on my break, man. You can't just come back here."

Bosch glanced around as if looking for a way out. He did this so that his jacket would open, revealing the badge clipped to his belt. The badge was authentic, but it said RETIRED across the bottom of the shield where for many years it had said DETECTIVE. He believed he was far enough away from the table that it could not be read by Boatman or any of the others.

"Okay," he said. "I thought it would just save some time. But I'll go back to the office at the clubhouse and get it set up."

He started to walk back toward the open gate in the fence he had entered through. As expected, Boatman stopped him. He wasn't keen on bringing management into whatever this was.

"Okay, hold on, hold on," he said.

Bosch turned around and saw that Boatman was now sliding off the bench. He walked around the table and to Bosch. Harry noted that his skin was clear and his face fuller than in the mug shots. It looked like he was clean. According to the arrest reports Bosch had reviewed, Boatman was thirty-five years old. Whether or not he had stopped using, his years of addiction had added years to his appearance and demeanor. He looked at least forty, with thinning brown hair and stooped shoulders. And though his arms were well-tanned from his work outside in the sun, his complexion was sallow. Most telling of all, his eyes were still dead.

"What's this about?" he asked. "We don't need to get management involved."

"Is there anywhere private we can talk?" Bosch asked.

"Not exactly. But let's get out of here. This is fucked up, man. I mean, I work here, and I don't need the fucking police coming around."

Boatman led Bosch around the grounds maintenance enclosure into an area under a wind-billowing canopy that protected new sod from being burned by the sun. There were four-foot-high stacks of sod squares on wooden pallets ready to be moved anywhere on the course that replanting was needed.

He abruptly turned around to face Bosch.

"All right, now what is it?" he demanded. "I am totally clean. Been that way for two years, four months, and six days."

"I don't care if you're clean or not, Jonathan," Bosch said. "This is not about your history with drugs."

"Then what is it, and what's my mother got to do with it?"

"Remember the burglary at your mother's place? I was talking to her about it yesterday and your name came up, and I thought I would check in with you, see what you remember."

Boatman put both hands on his hips and adopted what he thought was an intimidating stance. He was a solid three inches taller than Bosch and he mistakenly thought that his height and his age were an advantage.

"You come all the way out here to talk about *that*?" he said. "A ten-year-old burglary where a fucking phone was taken?"

"More like six years ago," Bosch said calmly. "And there was more than a phone taken."

"Whatever. Who gives a fuck? I wasn't even there. Why do you come to my place of work and ask me this shit? Are you trying to get me fired, motherfucker? I don't care how old you are, I'll knock your fucking head—"

Before he finished the threat, Bosch pistoned his left fist under Boatman's chin and into his throat. Boatman bit off his last word, stepped back, and leaned over, trying to get a breath down his windpipe. Bosch put his hand on his shoulder to steady him.

"It's okay," he said. "Relax and it'll come back. Just relax."

Boatman's legs went out and he landed butt-first on the ground. Bosch gently guided him down so that he was lying on his back.

"You just lost your breath, that's all," he said. "Just take it easy and it'll come back."

Boatman's face was almost purple, but then Bosch saw his skin begin to turn red and his breathing start to return to normal.

"That's it," he said. "You're all right. Just keep breathing."

"Fuck you," Boatman said.

His words came out strangled and high-pitched.

"You were threatening me and I had to stop it," Bosch said.

"I wasn't…," Boatman said.

He stopped talking, realizing it was too soon. Bosch was crouched next to him, ready to strike again if Boatman was foolish enough to attempt to retaliate.

He didn't. He relaxed and eventually turned his head to see if any of his coworkers had seen him laid low by an old man.

"What the fuck do you want?" he finally asked.

"I want to know if that was you who did the burglary."

"Why would I rip off my own mother?"

Boatman started to get up but Bosch put his hand on his chest and pushed him back down.

"Stay down," he said. "You ripped her off for drug money. It was crystal meth, right?"

"I'm not talking to you, man," Boatman said. "I'm not telling you shit."

"You sure? I mean, it doesn't matter. It's long past any statute of limitations. If I had still been a cop back then, things might've been different. But you got lucky and got away with it. You can't be charged now. So you might as well tell me."

"Like I said, I'm not telling you shit."

He looked away from Bosch, refusing to give him his eyes.

"It's okay, Jonathan," Bosch said. "You just did."

"Wrong, asshole," Boatman said.

"So what did your mother say yesterday when she called you after I left?"

"She said you're an asshole."

"Really? That hurts."

"Yeah, good."

Bosch patted him on the cheek.

"You be good now, Jonathan," he said.

His knees cracked as he got up. He stumbled a bit getting his balance and tried to hide his own physical exhaustion from the encounter. He turned from Boatman and started back toward the parking lot.

"Fuck you, old man!"

Boatman had yelled it loud but without much conviction. Bosch didn't even bother to look back. His acknowledgment was a simple wave and then he made a turn and was out of Boatman's sight.

He knew that Boatman would most likely be on the phone to his mother within minutes. That was okay with Bosch, too. He wanted Sheila Walsh to know that this was not over. Not by a long shot.

15

BALLARD WANTED TO get away from Ahmanson to think. She drove up to Abbott Kinney in Venice and ordered a harvest bowl at the Butcher's Daughter. Since her breakup with Garrett Single, the paramedic, she had tended to eat vegetarian when on her own. Single had prided himself on his barbecue skills, and it had been a consistent part of the relationship. She had spent the last three months on a cleanse of him and all red meats. She now preferred watermelon radish to brisket and, like the butcher's daughter, could not see herself going red again.

She was casually making a list as she ate. Then she got a call from one of the first entries on the list. Nelson Hastings.

"Just checking in," he said, "seeing if there's anything I can put in front of the councilman today."

"I was going to call you," Ballard said.

"Really? What's up?"

"I wanted to ask you, how far back do the councilman's campaign records go?"

"If you mean our quarterly CDRs, we keep them from day one. What's this about?"

"What's a CDR?"

"Campaign donation report. We file them in accordance with the law. But again, what's this about, Detective?"

His voice had an urgency and higher pitch than usual. Ballard guessed that the most likely place that elected politicians ran afoul of the law was in the area of money. She quickly tried to allay the concern.

"This has nothing to do with campaign contributions," she said. "I was wondering about personnel, volunteers, that sort of thing. How far back do you keep records?"

"Well, we keep some," Hastings said. "I'd have to check. Is there something specific I would be looking for?"

Ballard noted that his voice had returned to its regular, modulated tone.

"Laura Wilson," Ballard said. "She had a 'JAKE!' campaign button in a drawer and I was just wondering if she might have volunteered for him. She wouldn't have had the money to make a campaign donation, I don't think, but her parents were active in Chicago politics. I thought maybe she could have gotten involved when she came out here."

"I thought you told me that she was killed eleven years after Sarah," Hastings said. "That would be, what, '05? '06? Jake didn't get to the council till six years ago."

"Right, but he ran unsuccessfully in '05 in a special election to fill the same seat he has now. Laura lived in the district where he was running, so I thought maybe..."

"Well, that's before my time. I'd have to see what records we have. What would it mean if that was the case and she was part of the campaign?"

"I don't know yet. We're looking for connections between

the victims, and if she worked for Jake, then that's a pretty interesting connection. We'd have to see where it led."

"Yes, I see what you mean. Let me do this: I'll see what we've got in our records and get back to you as soon as I can. Okay?"

"That would be great. I'm not at the office right now, but when I get back, I could shoot you over a photo of her if that would help."

"It may, but I think the councilman will know. He never forgets a supporter's face."

"Good. If you can run the name by him—"

"Don't worry, I will."

"Thank you."

Ballard hung up and immediately called Darcy Troy at the DNA lab. She knew she might be stepping on Tom Laffont's toes, since she had assigned him the medical angle to work, but she wanted to keep things in motion.

"Darcy, it's Renée. Have you heard from Tom Laffont today?"

"Uh, no, was I supposed to?"

"Not necessarily, but I thought he might have called. On the Wilson case, are you able to see if they still have the specimen swabs they got the DNA from?"

"I can check. It should be there unless there was a destroy order from the District Attorney's Office, and that is only supposed to happen when a case is closed."

"Good. Can you see what's there? And then I need a favor."

"You want further analysis."

"I do. I want to know more about the blood. In '05, they were just interested in finding DNA. I want to know why this guy had blood in the urine. The reports in the murder book are very general. Could be kidney disease, could be bladder. I'm thinking all these years later, we might be able to learn more with serology sciences, you know?"

"I do, and I'll see what we've got."

"How long?"

"It's not what I do, but I think I can honcho something. If there is still material. Sometimes they use up everything processing for DNA."

"Fingers crossed. Thanks, Darcy."

"You got it."

Ballard disconnected and reminded herself to tell Laffont that she had already put this in play. She packed everything she had on the table into her backpack, put cash down on her check, and left the restaurant.

It took her twenty minutes to get back to the Ahmanson Center. As she was getting out of her car, she took a callback from Nelson Hastings.

"You find out anything, Nelson?"

"Nothing that I think will be helpful to the investigation. Our staffing records, CDRs, and donor lists are complete back to Jake Pearlman's successful election to the council six years ago. Everything before that apparently was not kept, because he lost the election. I asked around the office and even inquired with the councilman to see if anyone remembered Laura Wilson and came up empty."

"It was a long shot. Did the councilman have a campaign manager back in '05? Maybe he or she would remember if Wilson was a volunteer or something."

As Ballard asked the question, she saw Bosch's green Cherokee pull into the center's parking lot.

"I'll get you the name and contact info," Hastings said. "But I think the councilman would remember if someone working on his campaign had been murdered. And to be quite honest, an African American volunteer or supporter would have been remembered as well."

Ballard nodded.

"I think you're probably right," she said. "Thanks for your efforts. If you could shoot me an email with the name and number of the campaign manager from '05, that would be great."

Ballard saw Bosch pop the hatch of his car and start to pull out boxes. She knew from the red tape on them that they were evidence boxes from property division. She started walking that way.

"Detective Ballard, can I bring up a delicate matter with you?" Hastings said on the phone.

"Uh, sure," Ballard said. "What's up?"

"You seem to be going down this road of connecting this woman's death to the councilman or the campaign, and I just want to caution you to move carefully. Any hint that the councilman could have been involved in this is ridiculous and I'm sure you agree, but if it leaks to the media, it could blow up. So be careful, Detective Ballard. What you have is a ten-cent campaign button of which hundreds, if not thousands, were likely printed."

Ballard stopped in the middle of a parking lane to respond. She saw that Bosch had noticed her approaching and was waiting at the back of the Cherokee.

"Of course we are proceeding carefully and cautiously, Nelson. And my question about this does not reflect in any way on the councilman. You can tell him that."

"I will, Detective."

Hastings disconnected and Ballard continued toward Bosch. He read her face as she approached.

"What?" he said.

"Nothing," Ballard said. "Just more bullshit from the city councilman's guard dog. I see you went by property."

"Yeah, and they gave me a box from the Wilson case. They said you ordered it and I could save a messenger run if I delivered it. Can you carry one box?"

"Sure."

Ballard slung her backpack over her shoulder and leaned into the back of the Cherokee to get the box from the original Wilson investigation. It was 24 x 24 x 24 and not heavy. She lifted it and then put it down on the bumper and looked at Bosch.

"Did you talk to the meth addict?" she asked.

"Yeah, I did," Bosch said. "He's clean now, but he all but admitted that he committed the burglary at his mother's house. Now that I know it was him, it changes my thinking on McShane. He could have been in that house anytime between the murders and the burglary."

"Look, Harry, you can't do this."

"Do what?"

"Wander off on your pet case when I specifically told you I need you on Wilson."

"Pet case? Four people—a whole family—murdered and buried in a hole out in the desert, and that's a pet case."

"Look, it's a big case; it's an important case. But Wilson has got to take priority at the moment. I'm not stopping you from working Gallagher but I need you in the short run on Wilson. And I don't want to be like some kind of a shrew ordering you around. Can't you just do this for me?"

"I'm here. I'm ready to work. What I did today will get Sheila Walsh thinking: *What is Bosch doing? What is he up to?* I'll let that percolate while I work on Wilson and then I'll come back around. I'm playing the long game with her. So, what do you want me to do?"

"Let's get this stuff in and then we can talk."

"Fine."

"Good."

Ballard then lifted her box and stepped back so that Bosch, balancing a stack of two boxes with one hand, could use the other to close the hatch.

"Let's drop these at the pod, but then you and I go somewhere to talk," Ballard said. "I want your take on a couple things."

"Roger that."

"You gotta stop saying that. Everybody has to stop saying it."

"What's wrong with it?"

"When influencers are saying it on TikTok, it's jumped the shark."

"I don't know what one word of that means."

"Which is a good thing. You okay with those?"

It looked to her like Bosch was struggling with the weight of his two boxes.

"I'm good," he insisted.

"You want to get coffee?" Ballard asked.

"You read my mind."

"All right. There's a break room on the second floor that nobody from the pod knows about yet. It's for the academy trainers but they're all at Elysian today for a graduation. We'll go there."

"Roger that."

16

AFTER DROPPING OFF the property boxes at the pod, Ballard and Bosch went up to the break room on the second floor. Over black coffee Ballard updated Bosch on what was happening on the Wilson case. She showed him the photo of the junk drawer in the victim's walk-in closet and asked for his take on it. Bosch saw through her reserve as she mentioned this. He knew that beneath her neutral delivery of the information, there was something exciting to her about this angle of investigation.

"Well, I don't believe in coincidences until there is no other explanation," he said. "It needs to be checked out. Have you—"

"I asked Pearlman's chief of staff to look into it," Ballard said. "He couldn't find any records from his failed run for the council. Pearlman himself said he didn't remember Laura, and none of his current staff go back that far. Hastings said he would let me know who Pearlman's campaign manager was in '05, and I'll follow up on that. I got the idea that it was sort of a seat-of-the-pants operation, a way for Pearlman to get his name out there but he knew from the start that there wasn't much of a chance he would win."

"What about Wilson? Anything else in her place that showed she was politically involved or motivated?"

"In the apartment, no. But her father was listed in the murder book as a ward committee member in Chicago. So politics was in her upbringing. She could have taken an interest in it out here. Her apartment was in the district Pearlman was running in."

Bosch didn't respond. He took a sip of his coffee and thought about how to proceed with this angle and if it was worth the expenditure of time when there were other angles to follow. But like Ballard, he found something about the campaign button intriguing. Eleven years after Pearlman's sister is murdered, his campaign button is in the home of a woman killed by the same perpetrator.

It could easily be a coincidence. Ballard said there were hundreds of such buttons distributed back then. But it didn't feel like a coincidence, and Bosch understood Ballard's hunch all too well.

"When you talk to the campaign manager, maybe he'll remember how many of those things were made," he said. "And since Wilson's father was in politics, you might want to ask him if his daughter mentioned getting involved out here."

"Her father's dead," Ballard said. "Covid. I talked to her mother but that was before this came up. I'll call back and ask about politics. I'll also ask who cleared out Laura's apartment after her death. It's pretty unlikely, but maybe somebody has all her stuff."

Bosch nodded. He hadn't thought of that. Parents who lose children often hold on to any reminder of them.

"Good idea," he said. "Anything new on the blood angle and the DNA?"

"Nothing yet," Ballard said. "But on my way back from lunch, I got an email from Darcy Troy in the lab. She checked the cold storage at serology, and the swabs from the Wilson case—from the toilet—are still there, and there's enough left for further testing. She hopes to get back tomorrow with more on what exactly was wrong with our doer."

"That's good," Bosch said.

"It wasn't something they pursued back in the day."

"They were probably just happy to get the DNA out of it."

"Well, their oversight could be to our benefit. Obviously, the technology has advanced since 2005, and we might be able to detect things they couldn't."

"Let me know about that."

"Roger that, I will. Shit—now *I* said it!"

Bosch smiled while Ballard got up and dumped her empty cup in the trash. They went down the stairs and back to the pod. As they approached, Bosch saw that the property box Ballard had left on her desk had been opened and Colleen Hatteras was standing over it, holding up what looked like a pink nightgown. There was no one else in the pod.

"Colleen, what are you doing?" Ballard asked.

"I just needed to see it," Hatteras said. "To feel it."

"First of all, you shouldn't have done that after what we talked about before. And second, and most important of all, you should have worn gloves."

"Gloves don't work."

"What?"

"I need to be able to feel her."

"Put it back in the box. Now."

Hatteras did as instructed.

"Go back to your workstation," Ballard ordered.

Hatteras sullenly stepped back from Ballard's station. She turned and went back to her own.

Ballard threw a glance at Bosch. She looked as upset as he had ever seen her. He moved to his workstation, checked the red tape on the boxes from the Gallagher Family case, and saw that they had not been tampered with. He sat down but noticed that Ballard was still too agitated to sit down.

"Colleen, I want you to go home," she said.

"What?" Hatteras said. "I'm right in the middle of the ancestry search on this."

"I don't care. I don't want to see you anymore today. You need to go and I need to think about this."

"Think about what?"

"I told you this morning I didn't want to go down that road, but you went there anyway. This is a team, but I'm in charge of the team, and you directly ignored my order."

"I didn't think it was an order."

"It was. So, go. Now."

Ballard dropped out of Bosch's sight as she sat down. He couldn't see Hatteras but heard her open and sharply close a desk drawer and then roughly pull a zipper closed on what he assumed was a purse. She then popped up into view and headed toward the exit. Ballard said nothing as she passed the end of the pod.

Hatteras was halfway to the aisle that led to the exit when she pirouetted and came back toward Ballard.

"For what it's worth, he's close," she said. "Her killer is very close."

"Yeah, you said that about McShane, too," Ballard said. "I'll take it under advisement."

"I didn't say McShane was close. This is so typical."

"Just go home, Colleen. We'll talk tomorrow."

Hatteras pirouetted again and headed to the exit. Once she was gone, Ballard sat up straight in her seat so she could look over the partition at Bosch.

"What do I do about her?" she asked.

Bosch shook his head.

"I don't know," he said. "I don't know how valuable the heritage stuff she does is."

"Very valuable," Ballard said.

"Can you get anybody else? What about Lilia?"

"Colleen knows it like the back of her hand. But this psychic shit is a problem. Did she open your boxes?"

"No, they're safe."

"This is heading toward a bad end. This whole being-in-charge thing is a pain. I just want to follow cases."

"I get it."

She slumped down out of sight but before long she stood up again.

"I have to get out of here, Harry," she said. "I'm going up to the Valley and I need a partner."

Bosch stood up, ready to go.

17

THEY TOOK BALLARD'S city ride and were all the way onto the 405 North before Bosch asked what they were doing.

"I made a case list at lunch and there's an interview I want to cross off," Ballard said. "Due diligence as much as anything and now's as good a time as any. I needed to get out of there."

"Cool," Bosch said. "Who's the interview?"

"A guy named Adam Beecher. He and Laura Wilson were in the same theater group out in Burbank. Back then, the ODs leaned on the theater director, a guy named Harmon Harris, because they heard he and Wilson had an affair a year before her death. They thought maybe there was bad blood between them. Harris denied the affair and they dropped it when he offered up Beecher as an alibi."

She knew that Bosch would know that OD was cold case lingo for *original detective*.

"Beecher confirmed he was with him the night of the crime," he said.

"Right," Ballard said. "And I would've left it there but I happened to google these guys at lunch, and it turns out that a few years back, Harmon Harris got #MeToo'd out of the business. It was part of an *L.A. Times* series on the entertainment business. The sexual assault and harassment complaints about Harris came from both men and women. I guess he was a real Hollywood player, and that kind of scratches the I'm-innocent-because-I'm-gay angle."

"Right."

"The *Times* story also reported through anonymous sources that Harris would extort closeted gay actors who came through his classes and theater. He would threaten to derail their careers by spreading word around that they were gay."

"So you're thinking maybe the alibi confirmation was extorted from Beecher. Does Harris still run the theater?"

"No, he's dead. Car accident last year—a month after he was exposed. He hit an abutment on the one-oh-one."

"Suicide?"

"Most likely. Anyway, like I said, I hope I'm just checking this off a list. I don't want a 'cleared other.' I don't want to tell Jake Pearlman that we found the killer but he's beyond the reach of earthly law."

"I get that. What about the ODs on Wilson? Have you talked to them yet? I saw in the Pearlman chrono that the originals on that case are dead."

"I've tried on Wilson. One's dead. The other hasn't called me back. He's up in Idaho."

Many retired LAPD officers moved as far away from the place they had worked as was possible and affordable. Idaho was a favored spot, called Blue Heaven by many for its low crime, clean air, conservative politics, and don't-tread-on-me attitude. One reason Ballard liked Bosch was his decision to stay in the city he had dedicated so many years to.

"I've left two messages," she said. "I think he's one of those guys who's not going to call. If he couldn't solve it, nobody can. I hate that shit."

It wasn't the first time she had encountered the issue when working cold cases, and she couldn't understand it—putting a detective's pride in front of justice for a victim and a family who had lost something precious. She also believed it had something to do with gender. Some of these old bulls didn't like the idea of a female detective taking up their failed investigation and solving the case. She had to admit to herself that it was partially for this reason that she was not vigorously pursuing Dubose.

"What's the Idaho guy's name?" Bosch asked. "Maybe I knew him back in the day."

"Dale Dubose," Ballard said.

"I don't remember him. But let me give it a try. I'll ask around, see if anybody knows him and can get a call through that will be answered."

"Thanks. Not sure what it will get us, but you never know. Sometimes these old guys take stuff with them after they retire. They shouldn't, but they do."

"Funny. So was Dubose at Hollywood or RHD? I don't remember that name at all."

"No, the case was flipped to Northeast. Apparently Hollywood had caught two homicides earlier in the day and had everybody going full field on them. The detective lieutenant threw it over the fence to Northeast."

Hollywood and Northeast Divisions were contiguous. It was not unusual for cases to be moved one way or the other, depending on caseloads and personnel availability.

"All right, well, I'll see if I can get to Dubose," Bosch

said. "I want to ask why they did nothing with the blood in the urine."

"I kind of give them a pass on that," Ballard said. "There was only so much they could draw from the serology back then. Even if they had a list of everybody in L.A. with kidney and bladder disease, what do you do with that? It would be thousands."

"They could have at least looked for criminal records, sex offenders, narrowed it down from thousands."

"True. But remember, they were working out of Northeast, not Homicide Special downtown. They were second tier."

"Doesn't matter. I was second tier, and everybody counts. You know what this is? She was Black and they didn't run the lead out. This guy up in Blue Heaven, shoot me his number. I'm going to call him."

"And say what? You'll get his voice mail."

"I'm going to say, if he doesn't call me back, I'm going to come up there to see him. And he won't like that."

"Okay, Harry. Thanks. I'll send you the number after this interview."

Ballard merged onto the 101 and skirted the northern slope of the Santa Monica Mountains before exiting in Studio City. She headed to the address she had gotten from Adam Beecher's driver's license, a house on Vineland in the foothills.

She suddenly realized something.

"Damn. I'm sorry, Harry," Ballard said. "I just realized we should have driven separately. We're practically in your neighborhood, and now you'll have to go all the way back to Ahmanson to get your car."

"It's not a big deal," Bosch said. "You got to fill me in on the case."

"And get you pissed off about Dubose. I'll tell you what. After the interview, I can drop you off at home and then I'll come get you on the way in tomorrow."

"Well…let's decide that when we're done. I have to think about whether I need my car tonight."

"Okay. Hot date?"

"Uh, no. But speaking of hot dates, I was going to ask you: How are you and the fireman doing?"

"He's a paramedic, actually, and he's gone."

"Oh, sorry, I didn't know. I hope it was your call."

"It was."

"Too many hours apart?"

"No, the opposite, actually. He was three on, four off, and all he wanted to do when he was off duty was barbecue brisket and sit around watching *Chicago Fire* reruns."

"Hmm," Bosch said.

Ballard knew she could tell Bosch more, but she didn't go on. She wanted to stay focused on the case and the interview with Adam Beecher.

She pulled over in front of a house built on a lot that sloped so steeply right to left that one side of the house was two stories and the other side just one. The front door was up a curving stone-and-stepped path to the upper level.

"Harry, you going to be all right going up?" Ballard asked.

"Not a problem," Bosch said. "So this guy's still an actor?"

"No, not anymore. I looked him up on IMDb and he had a few roles on network TV ten, twelve years ago. His recent credits all say 'Locations Department' on various shows shot here in L.A."

"Must be pretty good at it. This neighborhood is seven figures easily."

"It could be rented. Shall we?"

Ballard opened her door. The slope was so severe that the door immediately slammed shut under its own weight. She tried again, putting her foot out to push it all the way into a holding position. Bosch struggled to get out as well, and then came around the back of the city car.

"He knows we're coming?" he asked.

"Nope," Ballard said. "Wanted it to come out of the blue."

Bosch nodded his approval.

"Hope he's home," Ballard said. "It was a lot easier catching people at home during the lockdown days."

Ballard got to the front door and then waited for Bosch to catch up. He had taken the steps up slowly and was huffing by the time he reached her.

"You okay?" she asked.

"Never better," he said.

Ballard punched a Ring doorbell, knowing that they were on camera. It wasn't long before the door was answered by a man in blue jeans and a denim shirt.

"Mr. Beecher?" Ballard asked.

"That's right," he said. "What can I do for you?"

Ballard badged him and identified herself and Bosch as her partner.

"We'd like to come in and ask you a few questions," she said.

"About what?" Beecher said. "I'm actually working and have a Zoom in, like, twenty minutes that I have to prep for."

"This won't take long, sir. May we?"

"Uh, I guess."

He stepped back and opened the door for them. They entered a neat and expensively furnished living room with a dining area and kitchen beyond and a hallway toward the back of the house. There were large canvases framed in wood on the walls, all studies of the male figure.

"Is this about the robbery?" Beecher asked.

"What robbery is that?" Ballard asked.

"The Tilbrooks next door. Their house got hit a few nights ago. First time out to the movies in more than two years, and their house gets robbed while they're gone. What a town, right?"

"That would be a burglary and we're investigating a homicide."

"A homicide? Shit. Who?"

"Can we sit down, sir?"

"Sure."

He gestured to the couch and chairs configured around a coffee table that appeared to be a two-inch-thick cut of redwood. There was a small sculpture on the table. An angel sitting in repose, one of his wings broken on the ground at his feet. Ballard sat down in the middle of the couch, on the front edge of the cushion, pulling out a small pad from the pocket of her Van Heusen sport coat. Bosch took a black leather chair off the corner of the coffee table, and that left Beecher the twin in the matching set.

Ballard began the questioning.

"Mr. Beecher, we have reopened an investigation into the 2005 homicide of Laura Wilson. You were acquainted with her, correct?"

"Oh, Laura, yes, we were in theater together. Oh my god, I think about her all the time. It so bothered me that they never caught anybody. I can't imagine what her family has gone through."

"You were questioned back then by Detective Dubose. Do you remember that?"

"I do, yes."

"You told Detective Dubose that you were with Harmon Harris on the night of the murder."

Ballard watched as Beecher's face darkened and his eyes flitted away. He obviously didn't think of Harmon Harris in the affectionate way he thought of Laura Wilson.

"I did, yes," he said.

"We are here because we want to give you the opportunity to retract that statement if you wish," Ballard said.

"What do you mean, that I lied?"

"What I mean is, if it wasn't true that you were with him, then now is the time to set the record straight, Mr. Beecher. This is an unsolved homicide. We need to know the truth."

"I have nothing to set straight."

"Are you still in the theater, Mr. Beecher? An actor?"

"I rarely act. I just got too busy with my other work."

"What work is that?"

"I'm in locations for L.A.-based productions. It's more work than I can handle, to tell you the truth."

Ballard noted that he could not acknowledge that he didn't quite make it as an actor. He claimed something else had pulled him away from that work.

"You know that Harmon Harris is dead, right?" she said.

"Yes," Beecher said. "That was a tragedy."

"He drove into a concrete pillar on the freeway a month after being outed as being abusive to his students and employees at the theater. It was a story in the *Los Angeles Times*. Did you know about that, too?"

Beecher nodded vigorously. His hands were gripped together tightly in his lap.

"Yes, I knew about that," he said.

"The article anonymously quoted three different men who said that Harris threatened to spread the word in the industry that they were gay if they did not have relations with him. You read that, too, right?"

"Yes."

"You're gay as well, sir—correct? Your alibi for him was that you spent the night together on the night Laura Wilson was murdered."

"Yes, all true, but what's it got to do with the new investigation?"

"Were you extorted in any way by Harris to provide an alibi for him?"

"No, I wasn't!"

"Were you an anonymous source for that *Times* article?"

"I was not! I think you really need to go now. I have a Zoom."

Beecher stood up but Ballard and Bosch did not.

"Please sit down, Mr. Beecher," Ballard said. "We have more questions."

"My Zoom is in, like, five minutes," Beecher complained.

"The sooner you sit down, the sooner you will get to your Zoom."

Beecher had moved behind his chair and put his hands on it as if for support. He bowed his head and then raised it angrily.

"I want you to leave," he said.

"Sit down," Bosch said. "Now."

Bosch's first words in the house gave Beecher a jolt and he looked at Bosch as if scared.

"Please," Ballard offered.

"Oh, whatever," Beecher said.

He came around the chair and dropped into it.

"Laura's father died of Covid last year," Ballard said. "He never saw justice for his daughter. Her mother is still alive and waiting for justice. We need your help, Mr. Beecher. We need the truth."

Beecher ran both hands through his thick dark hair, messing up what had been a carefully composed front wave.

"You're barking up the wrong tree," he said.

Ballard leaned a few inches forward. It was not a denial or an admission that he had lied. But she took it as an indication that there was a new story to be told.

"How so?" she asked.

"Harmon didn't kill Laura," Beecher said. "There is no way in the world that happened."

"Is that why you gave him an alibi?"

"He had an alibi but he couldn't use it."

"Which was?"

"He was with someone else, not me. But that person couldn't go to the police. He was a famous guy and he couldn't risk it coming out that he wasn't straight. His career would have been over."

"You knew this man?"

"At the time I knew of him. A lot of people did. So Harmon made me say I was the one with him that night, end of story."

"Who was it who was really with him that night?"

"I'm not telling you. It's the same risk today that it was back then. He's still a star. I'm not going to ruin his career."

"We would keep it confidential. We wouldn't even put it on paper."

"No. Nothing stays a secret forever, but if I told you, it would be a betrayal. Not just of him, but of all of us."

Ballard slowly nodded. She instinctively guessed that they had gotten all they could from Beecher. He had admitted that he lied but confirmed the alibi of Harmon Harris.

"Okay, let me ask you this," Ballard said. "If you weren't with Harris, how do you know he was actually with this other person? This Mr. X movie star."

"Because I asked him."

"You asked Mr. X?"

"Yeah, I wasn't going to just take Harmon's word and lie to the cops. I went to him and asked. He confirmed. End of story, and you have to leave now."

"You know, we could charge you for lying to us back then."

"After seventeen years? I really doubt that."

Ballard knew her threat had backfired almost as soon as she said it. She could think of no other way to get the name she needed from Beecher.

"Are you still in touch with Mr. X?" she asked.

"No, not really," Beecher said. "He's gotten so big you can't get near him even to say, 'Hey, you remember me?'"

"Could you reach out and get him to call us anonymously? I just want to confirm this and move on with the investigation."

"No. It's impossible for him to be anonymous. You'd know who you're talking to within ten seconds."

Ballard nodded and glanced over at Bosch. It was her signal for him to ask any questions he might be sitting on. But he gave a slight shake of the head. He had nothing to ask that hadn't already been asked.

"Okay, Mr. Beecher, thank you for your cooperation," she

said. "I'm going to leave you my card, and I hope you'll call if you think of any further information to share with me."

"Fine," Beecher said. "But I don't think I'll be calling you."

All three of them stood up and headed toward the door. Beecher opened it and then stepped back to let Ballard and Bosch out. As Bosch passed him, Beecher spoke.

"You don't talk too much, do you?" he said.

"I usually don't have to," Bosch said.

18

BOSCH WAS LISTENING to the King Curtis live album recorded at the Fillmore West just a few months before he was murdered in 1971. He popped the volume two notches for "A Whiter Shade of Pale" and thought about all the music not recorded by the sax player because of his early demise in a fight in front of his New York apartment. Parker, Coltrane, Brown, Baker—the list of those who left the stage in mid-song was long. It got Bosch thinking about the Gallagher family and all that was lost with them. The kids never even had the chance to leave a song behind.

There was a short honk from outside the house and Bosch lifted the needle off the record and killed the power to the stereo. He grabbed his keys and went out the front door. Ballard was in her city ride at the curb, the passenger door already open. It told Bosch that something had her in a hurry this morning. He got in quickly and pulled his seat belt on.

"Morning," he said.

"Good morning," she said. "Was that Procol Harum you were playing?"

She said it with surprise in her voice as she pulled away from the curb and headed down to Cahuenga.

"Close," Bosch said. "It was a cover by King Curtis."

"My father loved that song," Ballard said. "He'd sit on the beach after surfing and play it on this toy flute he had."

"First time I heard it was on a harmonica. A guy in Vietnam. It sounded like a funeral song to me. And that guy, he never made it home."

That ended the conversation and Bosch became self-conscious about the buzzkill. Ballard rescued him by handing him a piece of paper he knew came from her notebook.

"What's this?"

"My case list. Look it over and pick something to run with. Pick more than one."

Bosch studied the list. There were several entries but some had already been crossed out as completed.

"'Photo to NH'?" he asked.

"I was supposed to send Nelson Hastings a photo of Laura Wilson," Ballard said. "But he already asked about her in the office before I got to it."

"I'd still send it. Sometimes a face is more memorable than a name."

"Yeah, but no one in the current office was around during that first election. I need to remind Hastings he has to get me the name of the campaign manager. I'll see if he wants the photo then."

"'Juanita'—is that the victim's mother?"

"Yes, in Chicago. We need to find out what happened to Laura's belongings, see if the campaign button can be located."

"Right, how about I talk to her, and I'm also going to get to Dale Dubose."

"Great."

"What else?"

"When we get in, I want to call Darcy Troy. She texted me on my way over. She has some preliminary info on our suspect's health that she wants to share. I didn't want to do it while driving and because I want you to hear it."

"That's why you're in a hurry?"

"I didn't say that, but, yeah, I want to find out what she's got and I want you there. We can go into the interview room and call her. You can deal with Juanita afterward. Cool?"

"Cool."

They had gotten to the 101 and were heading south, the spires of downtown in the mist ahead. They would end up taking three freeways to get to Westchester and the Ahmanson Center.

"So," Bosch said. "You've had a night to sleep on it. What do you think about Beecher?"

"Well, I really don't like being unable to confirm his story," Ballard said. "But he wasn't going to give up Mr. X and we had no leverage to make him."

"What's your gut say?"

"My gut says it's a true story. And I have to tell you, I went down an internet rabbit hole last night, trying to check associations and crossing points between Harmon Harris and people in the business on the level that Beecher was talking about."

"Are you going to tell me Brad Pitt is gay?"

"No, I'm going to tell you I wasted two hours that I could have used for sleep. I came up with nothing and nobody I could even hazard a guess at. What's your gut say?"

"To quote Beecher, I think we're barking up the wrong tree. We needed to do it, due diligence and all of that, but I don't see Harmon Harris doing this and I think Beecher was believable."

"Then we're done with it. We move on."

They got to the Ahmanson Center by eight o'clock and were the first members of the OU Unit to arrive at the pod. After a stop at the break room, they took their coffees into the interview room and closed the door so they could talk to Darcy Troy in private.

"Think Colleen's going to come in today?" Bosch asked.

"I don't care, as long as she keeps her hands off the property boxes."

Ballard made the call on her cell and put it on speaker. Troy picked up right away.

"Hey, Renée," she said.

"Darcy," Ballard said. "Thanks for running with this. I'm here with Harry Bosch, who is one of the cold case investigators working with me."

"Hi, Harry," Troy said.

"Hello," Bosch said. "Nice to meet you."

"Oh, we've met," Troy said. "It was many years ago, when I first came on in the DNA lab."

"Oh, okay," Bosch said, slightly embarrassed. "Then good to meet you again."

"So, you have an update for us?" Ballard asked.

"I do," Troy said. "I would term this preliminary because there's more we can do, but I knew you were moving quickly, so let me tell you what we've got right now. As you know, they really didn't do much with this when the case first came in, what, seventeen years ago. But there was enough of the sample stored here to allow for further analysis."

"We got lucky," Ballard said.

"We did," Troy said. "So we ran a basic urine cytology test on what we had, and it does show high levels of albumin and renal epithelial cells. These are clear signs of damage somewhere in the kidneys, bladder, or urinary tract. Most of the time it signals what is called clear cell renal cell carcinoma. This man likely had a tumor in one or possibly both kidneys, but of course we can't be sure, since we don't have him to examine."

"Would he have known he had cancer?" Ballard asked.

"He would have eventually," Troy said. "But we can't tell what he knew from what we have to go on now."

"Would it have been fatal?" Ballard asked.

"If untreated, yes," Troy said. "But if caught early, it can be treated. And if it is contained in only one kidney, the damaged organ can be removed. After all, we have two."

"What about transplant?" Bosch asked.

"That, too," Troy said. "But people are not really considered for organ transplant in cases of cancer unless it's caught super early. Transplant is normally considered where the kidneys are damaged by disease other than cancer. I should say here that I'm not an expert on this by any means. Most of what I'm telling you I researched last night."

"We really appreciate this, Darcy," Ballard said.

"We girls have to stick together, Renée," Troy said. "No offense, Harry."

"None taken," Bosch said. "What could be the cause of this cancer?"

"Oh, well, now you're opening up a whole can of worms," Troy said. "Again, we have an unknown subject and know nothing of his life and experiences. This could be a hereditary predisposition, or it could have been some sort of toxic exposure. I know you're trying to identify this guy. I would say that it could be somebody who worked in an industry where there was prolonged exposure to carcinogens. I know that doesn't really help you, but it's the best I've got considering what we do know — which is not much."

"Well, we know a lot more than we did before this call," Ballard said. "You said there's further work you can do on this?"

"Just a deeper dive into it — more analysis on the specimen we have," Troy said. "We may be able to narrow down exactly what this person's illness was. But this time it won't be quick. I would need to find an oncology lab and send it out. I have to make some calls later but likely it will be County-USC."

"Really appreciate it, Darcy," Ballard said again.

"You got it," Troy said.

All three said their goodbyes and disconnected. Ballard took a drink of coffee and then asked Bosch what he thought of the new information.

"It's good stuff but it's sort of after-the-fact," he said. "Dubose and his partner missed the chance to put together a list of people with kidney disease back at the time of the killing. I don't see how we could do that now. So after we arrest the guy, we use it to tie him in. But we'll already be able to do that with DNA."

"So there's no way at all to use this to identify him?" Ballard asked.

"That's the hard part, because we don't know when he sought treatment, or if he even did seek treatment. Maybe he never knew and got sick and died."

Ballard nodded.

"What about you?" Bosch prompted.

"I just think there has to be a way to use this as a search tool," Ballard said. "The others may have some ideas when we bring them up to speed."

"Maybe Colleen can tell you whether the guy's dead or alive."

"Harry, please. It's not funny. I don't know what I'm going to do about her. I think I'm going to ask Lilia to take over the hereditary part of this."

"But you said Hatteras was the best on your team."

"She is, but I can't have her disobeying direct orders. The psychic bullshit I can actually deal with. But when I tell her not to handle property and evidence and she does exactly that, then I have to do something."

"I guess so."

Ballard stood up, ready to go.

"Okay," Bosch said. "I'm going to call Juanita Wilson. Do you have her contacts?"

"I have her number," Ballard said. "I'll text it to you."

They left the interview room and returned to the pod. Hatteras, Masser, Aghzafi, and Laffont were all at their stations. Bosch guessed they were working multiple days because they knew how important this case was to the longevity of the unit. He sat down at his station and made the call to Chicago as soon as Ballard sent him the number for Juanita Wilson. The call was answered right away.

"Mrs. Wilson?"

"Yes."

"My name is Harry Bosch. I'm with the Los Angeles Police Department cold case squad. You spoke with my colleague Renée Ballard yesterday."

"Yes. Have you made an arrest?"

"Not yet, Mrs. Wilson, but we're working very hard on the case. I wondered if I could ask you a few more questions."

"Yes, of course. I'm just so thankful that there is still an investigation. I thought you people had given up."

"No, ma'am, we aren't giving up. I know this must be very difficult for you to be thinking of those horrible times, but do you remember, after your daughter's death, what happened to all her property and belongings that were here in Los Angeles?"

There was a long silence before Juanita Wilson responded.

"Well, let me see," she said. "My husband and I went to Los Angeles to bring her home. And when we were there, we were allowed to go into her apartment after the police were all through. We packed all of her things in boxes and shipped them back here. And some of the furniture we put out in front of her building like a little garage sale and we sold it."

Bosch tried to control his anticipation. But Juanita's first answer gave him hope.

"How many boxes did you send back to Chicago? Do you remember?"

"Oh, there were quite a few. That's why we sent them. There was too much to take on a plane."

"And what happened to the boxes once they were in Chicago?"

"You know, for a long time I couldn't bear to open them and look through her things. So they were in the closet in her bedroom for the longest time. And then I started taking a look from time to time, you know, just to get a sense of her."

"Do you still have the boxes?"

"Of course, I couldn't throw those things away. They were my daughter's."

"I understand that. Mrs. Wilson, the crime scene photographer took what we call 'environmental photographs' of your daughter's apartment. These were photos that were not actually of the crime scene but of the rest of the apartment. Like what was on Laura's refrigerator and in the drawers of her bureau, things like that. And we have one photo that shows a campaign button for a man who was running for city council out here at that time. We think it might be important to the case."

"How would it be important?"

"Well, I can't really talk about it at the moment, but I'm wondering if you would be willing to look through the boxes you have and see if you find it. It is probably a long shot, but it would help us if you could. If you give me an email address, I could send you the photo that was taken back then. Is this something you think you can do?"

"I could, yes."

"When would that be?"

"As soon as I hang up this phone. If you think it will help the investigation, I'm going to do it right now."

She gave Bosch her email address and he wrote it down.

"Give me ten minutes and then check your email," Bosch said. "I'll send you the photo and I'll circle the button so you will know exactly what we're looking for."

He described the pin while looking at the photo of it.

"Send it to me," Juanita said. "I'll be waiting."

"One thing, Mrs. Wilson," Bosch said. "If we're lucky enough that the button is still there, I don't want you to touch it. Just identify it and then call me and we can talk about how to preserve it. But for now, I just want you to look for it but not touch it, okay? That's important."

"Okay. You'll send the email?"

"Yes, I have to scan the photo first, so it might take a few minutes."

"Good."

"Thank you."

Bosch disconnected. He thought there was only a slim chance that Juanita Wilson would find the campaign pin, but he felt his spirits boosted by her willingness to work with him. He believed that positive energy often paid off.

19

BALLARD HAD TAKEN Colleen Hatteras into the interrogation room to speak privately with her about the blurred line between her IGG work and her self-claimed empathic skills. Though this was Ballard's first position as a supervisor, she instinctively understood the boss-employee paradigm: Praise in public, criticize in private. She knew she had broken that unwritten rule when she had angrily sent Hatteras home in front of Bosch, but now she was calm and playing it right.

"The cases are too important," Ballard said. "We are dealing with victims and families. I'm sorry, but I can't risk these cases. If you're going to stay on the team, then I need you to put that psychic/empath stuff away."

"I don't understand," Hatteras protested. "What is the risk?"

"Colleen, come on. You know what I'm talking about. If we make a case through IGG, then that investigator—most likely you—will have to testify to a jury about how you made the connections and the identification of the suspect. You are a civilian. You've never been in law enforcement, and any smart defense lawyer is going to try to destroy your credibility. And if they destroy you, they destroy the case. It's called 'killing the messenger.'"

"You are saying I have no credibility because I have these feelings?"

"I'm saying a defense lawyer will challenge your credibility. And even if your feelings have had nothing to do with the case, it doesn't matter. The lawyer will kill you with the questions. Here's one: 'Answer this. Ms. Hatteras: Did you communicate with the victim in this case?'"

Hatteras took a moment to compose an answer.

"No, I did not," she finally said.

"'But you do call yourself a psychic, don't you?'" Ballard pressed.

"No, I never call myself that."

"'Really? But don't you get messages from the dead?'"

"Messages, no."

"'What about impressions?'"

"Well…"

"'When you held the nightgown worn by the victim of this case on the night of her murder, did you get a psychic impression? Can you share it with the jury?'"

Hatteras pursed her lips and her eyes got glassy as tears started to form. Ballard spoke quietly and sympathetically.

"Colleen, I don't want that to happen to you. I don't want it to happen to a case where a family has waited years for justice. I'm protecting you as much as them. You need to keep that part of you out of your work here. You are great at IGG and that's what I need from you. Do you understand?"

"I guess so."

"I really need a yes or no, Colleen."

"Yes. Yes."

"Good. So why don't you get back to it. I'm going to stay in here and make a call."

"Sure."

Hatteras got up and left the room, shutting the door behind her. Ballard looked at the case list she had put down on the table. She crossed a line through the entry about talking to Hatteras and surveyed what was left. The top entry was talking to whoever had been Jake Pearlman's campaign manager in 2005. She pulled her phone to call Nelson Hastings, but there was a knock on the door before the call went through. She disconnected.

"It's open."

Bosch came in and shut the door behind him.

"What did you do to her?" he asked.

"Who?" Ballard responded.

"Colleen. She just walked stiff-legged out of the room. Looked like she was about to cry."

"I told her she had to stow the psychic shit or she was off the team."

Bosch nodded as if to acknowledge that it had to be done.

"Must be fun being boss," he said.

"It's a blast," Ballard replied. "What do you need, Harry?"

"To go to Chicago. Juanita found the button."

"Holy shit, where?"

"She and her husband came out after the murder and cleared Laura's apartment. They boxed all the personal effects and sent them to Chicago. It's pretty much been in a box ever since."

"Did she handle it?"

"Not today, no. I told her not to. And she could not

remember ever handling it in the past. So it's there, and I want to go get it."

"Why? Just have someone in Chicago PD pick it up."

"Because that will take forever, first to get them to do it, then to get it shipped here. I know it's unlikely that there's a usable print or a dot of DNA on it, but if there is, then you will have chain-of-custody issues at trial. Every Chicago cop involved in the pickup and shipping will have to be brought in to testify. If I go, you just call me. It's good case management. But really, none of that matters because Juanita told me she wouldn't let the Chicago police in her house to collect the button. She lives in the fourteenth ward. You remember what happened there?"

"No, what?"

"That was where Laquan McDonald was shot by a cop a few years ago. Remember? Sixteen times in the back. They covered it up until a video came out, and the cop went to prison."

"Another bad apple making us all look bad."

Bosch nodded.

"I checked the airlines. I could get there tonight, go see Juanita in the morning, and be back here tomorrow afternoon."

"I'm never going to get approval or a travel voucher today, Harry. If I put in the request, I'll be lucky to hear back by the end of the week."

"I know. I'm going on my own. I already booked it."

"Harry, hold on. I don't want you using your own money to—"

"I go, I get the button, you put in an expense request. If you get it, I get made whole. If you don't, that was my risk, and I'm willing to take it."

Ballard said nothing. She was thinking and coming to the conclusion that Bosch's plan was best.

"If I'm gonna go, I need to get to the airport in an hour," Bosch said.

"That's not enough time for you to get home, pack clothes, and get back to the airport," Ballard said.

"I have a go bag in my car."

"Harry, what are you, seventy? And you drive around with a go bag?"

"I put it in this week. For this job. You never know where it's going to take you. So we're good? I'll need some gloves, tape, and an evidence bag. Probably a print kit, too."

"Hold your horses. I want to make sure this is legit."

Ballard got up and went to the door. She called out to Paul Masser and asked him to come to the interview room.

Masser stepped in and Ballard invited him to take the remaining chair. She then ran the scenario of Bosch going to Chicago past him and asked if he, as a former deputy district attorney, saw any procedural or prosecutorial hiccups in the plan.

"Let me think for a second," Masser said. "On its face it seems…kosher to me. Harry is a volunteer member of the unit. He has immense experience in cases and the finding and collecting of evidence. If the defense tries to challenge this, I think I'd be able to rely on Harry's experience to head off any suggestion of impropriety or incompetence. Would you go alone?"

Bosch and Ballard looked at each other and then Ballard nodded.

"Yes," she said. "Alone. I don't want to lose two people on this. Frankly, it's a Hail Mary."

"Well, then, I'd ask that you document the evidence

collection," Masser said. "Video it and note the date and time and all of that."

"Not a problem," Bosch said.

"Okay, then I think you're good," Masser said.

"Great," Ballard said. "Thanks, Paul."

Masser got up and left the room.

"I have the gloves and the other stuff in my car," Ballard said. "I'll walk out with you."

Her phone buzzed and she saw on the screen that it was Nelson Hastings.

"Let me take this first," Ballard said.

"I'll be at my desk," Bosch said. "Remember, I need to go."

Ballard answered as he walked out the door.

"Nelson, I was just about to call you, when I got—"

"The councilman is on his way. Surprise visit."

Hastings disconnected.

"Shit," Ballard said.

One of the things that helped Jake Pearlman get elected and then keep his job for a second term was his routine of making so-called surprise visits to people and places in his district. These, of course, were photo ops for the media, which was always invited. And Ballard knew that the heads-up from Hastings was to allow her time to prep for what was actually a no-surprise surprise visit.

She left the interview room to warn the team about what was coming.

20

BECAUSE OF A massive construction project to build Metro train access to the LAX terminal loop, two of the six parking structures were closed and Bosch had to drive out of the loop, park at a garage on Century Boulevard, and take a shuttle bus back to the American Airlines terminal. He then faced a long security line, and by the time he got to his gate, boarding was well underway, and Bosch was the very last passenger allowed on.

He had hoped for some downtime in the terminal to make some calls and reserve a hotel room for that night, as well as check on the lineups of performers in the Chicago jazz clubs.

His seat was midway through the economy cabin, and there was no room in the overhead bins for his carry-on bag. He stuffed it under the seat in front of his window seat, which left him little room for his feet. Cramped and crammed in, he had to turn sideways in his seat to dig the cellphone out of his pocket. It had been almost three years since he had been on a plane, and he realized he hadn't missed it at all.

His daughter worked a mid-watch shift, so he believed she would be awake but not working yet. As he was about to call her to inform her of his travels, he received an incoming call from an unknown number.

"Bosch."

"Leave my son alone."

It was a woman's voice and Bosch immediately knew who it belonged to. He turned toward the window and talked softly so as to not be overheard.

"Mrs. Walsh? He—"

"You just leave him out of this, you understand? You punched him! You punched my son!"

"Because he needed to be punched. Look, I know he was the one who broke into your house. He either told you or you figured it out later but by then you'd already called the police. So when McShane's prints came up, you were happy to lay the burglary off on him so the police wouldn't come looking for your son."

"You don't know what you are talking about."

"I think I do, Sheila. And I'm in the middle of something right now but we are going to talk very soon. I want the truth about how McShane's prints got there."

"Don't you come near me, and don't you come near my son. I have a lawyer and he'll sue your ass till you have nothing left."

"Listen to me, Sheila—"

She disconnected.

Bosch considered calling her back but decided to leave it. His approach to her son had obviously spooked her and that's what he had wanted. He would let that percolate for a while and then he'd come knocking on her door, lawyer or no lawyer.

Bosch looked around. The plane hadn't moved yet and there were no flight attendants in the aisle to tell him to stop using his phone. He quickly called his daughter.

"Hi, Dad."

"How's it going, Mads?"

Just then an announcement came blaring out of an overhead speaker as the plane's first officer addressed the passengers and gave the details of the flight plan and arrival.

"Sorry, hold on," Bosch said.

The pilot said it was a four-hour flight that would get in at Chicago O'Hare at 8 p.m. Central Time, with the two-hour time change.

"Okay," Bosch said. "Sorry about that."

"Are you on a plane?" his daughter asked.

"Yeah, I'm going to Chicago. About to take off."

"What's in Chicago?"

"I'm on a case. I sort of got recruited by Renée Ballard for the reboot of the Open-Unsolved Unit."

"You are kidding me. Why didn't you tell me?"

"Well, I just sort of started this week. I wanted to see how it goes first, then I was going to tell you."

"Dad, are you sure you should be doing this? I wish you had told me before you agreed to do this."

"Yes, I'm sure. This is what I do, Mads. You know that."

"And she already has you going to Chicago on a case."

"It's really just an errand. I'm picking up a piece of evidence. I'll just be gone a night but wanted to check in with you, see how things were going."

"Is Renée with you?"

"No, going by myself. I'm just making a pickup and then coming back. Nothing dangerous. Not even bringing a gun."

"You still shouldn't do this stuff by yourself. Why can't the Chicago police just send it to you?"

"That's a long story but, really, it's not a big deal, Maddie. I'll be in and out. I wouldn't even stay over if I could have scheduled it earlier. So never mind me. What's going on with you? How is SPU?"

She had recently been assigned to the Special Problems Unit at Hollywood Division. The unit followed a law enforcement strategy of attacking hot spots of crime by flooding the problem area with increased patrols and other tactics targeting the specific crime trend. It was a favored assignment among young officers because it wasn't always uniform duty. It also involved plain-clothes surveillance as well as decoy operations. Bosch knew his daughter was particularly proud of getting the assignment less than a year after graduating from the police academy.

"It's all good," Maddie said. "I've been decoying all week on Melrose. They're having a problem with drive-by purse snatchers. But so far nothing."

Bosch pictured his daughter walking the sidewalks of the hip shopping area with a purse loosely slung over her curbside shoulder, waiting for the robbers to drive up, grab it, and go.

"Cool. Just you, or are there other decoys?"

"Just me and a couple follow teams."

Bosch was glad to hear she was the solo decoy. He didn't want the follow teams concentrating on anybody else.

The plane jerked as it started to pull back from the gate.

"I think I gotta go, we're rolling."

"Okay, Dad. Stay safe and let me know when you're back."

"You, too. Shoot me a text when you get the bad guys, okay?"

"Will do."

They disconnected.

Bosch quickly made one more call, punching in the phone

number Ballard had given him for retired detective Dale Dubose in Coeur d'Alene, Idaho. He knew the call would probably go unanswered, so he wasn't worried about starting a conversation as the plane was taking off. Most departing planes at LAX taxied for a good fifteen minutes before getting the all clear to take off.

As expected, the call went to voice mail. Bosch cupped a hand over his mouth and the phone so he would not be overheard while he left a message.

"Dale Dubose, it's Harry Bosch with the cold case unit at LAPD. I need you to call me back about the Laura Wilson case or you're going to find me at your front door. I'll give you a day and then I'm coming up there. And I'll be pretty pissed off if I have to fly all the way up for a conversation that can be handled over the phone."

Bosch repeated his cell number twice and then disconnected. He hoped the tone of his voice on the message would convey to Dubose that ignoring the call was not an option.

He then turned his phone off and put it back in his pocket.

Fifteen minutes later, the plane was in the air and Bosch was looking down through the window at the cold, dark Pacific as the plane banked after takeoff and started to turn east.

21

AFTER GETTING THE alert from the front desk, Ballard went out to the entrance of the homicide archive to receive Councilman Jake Pearlman and his entourage. They came down the main hallway four wide—two men, two women—plus a pool videographer and two reporters. Ballard had not yet met Pearlman in person, as most of her interactions had been phone calls or Zooms or with Nelson Hastings.

"Detective Ballard?" Pearlman said as he approached.

He reached out his hand and they shook. Pearlman was clean-shaven with curly dark hair. His grip was firm. He was taller and trimmer than she had expected. Her impression from the Zoom videos was that he would be short and squat. This was probably because he used a fixed video camera that caught him from a downward angle. Pearlman wore his standard campaign look—blue jeans, black sneakers, and a white button-down shirt, sleeves haphazardly rolled up to the elbows.

"Welcome to the Ahmanson Center and the homicide archive," Ballard said. "Thank you for coming."

"Well, I had to see it," Pearlman said. "And I had to finally meet you in person."

The councilman introduced his entourage. Ballard already knew Hastings. He was slightly shorter than Pearlman, with close-cropped brown hair. He carried himself with a precise military bearing. The women were Rita Ford, the councilman's political adviser, and Susan Aguilar, his policy adviser. Both women were mid-thirties and attractive, dressed in conservative, professional suits. Ballard considered that politics and policy might be the same thing or at least overlap in terms of advisement but didn't ask the question.

"Well, if you'd like to come back, I'll show you what we're doing," she said.

"Of course," Pearlman said. "And I want to hear the latest on Sarah's case. You don't know what it means to me just to know that progress is being made."

"I'll be happy to sit down with you after the walk-through."

"Then please lead the way."

They entered the archive and Ballard slowly led the group by the rows of shelved murder books and told them the somber statistics and facts that they already knew, since it had been their pressure on the police department that resulted in the Open-Unsolved Unit being reborn.

Eventually, they came to the pod and Ballard introduced each of the investigators on the team and explained what his or her specialty was. She also pointed to Bosch's empty spot and noted that their most experienced investigator was in the field, not mentioning that he had extended the field to Chicago.

As she made the introductions, she saw Hastings come up behind the chair where Ted Rawls sat and briefly put his hands on his shoulders. That, plus the fact that Rawls had conveniently arrived at the pod just minutes before Pearlman, confirmed what

Ballard already knew: Rawls was tight with Hastings and, by extension, Pearlman. Hastings most likely gave Rawls the same heads-up she had gotten. And he probably got the first call.

The councilman asked a few questions of the investigators, primarily for the video camera, and then Hastings said it was time to move things along.

"The councilman's schedule is very tight," he said. "And I know he wanted a few minutes alone with Detective Ballard to get an update."

Ballard wheeled Bosch's desk chair around to her pod and invited Pearlman to sit down. Hastings stood a few steps behind them, ever on watch, while Ford and Aguilar engaged Hatteras in a discussion of her role as the team's investigative genetic genealogy specialist.

While Ballard was worried that Hatteras might start talking about her empathic feelings, she shut out the distraction to focus on her briefing with Pearlman.

"Before I tell you where we are with the investigation, I want to start with a couple questions," Ballard said. "You don't remember a young woman named Laura Wilson having any involvement in your 2005 campaign, correct?"

"Yes, that's what I told Nelson," Pearlman said. "I don't re-member the name and I don't remember an African American woman among our volunteers back then. Now I have major support in the Black community, but that first election was, well, not very well-thought-out or executed."

Ballard opened the Laura Wilson murder book, where she had placed one of the actress's 8 x 10 headshots with her résumé printed on the back side. She handed the photo to Pearlman.

"That's Laura Wilson," she said.

Pearlman took the photo and Ballard studied him for a reaction as he looked at it. She saw no recognition in his eyes and then Pearlman slowly shook his head.

"So sad," he said. "She was beautiful, but no, I don't recognize her."

"Who ran your campaign back then?" Ballard asked.

Hastings stepped in close to the pod and leaned down to speak quietly.

"I thought this was going to be an update from you," he said. "Not a Q and A. The councilman has to get back to City Hall in an hour."

"I'm sorry," Ballard said. "That was my last question, and then I can bring you up to speed."

"Let's just proceed with the update," Hastings insisted.

"It's all right, Nelson," Pearlman said. "I wouldn't call it much of a campaign, but what there was of it was run by our friend Sandy Kramer."

"Kramer no longer works with you?" Ballard asked.

"No, he left politics a long time ago," Pearlman said. "Last I heard, he was selling tuxedos in Century City."

"Do you still have a number for him?" Ballard asked.

"I'm sure we could dig one up for you," Pearlman said. "I'll have Nelson look in the old Rolodex. Now, how close are you to cracking this case and bringing some justice to my sister and my family?"

Ballard didn't tell Pearlman everything about their progress but provided enough details for him to know that the case had the most important thing going for it: momentum.

"We have several irons in the fire and it's my hope that we will be able to identify a suspect soon," she concluded.

She knew as soon as she said it that she had just made a political promise and that there would most likely be retribution if she didn't deliver on it.

"This is good to hear," Pearlman said. "I look forward to that phone call. I've been waiting many years for it."

Hastings came back to the pod and put a hand on Pearlman's shoulder, a wordless reminder that they were on the clock. The councilman ignored it and asked another question.

"So, the campaign button," he said. "Is that just a coincidence? Because it's sort of weird, you know?"

"Well, we can't dismiss it yet," Ballard said. "We have actually located the button and we're going to see what it brings us. That's where my in-the-field detective is at the moment."

"Fantastic," Pearlman said. "Let me know about that. Meantime, do you have everything you need here? What can I do?"

"I appreciate that, Councilman," Ballard said. "The one thing I've found since we started over here is that we need secured storage. We bring in evidence and property from the old cases and have no place to secure it. We've been using the second interview room for some storage, and, of course, this is a police facility, so things should be pretty safe, but most squads have a place to keep things locked up and secure."

Before Pearlman could respond, Hastings leaned in with a verbal prompt this time.

"Jake, we really gotta go," he said.

Pearlman stood up and Ballard followed.

"You mean like a safe or something?" Pearlman asked.

"Yes, an evidence safe would be good," Ballard said.

Pearlman turned to Hastings.

"Nelly, remember that," he said. "We need to get a safe in here."

"I'll remember," Hastings said.

Pearlman turned back to Ballard and put out his hand. The videographer focused on their hands as they shook.

"Thank you for what you're doing, Detective," Pearlman said. "It means a lot to me, but more importantly, it means a lot to this city and this community. We can never forget our victims."

"Yes, sir," Ballard said dutifully.

She walked the group out and then returned to her workstation, expecting the others to crowd around and ask questions about the high-powered visit. But only Colleen Hatteras poked her head up over the partition.

"So, how did that go?" she asked.

"I guess okay," Ballard said. "We just need to break open his sister's case and then we're made in the shade."

"We will."

"Anything on IGG?"

"I've got one hit through GEDmatch so far. A distant cousin to our unknown suspect. I'm going to reach out today, but I'm hoping we get something better. Something closer."

"Good. Let me know."

Hatteras dropped back out of sight and Ballard went to work. Not believing that Hastings or anyone else in Pearlman's crew would move quickly to get her a contact number for Sandy Kramer, Ballard started looking on her own. She guessed that Sandy was a nickname or a diminutive for a given name such as Alexander. As she expected, DMV records didn't help. There were too many Alexander Kramers for her to confidently pick a winner. There were also several entries under Sandy or other alternatives, like Sandor and Sundeep.

Her next move was to google tuxedo shops in Century City

and start making phone calls. When she had exhausted all the internet listings and hadn't come across a salesman named Kramer, she moved on to Beverly Hills, which was adjacent to Century City.

She hit pay dirt on her third call, this one to a place on Beverly Drive called Tux by Lux. She was told that a salesman named Alexander Kramer was on his day off but would be back at ten the next morning. Ballard guessed that selling tuxedos in Beverly Hills required a more formal name than Sandy.

Ballard disconnected. She planned to be in Beverly Hills the next morning when Kramer came to work.

22

BOSCH WAS SQUINTING through the sharp morning light and a slight hangover, looking for address numbers on a small blond-brick house at the corner of South Keeler and West 43rd Street. He was far from the DoubleTree near the lake, where he had spent the night. And even farther from Los Angeles. He was sitting in the back seat of an Uber in a mixed neighborhood of small homes and one-floor warehouses and manufacturing businesses.

"This has got to be it," the driver said.

"I don't see any numbers," Bosch said.

"Yes, but it's got to be it. My GPS says so, and this will be the best I can do for you, sir."

"Okay, I'm getting out here. You want to wait around? I'll be out in less than thirty minutes and then I go to the American terminal at O'Hare. I'll pay you to wait. I don't want to miss my plane."

"No, man, I don't wait 'round here."

"You sure? Fifty bucks, just to wait a half hour. Then the airport run on top of that."

Bosch saw the driver's eyes in the mirror. He was considering the offer. The ride app had said his name was Irfan. Bosch wasn't sure why he was uncomfortable staying in the neighborhood. It was certainly a mid- to low-income neighborhood, but there was nothing that indicated possible danger. No graffiti, no gangbangers hanging on the corners.

"Make it eighty, Irfan," Bosch said. "Cash."

The driver looked at him in the mirror.

"Make it a hundred," he said. "And a five-star rating."

Bosch nodded.

"Done," he said. "Now, you want me to rip a hundred-dollar bill in half like they do in the movies? Give you half, I keep half?"

"No, but you pay me as soon as you get back in the car," Irfan said. "Cash. Or I leave you right here, and good luck to you getting another ride. Nobody will come here and you will miss your plane."

"Deal. I only have twenties anyway."

Irfan didn't appear to see the humor in that. Bosch cracked the door and was about to get out with his backpack, when he hesitated.

"Irfan, what is wrong with this neighborhood that no driver would come out here?" he asked.

"Too many guns," Irfan said.

Bosch thought that might be an issue for most neighborhoods in most big cities, but he let it go and got out.

The house's exterior, front lawn, and bushes were kept neat and clean. The blond brick gave a sense of resolute sturdiness, as though the place was a fortress against cold and heat.

Juanita Wilson was expecting him and opened the door

before he got to it. She was an old lady and she weakly smiled at him.

"Mrs. Wilson?" Bosch asked. "I'm Harry Bosch. We spoke on the phone."

"That's me—Juanita," she said. "Please come in."

Bosch entered and lightly shook her hand. She seemed thin and frail and wore a loose housedress to disguise it. Her hair was hidden in a turban-style head wrap made of cloth striped with red, black, and green. Even so, Bosch saw a resemblance to the photo Ballard had of Laura Wilson. The eyes matched.

He thanked her for her help and for allowing him to intrude on such short notice. He explained that the sooner he got back to Los Angeles, the sooner the campaign button could be examined for fingerprints and DNA, and the investigation could proceed. It was for this reason that he had booked a flight that would get him back by midafternoon.

"In other words, I'm in a bit of a hurry," he said. "I want to get this back and have our techs look at it as soon as possible."

"I understand," Juanita said.

She led him through the small house and back to the bedroom that had been her daughter's. It was small but had a nice glow from the sun through a window with the curtains drawn open.

It looked to Bosch as though half the room had been preserved as Laura had left it, and half had been rededicated as a home office. A folding table with a desk chair held rubber-banded stacks of mail along with other assorted paperwork.

"My husband set up in here after Laura went to L.A.," Juanita said. "But we kept the rest for her when she would come home to visit or in case she gave up on her dream and wanted to come back. And then...we just left it."

Bosch nodded that he understood. He saw a cardboard box on the bed and pointed to it.

"Is that where you found the pin?" he asked.

"Yes, right in that one," Juanita said. "There were some clothes on the top and some scripts I think she was working with at the time. But when I lifted them out, I saw the button right away in a shoebox."

Bosch pulled out his phone and turned on the video camera.

"Mrs. Wilson, can you show me without touching the button?" he asked.

He followed her on camera as she went to the box, spread the cardboard flaps, and then pointed down into it. He moved in to see that there was a shoebox within the larger box. Its top was off and it was filled with small items that Bosch recognized from the crime scene photo of Laura Wilson's junk drawer. He brought his phone down and then zoomed in on the campaign button that said "JAKE!"

"If I give you my phone, would you please video me as I retrieve the button, Mrs. Wilson?" Bosch asked.

"If you want," Juanita said. "I'm not all that good with a camera."

"It'll be fine. I just want to be able to document chain of custody."

"Chain of custody?"

"Who had possession of the item and when. That once it was collected, it was maintained in police control."

"I understand."

Bosch handed her the phone and she recorded him putting on

rubber gloves from his backpack and opening a plastic evidence bag. He then reached into the box and removed the campaign button from the shoebox. He bagged it, sealed it, and put it in the side pocket of his sport coat.

He reached for the phone, spoke the date and time of day, and then turned the recording off. He played the beginning of the video to check that Juanita had gotten what he needed.

"That should do it," he said. "Thank you."

"What else can I do?" Juanita asked.

Bosch hesitated. He had both a print kit and swab kit in his backpack. Ballard had given them to him when she walked him out of the Ahmanson Center. Under evidence protocols, he knew he should take Juanita's fingerprints and a DNA swab so she could be excluded from anything that might be found on the campaign button. But he was hesitant about putting this frail Black woman through that and possibly making her feel victimized by the investigation of her own daughter's murder. He decided to pass on the protocols.

"You said you didn't even touch the button, right?" he asked.

"No, I saw it there and didn't go near it, like you told me," Juanita said. "Is something wrong?"

"No, not at all. Everything's good. Then I think that's it and I can get out of your hair."

"What happens now?"

"Well, I go back to Los Angeles and, like I said, I'll get this into forensics today. If we get lucky, we get a print that is not your daughter's and run it down, see who handled the button, maybe find out who gave it to her. Either Detective Ballard or I will keep you informed of our progress."

"Okay. Because I'm not sure how much more I can wait, you know?"

"I know it's difficult. You have waited a long, long time, and believe me, I know what that's like."

"No, you don't understand. I'm on a clock, Detective Bosch. I have cancer. A terminal cancer and I want to know before...the end."

Bosch realized that she was not an old lady as he had initially thought. She was sick. He guessed that the head wrap probably hid the baldness that was the result of the brutal assault of anti-cancer treatment. He was immediately embarrassed by his gaffe in saying he would get out of her hair.

"I'm sorry," Bosch whispered.

"I had given up and was prepared to die," Juanita said. "Then the woman detective called and it gave me hope. I will hang on, Detective Bosch, until you can give me an answer."

"I understand. We will move quickly. That's all I can promise."

"That's all I need. Thank you."

Bosch nodded. Juanita led him back to the front door, where they shook hands and said goodbye. From the front stoop Bosch saw no car waiting for him on the street.

"Shit," he whispered. "No stars for you, Irfan."

He walked down the steps and pulled his phone to open the ride app and try to get another car. Movement in his peripheral vision drew his attention and he looked up to see Irfan's car gliding to a stop at the curb. His window was down.

"I went to refuel," he called.

Bosch got in the back seat. He handed five twenties over the seat to the driver.

"Hold here for a second," he said.

Irfan did as instructed. Bosch plugged in his earphones and turned on the music he had downloaded to his phone the night before. He had gone to see the Pharez Whitted Quintet at Winter's Jazz Club near the Navy Pier. The set had been a tribute to Miles Davis, and Bosch had enjoyed it and stayed too late. But he wanted to hear Whitted's own music and had downloaded three albums when he got back to his hotel room. Now a song called "The Tree of Life" played in his ears while he looked back at the house Laura Wilson had come from.

Modest was an understatement. He thought about Laura's humble beginnings in the blond-brick house and the dream that took her to L.A., only to have everything she had and had hoped for taken away. It made Bosch angry. He felt an old familiar fire start to burn inside.

"Okay, Irfan," he finally said. "Take me to the airport."

23

TUX BY LUX was on Beverly Drive south of Wilshire, which put it on the more economical side of Beverly Hills. It looked like a business that moved a lot of product, as opposed to the by-appointment-only salons on Rodeo Drive that catered to clients headed to the Oscars and the *Vanity Fair* after-party.

Ballard sat in her city ride, sipping her coffee from Go Get Em Tiger, and waited for the front glass door of Tux by Lux to be unlocked for the day. It was 9:50.

Her phone rang and she saw it was Bosch. She took the call but kept her eyes on the glass door.

"Just checking in," Bosch said. "I have the campaign button and am at the airport ready to board."

"Sounds good," Ballard said. "How was Juanita?"

"Fully cooperative but sick. She's dying."

"What?"

"Terminal cancer. I don't know how much time she's got left, but it didn't look like a lot. No pressure but she said she's hanging on because you gave her hope. She wants to live to see somebody get charged."

"Oh, great, no pressure at all. What kind of cancer?"

"I didn't ask. The kind that shrivels you up in the end."

"God. Well, all we can do is do what we can do. I hope we make a case and she's still alive to know it."

"You in the car? I hear traffic."

Ballard told him what she was doing, and as she spoke, she saw a man in his forties come to the glass door of the tuxedo store, unlock it at the bottom, and enter.

"I think he just opened the store," she said. "I should get in there before any customers do."

"I'll let you go," Bosch said. "But when you get back to Ahmanson, can you prime forensics on what's coming? Maybe they can send a print car out to do it right there so we know whether this was a complete waste of time."

"Will do."

"Good luck."

They disconnected and Ballard got out of the car. She was pleased that she had not said "Roger that" to Bosch's request about forensics.

Ballard entered the store, carrying a file with two photos in it. Racks of tuxedos lined the wall on the right, and floor-to-ceiling shelves of white shirts lined the left. There was a mirrored fitting area in the back and a checkout station in front. Two glass cases with bow ties in one and assorted cuff links in the other extended from either side of the cashier's desk.

There was no sign of the man Ballard had seen unlock and enter the store.

"Hello?" she called out loudly.

"Hello?" a voice came back. "I'll be with you in one moment."

Ballard walked over to the glass counter and looked down at the cuff links. They ranged from the tasteful and exquisite to the off-putting and tacky. She was leaning over a pair that were silver silhouettes of a woman posing with arms back and chest out, an image familiar from the mud flaps of 18-wheelers.

"How can I help you?"

Ballard turned and saw the man she had seen unlock the store. She pulled her badge off her belt and held it out to him.

"Renée Ballard, LAPD. I'm looking for Sandy Kramer."

He raised his hands.

"You got me!"

He then dropped his arms and put his wrists together for the handcuffs. Ballard gave a perfunctory smile. It wasn't the first time someone she badged had reacted this way, thinking they were being clever.

"I need to ask you some questions about a homicide investigation," she said.

"Oh, shit, my bad," Kramer said. "I guess I shouldn't have been joking, huh? Who's dead?"

"Is there a place we can talk privately? I'd rather not be in the middle of this when a customer comes in."

"Uh, we have a break room in the back. It's kind of small."

"That will be fine."

"I don't have any appointments till eleven. I could just put a sign on the door and lock up. How long will this take?"

"Not that long."

"Okay, let's do it."

He went behind the counter, took out a pad for writing down alteration instructions, and wrote "BACK BY 10:45" on it. Using a piece of hemming tape from a tool basket, he attached the sign to the front glass. He then reached down and locked the door.

"Follow me," he said.

They went around a curtain in the fitting area and into a space that was half storage and half break room. There was a table with two chairs, and Kramer offered one to Ballard. She pulled it out and sat down. Kramer did the same.

"Now, what murder?" he asked.

"We'll get to that," Ballard said. "First, tell me, when was the last time you spoke to Jake Pearlman?"

"Oh my god, is Jake dead?"

His surprise seemed genuine to Ballard. She had wanted to know if he had been tipped to the investigation by Pearlman or anyone else on his team.

"No, he's not dead," she said. "Can you remember the last time you talked to him?"

"Uh, well, it's been a while," Kramer said. "I called him when he won the election. So that would've been four years ago?"

"He got elected six years ago."

"Wow, time flies. Well, whenever it was, I called and congratulated him. I remember I told him he would be going to a lot of black-tie events now and I offered him a discount here. But that was it. He never took me up on it."

"What about Nelson Hastings? Did you talk to him lately?"

"Hastings? Forget it. I have no reason to talk to him. I can't remember the last time."

"But you know him?"

"More like knew. We all went to school together. Hollywood High—and I do mean high."

He laughed at his own inside joke. But it was a nervous laugh. Ballard read his tone when he spoke about Hastings as bordering on enmity.

"Did you have a problem with Hastings?" she asked.

"More like he had a problem with me. He wanted Jake to himself and eventually pushed me out. I'm just not that competitive. So now he's running the Jake show, and I'm here."

Ballard nodded.

"So, let's go back to 2005," she said. "You ran his campaign back then, correct?"

"I did, yeah," Kramer said. "But I'm not sure I would call it a campaign. That sounds so big and planned—all the things that ours was not."

"It was a small operation?"

"When Jake ran for president of the senior class at Hollywood High, we probably had a better machine. I mean, the '05 campaign was held together by spit and Scotch Tape. We didn't know what we were doing, and it failed as it deserved to fail. Jake stayed in politics, retooled, and then came back and won that seat. I was long gone by then. So tell me who died and what it has to do with me. I'm getting worried here."

"Laura Wilson died. Was murdered. Does that name sound familiar to you?"

"Laura Wilson—I don't think so. Let me think for a minute."

"Sure."

Kramer seemed to ponder the name, but he didn't take the minute he'd asked for.

"Are you saying she had something to do with the campaign?" he asked.

"I'm trying to find that out," Ballard said. "Did you know all the volunteers?"

"Back then, I did, yes. I recruited them. But there were not very many and I don't remember any Laura Wilson."

"Let me show you something."

She opened the file on the table and proffered the 8 x 10 headshot of Laura Wilson. Kramer leaned in to look at it without touching it.

"No, don't recognize her," Kramer said.

"Is it possible she could have been a volunteer?" Ballard pressed.

"A Black girl, I would remember. We could've used one but we didn't have any."

"You're sure."

Kramer pointed emphatically at the photo.

"She was not part of the campaign," he said. "I recruited all the volunteers. She wasn't one of them."

"Okay," Ballard said. "Take a look at this photo."

She slid an 8 x 10 copy of the photo of Laura's junk drawer across the table to Kramer.

"You see the campaign button there?" she asked.

"Yep, right there," Kramer said. "It's a beauty."

"Did you have those made?"

"Of course. They were the deluxe—with the freedom ribbons attached. I remember we debated the extra spend but Jake liked the ribbons. Made the button stand out."

"Who got them?"

"Well, we had them at the office for walk-ins. And we also went door-to-door in the district. We didn't give everybody a button, but we did give them to people who expressed support for Jake."

"How many did you have made, do you remember?"

"I think it was a thousand, but we didn't give them all out. I remember after it was all over, I had a couple bags left and just dumped them. In fact, I think the last time I talked to Nelson was when he called me up and asked for the buttons because Jake was going to make another run at it. I told him I dumped them years ago and he just hung up on me. Great guy, that Nelly."

"Back in '05, do you remember if the campaign sent people door-to-door in the Franklin Village area? More specifically, Tamarind Avenue—that neighborhood?"

"If it was in the district, I am sure we did. We went out every night. The whole staff and all the volunteers we could get. We'd meet at that deli on Sunset...I can't remember the name. It was like a hundred years old, but they closed for good during the pandemic."

"Greenblatt's."

"Right, Greenblatt's—what a loss. I loved that place. They had a room upstairs and we would all meet there at six every night. We'd order sandwiches and a beer, expensing it to the campaign, and then we'd divvy up the neighborhoods so there wouldn't be any overlap. We'd hand out buttons and pledge cards and then we'd split up to go knock on doors. Grassroots, man. But the truth was, I didn't know shit about running a campaign. It was fun, though."

"Who got Tamarind Avenue?"

"Oh, man, I can't remember that. All I can tell you is we tried to hit every neighborhood at least twice. But I have no records, and that was way too long ago for me to remember who went where or what street. Are you trying to say someone from the campaign killed this woman?"

"No, I'm not saying that. I'm really just running down a loose end. This photo is from her apartment. She was murdered there the Saturday before the election, and that button was in her junk drawer. That tells me someone from the campaign probably knocked on her door at some point leading up to the election. It may not mean anything at all, but we have to ask questions and follow leads wherever they go."

"Got it. I wish I was more help."

Ballard put the photos back in the file and closed it.

"I take it you've talked to Jake and Hastings already," Kramer said.

"Yes, we have," Ballard said. "I saw them both yesterday. You really don't like Hastings, do you?"

"That obvious, huh?"

"Yes. But at one time you all were good friends?"

"We were, yeah. We were tight as a fist, we used to say. But Nelson got between me and Jake and pushed us apart. It started during that campaign, and then after we lost, I got blamed. Not by Jake but by Nelson, and that always rubbed me wrong, because he was only the driver. He didn't write positions, didn't strategize media buys. He did nothing except drive, and then he dumps it all on me, that I was the reason we lost."

Ballard froze. She tried not to show what was going on behind her eyes, but she was sure that when she had spoken to Hastings about the 2005 campaign and the button in Laura Wilson's drawer, he had said the election was before his time on Pearlman's staff.

"Wait a minute," she said. "Nelson Hastings was Pearlman's driver during the 2005 campaign? He was around back then?"

"Yeah, he was there," Kramer said. "He had just gotten back from Afghanistan and was out of the army and Jake said he needed a driver. We didn't pay him anything. He was a volunteer."

"Did he do any of the knocking on doors?"

"We all did that. Even Jake. It was required."

Adrenaline was beginning to course through Ballard's blood. She had caught a discrepancy, possibly even an outright lie, in the net she had thrown. She felt the investigation suddenly had a solid new direction.

"Before I leave, I just want to ask you something," she said. "Back in high school, did you know Jake's sister?"

"Sure," Kramer said. "We all did. Sarah. That was horrible, just horrible."

"You were around the family when she was murdered?"

"Yeah, I was over there. Jake was my friend. But what could you say, you know? It was just a nightmare."

"Who else among his friends was there for him?"

"Well, there was me. And Nelly. Another guy, named Rawls, who became a cop was part of our group."

"Rawls, was he part of that tight fist you mentioned?"

"He was. And so, yeah, we tried to do what we could, but we didn't know how to help. We were just kids."

"I understand that. Did the police back then talk to you all?"

"I think so. They talked to me, that's for sure. I had gone out on one date with Sarah, but it was a long time before. But they still gave me the third degree. Are these cases somehow connected? Sarah and the girl who had the button?"

"We don't know. It's probably just a grim coincidence. I was curious about it. It's still a big thing for Jake."

"And always will be, I'm sure. Sarah was great. She was smart and beautiful and had a lot going for her. I never understood why someone would want to take all of that away."

Ballard nodded.

"Well, it's almost time for your appointment," she said. "I think I'll let you get ready for that. I appreciate your time, Mr. Kramer. Could you do one thing for me?"

"Sure," Kramer said. "What do you need?"

"I need you to keep this conversation between us. Is that a problem?"

"Not at all, Detective."

Ballard gave Kramer her cell number and told him to call if he thought of anything else she should know. She was almost hyperventilating by the time she got back to her car. She started the engine and cranked up the air conditioning. She composed herself and then reached over to the passenger seat to get her case list. She studied it for a moment, trying to modulate her breathing. She focused on one entry on the paper.

Hastings—send photo of LW

She realized that she had never done that. And that raised a big question.

She checked the dashboard clock, did the math, and realized that Harry Bosch was in the air and it would still be a few hours until she would be able to talk to him. She knew she had much to do before then.

She dropped the car into drive and pulled away from the curb.

24

BOSCH DROVE INTO the north parking lot of the Hawthorne mall and easily spotted Ballard's city ride. It was the only vehicle in the vast sea of asphalt that surrounded the abandoned mall. He drove directly to her and parked so that their driver's-side windows faced each other and they could talk without getting out of their vehicles. In LAPD slang, it was called a "69 meeting" because of the positioning of the cars.

Bosch's window was already down because the old Cherokee's air-conditioning did little to effect climate change in the car. Ballard's window glided down upon his arrival.

"Harry, how was the flight?"

"Fine. I listened to some good music. So what's with the code sixty-nine?"

"I didn't want to talk at Ahmanson. Rawls was in today and he's a pipeline to Hastings and Pearlman. In fact, he's been coming in a lot this week and I think that's because Hastings wants to know what moves we're making."

"Really? Can't Hastings just call you anytime he wants?"

"He could, yeah. But he wants to hide how closely he's paying attention, because Hastings is our guy."

"What do you mean? The killer?"

"I'd bet my badge on it, Harry. We get his DNA, and it's going to match."

"Tell me how you got there."

Ballard recapped the interview she conducted that morning with Sandy Kramer and how one of her very last questions to the tuxedo salesman revealed that Hastings had lied to her when he said that the Laura Wilson murder occurred before his time working for Jake Pearlman.

"He's been with Pearlman all along," she said. "And that's not a little lie. That is a lie meant to throw me off. That makes it a big lie."

"Okay, I get it," Bosch said. "That's suspicious, but it doesn't get you to handcuffs. You have anything else?"

"I do. After talking to Kramer, I started going back over my interactions with Hastings on this case. He's always been the point man. He's the one who calls and wants updates, supposedly for Pearlman. But now I think he was trying to see how close we were getting to him."

"Still no handcuffs."

"Look at this."

She handed a piece of notebook paper to him. Bosch looked at it and realized it was her case list.

"Your list," he said. "I already saw this."

"I know," Ballard said. "But I never sent Hastings a photo of Laura Wilson and didn't scratch it off the list."

"And what does that mean?"

"Okay, I've had two phone conversations with Hastings this week about the Wilson case. I've been going over the first conversation in my head. I asked him if he knew the name

Laura Wilson and to check what campaign records there might be about her working as a volunteer or making a donation or whatever. I also asked him to check with the staff, including the councilman. I am ninety-five percent sure I never said Laura was Black. The plan was to scan a photo and send it to him. But I never did. I forgot."

"Okay."

"So then in the next conversation, he reports back that there are no records and nobody, including Jake, can remember a Laura Wilson being a volunteer or otherwise. And then to underline this, he said that Jake said he would have remembered if he had an African American woman on staff or as a volunteer."

"But you're sure you hadn't told him Laura was Black."

"Exactly. And then when Jake came by the unit yesterday, he said the same thing: that he would have remembered an African American on the campaign."

Bosch nodded. Ballard had told him before he'd left for the airport that she had been tipped that Pearlman was on his way for a surprise visit to the unit.

"Could Hastings have figured out she was Black on his own?" he asked.

"Well, anything's possible," Ballard said. "But I didn't tell him. I'm sure of it."

"Other than that, how was the surprise visit?"

"He and his entourage were there for about thirty minutes tops. I showed them around, they took some video, and I got about five minutes with Pearlman to ask about Laura. And that's another thing, Hastings kept interrupting and saying Jake had a tight schedule and had to go. Another sign he's trying to block the investigation. He clearly didn't want me asking Pearlman questions."

Bosch could tell by her urgent tone that Ballard was flying on adrenaline. He was beginning to feel the charge, too.

"What do you think, Harry?" Ballard asked. "What are the moves?"

"Simple. We get his DNA," Bosch said. "That's what you're thinking, right? If the DNA matches, game over. Handcuffs."

Ballard nodded.

"We do it on the down-low," she said. "Surreptitious collection. We can't let anybody know about this. Rawls is a leak right back to Hastings, and the more people who know, the more things that can go wrong. That's why I wanted to meet you off-site."

"Got it," Bosch said.

They both were silent for a long moment until Bosch spoke again.

"I'll do it," he said.

"You'll do what?" Ballard asked.

"Follow Hastings and get his DNA."

"By yourself?"

"You can't do it. You have to run the unit and Hastings knows you. He doesn't know me. I wasn't there for the surprise visit. I'll watch him and make the collection. If it's a match, we run a game on him. We bring him in for an update on the case and get him on record saying he didn't know Wilson and had never been to her apartment."

"Good. That sounds right. How do I explain you not being at the pod working the case? When you stop showing up, the others will ask me."

"Then we run a game on them, too. I have the campaign button. I bring it in, and you hit the roof because I went to Chicago without permission. You've already shown that you're willing to send anybody who fucks up home."

Ballard paused as she ran a possible scenario through her mind.

"You know, that could work," she said.

"Wat a minute, Masser knows you sent me," Bosch said.

"He's not here. He had to take care of something and left."

"Then let's go do it. I want to be on Hastings when he punches out tonight and his weekend starts."

"There's one other thing."

"What?"

"When this started to tumble together with Hastings, I looked him up. Pearlman has a website for his constituents and it has a section on his staff. Photos, mini-biographies, and their scope of duties, all of that. For Hastings, the bio says he's a disabled vet, and I was thinking about the blood in the urine and the cancer. Kramer told me that when Hastings joined that first campaign, he had just gotten out of the military."

Bosch thought about this. It could lead to another way to tie Hastings into the case.

"I know a guy at the military archives in St. Louis," he said. "He can pull his service records and we can see what's there."

"So you'll handle that, too?" Ballard asked.

"I think anything to do with Hastings should be handled away from the pod."

"Right."

"What else?"

"That's it as far as I know."

"So why don't you go back to Ahmanson and I'll come

wandering in afterward. I'll sit here and call St. Louis first. Do we have a DOB for Hastings?"

"I'll shoot it to you. I pulled it off DMV today because I wanted to know his home address."

"Did the tuxedo guy say which branch of the military Hastings was in?"

"He said army but that could have just been a general catchall."

"I'll tell my contact to start there."

Ballard was looking down at her phone, pulling up Hastings's date of birth. After she sent it to Bosch, she looked up through the windshield. She was facing the abandoned mall.

"What's with this place?" she asked.

"It's been abandoned for more than twenty years," Bosch said. "After the aerospace companies moved away from this area and LAX, it fell on hard times. They closed it down and it just sits here empty. They use it to film movies now."

"Strange—a big empty mall like that."

"Yeah."

"I'll see you back at Ahmanson."

"I'll be there."

She dropped her car into gear and drove off, cutting across the empty parking lot to the exit.

Bosch pulled his phone and looked among his contacts for the number for Gary McIntyre, an NCIS investigator at the National Personnel Records Center in Missouri. He had made contact with McIntyre on several cases over the years. Bosch knew McIntyre would be willing to help if he was still there.

The call was answered by a female voice.

"I was calling Gary McIntyre," he said.

"Gary's not here anymore," the woman said. "This is Investigator Henic. How can I help you?"

"This is Harry Bosch, Los Angeles Police Department. I usually deal with Gary. I need to get the service package for a suspect we have out here in a double homicide investigation."

"Gary's been gone a long time. What was your name again?"

"Harry Bosch."

"Let me see if he's got your name in the contacts he left me."

"It should be there."

Bosch heard typing on a keyboard, then a few moments of silence before Henic reported her findings.

"He's got you down here as working for San Fernando PD."

"I was there for a couple years, then I came back to the LAPD. I work cold cases now."

"How can I help you?"

"I want to get the package for a guy named Nelson Hastings, DOB three-sixteen-seventy-six."

"Okay, I've written it down."

Now came the hard part. Bosch needed the information sooner rather than later and had to finesse Henic's cooperation.

"Did you say your name is Henic?" he asked. "I want to update my contacts."

"Yes, sir," she said.

"Could you spell it? I want to make sure I have it right."

"Hotel-Echo-November-India-Charlie."

"Thanks. How about a first name?"

"Sarah with an *h*."

"So, Sarah with an *h,* what kind of time frame are we talking about on this? I've got a clock on this case."

"Well, you're on the list. We usually take these in the order they come in. What sort of a clock?"

"If we're right about this guy, he's a serial killer. We need to take him down before he kills somebody new. And I need the military history to see if he can be placed in certain locations during certain years. We get that, and we can start pulling the net closed and get him off the street before he hurts somebody else. Nobody wants that on their conscience. You know what I mean?"

There was a beat of silence before Henic responded.

"I get it," she finally said. "Give me twenty-four hours, and I'll get back to you. Gary has your number and email on here. Those are still good?"

"Still good," Bosch said. "So…tomorrow's Saturday. Does that twenty-four hours carry over to Monday, or do you think I'll hear something tomorrow?"

"I'm on duty tomorrow. You should hear from me."

"Many thanks, Sarah with an *h*."

Bosch disconnected and started his car. He then headed across the parking lot and back to the Ahmanson Center.

25

BALLARD WAS BACK at her workstation, writing up notes on her conversation with Kramer, when Bosch came up behind her chair and put down the evidence bag with the campaign button sealed in it.

"What's this?" she asked.

"Evidence," Bosch said. "You need to get that into the print lab as soon as you can."

"I know what it is. How did you get it?"

"I didn't want to wait for the wheels of bureaucracy to turn. I went to Chicago and got it."

Now Ballard raised her voice.

"You went to Chicago?"

"I just said I did."

Ballard threw the pen she was holding down on the desk. It was a move that, along with her raised voice, was certain to draw attention in the pod.

"Harry, follow me."

She got up and walked to the interview room for a private conversation. Bosch followed, head down, like a condemned man. They entered and Ballard closed the door loudly. She immediately brought a hand to her mouth to stifle a laugh.

"That was so good," she whispered. "They were all watching."

"Well, you do need to get that button into forensics," Bosch said.

"I will. Did you call your guy in St. Louis?"

"I did but he's not there anymore. It's a she now. I talked to her and she promised to get back within twenty-four hours. We'll see. My other guy would have dropped everything, and he trusted me enough not to redact stuff. We'll see with this new one."

"Okay, let me know what you hear. You ready to go back out there?"

"Yeah. But you should raise your voice one more time, don't you think?"

Ballard smiled and brought her hand up again before it turned into a laugh. Then she dropped the hand and spoke loud enough to be heard through the door.

"Go home. Now!"

Bosch nodded and whispered.

"That should work."

He opened the door and walked out, adopting the same head-down countenance. Ballard watched from the doorway as he bypassed his workstation and headed straight for the exit. She shook her head as though frustrated to the limit by Bosch's infraction.

After Bosch was gone, she returned to her workstation but stayed standing as she put her laptop and the evidence bag in her backpack. She was aware that Colleen Hatteras was watching her.

"Colleen, if anybody's looking for me, I'm going downtown to the lab," she said.

"Okay," Hatteras said. "Are you coming back?"

"Probably not."

"I wanted to give you an IGG update."

"Did you make a connection?"

"No, not yet."

"Then let's see where you are Monday morning. I need to get to the lab."

Hatteras frowned. She wanted the moment.

"Maybe something will break by then, Colleen," Ballard said. "We'll talk first thing Monday."

"Fine," Hatteras asked. "Did you just fire Bosch?"

She blurted out the last part and Ballard was pleased to know that the interview room play had worked.

"I'm not sure yet," she said.

"I think he's a good man at heart," Hatteras said. "I feel it."

"Well, he's got to be a better team player or he's out."

"I'm sure he will be. My sense is he knows that."

"Then, good."

Ballard threw a backpack strap over her shoulder and looked at the others in the pod. They all had their heads down and were acting like they were deep in work and had not been listening to the skirmish with Bosch.

"Hey, everybody," she said. "I just want to say I appreciate all the hours and days put in this week. It's been above and beyond the call and you should know it does not go unnoticed. Have a good night."

With that she turned and headed to the exit.

26

BOSCH POSITIONED HIS car at the curb on Los Angeles Street, a half block from the exit gate at the City Hall parking garage. Ballard had also run a DMV vehicle registration on Nelson Hastings and passed on the descriptors and license plate number of his personal vehicle. Unfortunately, Bosch was waiting for a black 2020 Tesla Model 3 and was well aware that the color, make, and model he was looking for was very popular on the streets of L.A. He would need to confirm he had the right car by license plate number and had already followed two cars out of the garage, only to catch up and then eliminate them.

It was now 6:40 p.m. He had been waiting and watching for two hours and was worried that he had missed Hastings's exit. He pulled his phone, did an internet search, and then made a call. A woman answered.

"Councilman Jake Pearlman's office, how can I help you?" she asked.

"Yes, is Nelson still there?" Bosch asked.

Bosch said it in a casual voice that he hoped suggested familiarity.

"He is here but he's in a meeting with the councilman,"

the woman said. "Can I take your name and ask what this is regarding?"

"Uh, it's just a streetlight issue," Bosch said. "He knows about it. I'll call back Monday."

He disconnected. At least he knew he had not missed Hastings's exit. He settled in for a longer wait, keeping an eye on his sideview mirror for a traffic cop who had already told him once he was in a no-parking zone and needed to move on.

Twenty minutes further into the vigil, Bosch got a call and recognized the 208 area code for Coeur d'Alene, Idaho. He accepted the call.

"This is Bosch."

"It's Dubose. You left me a message."

"I did. And my partner left two before that. Made us wonder why retirement up there keeps you so busy you can't find time to return a call from your old department."

"Fuck my old department, Bosch. It never gave one shit about me. I'm returning the calls now. What do you want?"

"I want to solve the Laura Wilson case."

"We worked Wilson hard. But sometimes the breaks don't go your way. We never solved it, end of story."

"Not for her family. The story doesn't ever end."

"Yeah, that's too bad. But everything we did, everything we knew about the murder, is in the book. I got nothing to add. Goodbye."

"Don't hang up."

"I can't help you, Bosch."

"You don't know that. Not until you hear me out. There's another murder."

Dubose said nothing and Bosch waited.

"When?" Dubose finally said.

"It was eleven years before, actually," Bosch said. "We just connected it through DNA."

"Where?"

"Hollywood Division. The foothills, like Wilson."

"Black girl?"

"White. Does that make a difference?"

"No, I was just trying to get the details."

"Did you think race had something to do with Wilson's murder?"

"Not that we knew."

"Did it play a part in the investigation?"

"What are you saying, Bosch?"

"Nothing. I'm just asking questions. Tell me something about the investigation that's not in the murder book."

"There's nothing."

"There always is. Reports not written, dead ends not explained. Why didn't you run with the blood in the urine?"

"The what?"

"You heard me. You got the DNA off blood in the urine. It meant there was disease but there's nothing in the book about a follow-up."

"Are you fucking kidding me? What were we supposed to do? That could have meant anything. A solid punch in the gut will put blood in your piss. What, we were supposed to go to every hospital and dialysis clinic in the city and say, 'Give us a list of your patients'? Fuck you, Bosch. We did the due diligence on the case and—"

"Nelson Hastings. That name ever come up?"

"Nelson...who?"

"Hastings. The name's not in the book. He was around thirty at the time, just out of the military. Does the name mean anything to you?"

"No, never heard of him."

"Think you'd remember if he had come up?"

"If he came up, then his name would be in the book. We left nothing out. Are we done?"

"Yeah, sure, Dubose. We're done."

"Good."

Dubose disconnected.

Bosch had kept his eyes on the garage exit during the call. He never saw a black Tesla emerge. He now started to grind on the conversation with Dubose. The fact that the retired detective had brought up checking hospitals and dialysis clinics told Bosch that Dubose and his partner had probably considered such an avenue of investigation and had dismissed it. His upset with Bosch was probably based in his guilt for not pursuing it. The stone left unturned—Bosch knew that detectives carried such guilt and regret all the way to the grave.

He was about to call Ballard and tell her about the call from Dubose, when he saw a quick procession of cars come out of the City Hall garage. The third one in line was a black Tesla. Bosch put down his phone, pulled his car away from the curb, and followed. There was a red light at 1st Street and he caught up, confirming the license plate number. It was Hastings's car, but the glass was tinted too dark for him to be able to confirm it was the man whose photograph was on the staff page of the city councilman's website.

The Tesla turned right on 1st and headed north and out of downtown, the driver choosing surface streets over the rush-hour-choked Hollywood Freeway. One-car follows were always difficult, especially when the one car was a thirty-year-old Cherokee with distinctive square body styling. Bosch hung back as much as he could but knew that if he missed one traffic light, he could easily lose Hastings. Bosch had gotten his home address from Ballard, but he was hoping there would be a stop-off somewhere along the way that would result in a DNA deposit on a coffee cup, food wrapper, or pizza crust. Shed skin cells contained the needed DNA. All Hastings had to do was handle an object and leave it behind for collection.

The Tesla eventually made its way up to Sunset Boulevard and then headed west toward the descending sun. Bosch knew from the data Ballard had sent that Hastings lived on Vista near the lower entrance to Runyon Canyon Park. He was disappointed that home appeared to be the Tesla's destination. That meant there would likely be no DNA collection this night.

But then the Tesla drove past Vista without making the turn. A few blocks later, it stopped at the curb in front of the Almor Wine & Spirits shop. Bosch pulled to the curb a half block back and watched as a man jumped out of the car and went quickly into the store. Bosch pulled up and into the parking lot on the side where the Tesla driver wouldn't see his car when he left. Bosch put on a Dodgers cap, got out, and went into the shop. The hat would give him some degree of camouflage, but he was banking on Hastings's not having seen him before or having looked up a photo when he learned from Ballard about the latest addition to the Open-Unsolved Unit. Even if he had looked at a photo, it would be an old one from Bosch's LAPD file.

Once in the store, Bosch confirmed the driver was Hastings and was at least momentarily relieved that he hadn't blown the surveillance.

Hastings was standing in front of the red-wine racks. Bosch moved into the shop and stood near a floor display of white wines. Over the top of the display, he saw Hastings reach for a bottle of red and hold it in his palm while he read the back label. He soon put the bottle back on its shelf and picked up another. He read the back label of this one as well and seemed to like what he saw. He turned and went to the counter to purchase it.

Bosch noted the location of the first bottle Hastings had handled. He knew he could come back for it. But at the moment he wanted to be in place to continue following Hastings. He turned and left the shop to return to his car.

Bosch knew it was likely that Hastings was simply headed to his nearby home to start off the weekend with a bottle of wine. But he couldn't risk losing him if not. It was important to know where Hastings was located, should it be decided to confront or even arrest him during the weekend. Bosch had to see the surveillance through.

A few minutes later, Hastings left the shop, carrying his bottle by the neck. He did not look back in Bosch's direction and hopped into his car. Bosch could only see the back end of the Tesla past the front corner of the shop. When it disappeared as Hastings moved back into traffic, Bosch drove out of the lot and followed.

Hastings didn't go home. He continued west on Sunset, crossing Fairfax and Crescent Heights and then cruising the length of the Strip until he got to Sunset Plaza and turned north again into the hills. He soon made a turn onto St. Ives and immediately parked at the curb in front of a house.

Bosch drove past St. Ives and several homes up the hill before making a U-turn and coasting back down to the corner. He held in a position where he had a narrow and partially hidden view of the Tesla and the entrance to the house it was parked in front of. He waited and watched but Hastings didn't get out of the car. Bosch began to wonder if this was a ploy by Hastings to determine whether he was being followed.

But then the house's garage door started to open and Bosch saw a car coming up Sunset Plaza with its turn indicator flashing. He quickly slapped down his window visor and rubbed his forehead with a hand in front of his face as the car turned in front of him onto St. Ives. He zeroed in on the license plate as it passed and watched as the car pulled into the garage. Hastings got out of his car and walked toward the garage, bottle of wine in hand. Hastings entered, and a few moments later the garage closed.

Bosch quickly grabbed a pad and pen out of the center console and wrote the license plate number down. He then called Ballard.

"Harry."

"Where are you?"

"Home. What's up?"

"Can you run a plate for me? Hastings didn't go home. He bought a bottle of wine and brought it to a house above Sunset Plaza. I saw a car pull into the garage and I got the plate."

"Give it to me and I'll call you back."

Bosch disconnected after reading the number off his pad. He checked the house and saw no activity behind the drawn curtains. His gut told him that Hastings had arrived for a romantic dinner with someone and was probably in for the night. Bosch knew that there was a possibility that Ballard would want to continue the surveillance in the morning and possibly through the weekend.

He knew from memory that there was a Midway car rental on Sunset near Book Soup. He looked it up on his phone and called to reserve a car. He knew it would be pressing his luck to continue following Hastings with a 1992 hunter green Cherokee. He needed to switch things up.

Ballard had called while he was on the phone with Midway and he had ignored it. He called her back after securing the rental reservation.

"Is that house you're talking about on St. Ives?" she asked.

"Yep," Bosch said. "What did you get?"

"The plate is registered to Rita Ford on St. Ives. She's Pearlman's political adviser. Short, white, long dark hair—that her?"

"I didn't see her, because she pulled into the garage. Just got the plate."

"Well, looks like we have a little interoffice relationship going. I wonder whether Pearlman knows. It could blow up on him if it ever goes sideways or becomes public knowledge."

Bosch didn't offer an opinion. He didn't care about something that to him amounted to gossip.

"My gut tells me that Hastings is in for the night," he said. "He may go home later but my guess is probably not. Not if they're drinking a bottle of wine."

"Good point," Ballard said.

"So, you want me to stay or pick it up in the morning? I just rented a car. I'll have a different look tomorrow in case you're worried about the Cherokee."

"That's smart. You make the call. Leave if you want to."

"I saw him holding a bottle of wine in the shop. I could go back and get it, drop it off so you can have them look for a palm print in the morning."

"Wow, yes. Go get that bottle, Harry, and let's hope nobody beat you to it."

Bosch hesitated for a moment but then put words to something else he had been contemplating.

"And, you know, since he's here with her…"

He stopped.

"What?" Ballard asked.

"I was thinking about his house," Bosch said. "Maybe I could see if there's something there."

"Harry, don't even think about it. You're not a private eye anymore and we need to do this by the book. There are rules to surreptitious collection. The item collected must be discarded in public. Don't go into his house. I mean it."

"What if I swing by and just check the trash cans? The courts have ruled that trash is fair game."

"If it's out on a public street. So Harry, don't go near his house. I want to hear you say you won't."

"I won't go by his house, okay? It was just a suggestion."

"A bad one."

"Okay, so you'll be home? I'm going to go get that bottle of wine."

"I'll be here."

Twenty-five minutes later, Bosch pulled up in front of Ballard's apartment complex in Los Feliz. Ballard was waiting in the street because he had given her a heads-up call. She had her dog, Pinto, on a leash at her side.

Bosch handed the bottle of Portlandia Pinot Noir out the window to her. It was in a brown paper bag from Almor Wine & Spirits.

"Tell them there could be a palm print on the front label," he said. "He held it in his palm when he was reading the back label."

"Got it."

She opened the bag, pulled the bottle up by the neck, and studied the front label.

"Looks like good stuff," she said.

"Must be," Bosch said. "But too expensive for him. He went with something cheaper."

"Rita Ford is not worth the good stuff—I wonder if she knows that."

"There's probably a lot she doesn't know about Hastings."

"Thanks for this, Harry. I'll see who's working tomorrow and take it in first thing. Maybe they'll have something on the campaign button by then."

"Let me know."

"And I'll add this to your expense report."

She smiled and Bosch nodded.

"Yeah, put it on there," he said.

Ballard stepped back and Bosch drove off.

He was in his daughter's neighborhood. He decided to drive by her house, even though he assumed she was still working her mid-watch shift. The small house she shared with her boyfriend was dark. Bosch idled for a few moments and then drove on, pulling his phone up to call her.

The call went to message.

"Hey, Mads, just wanted to let you know I'm back in L.A. I'm around if you need anything or want to grab a coffee or a beer or dinner. Be safe. I love you."

He disconnected, knowing she probably wouldn't call him back or take him up on his offer. He continued driving into the night.

27

BALLARD GOT INTO the car, lowered the window, and composed herself.

"Shit," she said.

She pulled her phone and called Bosch. He answered right away and Ballard could hear traffic noise in the background.

"Harry, it's me. Where are you?"

"In my rental, following Hastings to City Hall."

"City Hall—are you sure? It's Saturday."

"I won't be sure till he gets there, but it looks like he's heading downtown. He left Rita Ford's place about eight, went home, and then came out a little while later in casual Saturday clothes."

"What does that mean?"

"Jacket, dress shirt, no tie."

"No other stops?"

"Not so far. Anything from the lab?"

"I just left. And it's not good."

"No prints on the button?"

"No, there's a print. But it belongs to Laura Wilson."

"Okay. What about the wine bottle? Did you—"

"It's a smudge. It's useless."

"What about DNA?"

"I dropped the bottle and the pin off at serology. Darcy's off but I called her. She said she'd come in to swab them. But don't get your hopes up. She said we got lucky with the windowsill palm print because the guy was probably nervous and sweating. I doubt Hastings broke much of a sweat picking out a bottle of wine."

Bosch didn't respond.

"Are you there, Harry?"

"Yeah, I'm just thinking. You don't want to go through his trash until it's out on the street. So maybe we should bring him in."

"What, arrest him? We have nothing."

"No, bring him back to Ahmanson. I don't know, we make something up, tell him he needs to come in for an update."

"And you're sure he'll come running all the way out to Westchester on his day off?"

"You tell him it has to be in person because of something sensitive we discovered about the councilman. We know his number one priority is protecting Pearlman. He'll come. And then we put him in a chair with arms so we get his palms when he gets up. We give him a cup of coffee, put some snacks and a pack of gum on the table. We give him some kind of document to read, not keep. You know, we carry out the charade, then he leaves and we hopefully have a palm print and his DNA."

Ballard considered the idea for a few moments.

"What do you think?" Bosch prompted.

"That could work, but if he's the guy, he'll know if we are

194

feeding him a bullshit story," Ballard said. "We need to come up with something important enough to draw him out, but then he's also got to believe what we tell him."

"You said Hastings and the tuxedo guy don't talk, right?"

"Kramer. And yeah, not in years. Hastings pushed him out of the Pearlman universe and Kramer's still bitter."

"Okay, so that's where we build the story. It's something Kramer told you. An accusation or just some sort of story that will hurt Pearlman politically if it comes out. We phony up an affidavit from Kramer."

Ballard nodded as Bosch talked, even though they were on their phones.

"And it will be unlikely that Hastings checks it out with Kramer, because they don't talk," Ballard said. "We could say Kramer kept records from that first campaign and there's something there connecting Pearlman to Laura Wilson. It could be a note or a phone message or something. We'll think it through before we meet."

She started the car and headed back toward the 10 freeway.

"So you'll set it up?" Bosch asked.

"I'll try to get him out to Ahmanson today," Ballard said. "It'll be good that it's Saturday. No one else around. I'll tell him we need to keep it private."

"But what if he wants you to come to him? What's the fallback position?"

"I'll just say no. Pearlman might be coming in on a Saturday, too. So it's gotta be Ahmanson. If he balks at Ahmanson, I'll suggest a coffee shop and I'll be late so he'll get a head start drinking his coffee and will toss the cup when we're finished talking."

"Good. He just pulled into the City Hall garage. You want me to stay with him, just in case he comes back out?"

"No, let's meet at Ahmanson and work out the story. We can set up the meet."

"I don't think he ever saw me on his tail. But just in case, I don't think I should be part of the meeting with Hastings. I'll hang back."

"Yes, play it safe."

"Okay, I'll see you there."

Ballard disconnected. It took her forty minutes to cut through downtown and then out to Westchester. When she finally got to the pod, she found Colleen Hatteras at her station.

"Colleen, it's Saturday. What are you doing here?"

"I just wanted to work on this before the update Monday."

"What update?"

"Remember, we were going to meet first thing to go over the IGG stuff on Pearlman-Wilson?"

"Oh, right."

"What are you doing here?"

"Just…work. I had to go by the lab this morning and I was going to write up some reports and check on a few things. Let me go get a coffee and then we can talk IGG. I'll get you out of here so you can enjoy your weekend."

"Uh, okay. I'd probably have more information by Monday but now is good. How was the lab? Good news?"

"No, not good news. That's why I'm hoping IGG is going to come through."

"What about Harry? Is he coming back?"

"Actually, he is. I talked to him and he sees the light. Everything's fine now."

"Good. I like Harry. He's a good soul."

"Yeah. I'll be back. Set up what you want to show me."

Ballard left her backpack on the floor next to her chair and went to the break room. No coffee had been made, which was good. It gave her a legit reason to stay away from Hatteras and the pod. She started brewing a pot and then pulled out her phone to text Bosch.

> Hang back, Harry. Colleen is in the
> office. I'll try to get rid of her. I'll text
> you when it's clear.

Once the glass pot was filled, Ballard poured herself a cup and returned to the pod. Colleen had already pulled a second desk chair over to her station so Ballard could sit next to her and view her screen.

"Give me another minute," Ballard said. "I have to write a quick email."

Ballard pulled her laptop out of her backpack and opened it on her desk. She then composed a bait email to Hastings that she hoped would lead to an in-person meeting.

> Nelson, something's come up. I know
> it's Saturday but I found records from
> JP's first campaign and there is
> something we need to talk about.
> Any chance you can come to Ahman-
> son or meet me somewhere away
> from City Hall? Let me know.
> RB

She read the email over and realized the reference to City Hall revealed that she knew he was working there on a Saturday. She edited it out and then sent it to Hastings. She then grabbed a notebook and a pen to take over to the IGG briefing with Hatteras. But before she could even get up from her chair, she received a cell phone call from Hastings.

"Detective Ballard, what are we talking about here?" he asked.

"Uh, I don't want to discuss it on the phone," Ballard said. "Can we meet today?"

"I'm at work today. You'll need to come downtown."

"No, I don't want to be in City Hall for this. There may be others around and I don't—"

"I understand. I can leave the office at two. You know the Grand Central Market on Broadway?"

"Sure. I can meet you there."

"There's a G&B Coffee right at the Hill Street side entrance. Meet me there at two fifteen."

"Okay."

"You're sure we can't discuss this on the phone right now?"

"I'd rather not. You'll understand why."

"Okay, then. See you at two fifteen at G&B."

He disconnected. Ballard sat for a moment, feeling the rising pressure of having three hours to come up with a story that would not make Hastings suspicious of the need for a face-to-face meeting.

"Are you ready?" Hatteras said from the other side of the partition.

"Coming," Ballard said as she got up from her station.

She walked around to the next cubicle and sat down next to Hatteras, who had her laptop connected to a 28-inch LG screen.

This allowed her to work on a large digital canvas when looking at DNA family trees and toggling through the color-coded graphics of a person's chromosomes and estimated geographic ancestry.

"You seem tense," Hatteras said.

"Don't try to read me, Colleen," Ballard replied, bristling. "I'm not in the mood. Just tell me what you've got."

Hatteras nodded and looked hurt.

"Fine," she said. "So, we have previously discussed the IGG basics, right? Centimorgans, shared matches, most recent common ancestors—all of the things we use to find potential ancestors to our sample DNA?"

"Yes, I remember all of that. But I'm not a geneticist or a genealogist, so please just keep this simple and tell me whether you're narrowing in on any potential relatives for our suspect."

"Well, we're getting closer. I can say that."

For the next twenty minutes, Hatteras went through her IGG findings and what they could mean. The DNA profile obtained from the palm print found on the windowsill in Sarah Pearlman's bedroom had been uploaded to GEDmatch's database. GEDmatch then generated comparisons with hundreds of thousands of other users' raw autosomal DNA data files, which had been uploaded to various consumer genealogy platforms such as 23andMe, AncestryDNA, and more.

So far, there were four hits to users who shared at least some DNA with the man who had left his partial palm print on the sill.

"That means we're now up to four possible leads to our suspect," Hatteras said. "The next move would normally be to start building a family tree around one or all of them to see how they might be related to him. But here's where we got lucky. One of these people has already started a family tree and it's available to us. It also seems to include the other three people whose matches came up. When you start to build a family tree, you can either keep it private or put it out there for other users who may be looking for you to see. This one is public—at the moment."

Hatteras pointed to her big screen. A genetic family tree looked more like a corporate flowchart than an actual tree. This one was labeled Laughlin Family Tree, and the section Hatteras had enlarged was shaped like an hourglass composed of male and female ancestor icons with names, birth and death years, geographic locations, and in some cases thumbnail images. Some icons appeared blank, as relatives on the distant branches of the tree had not yet been identified. It was most definitely a work in progress that had stalled because of a lack of new connections.

"That doesn't look like it shows anyone in L.A.," Ballard said.

"I said we got lucky, but not that lucky," Hatteras said. "This tree reflects a distinctly Midwest settlement of the family. It shows known genetic relatives in Kansas, Missouri, Ohio, and places in between. But hold on, all is not lost. Judging by the number of centimorgans these people share, I'm guessing these are second or third cousins to our unknown suspect. And some of these unknowns you see at the top here could well be the family member who headed off to the West Coast."

"But wouldn't you have gotten a hit from out here?"

"Only if a relative out here submitted their DNA and allowed it to be shared with GEDmatch. We can only work with what's been entered into the DNA platforms. That's why a personal connection is important. You can directly ask if they've heard in family lore about someone like a grandparent or great-uncle having moved out here a while back."

"Have you made contact yet with any of them?"

"I've messaged all four of the matches through the GED-match portal and have gotten responses from three. This is quite good, because you'd be amazed by how many people don't respond or respond once and then just ghost you because you're law enforcement connected. It's kind of ironic, because on most of these platforms, you have to click a box that opts you in to law enforcement searches. But then when you come calling, some of them ignore you. So three out of four is not bad at all."

"So then, the three who responded—what did they say when you asked about the West Coast?"

"That's what I was checking for today. I've only gotten one reply so far to that question and it was a negative."

"Meaning what?"

"That she knew of no relatives in Los Angeles or California. But she did say she would try to find out."

"That's not a lot of help."

"Actually, in a way it is. We can definitely get an informative read off what we have here. These four DNA relatives are in a fairly tight geographic cluster. Not a lot of spreading out across the country over the decades, as is usually the case. So what this tells me is we are likely looking for a family member who moved away to the West Coast at least a generation or two ago. Because we have two crimes separated by eleven years, it leads me to conclude that this wasn't a tourist, but more likely a resident here but with roots in the Midwest."

"Okay. So how will the person who responded to you try to find out more if it's not on here?"

"If you look at the tree, this is the one who answered me. Shannon Laughlin. You can see here that she has one living grandparent. It's her grandmother on her mother's side. Edith McGrath. She will likely go to her and ask if anybody she knows of in her line—a brother, cousin, anybody—moved west."

Ballard felt the phone in her pocket vibrate.

"Hold on a second," she said.

She pulled the phone and checked the text. It was from Bosch.

I'm here. Just heard from St. Louis.
We need to talk.

Ballard quickly typed a response.

Go to the upstairs break room. Meet
there in 5.

She put the phone away and turned her attention back to Hatteras.

"So, you'll follow up with Shannon Laughlin about her grandmother?"

"I will."

Ballard pointed to the screen.

"And meantime, all we know for sure is that our suspect will have Midwestern roots," she said.

"That's correct," Hatteras said. "And I'm going to keep at it."

"And how are you identifying yourself with these people?"

"I'm saying I'm a genealogist looking at cold cases for the police department. As you know, there's a lot of anti-police sentiment out there lately, so I'm just trying to tread slowly and gently and hopefully gain their trust. It's better, I think, that I don't outright say I'm LAPD."

"I think that's fine. But keep in mind you aren't actually LAPD. You're a civilian volunteer."

"I understand."

"Okay, Colleen, good stuff. Keep at it and let me know when you make the next link."

Since the meet with Hastings was now going to be downtown, Ballard did not see the need to get Hatteras out of the building. She could work here all day if she wanted.

"I will," Hatteras said. "And, um, Renée?"

"What?" Ballard said.

"Is there anything going on that the rest of us should know about? Feels a little bit like high school, the way you and Harry have kind of teamed up and are whispering all the time. And like that fight you two supposedly had yesterday. That felt like a show you put on for all of us."

"No, Colleen, there's nothing anybody else needs to know. There are just some things about the case that are sensitive...politically. Plus, Harry Bosch and I have worked cases going back several years, so we have a shorthand and a level of trust that is already built in. Is that okay?"

"Uh, sure, yes. I was just curious. I didn't mean—"

"Okay, well, you just do what you do and get me some results, Colleen. And thanks for updating me. I'm going to head out now."

"I thought you said you had some reports to write."

"I changed my mind. I'll do it from home. You should go home, too. It's the weekend, Colleen."

Ballard got up and went back to her workstation, returned her laptop to her backpack, and then headed toward the exit. She did not look back at Hatteras but had the feeling that she was being watched the whole way.

28

BOSCH WAS AT the table, looking at his phone, when Ballard entered the second-floor break room. He spoke first.

"Did you bait Hastings? Is he coming in?"

"No, we're meeting downtown at two fifteen. Grand Central Market. What did you get from military archives?"

"I just emailed two files to you. Open up the one called 'St. Louis.'"

Ballard sat down and opened her laptop. While she put in her password and went to her email, Bosch told her what Henic had sent him. He tried to contain the energy that he felt building inside.

"The new woman at the military archives in St. Louis called the old guy I used to deal with," he said. "He vouched for me, said I was good people. So I got the whole military file on Hastings, no redactions."

Ballard was across the table from him and looking at her screen.

"Okay, what am I looking for?" she asked.

"First, you have his postings, and then on page four you have a field action report," Bosch said. "He lost part of his foot in

Afghanistan. And that's what got him his disabled vet status. Honorably discharged in '04."

"So he was here for Wilson."

"Right."

"He's missing half his foot..."

"He must have a prosthetic. From what I saw last night and today, he's got no limp."

Ballard was squinting as she looked at her screen.

"You need glasses, Renée," Bosch said.

"No, I don't," she said. "What was it, IED?"

"Doesn't say in the field action report. When I was in Vietnam, some guys shot themselves so they could get the hell out of there."

"In the foot?"

"Most of the time."

"They must've really wanted out. Is that what you think Hastings did?"

"I have no idea. I was just talking about Vietnam."

"Whether he did or he didn't, what's that got to do with Sarah Pearlman and Laura Wilson?"

"Nothing. Now open the second file."

While Ballard did so, Bosch told her how he got the second file.

"Remember I said I got the military file without redactions? Hastings's Social Security and military serial numbers were in the first file. I used them to access his VA file, and that's what you have there."

"Goddamn, Harry, we shouldn't have this. We should have gotten a search warrant first."

"No one's ever going to know we got it, and it will never come up in court. Scroll through it until you get to 2008."

"Shit, I can't believe we're doing this."

It was Ballard's last protest before following his directions. Bosch got up and came around the table to be able to see her screen.

"Okay, 2008," Ballard said. "Says he came into the Westwood VA hospital for urinalysis. I can't read these results."

"They don't mean anything," Bosch said. "Since '08, he has come in annually for a urinalysis test."

"Is this about kidney disease?"

"It's about this."

Bosch leaned over her shoulder and pointed to a word in the treatment notes from Hastings's 2008 visit.

"Nephrectomy," she said. "What is that?"

"I had to look it up," Bosch said. "It's the surgical procedure for removing a kidney."

Ballard turned from the screen to look at him.

"Harry," she said. "It's him."

29

BALLARD STOOD ON the sidewalk on 1st Street near the corner of the Grand Central Market building. She was in a blind where Hastings would not be able to see her. It was 2:25 and she was waiting on the go-ahead from Bosch. An earlier text from him reported that he was in place and had eyes on Hastings, who had ordered and received a coffee and was looking at his phone while waiting for her.

The key was to make sure Hastings didn't leave with his coffee cup. They needed that for his DNA.

Ballard paced in a small pattern next to the wall of the GCM's parking garage while going over the story in her head. The news that Hastings had had a kidney removed in 2008 shot new momentum into the quiet investigation she and Bosch were conducting. The stakes had grown exponentially in the last few hours and she was now sure that she would be sitting very soon having coffee with a serial killer. She had to be careful not to stir any suspicion in Hastings, nothing that would cause him to flee or otherwise act out after their conversation.

At 2:31 the green-light text came in from Bosch.

He's halfway through his cup. You're
good to go.

She put her phone away and immediately rounded the corner onto Hill Street. The open entry to the massive gathering of food and beverage stalls and butcher and produce shops was on the left. Across the street was the lower landing of Angels Flight, the block-long funicular that carried passengers up and down steep Bunker Hill. Ballard could see Hastings at a small stainless-steel table with his back to her approach.

She tapped him on the shoulder.

"Sorry I'm late," she said. "Airport traffic. Do you want a top-off?"

She had to ask the question even though she was hoping for a no.

"I shouldn't even be drinking coffee this late in the day," Hastings said. "It'll have me up all night."

"Okay, I'll be right back," Ballard said.

There was no line for midafternoon coffee. Ballard quickly ordered a cup of plain black coffee at the counter. As she waited, she casually looked around and saw Bosch at a table by the neon mural on the east wall of the market. He was in Hastings's blind, even though there was no evidence to suggest Hastings knew who Bosch was.

Coffee in hand, Ballard sat down at the table with Hastings. She noticed that his cup was almost empty. The barista had written "Nelson" on the side of the paper cup, which would make it easy to identify should he throw it in the trash. But like her own cup, it had a corrugated paper sleeve around it. While that would be an impediment to collecting fingerprints from the cup, she anticipated that they would still be able to collect Hastings's DNA through saliva and epithelial cells.

"Thanks for seeing me on such short notice," she said.

"Not a problem," Hastings said. "So, what's so important you could only tell me face-to-face?"

Ballard nodded and took a sip of hot coffee to buy some time as she mentally went over the script she had worked out with Bosch.

"As I said, it's a delicate matter," she said. "I'm well aware that the Open-Unsolved Unit is in existence only because of Councilman Pearlman and that any perceived hint of scandal could hurt him as well as the unit."

"What perceived hint of scandal, Detective?" Hastings pressed.

"I talked to Sandy Kramer. And while it was pretty clear that there is no love lost between you two, Kramer is still loyal to Jake Pearlman."

"Exactly right, no love lost. Why would you talk to that asshole?"

"This is a homicide investigation. It goes where it goes."

"You talked to him about the girl with the button in her drawer?"

"The woman, yes. Laura Wilson."

"The woman. Okay, what did Kramer say?"

"Well, when I asked him about Laura and showed him the photo, he said he remembered her."

"That's it?"

"No. He said he thought she might have volunteered and that I should ask Jake because he knew her, too."

Hastings immediately pushed his cup to the side of the table like he was finished with it. And he shook his head.

"No way," he said. "I would have seen it. I don't know what he is now, but Kramer was a drunk back then. That was why he eventually had to go when Jake got serious about politics."

"How can you know for sure?" Ballard asked. "You weren't there then."

"I was there, and I'm telling you, there was no Laura Wilson."

"You told me that the 2005 election was before your time with Pearlman."

"No, what I said, or at least what I meant, was that it was before my time as chief of staff. I was there back then. I was Jake's driver. I had just gotten out of the VA and needed to restart my life, and he said he needed a driver. Believe me, if Laura Wilson was part of the campaign, I would have known, because first of all, it was a small operation, and second, she was Black."

Ballard paused for a moment. She did not recall the exact words of the phone conversation earlier in the week when Hastings used the phrase *before my time*. But he had just corrected the record and it matched what Kramer had told her. This caused her to go temporarily off script.

"When I talked to the councilman about Laura, he said he didn't know her," Ballard said. "But somehow he knew she was Black before I even showed him her photo."

"That's because I told him," Hastings said.

"Okay, and how did you know? I never got around to sending you the photo."

"I know you didn't. But I did what any good chief of staff would do. I don't go into any meeting with my boss without being prepared. You didn't send me a photo, and so I went online and googled 'Laura Wilson murder Los Angeles.' And what came up? A photo of her that ran in the *Times*. Poor kid finally got famous as a murder victim. There was a whole story on it."

Ballard had seen the newspaper clipping, including the photo, in the Laura Wilson murder book. Hastings had again talked his way out of one of the inconsistencies that had bred her suspicion. She felt the interview falling apart and Hastings doing the one thing she didn't want. He was growing suspicious. She tried one more time to put him on the defensive.

"When I asked you if Pearlman had a campaign manager on that first run for office, you said you'd get me the name and contact," she said. "But you knew right then it was Kramer and didn't tell me. Why?"

"I just told you why," Hastings said. "Kramer's an asshole. A drunk. And I was concerned that he'd be vindictive because of the way we moved him out of the picture. It turns out my concerns were well founded. He's given you a line of bullshit that has taken you completely off course."

"I told you, it goes where it goes. If Kramer is lying I'll deal with him."

"What's this really about, Ballard? Are you trying to make some kind of a play at Jake? Are you trying to threaten him? Is it you or the department?"

"I can assure you, it is no play. It is no threat. I am conducting a full field investigation. No stone left unturned. Why do you think I wanted to meet away from my team and yours? I thought you would appreciate—"

"Then what does Sandy Kramer want?"

Before Ballard could answer, a man came to the table. He wore an apron and gloves and carried a trash can. He wore a mask over his mouth and nose as other employees in the market still did.

"Finished, sir?"

He pointed to Hastings's coffee cup. Ballard looked up and saw that the man behind the mask was Bosch. Hastings barely looked up at him.

"Take it," he said. "I'm done."

The second sentence was directed at Ballard. Bosch took the coffee cup in his gloved hand and walked away from the table. Hastings fixed Ballard with a hard stare.

"You know what?" he said. "I don't even care what Sandy Kramer wants. Fuck him and fuck you, Ballard, if you think you're going to make a move against Jake or me. This is weak and I'm out of here."

He got up and started walking way.

"You have this completely wrong," Ballard called after him.

He didn't stop.

30

BOSCH GRABBED THE key off the rear tire of Ballard's Defender, unlocked the vehicle, and placed the evidence package on the back seat floor. He relocked the vehicle and put the key back. He was heading back to the market when he got a call from Ballard.

"He left," she said. "Where are you?"

"By your car," Bosch said. "I put the cup on the floor in the back seat."

"I went off script and he got mad. He headed back through the market. Can you pick him up?"

"Hold on."

Bosch changed directions on 3rd Street. Instead of going up to Hill, he went down to Broadway and waited at the corner to see if Hastings emerged from the south side of the block-long food court.

"I don't have him," he said.

"He should be coming out," Ballard said. "He just walked away less than a minute ago."

Bosch knew that there were no through-aisles in the market. It was a maze of crowded shops and food concessions, and

Hastings would need to move around people and shift from one aisle to another as he made his way through. Not enough time had passed for him to get to Broadway.

"What happened?" he asked.

"I'll tell you later," Ballard said. "Let's just see if—"

"Got him."

Hastings had left the market and was jaywalking across Broadway. Bosch could see he was talking and then he reached up to his ear. Bosch saw the earbud and knew he had been on a call.

"He just made a call," Bosch said.

"He's probably trying to find Kramer," Ballard said. "This whole thing just blew up."

"He looks pretty hot."

"You're going to stay with him? He may try to confront Kramer."

"I got him. Wherever he goes."

"Okay, let me get to my car and head to the lab. If I'm lucky, I'll be able to catch Darcy while she's there. You stay with Hastings and I'll call you back."

She disconnected without waiting for Bosch's reply. Bosch hung back nearly half a block as he followed Hastings on the four-block walk back to his office in council chambers. Hastings walked down 3rd to Spring and turned left. As he turned the corner, Bosch saw him reach up to the earbud again. He was getting a call.

Bosch picked up his pace, falling into a trot until he reached the corner. He made the turn and walked briskly to catch up close enough to overhear Hastings's part of the phone conversation.

At the 2nd Street intersection, Hastings had to stop and wait for a green light. The Civic Center was largely deserted because it was a weekend and all the city offices and courts were closed. But Bosch was able to use two pedestrians who were waiting for the light as camouflage when he caught up to Hastings.

At first Hastings stood silently, like he was listening or waiting for someone to speak. Then he started speaking in tight, angry bursts. Because he was aware that others were waiting to cross with him, he dropped his voice so low that Bosch heard nothing. But as soon as the light changed and he stepped into the crosswalk, his voice returned to its sharp tone of command.

And Bosch was able to hear almost every word he said.

"Listen, motherfucker, you call her back and tell her you lied."

There was another pause during which Hastings flung a hand out in a dismissive gesture.

"Bullshit—you're the liar. You call her back and tell her what I told you, or I will destroy you. You understand, asshole?"

There was a beat of silence and then Hastings signed off with one word.

"Good."

Hastings put his finger to his ear to end the call and continued toward City Hall. Bosch once again held back and finally stopped the tail when he watched Hastings go up the stone steps of the historic building. He called Ballard to report on what he had seen and heard.

"He's back at City Hall," he said. "Along the way, I think he had somebody find Kramer and put him on a call. He never used the name but he was angry and told somebody to 'call her back' and change the story."

"It was Kramer," Ballard said. "He just called me and said he just talked to Hastings. He was going apeshit."

"So was Hastings. You straighten Kramer out?"

"I did. I explained that we were just trying to get a rise out of Hastings. I think he's cool with it. He doesn't like the guy, remember?"

"How far did you go off script?"

"I'm pulling in at the lab and I've got Darcy Troy waiting for me. Let me drop this off and then I'll call you back. Or if you want, we can meet somewhere."

"I could eat. Meet me at Traxx."

"Is that back open?"

"Yeah. You want anything?"

"I'll get something to drink when I get there. I already ate."

It took Bosch ten minutes to get over to Union Station and the restaurant inside its huge waiting hall. It was after the lunch rush and the restaurant wasn't crowded, but the waiting hall was packed with travelers embracing a postpandemic world, whether the threat of the pandemic was actually over or not.

Bosch was halfway through a grilled cheese sandwich and a side of fries when Ballard slid into the window booth across from him. She took a french fry off his plate in the same fluid motion. Bosch pushed his plate toward the middle of the table.

"Dig in," he said. "I can't eat all of this."

She took another fry as the waitress came to the table.

"I just want an iced tea and some ketchup," she said.

Bosch let her settle for a moment before going right to the case.

"So Darcy has the cup?"

"She does. She's putting a rush on it. I think I've used up the next three months of favors with her. Especially getting her to come in today."

"It'll be worth it when we bag this guy. When will she know?"

"She's hoping the sequencing is done by tomorrow, and then she'll put it into CODIS and see if it draws a match."

"She can't directly compare what we get from the cup to what they got from the palm print?"

Ballard shook her head.

"Legal protocol handed down by the D.A.'s Office," she said. "Makes it harder to challenge in court if you don't go outside the bounds of usual procedure. Skipping it and going to a one-to-one comparison can look like the fix was in. A defense lawyer like your brother, Mickey, could blow that up in court."

"Half brother. So tomorrow we'll know."

"If we're lucky."

Bosch nodded and took another bite of his sandwich. He spoke with his mouth full.

"So you went off script with Hastings."

"Yeah. He sort of got to me when he knocked down all three strikes I had against him."

"What strikes?"

"He corrected what he meant when he said the Wilson murder was before his time with Pearlman. He now says he meant before his time as chief of staff. He acknowledged today that he was Pearlman's driver back then. So I went off script when I asked him how he knew Wilson was Black when I didn't tell him."

"And?"

"He had an answer for it. I didn't send him a photo, so he googled her and found a *Times* story on her murder that had her photo. He was right. The same clip is in the murder book."

"Look, none of that matters now with the missing kidney. The DNA match will come back and we take him down."

"I know, I know, but he's good. He shifted the conversation, so when I got back on script and brought up Kramer and him not giving me the name of the campaign manager when he clearly knew it, he went ballistic."

"Yeah, I heard Hastings's side of it. What did Kramer tell you he said to Hastings on the call?"

"He told me he denied saying that Pearlman knew Laura Wilson, but Hastings didn't believe him. He just yelled and threatened to destroy him."

"I think you need to call him."

"Who?"

"Hastings. Tell him that Kramer just called you and changed his story. Maybe that will calm him down. We kind of left Kramer's ass blowin' in the wind on this. Hastings should know there is no threat."

"Like, now?"

"Yeah, call him, see if he answers. We have to give Kramer some cover."

Ballard pulled her phone and called Hastings. He answered and she quickly explained that she now knew that the information she had received about Pearlman knowing Wilson was wrong. She apologized for not confirming or debunking the intel before bringing it to him. She then listened quietly for almost a minute as Hastings had his say and disconnected without giving her a chance to respond.

"Sounded like that went well," Bosch said.

"Right," Ballard said. "Let's just say that I hope we get that DNA back before he can have me fired Monday."

Bosch nodded.

"Let's hope Darcy comes through," he said.

Ballard leaned back and looked out the window into the waiting hall. Union Station was one of the city's lasting beauties.

"Think how many people have come through this place to get to this city, Harry," she said. "People like Laura Wilson, bringing their hopes and dreams."

"She came from Chicago by train?" Bosch asked.

"She kept a journal. It was in the murder book. She took the train to save money. It took two days and she saw the Rocky Mountains. Then she got here and got killed. How fucking unfair was that?"

"Murder is never fair. I'd like to read that journal."

"I have it at my desk at Ahmanson."

Bosch joined her in looking out the window into the hall. Dozens of people from all walks of life moved across the Spanish-tile floor, either heading away from L.A. or having arrived at their destination, suitcases and dreams in hand. He pictured Laura Wilson arriving and moving wide-eyed through the great hall to the doors that opened to the City of Angels. She could not have known that it was her final destination.

31

THE OCEAN WAS as smooth as a fitted sheet on a bed. Ballard had brought both surfboard and paddleboard with her so she would be ready for any kind of surface. She had found a parking spot on the Pacific Coast Highway at the west end of La Costa Beach in Malibu and was close enough to the water to be able to tell it was a paddle day. This was good. It meant Pinto would get to ride with her rather than being leashed to a tent pole while she rode the bigger waves.

It was a Sunday but early enough that the beach was not crowded. Ballard opened the Defender's hatch and sat on the tail while working on her wet suit. Pinto was still in his travel crate next to her.

She was just about to slide her phone into its waterproof case, when it started to buzz. The caller was Darcy Troy and Ballard's pulse quickened.

"Darcy, give me the good news," Ballard said.

This was met with silence.

"Darcy? Hello?"

"I'm here. And I don't have good news, Renée. We got a good sample from the cup, and I'm sorry but it is no match to the two previous cases."

Now it was Ballard who went silent. She had fully invested in Hastings as their guy.

"Renée, you still there?"

"I don't understand. He's the guy. He lost a kidney. He's been shaky on his stories. I can't believe this. Are you sure, Darcy? Could there be some kind of mistake?"

"No, no mistake. I'm sorry. But what do you mean when you say he lost a kidney?"

"We have his VA records. Three years after the Laura Wilson murder, he had a radical neph-whatever-you-call-it."

"Nephrectomy. Removal of a kidney. But that doesn't mean he had kidney disease. He could have donated a kidney. I mean, I'd have to look at the medical records or get somebody more qualified to look, but—"

"Oh, shit. We didn't—I need to call Harry Bosch. Darcy, you're a genius. I'll call you later. And thanks so much for giving up your weekend for this."

Ballard disconnected. She immediately called Bosch and started unzipping her wet suit as she waited for him to answer.

"Ballard. What's up?"

"Good and bad news. The DNA from Hastings does not match the case DNA."

"Is that the good or bad news?"

"The bad. The good news is that he could have donated a kidney to a friend or relative. And that person would be the one with kidney disease and could be our new suspect."

Bosch was silent.

"Harry?"

"Just thinking. We don't have much of a choice. We have to go to Hastings."

"Follow the kidney."

Ballard smiled but heard no reaction from Bosch.

"That was supposed to be funny, Harry."

"Yeah, I know. So, where are you?"

"Well, I was about to go paddling. I'm in Malibu."

"Do you want to wait till tomorrow?"

"Not really. We have new momentum. Let's go see him."

"If we can find him."

"Well, we know where he lives and works and where he's been shacking up. I can also just call him."

"I think it would be better if he doesn't know we're coming. You never know, he could call somebody if he knows why we're coming."

"Agreed."

"When?"

"I can get back in an hour. I'll change, drop off the dog, and then come get you. Let's say noon."

"I'll be ready."

They disconnected and Ballard finished peeling off her wet suit. She looked at Pinto in his crate.

"Sorry, boy," she said. "Mom's gotta go to work. We'll come back next week and get on the water. I promise."

She threw her wet suit into the back of the SUV and put her sweats back on over her one-piece. She turned and looked back at the ocean. She saw the silhouette of Catalina emerging on the horizon through the marine layer. It was going to be a clear and hot day.

"Damn," she said.

32

BALLARD AND BOSCH went to Hastings's house first and found no one home. From there, they went west to Sunset Plaza and the home of Rita Ford. The black Tesla that Bosch had previously followed was there, parked in the same spot at the curb on St. Ives as before.

"Bingo," Bosch said.

They pulled into the driveway and parked. Rita Ford answered the door.

"Detective Ballard, this is a surprise," she said. "What brings you here?"

"We need to see Nelson Hastings," Ballard said.

"Why do you think he would be here?"

Ballard pointed out to the street.

"Because that's his car and because we know he is," she said. "We need to talk to him, Rita. It's important."

"Just a moment," Ford said.

She closed the door. Ballard looked at Bosch. They were expecting a cold welcome.

When the door reopened, Hastings was standing there.

"What are you doing here?" he demanded.

"We need your help," Ballard said.

"You want my help? Jesus Christ, one minute you have me down as suspect number one, and now you want my help?"

"What makes you say we suspected you?"

"Come on, Detective. That charade yesterday where you tell me a bullshit story from Kramer after trying to catch me in lies from my earlier statements? I'm not stupid. You've got it in your head that someone from Jake's circle killed Laura Wilson and Sarah Pearlman and that someone was me."

"We don't think that, Nelson. Can we come in? We really need you to help us with this."

Hastings pointed at Bosch.

"And you, I know who you are," he said. "You followed me from G&B's. Yeah, I saw you. My guess is you're Bosch. Well, you fucked up, Bosch, along with her, and tomorrow you'll both be gone."

"I fucked up," Bosch said. "Not Renée. And if you let us in, we can explain it and you can help us catch the murderer of your friend's sister."

Hastings shifted his stare from Bosch to Ballard but didn't move or say anything. Then the stare came back to Bosch. Hastings shook his head like he couldn't believe what he was about to do and stepped back from the door.

"Ten minutes," he said. "That's how long you have to convince me not to have you both fired and maybe even prosecuted."

Bosch almost told him he couldn't be fired because he was a volunteer, and that any effort to charge him or Ballard with a crime would be laughed out of the D.A.'s Office along with Hastings.

But he let it go. They followed Hastings into the house,

and he led them to a living room furnished in bright oranges and yellows. Rita Ford was sitting on the couch upholstered in white-and-yellow stripes.

"We need to talk privately with Nelson," Ballard said.

"Fine," Ford said in an insulted tone.

She got up and left the room. Hastings gestured to the now empty couch, and Bosch and Ballard sat down. The room had a glass wall with a view that extended over the top of the Sunset Boulevard shops a block below and out across West Hollywood.

Hastings stayed standing, arms folded tightly across his chest.

"So," he said. "Just so we are clear, you two detectives have obviously been following me, *investigating* me, and suspecting me of *murdering* my best friend's sister. Do you admit that?"

"I would like to know how you know all of that," Ballard asked levelly.

"What does that matter?" Hastings said. "Is it true, or are you going to sit there and deny it."

"Hastings, why don't you sit down and cool off," Bosch said.

"Don't fucking tell me what to do, old man," Hastings shot back.

"Look, we're sorry if you got your feathers ruffled because we were just doing our jobs," Bosch said. "Sure, we were looking at you, and for good reasons that we can tell you about if you're interested in listening. So again, why don't you sit down and help us catch a killer. Wouldn't your best friend want that?"

Hastings held up his hand to stop all discussion. He briefly closed his eyes and went through some sort of internal calming exercise. He then opened his eyes and sat down on a chair with puffy orange cushions.

"What do you want?" he said.

Bosch looked at Ballard and nodded. She was lead.

"You had a kidney removed in 2008," she said. "Why?"

Hastings shook his head like he couldn't comprehend what the question had to do with the subject at hand.

"First of all, how do you know that?" he asked.

"We're detectives, Mr. Hastings," Ballard said. "We find things out. You lost a kidney. Why?"

"Okay, look, I didn't *lose* a kidney," Hastings said. "I gave it away."

Ballard nodded.

"Sorry, poor choice of words," she said. "You *gave* someone a kidney. That was a very unselfish thing to do. It must have been someone very close to you. A family member?"

"I'm surprised you don't already know," Hastings said. "I gave it to Ted Rawls."

In the movies, the detectives always look at each other to underscore for the viewer the significance of a witness's revelation. Ballard and Bosch couldn't help exchanging a look, and this underscored the significance for Hastings.

"What?" he said. "Are you saying Ted's the one? No way."

"We're not saying that," Ballard said. "I just didn't know that Ted had that kind of a health situation. If I had, I would have questioned why the councilman wanted him on our team."

"The guy wanted to be a cop his whole life," Hastings said. "LAPD wouldn't take him but Santa Monica did. Then he gets sick and is forced to quit his chosen profession. So yeah, I gave him a kidney. I had an extra one."

"What sort of issue did he have with his kidneys?" Ballard asked.

"Cancer," Hastings said. "Took both kidneys, his spleen. He almost died. But he fought his way back, started a small business, and built it up. He's amazing. But he never gave up on the dream of being a detective. So when he saw the press conference on TV where Jake announced the reboot of the cold case team, he came to me and said, 'Put me on.' I talked to Jake and we agreed. Jake went to you with it."

"And he conveniently left out his medical history," Ballard said. "You must have known that the LAPD would not have accepted the liability of that."

"Jake didn't want to give you any reason to push back on him," Hastings said. "So Ted got added to the team. And now you're saying he had something to do with Sarah and the Wilson girl? That is ridiculous."

"Again, we're not saying that," Ballard said.

"Then what are you saying?" Hastings said. "Why all these questions about Ted?"

Ballard paused for a moment and looked back at Bosch. He knew she was trying to decide whether to trust Hastings not to pass on what she told him to his friends Jake Pearlman and Ted Rawls. Bosch nodded, giving her the go-ahead from his view of things.

"I told you that DNA from the Laura Wilson case matched her killer to the Sarah Pearlman case," Ballard said.

"Yes, you told me," Hastings said. "And Wilson had a 'JAKE!' button. It's thin, Detective Ballard."

"The DNA sample from the Wilson case came from blood found in urine on the toilet seat in her apartment," Ballard said. "The blood also told us something else. That the killer had kidney disease."

As staunch a defender of Rawls as he was, even Hastings blinked at the revelation. He was quiet for a few moments and then spoke in a reserved voice.

"So when you found out I was missing a kidney...," he said, his voice trailing off.

"Plus, I thought you had lied when you told me that the '05 campaign was before your time," Ballard said.

Hastings nodded.

"And I knew Laura Wilson was Black before you told me," he said.

Ballard let him sit with that for a moment and then continued.

"When was the last time you talked to Ted Rawls?" she asked.

"Uh, yesterday," Hastings said. "He...I called him because I was upset about our conversation. He told me it was probably a setup, that you were getting my DNA. And I remembered the guy there who came up and took my cup. You, right?"

He looked directly at Bosch, who nodded.

"I'm sorry I called you an old man," Hastings said. "That wasn't cool at all."

"Don't worry about it," Bosch said. "I am an old man."

"What else did Ted tell you?" Ballard asked.

"I don't really remember," Hastings said. "I kind of went dark when he said, 'She's looking at you, man, and you'd better be careful.'"

"Anything else that you can remember?" she pressed.

"No, I just wanted to get off the phone," Hastings said. "I was so angry once I realized what that meeting between us had really been about."

"Who else have you talked to about this?" Bosch asked. "Did you tell the councilman?"

"No, I was going to tell him all about it tomorrow when I told him you needed to be fired," Hastings said. "I talked to Rita about it, but she hasn't told anyone."

He held Ballard's eyes for a long moment.

"You can't talk to anybody else about this," Ballard said. "Not the councilman and certainly not Ted Rawls. Rita, too."

"We keep quiet while you do what?" Hastings asked.

"Continue the investigation," Ballard said. "We're very close, and you and the councilman will be the first we call when we get there."

"What if Ted calls me?" Hastings said. "What do I say?"

"Just don't take the call," Bosch said. "If you talk to him, he might be able to read that you know something."

"My god," Hastings said. "I really can't believe this."

Ballard stood up and Bosch did the same. He knew that she understood that they had to get moving on Rawls—if it wasn't already too late.

Hastings remained seated and looked like he was deep in thought.

"I just realized something," he said.

"What?" Ballard asked.

"That I gave my kidney to the guy who killed Sarah," Hastings said. "And Laura Wilson and who knows who else. I kept this guy alive to do that."

"Nelson, we don't know that yet," Ballard said. "We are working this one step at a time. You've been very helpful but we need to continue our work. I promise I will personally keep you in the loop."

Hastings was staring blankly at nothing.

"Are you okay, Nelson?" Ballard asked.

"Yeah," Hastings said in a flat voice. "I'm just dandy."

They left him there with his thoughts. Bosch looked around for Rita Ford as they were exiting the house but didn't see her. It looked like Hastings was on his own for now.

33

THE FIRST THING Ballard did after she and Bosch got back in her city car was call Paul Masser on his cell.

"Paul, I need you to come in," she said.

"Really?" he said. "It's Sunday—what's going on?"

"I need a search warrant and I want it to be ironclad. It can never come back on us in court."

"And you need this today?"

"I need it ten minutes ago. Can you come in? I'll have it roughed out for you. I promise, you'll be in and out."

"Can't you just email it to me? I can go over it on my phone?"

"No, I want you at the pod so we can do it together."

"Uh, okay. Give me an hour and I'll be there."

"Thank you. And, Paul, don't tell anyone on the team that you're rolling in to work. No one."

She disconnected before he could ask her what was going on. She started driving down the hill to Sunset.

"You don't need me for that, right?" Bosch said. "You and Paul will write it up."

Ballard looked over at him.

"I guess," she said. "But you've written more search warrants than Paul and me combined. Where do you have to go?"

DESERT STAR

"I was thinking I'd get my car and go sit on Rawls," Bosch said. "If I can find him."

Ballard nodded. It was the right move.

"Good idea," she said. "I can get his home address out of my team files. He also has an office above one of his stores, the first one he opened in Santa Monica. It's the flagship and he runs all the others from there. You can look that address up. It's called DGP Mailboxes and More."

"Got it," Bosch said. "DGP?"

"I once heard him tell the others in the pod that it stood for Don't Go Postal, but nobody's supposed to know that."

"Nice. Thoughtful. What about his car?"

"I have copies of all the paperwork he filled out when he joined the team, including a description of car and plate number for security at Ahmanson."

"Good, get that to me, too. Let me out on Sunset and I'll grab a Lyft back to my place. Save you some driving."

"You sure?"

"My car's in the opposite direction of Ahmanson. You need to get there and start writing."

Ballard had a green light and made the turn from Sunset Plaza onto Sunset Boulevard. She pulled to the curb in front of a real estate office. Bosch paused before getting out as he looked at the glass facade of the business.

"What?" Ballard asked.

"Nothing," Bosch said. "I worked a case that involved that place when it was a high-end jewelry store. Two brothers were murdered in the back room."

"Oh, I remember that."

"That one ended up being about bent cops, too."

Bosch got out of the city car and looked back in at Ballard before closing the door.

"I'll call you when I get eyes on Rawls."

"Roger—I mean, sounds good."

"That was close."

"Caught myself."

"Good luck with the warrant."

He closed the door, and Ballard pulled back into traffic, drawing a horn from a driver who thought she had cut him off. She checked her rearview and saw Bosch standing on the sidewalk looking at his phone. He was summoning a ride.

An hour later, Ballard was at her workstation at Ahmanson. She was putting the finishing touches on the probable cause statement that would be included in an application for a search warrant allowing her to take a DNA swab from the mouth of Ted Rawls.

Paul Masser arrived. He was wearing shorts and a tucked-in polo shirt.

"Oh, shit, I pulled you off the golf course?" Ballard said.

"Not a big deal," Masser said. "I was on the seventeenth green at Wilshire when you called. I would have had to walk in from there. So I just played the last hole, took a quick shower, and came directly here."

He gestured to the golfing outfit he was wearing.

"I got these in the golf shop because I didn't have anything in my locker to change into."

"Well, I have the PC statement. I'll print it and you can start."

A search warrant was all about the probable cause statement. It had to convince a judge that there was enough legal cause to allow for a search and seizure of a citizen's property or person.

Everything else in a search warrant was largely boilerplate. The judge it was submitted to would likely skip over all of that and go directly to the PC.

"Who's up today?" Masser asked. "Did you check yet?"

"No," Ballard asked. "Why don't you do that while I get this from the printer."

Masser was inquiring about which judge from the criminal courts division was up on rotation to handle after-hours search warrant requests. This was a key question because judges had particular viewpoints and practices that became known to the trade—the lawyers who appeared before them and the police officers who went to them for search warrant approval. Some judges were fierce defenders of the Fourth Amendment protections against unlawful search and seizure. Others were fierce law-and-order judges who never saw a search warrant application they didn't like. In addition, they were elected to the bench. While they were charged with wielding their power without personal or political bias, it was a rare judge who didn't occasionally peek out from under the blindfold at the possible electoral ramifications of a ruling—like whether to allow the state to take a DNA sample from an ex-cop suspected of being a killer.

Ballard came back from the printer and handed Masser the two-page PC statement just as he was hanging up his desk phone.

"Judge Canterbury is up," he said. "And that is not good. He's very strict on search and seizure."

"I've heard," Ballard said. "I might have another way to go."

Most detectives worked on establishing a relationship with a go-to judge whom they could count on to be sympathetic when it came to questions of probable cause. It was a form of judge shopping, but it was practiced widely. Ballard, from her years on the midnight shift at Hollywood Division, had woken more than a few judges up in the middle of the night to get a search warrant signed. She had a few names on her contact list that she could call if she and Masser didn't want to go to Judge Canterbury.

Ballard pointed to the document now in Masser's hands.

"You're going to be upset by what you read," she said. "And I don't want you repeating any of it to anybody. Clear?"

"Yes, clear," Masser said. "Now I can't wait."

She left him at his workstation and went back to hers. While Masser was going through the PC document, she opened one of the original murder books from the Pearlman case and started leafing through the transcripts from the interviews conducted by the original detectives. Her memory was correct. There were apparently no interviews with Nelson Hastings or Ted Rawls. And this carried through to the original lab reports. Neither one of them had ever had their palm print compared to that found on the windowsill in Sarah Pearlman's bedroom.

This was a serious flaw in the original investigation. Hastings and Rawls were close friends of Jake Pearlman's and were acquainted with his sister. They should have been interviewed and printed—as Kramer had been. The fact that they weren't interviewed contradicted what had appeared to Ballard to be a tight and thorough investigation. Since the ODs on the case were no longer available, Ballard felt there was only one person she could talk to for clarification of this issue.

She called Nelson Hastings.

"Did you arrest him?" he asked immediately.

"No, and we're not there yet," Ballard said. "We are proceeding carefully."

"Then, what do you need from me?" Hastings asked.

"I'm reviewing interview transcripts from the original investigation. There is no interview with you or Ted Rawls. I don't understand that. You were Jake's friends and I assume you both knew Sarah. Do you remember this? Why didn't they interview you?"

"I was out of town with my parents when the murder happened," Hastings said. "They talked to my parents and confirmed it, so they never talked to me. And Ted wasn't around then."

"What do you mean?"

"I mean, he was around, but he wasn't as tight as Jake, Kramer, and I were. He was sort of the new guy. It was our senior year and we were all about to graduate. We had gotten our college acceptance letters and the three of us got into UCLA. Then that summer, we heard Ted got in, too, so we kind of started including him in stuff. We took him under our wing because we'd be going to college together. Only that didn't happen."

"Why not?"

"Well, for one thing, I changed my mind, joined the army, and never went to UCLA. And neither did Ted. Something happened and he ended up going to Santa Monica Community College, and then he joined the cops out there."

"Could it have been a lie about getting into UCLA? He only said he got in so he could get close to you guys?"

"I don't know, maybe. You mean like he glommed on to us so he'd hear stuff about Sarah and the investigation? That's sick."

"It's possible. But at the time of the murder, he wasn't close enough to Jake that the detectives would want to talk to him?"

"Yeah, exactly."

"Did he know Sarah?"

"He could have. She went to an all-girls school, so she'd come to our dances and events to meet boys. Jake would bring her. So Ted could have known her, or at least known who she was, from that."

Ballard noticed that Masser was now standing next to her. She saw that he had red-lined her probable cause statement. She held a finger up, indicating she was almost finished with her call.

"I have one more question," Ballard said. "In '05, Rawls was a cop in Santa Monica. He wasn't part of the Pearlman campaign, was he?"

There was another silence before Hastings answered.

"You're thinking about the campaign button," Hastings said. "The answer is yes. He was a volunteer. Kramer recruited him. He'd work his shift for Santa Monica and then come meet us at Greenblatt's, where we would gather all the volunteers before going out to canvass. He did that several times. Knocked on doors."

"So he could conceivably have knocked on Laura Wilson's door and given her the button," Ballard said.

It was a statement, not a question.

"Yes," Hastings said.

"Thanks for your time," Ballard said. "I'll be in touch."

She disconnected and held out her hand to Masser for the document.

"You don't have it, Renée," he said. "I'm sorry."

She looked at the printout. He had drawn a red box around the statement of facts in support of the search.

"What's wrong with it?" she asked.

"It's weak," Masser said. "The DNA collected in the Wilson case indicated kidney disease. Rawls got a kidney from Hastings because he had kidney disease, but there is no linkage between Rawls and Wilson. Her having a campaign button from Pearlman is nothing. It could be happenstance. There were probably thousands of those buttons. And I'm afraid that's how Canterbury or any other judge will look at this. You're asking for a swab of his DNA, to search his home, his car, even his desk here. You want the moon, Renée. And I'm sorry, but if I was still a D.D.A., I wouldn't let you go with this to a judge."

"Well, that's what you're here for."

"Let's just look at the DNA. Have you thought about surreptitious collection?"

"He's a cop and he already knows we did that with Hastings. He'll be too careful now. I mean, go look at his desk. It's so clean it looks like nobody sits there. He probably came in here yesterday and cleaned it after he figured out what we were doing with Hastings."

"Well, this is all hard for me to wrap my head around. Are you sure you're looking at the right person?"

"We're sure he's a suspect, but that's what we need the search warrant for. To gather evidence that either proves or disproves the suspicion."

"We?"

"Harry Bosch is working this with me. He should be watching Rawls right now. So...what if..."

She didn't finish because she was still thinking it out.

"What?" Masser said.

"That was Hastings I was just talking to," Ballard said. "He confirmed that Rawls was a volunteer with the campaign back in '05. He knocked on doors and handed out those pins."

"Did Hastings say he knocked on Laura Wilson's door or was even in her building? Anything that directly connects Rawls to Wilson?"

"No, nothing that close. He did join Jake Pearlman's social circle almost immediately after his sister's murder."

Masser shook his head.

"These are pluses to the document," he said. "But it's not enough to get it by Canterbury. Do you have a go-to judge you could take it to? My go-to retired two years ago."

Ballard thought for a moment before answering. She had a judge in mind, but it was complicated. Judge Charles Rowan was often more interested in Ballard as a woman than as a detective. Going to his house to get a search warrant signed would require a dance that she wasn't keen on or proud of. Prior to Rowan, she'd had a female go-to with whom no dance was required. But Carolyn Wickwire had lost reelection when a popular ex-prosecutor ran against her, claiming she was weak on crime.

"I have a judge I could go to, I think," Ballard finally said.

"Well, let's add in what you got from Hastings and pad this a little bit," Masser said. "And we'll see what happens."

34

TED RAWLS'S FLAGSHIP DGP store was on Montana Avenue in Santa Monica. Bosch cruised by slowly and saw a man inside the front room of the shop, using a key to open a mailbox. Bosch checked his rearview and then pulled to a stop to watch for a moment. He had already cruised by Ted Rawls's home on nearby Harvard Street but there appeared to be no one home.

The DGP shop was on the ground level of a two-story structure called simply enough the Montana Shoppes & Suites. It was a block long with retail shops running side by side on floor one and small offices on the second level. Staircases at the east and west ends allowed for access to the walkway that ran the length of the building in front of the offices.

The DGP store was divided into two sections. Up front behind the plate glass window was the bank of private mailboxes accessible to customers 24/7 through a front door with a key card lock. Beyond the mailbox room was the shipping and packaging center with a counter and displays of cardboard boxes and shipping materials.

Bosch watched the man take a small package out of his

mailbox, close it, and then leave. He then saw a man appear from the back of the business and take a seat behind the counter. It wasn't Ted Rawls, but this didn't mean Rawls was not there or in the office he kept directly above the store.

Bosch started cruising again and turned left on 16th Street. He then took another left into the alley that ran behind the shopping center. He cruised slowly, reading the names of the businesses stenciled on the rear doors. There were no cars in the alley and No Parking signs were spaced every fifty feet or so, as were dumpsters pushed up against the rear walls of the businesses. Bosch checked for security cameras but did not see any back here.

When he got to the door marked DGP, he slowed even more and looked up at the windows of the office on the second floor. They offered no clue as to whether Rawls was in. Venetian blinds had been pulled tightly closed behind the glass.

He picked up speed and continued to the end of the alley at 17th Street, then turned left and drove back out to Montana. He saw a streetside parking place opening up and quickly claimed it, swinging the Cherokee in behind a compact van. The spot gave him a solid view of the shops and the walkway to the offices on the second floor. He decided it was the best he could do for the moment. Rawls knew him. He couldn't go into the DGP store or the office without possibly revealing himself to the suspect. He decided he would wait until he heard from Ballard about the search warrant and learned what the next move should be.

He put KKJZ on the radio and caught an Ed Reed cover of the old Shirley Horn song "Here's to Life." Reed sang it slowly, his voice carrying the experience of his years.

He had to turn the radio down when his phone buzzed and he saw it was Ballard.

"Harry, what's happening?" she asked.

"I haven't found Rawls yet," Bosch said. "Looked like nobody was home at his house. No car, no sign of life. Now I'm watching the office on Montana. I haven't seen him or his car. How about you? Sounds like you're driving."

"I'm heading to Brentwood."

"What's in Brentwood?"

"Charlie Rowan. I've got the search warrant app. Masser helped me write it."

Bosch knew she was talking about Los Angeles County superior court judge Charles Rowan.

"Is Rowan up on rotation, or is he your judge?" he asked.

"My go-to," Ballard said. "Masser thinks it's going to be a squeaker, and I'm hoping I can use my charms with Rowan to push him across the finish line."

"Yeah, I remember back in the day, he had a reputation. You want me to meet you there?"

"Thanks, Harry, but you're not my father. Dealing with guys like Rowan is nothing new. I can handle him."

"Sorry I asked."

"I can come to you afterward. Brentwood's nearby."

"We have to figure out if Rawls is even here. He may have figured out from what Hastings told him that we were only a few moves away from getting to him."

"That's what I was thinking. Once I get this signed, we'll knock on doors and figure out if he's flown the coop."

"Okay, I'll be here."

They disconnected. Bosch looked across the street at the

DGP store. He had a viewing angle through the front window to the shipping counter, where it looked like the employee was reading a book while waiting for the next customer.

Bosch liked the vantage point he had and wasn't sure the parking space would be available if he left it to drive another circuit around the building. Montana was a major shopping area and parking spaces weren't left open for long. But that back door bothered him. He didn't know whether there was an interior stairway that connected the shop with the office above it. Either way, it was impossible for a single set of eyes to keep a complete watch on the business and office. He was hoping Ballard would get there soon with a signed search warrant.

35

JUDGE CHARLES ROWAN'S eyes lit up when he saw Ballard at his front door.

"Renée! My favorite detective in all the City of Angels. How are you, my dear?"

"I'm doing fine, Judge. How are you?"

"Better now that I get to look at you. What have you brought for me?"

He actually took a step back to better appraise her, his gaze lingering on her for too long. Ballard was disgusted but maintained her all-business front.

"I think you know," she said. "I've got a search warrant app on a case that is breaking as we speak. Can I tell you about it?"

"Of course," Rowan said. "Come in, come in."

Rowan stepped further back but opened the door only enough for Ballard to pass close by him as she entered. Her discomfort level went up another notch.

Rowan was well into his sixties, easily two decades older than Ballard. He had a full head of silver-gray hair and a matching beard. His prodigious ear hair was a match in color as well.

She had been in Rowan's home before and knew he lived alone after several failed marriages. She also knew to turn to the right, where the dining room was located, as opposed to the living room, where the judge might try to sit too close to her on the couch.

"Don't you want to be comfortable in the living room?" Rowan asked.

But Ballard was already to the dining room.

"The table here is fine, Judge," she said. "My partner is sitting on a location by himself and I don't want to leave him hanging. It could get dangerous. So, if I could get you to take a look at this, I'll be able to get back out there."

"Of course," Rowan said. "But first things first. What can I get you? A glass of iced tea, a Chardonnay, what would you like?"

"Really, Judge, what I would like is for you to read the warrant and hopefully find that everything adds up and is in order."

She gave him the most winning smile she could manage under the circumstances. She then put the warrant application down on the table and pulled out the chair for him. She was going to remain standing.

Rowan looked at her and seemed to get the message that this wasn't going to turn into a social visit. He moved to the chair and sat down.

"Well, let me see what you have here," he said.

"I can talk you through it," Ballard said. "But if you just want to read it, everything is right there."

"Did you go through the District Attorney's Office with this?"

"Not exactly. I'm now running the cold case unit, Judge, and we have a retired deputy D.A. assigned to the unit who reviews and helps us write our warrants. He came in from home today to work on this because he knew time was of the essence."

"Really? What's this deputy's name?"

"Paul Masser. He worked in Major Crimes at the D.A.'s."

"I know him. A capable prosecutor."

"He is."

"So...let's see."

The judge started reading the first page and Ballard felt her guts tighten. The first four pages of the application were standard boilerplate legalese that was virtually the same on every warrant a judge was presented with. Rowan could have flipped through these to the meat of the application—the case summary and probable cause statement—but he wasn't doing that, and Ballard had to believe it was because she had deflected his attempt to turn this into a social visit, if not something more.

Still, she said nothing for fear she might anger the judge and cause him to reject the warrant. She shifted her weight from one leg to the other and just watched.

Rowan remained silent until he flipped to the third page and spoke without looking up from the document.

"Are you sure I can't get you something, Renée?"

"No, Judge, I'm fine. My partner's waiting out there."

"I understand. I'm going as fast as I can. I have to be thorough. I don't want this to come back and bite me in appellate court should I see fit to sign it and send you on your way."

"Of course, sir."

"Charlie. We're old friends, Renée."

"Charlie...then."

Finally, he got to the statement of facts regarding the case and then the PC statement. Ballard checked her watch. She was worried about what was going on with Bosch as he waited for her to get to Montana Avenue.

"Checking your watch does not help," Rowan said. "You may be in a hurry, but I can't be. Not when we are considering the search and seizure of a man's properties and body."

"I understand, sir," Ballard said. "I mean, Charlie."

She was now sure that Rowan was going reject the warrant because she had rejected him. She was chasing down a serial killer, and this judge would be so petty as to thwart that effort because his pride was bruised. Ballard wished she had just taken her chances with Canterbury.

"Renée, would you go into the living room?" Rowan suddenly asked.

"Uh, why, Charlie?" Ballard asked.

"Because in the living room is a door to my home office. On the desk you will find my stamp and its ink pad. Would you retrieve them so I can sign and seal this search warrant?"

"Of course."

Surprised and relieved, Ballard quickly crossed the entry hall and went through the living room to a set of double doors that opened to an office. She spotted the stamp that carried the seal of the superior court sitting on an ink pad on the desk.

On the way back to the dining room, she heard her phone buzz. It was Bosch. She didn't take the call. She wanted to get the search warrant signed and stamped and then get away from the judge. She'd call Bosch back after.

36

THE KJAZZ PRESENTER sent out best wishes to Ron Carter on his eighty-fifth birthday celebrated at Carnegie Hall in New York in the past week. He then played "A Song for You," a cover off Carter's *At His Best* album, released when the great bass player was a young fifty-nine years old.

The song went eight minutes long, and when it was over, Bosch turned off the radio so he could call Ballard again and see if she was heading to Montana Avenue yet. But before he could make the call, he saw the light inside the DGP store change. The far recesses of the store behind the shipping counter were momentarily illuminated, and Bosch guessed that someone had just opened the back door of the shop and let in daylight. He immediately started the engine and pulled out of the coveted parking space.

This time he drove by the western entrance to the alley rather than turning in. This gave him a two-second glimpse down the straightaway, and he saw a car parked about halfway down the alley, which put it in the vicinity of the DGP store. The car had its trunk open, preventing Bosch from identifying its make or seeing whether the plate number matched Rawls's.

He continued on to Idaho Avenue, took a left through a residential neighborhood, and drove down to 17th, where he turned left again and came up on the other end of the alley. This time he could see the distinctive BMW grille and the metallic-blue paint finish on the hood. Ballard had earlier texted him a description of a blue 2021 BMW 5 Series with a vanity plate reading DGP1. The car was too far down the alley for him to read the plate on the front bumper, but he could tell that it was only four characters long. He felt confident that it was Rawls's BMW and that he was inside the shop.

Because the BMW was pointed east, Bosch assumed that Rawls would drive out of the alley on the east side when he left his business. He put his car in reverse and backed down 17th Street and into the driveway of the first home south of the alley. The spot gave him a direct view of the alley's exit.

He had just put the transmission into park when a call came in from Ballard.

"Rawls is here," he said. "His car is in the alley behind the shop and I think he might be about to take off. Where are you? Do you have the warrant?"

"I got it signed," Ballard said. "I'm just leaving now."

"If he takes off, it's going to be tough to run a one-car follow on a guy probably looking for it."

"I understand. I'm on my way."

Bosch disconnected and focused his attention on the alley exit. He didn't like not having eyes directly on the BMW, but he also didn't want to leave his vehicle and risk being seen by Rawls or losing him if he drove off and Bosch was separated from his car.

Because he was looking to the right through the windshield,

he didn't see the man come up on his left side and rap his fist on the roof of the car. Bosch startled and turned.

"Didn't mean to startle you," the man said. "But do you mind telling me what you're doing here?"

"Uh, I'm waiting for somebody," Bosch said.

Bosch turned from him to check the alley, then looked back.

"Someone living in this neighborhood?" the man asked.

"It's not really any of your business," Bosch said.

"Well, I'm going to make it my business. This is my driveway, and I want to know why you're sitting in it."

"Sorry about that. I'll move out onto the street."

He started the engine.

"That's not good enough," the man said. "If you're hanging around here, then I need to know why or I'm going to call the police."

"Mister, I am the police," Bosch said.

He turned from the man and dropped the car into gear. He drove out onto the street and took a right. He cruised slowly past the alley and took a quick glance toward the BMW.

It wasn't there.

His eyes were drawn to a set of brake lights flaring at the far end of the alley as a car turned right onto 16th Street.

"Shit," Bosch said.

He hit the gas and drove up to Montana. At the stop sign he crept the car out into the intersection and looked down to his left. He saw the blue BMW pull out onto Montana and head west. Bosch did the same and started to follow, maintaining a block-and-a-half distance from the BMW. He guessed that Rawls was heading to Lincoln Boulevard, which in turn would take him to the 10 freeway and then anywhere he wanted to go.

He called Ballard again.

"He's on the move," he said. "I think he's heading to the freeway."

"Where should I go?"

"If he gets on the ten, he'll be heading toward the four-oh-five."

"I'm right by the four-oh-five."

"So jump on and head south. I'll call you back when we're heading that way. If we pull this off, you take lead. I think he made me."

"How do you know?"

"He turned around in the alley so he didn't have to drive by my location."

"Shit."

"One-car follow, what can I tell you."

"I know, my fault."

"No, not your fault. It just is what it is."

"What if he's just going home?"

"That would be perfect but I don't think it's happening. The college streets are east of here. He's taking a roundabout way if that's where he's going."

Up ahead, Rawls turned south onto Lincoln as predicted. Bosch reached the intersection, and as he made the same turn, he didn't see the BMW ahead. As he passed through the next intersection, he slowed and quickly looked one way and then the other. The BMW was nowhere to be seen.

"Shit," he said. "I think I already lost him."

"What?" Ballard said. "Where?"

"He turned onto Lincoln, and when I followed, he was gone. I'm checking side streets but don't see his car anywhere."

"We need to get that swab."

"I know that. So now it's my fault."

"I'm not blaming you, Harry. I'm just pissed. Where do you think he was going?"

"The freeway, and from there, who knows? Maybe he's going to the airport, or he could be driving south to Mexico or north to Canada."

Bosch had now passed through three intersections and had not seen the blue BMW.

"Where should I go now?" Ballard asked.

"Keep going to the four-oh-five and head south. I'll do the—"

He didn't finish the sentence. His phone flew out of his hand as he felt a sharp impact on the rear corner of the car. Suddenly he was in a counterclockwise spin. The Cherokee slid sideways through an intersection and then sheared off a stop sign before slamming into a parked car and coming to an abrupt stop.

Bosch was stunned for a moment and then a sharp pain in his right knee cut through the fog and brought clarity. He grabbed his knee and looked around, trying to get his bearings and determine what had just happened. Through the windshield he saw the blue BMW he had been looking for. It was sitting in the middle of Lincoln, its front passenger-side headlight shattered from the impact.

Bosch quickly formed an understanding of what had happened. Rawls had hit his car from behind with a PIT maneuver—a pursuit tactic designed to spin a car out by clipping the rear corner, changing the direction of its momentum, and swinging it into an out-of-control fishtail.

Only slightly damaged, the BMW didn't take off. It sat motionless in the middle of the street until the driver's door was suddenly flung open and Rawls got out. He came around the front of the car, and at first Bosch thought he was going to check the damage to his car. But he didn't even glance at the BMW's front end. Instead, he calmly started walking toward Bosch's car.

Bosch could see that he was carrying a gun down at his side.

"You gotta be kidding me," Bosch said.

He leaned across the center console and groaned as he felt pain in his ribs. He opened the glove box, reached in, and wrapped his hand around his own gun. Leaning back into his seat, he held the gun on his thigh. He had no idea what kind of confrontation was about to occur.

Rawls continued to advance, and as he got closer, he suddenly raised his gun up into a ready-fire position.

"No, no, no, no," Bosch said.

He raised his gun to aim, but Rawls fired first, and Bosch felt a searing pain spark through his brain.

37

BOSCH'S VOICE WAS cut off by a loud crashing sound followed by the squeal of tires on asphalt and then a final sound of crunching metal.

"Harry!" Ballard yelled into the phone.

She got no response.

"Harry? Are you there?"

There was still no answer, and then she heard his voice, but it was muffled and distant. She couldn't make out the words.

"Harry? Can you hear me?"

Then she heard him clearly, though it was also obvious he was not talking into the phone.

"No, no, no, no..."

And then came the shots. Clear, sharp reports. First one shot, followed by the shattering of glass, then a hail of gunfire. Too many shots in too few seconds to count. And then a final shot, muffled and spaced long enough after the others to be the coup de grâce, the kill shot.

"Harry!" Ballard yelled.

She yanked the wheel of her car into a U-turn. She hit the siren and code 3 lights hidden in the front grille and took off toward Santa Monica.

PART 2

HALLOWED GROUND

38

BOSCH WAS SITTING sideways on the examination bed, not wanting to lie down, because that might lead to him being admitted and spending the night, and he had no intention of staying any longer than the minimum. UCLA Santa Monica might be a great hospital, but he wanted to get home to his own bed.

He needed to call his daughter but he didn't have his phone. It had flown from his hand when his car was hit from behind. He waited for the ER doctor to come through the curtain, do a final check, and hand him a prescription slip before releasing him.

His injuries were minor, though technically he had been shot. He had bruised ribs, a knee contusion, and a handful of minor lacerations from flying glass, and a bullet had clipped the upper helix of his left ear. It was about as near a miss as he could possibly have had. If the bullet had been an inch more on target, he'd be spending the night in the morgue. For that he was certainly thankful. Otherwise, he was mostly upset. Ted Rawls was dead and whatever secrets he kept had probably died with him.

The wound had been cleaned and stitched closed with black thread by the ER physician, who needlessly warned him not to sleep with that ear on the pillow. Bosch could hear lots of activity and medical talk in the other curtained examination bays, but no one had been in to see him in more than twenty minutes. He decided he would wait another fifteen before he'd part the curtains and tell the supervising nurse he had to get back to work.

But that didn't happen. Five minutes before his self-imposed deadline, the curtain opened and Maddie entered, still in her uniform. She was far off her beat.

"Dad!"

He stood as she hurried to him. They hugged tightly while he did his best to protect his damaged ear.

"Are you okay? Renée called me."

"I'm good. Everything's fine. Really."

She pulled back and looked first at his face and then his ear.

"That's gotta hurt."

"Uh, at first it did, but now it's okay. The doctor said there aren't a lot of nerve endings up there."

The doctor had told him no such thing but Bosch didn't want his daughter to worry.

"And the guy, he's dead?" she asked.

"Unfortunately," Bosch said. "We wanted to talk to him and now…"

"Well, it's not your fault. Have you talked to FID yet?"

The LAPD's Force Investigation Division would investigate his actions, even though the shooting was in the city of Santa Monica. SMPD would do its own investigation as well.

"I gave a preliminary interview at the scene," Bosch said. "But I know there will be more. They're probably still at the scene, looking for witnesses and cameras and all of that stuff."

"Do you have to stay overnight?" Maddie asked.

"No. I've been waiting for the doctor to come in and discharge me. As soon as he does, I'm out of here. Aren't you supposed to be on patrol in Hollywood?"

"The captain let me go when we heard what happened. I'm so glad you're all right."

"Thanks, Mads. Tell you what, though, my car is still out there at the scene, and I don't think I'll be getting it back for a while. If I can get out of here, you think you can give me a lift home?"

"Of course, but Renée is in the waiting room, and she said she was going to need to talk to you after me. Case stuff, she said."

"Okay, then I'll get her to drive me and we can talk in the car."

"You sure?"

"Yes, no worries. And if you have to get back, we can talk later."

"I'll check in on you."

"I didn't even know you work Sundays."

"Yeah, I work Thursday to Sunday now."

"Cool. Maybe we can have lunch tomorrow or Tuesday. I have a feeling my knee will be too sore for me to want to go sit at a desk."

"Uh, yeah."

She seemed hesitant to commit.

"I just haven't seen you very much lately," Bosch said.

"I know," she said. "And it's my fault. I get so busy. But, yeah, let's do it. I'll check on you in the morning, and if you're too sore, we'll go for Tuesday."

"I'd like that, Maddie."

"Bye, Dad. I love you. So glad you're okay."

She hugged him again.

"Love you, too," Bosch said.

"I'll find Renée and tell her you're clear," she said.

And then she was gone.

Bosch now waited for both the doctor and Ballard. He tentatively reached a finger to his ear to see if it could bend without sending sparks of pain shooting through his brain.

"Don't touch that."

Bosch turned to see that the ER doc had entered. He went to a sink and washed his hands and then came over to Bosch. He looked at the sutures in Bosch's ear.

"This is going to look pretty nasty for a while, but something tells me you won't care," he said.

"The only thing I care about right now is getting out of here," Bosch replied.

"Well, you're free to go. I have a prescription waiting for you at the hospital pharmacy. Take it only to manage pain. If there is no pain, don't take it. Stay sharp."

"Got it. And thanks, Doc. I appreciate it."

"Doin' my job, just like you were doin' yours. But you should come back in a couple days and let me look at that, make sure there's no infection."

"I will. Thank you. What about the stitches?"

"We'll check them then, but I think we'll need to keep them in longer. You don't want that ear flopping over like my dog's."

"Right."

Ten minutes later, Bosch was in Ballard's car and they were pulling out of the emergency vehicle parking area outside the ER entrance. He had decided not to pick up the prescription and would manage the pain with over-the-counter measures.

"Let's get you home," Ballard said.

"Go by the scene first," Bosch said. "I want to see it."

"Harry, they're not going to want you there."

"Just a drive-by. It's five minutes out of the way, tops."

"All right. But no stopping."

"Doesn't FID or Santa Monica want to talk to you?"

"They already did. There will be more tomorrow but I was cleared to leave."

"Maddie said you had something to tell me."

"Yeah, the box."

"What box?"

"There was a box in the trunk of the BMW."

"The trunk was open when I saw the car in the alley. There could have been a box but I didn't see it. How big is it?"

"Sixteen by sixteen by six—it said it on the box. It's a shipping box like they sell in his shop."

"I could've missed it. What's in it?"

"It's filled with keepsakes. From his kills. There were more victims, most likely between Pearlman and Wilson, and then afterward. Probably a lot, and we'll be going through the box for a long time."

"Damn."

"And it's probably why he did himself at the end."

"Wait a minute, what?"

"He killed himself."

"No, I hit him. I saw it."

"You did, but that wasn't the fatal shot. You knocked him down in front of your car. But then he put the gun in his mouth. It was his last bullet."

Bosch thought about the shooting. It had been so quick

and intense that it was hard for him to remember every microsecond of detail. He knew the first shot from Rawls went through the windshield and ripped through his ear. He returned fire, getting off half a clip. The windshield shattered, allowing his remaining shots to fly true as Rawls continued his charge and fired back. One round hit Rawls in the right shoulder and he went down. He fell out of sight, and Bosch remembered hearing the last shot but didn't realize it was self-inflicted.

He had opened his door and tumbled out onto the ground. Blood was running down the side of his head, and at the time, he thought he had been more seriously injured than he was. Limping on the injured leg and not being sure of what he had left in his clip, he moved cautiously around his car and came up on the front from the passenger side. He saw Rawls dead on the ground, and he thought he had killed him.

"The FID guys didn't tell me that," he said.

"Well, that's what they told me," Ballard said.

Bosch went silent and stared out the window as Ballard drove. After a while, she got concerned.

"You doing okay, Harry?" she asked. "Don't get sick in my car."

"I won't," Bosch said. "I was thinking about that shop and the others Rawls had."

"What about them?"

"We know he started his business after he left the cops and got a new kidney and a new lease on life, right?"

"Right."

"So, why that business? What did it have to do with what he was really doing?"

"You think it helped him in some way? Maybe finding victims?"

"I don't know, but we should look at it. People rent those private mailboxes and most of them are legit, but I would bet some of them aren't. A lot of them do it because they have secret lives or at least compartmentalized lives. You want to have a place where you can get some things sent to you privately. Stuff you don't want sent to your home because your wife or your husband might see it."

"And he had access to all of it," Ballard said.

"That was what I was thinking. He was on the other side of that wall of private boxes and he could sort of see everybody's business. I don't know if that helped him in his own secret life of targeting women, and I guess it's another thing we'll never know because he's dead."

"I think we'll find that out when we start identifying other victims. And from what I know, I'm not too upset he's dead. I know people will think, he got away with it for so long— where's the justice in that? But I think there are untold lives out there that are now saved."

"I guess so."

"It's not a guess, Harry. It's the truth."

They were on Lincoln now, and the intersection where the shooting had gone down was barricaded by traffic control officers. Bosch could see that the green Cherokee had been put on a flatbed for towing to a police yard. As far as he knew, his phone was still in it somewhere.

They were waved by traffic control officers onto a side street and never got close enough for Bosch to see what else was happening inside the orange barricades. Ballard kept driving.

"Have you talked to the councilman yet?" Bosch asked.

"I talked to Hastings," Ballard said, "so he'd know what's going on. But I don't want to talk to Pearlman until we have a dead-bang DNA match to Rawls. Same thing with Laura Wilson's mother. I'll go by the coroner's office in the morning, pick up blood and prints, then go to the lab. Darcy Troy will be standing by to jump on the blood. I don't really have a go-to in latents, so we'll see what happens there."

"And what about the brass? You going to get blamed for having this guy on the Open-Unsolved team?"

"Hell, no. If they try to blame me, I have the emails from Hastings telling me in no uncertain terms to put Rawls on the squad. I'm not worried about that. I'm more worried about you, Harry."

"Me? Why?"

"I brought you on to the team and, what? In barely a week, you already got shot up and dinged up, plus your car's wrecked."

"It's not wrecked. That thing's a tank."

"Well, I hope somebody can find a new windshield some-where."

"There are plenty of parts out there."

"Then, good. I like you in that car, Harry. Like a square peg in a round-hole world."

Bosch thought about that for a little bit, then told Ballard his plan.

"I think I'm going to take a couple days off. Stay off the knee as much as I can. Then I want to get back on Gallagher."

"Sounds like a plan."

39

THEY MADE BALLARD sit in the waiting room for thirty-five minutes before she finally was told that the councilman was ready for her. It was Tuesday afternoon and the Rawls story had held firm in the news since Sunday night. It was the mystery that kept it afloat. Few of the details had leaked into the public discourse, largely because the LAPD was waiting for the confirmation of genetic linkage between Rawls and the murders of Sarah Pearlman and Laura Wilson. So far, the story had centered on the fact that an investigator with the Open-Unsolved Unit had exchanged gunfire with a murder suspect on a public street, leaving one man dead and another wounded. No names had been released or had leaked so far. But all of that would change in a few hours when the chief of police held a press conference in the plaza in front of the Police Administration Building. It was Ballard's job to give the councilman a heads-up on what the chief would be announcing.

She entered Pearlman's office to find the councilman waiting with Nelson Hastings and Rita Ford. There was a seating area to the right of the councilman's grand desk that consisted of two couches facing each other with a glass-topped coffee table between them. Pearlman and Hastings anchored the corners of one couch while Ford held a corner of the opposite couch. Ballard was signaled to sit in the remaining corner.

"Detective Ballard, I've been waiting for an update," Pearlman said. "What can you tell us?"

"Thanks for seeing me, Councilman," Ballard began. "At four o'clock this afternoon, the chief of police will be holding a press conference. He will announce that DNA and a palm print from Ted Rawls have been matched to the murders of your sister and Laura Wilson. This will bring those cases to a close, but investigation of Rawls and evidence gathered from his car and elsewhere is continuing. It is possible that he is linked to other cases as well. Several other cases."

Pearlman shook his head.

"Oh my god," he said. "Wow. Is it really over?"

"Yes, sir, as far as your sister's case," Ballard said. "The D.A. will review and approve our closing of the case. I know there is no such thing as closure, but maybe this will give you some measure of peace."

"And the other case?" Pearlman said. "He met her or picked her because he was door-knocking for me?"

"It looks that way," Ballard said.

There was a pause and then Hastings spoke.

"This cannot come back on the councilman," he said.

"I'm not sure what you mean," Ballard said.

"That last part, Detective," Hastings said. "You have no proof that Rawls met or targeted Laura Wilson while knocking on doors for a candidate. You have a campaign button that she could have gotten anywhere. So do not put that conjecture out in the media. If your chief chooses to do so, then he will no longer enjoy the support of this office."

"I will carry that message to media relations," Ballard said. "They'll be putting out the press release after the chief speaks."

"How are you handling the inclusion of Rawls on the cold case squad?" Hastings asked.

"How do you mean?" Ballard asked.

"I think you can count on some smart reporters asking how Rawls ended up on the squad," Hastings said. "And a follow-up question will be to ask what kind of background check was conducted."

"Well, I assume that kind of question won't come to me," Ballard said. "But if it does, I'm not going to lie to the media or anybody else. You told me that the councilman wanted him on the team. I spoke to my captain about it and we did what was asked. I still have the emails from you."

She wanted to make sure he understood that if he tried to throw her or the LAPD under the bus, it would likely backfire on him.

"Yes, the emails were from me," Hastings said. "*I* told you to put him on the team. Not the councilman. That is the truth and that is all you have to reveal if asked."

Hastings was willing to sacrifice himself to protect Pearlman. Ballard saw the valor in that—rare to find in politics. Her respect for Hastings grew in that moment.

"I understand," she said.

"When does the chief hold his presser?" Ford asked.

"At four," Ballard said.

"We should hold our own right afterward," Ford said. "So we're part of the same news cycle."

"Excellent idea," Hastings said. "Detective, a question for you. Would you be willing to stand with the councilman and state that his being instrumental in the reboot of the Open-Unsolved Unit led to the identity of the killer and to solving these two cases?"

"I'd have to get department approval," Ballard said.

"Then please do," Hastings said. "We would love to have you, and I'm sure you would want to show your respect for the man who led the charge in reinstating the unit after many years."

"I'll check with my captain and let you know," Ballard said.

Sensing that the meeting was over, Ballard stood up. Pearlman seemed to come out of a daze and stood up as well. It was then that Ballard saw tears on his face. While she had been parrying with Hastings and Ford, Pearlman had apparently been thinking about his lost sister and having to accept that it was someone from his life—a friend—who had killed her.

"Detective, thank you," he said. "When I pushed for the reinstatement of the unit, it was because I didn't want my sister's case forgotten. To know that we have solved the case validates everything I said about the unit's importance. That's the message I will convey at my press conference. I can't thank you enough, and I'll be sure to say that as well. I hope you will join us."

He put his hand out and Ballard shook it.

"Thank you, sir," she said.

As she walked the half block down Spring Street from City Hall to the PAB, Ballard reviewed the answers she had given during the intense meeting and believed she had acquitted herself well. She had no intention of asking permission to stand with Councilman Pearlman at a press conference—even if he was going to sing the praises of her and the unit. That would be mixing politics and police work, and that was a recipe for eventual disaster. She would take a pass on that.

When she got to the PAB, she saw a handful of television crews setting up in front of a lectern with a large gold replica of the LAPD badge affixed to it. On the badge was the image of City Hall, the iconic building Ballard had just come from—Old Faithful, as it was called by the denizens of the Civic Center. When the chief took the lectern for the press conference, the twenty-seven-floor tower would be reflected behind him in the glass facade of the PAB. It would be a reminder that politics and police work could never really be separated.

Ballard badged her way into the building and took the elevator to the tenth floor, where a pre–press conference meeting was scheduled in the media relations office just down the hall from the OCP—the Office of the Chief of Police.

The department's chief spokesperson was a civilian, a former reporter for Channel 5 News named Ramon Rivera. He welcomed Ballard into his office, and she was surprised to see the chief of police sitting there as well. They were going over the statement the chief would read at the press conference. A copy of the statement would be distributed to the reporters.

Ballard sat down and Rivera gave her a copy to read. The statement included the case details Ballard had given Rivera in an earlier phone call. It was a strict recitation of the facts of the case. That would be the easy part of the press conference. The difficult part would be anticipating what questions would be asked and deciding how to answer them.

A year earlier, the chief of police had urged Ballard to return to the department after she had resigned in frustration. It was his promise to give her the assignment of her choosing that had resulted in her getting the job running the reconstituted Open-Unsolved Unit. He now asked her the questions he anticipated the gathered media would hurl at him when he was finished reading the statement.

"Why was Bosch following Rawls by himself?" he asked.

"Following him wasn't the plan, actually," Ballard said. "But he had no choice. Bosch saw Rawls's car outside his place of business. He was keeping watch while I went to see a judge to get a search warrant signed. When Rawls took off before I got there, Bosch had no choice but to attempt a one-car follow. It's unclear whether Rawls knew he had a tail from the start or spotted Bosch's car while he was in transit."

"And you recruited Bosch for the Open-Unsolved Unit?"

"I did. He's the most experienced detective on the team."

"Did you know about his issues when he was with the department?"

"Issues, sir?"

"He'd been involved in several previous shootings. He didn't leave the department on good terms. Some might say he retired before the department retired him."

"Some of that I knew, yes. But I wanted to put together the best team of volunteers I could find, and he was at the top of my list. We solved this case largely because of moves he made."

"How would you feel if we had to remove him from the team?"

"I don't understand. It was his work that led us to Rawls, and now you want to kick him to the curb?"

"I'm not saying that. At least not yet. But we will have a perception problem with the unit when it is revealed that one of your selections was a killer. I'm sure you will agree that it's not a good look, Detective Ballard. And I'm wondering if we want to start over."

"You mean clean house?"

"For lack of a better term."

"First, I want to say that Rawls was not my selection. He was pushed on us by the councilman's office. I didn't want Rawls, but Councilman Pearlman's chief of staff made me take him. I talked to Captain Gandle about it and we agreed to take him on to keep the support of the councilman. But I still don't see why this should result in cleaning house. We have a good team. We have a former deputy D.A. who is our legal sounding board, an IGG expert, and other capable investigators, with Harry Bosch being the best of the bunch."

"Well, let's put that decision aside for now and go down and talk to the media. We'll see how things go before making any decisions."

Somehow Ballard felt that a decision had already been made. The chief stood up and Rivera did as well.

"Let me get the handouts from the printer," he said.

After Rivera left the room, Ballard stood and faced the chief of police.

"Sir, if you decide you need to start over with the unit, then you will have to do that without me. If Harry Bosch goes, I go."

The chief looked at her for a long moment before responding.

"Are you threatening me, Detective Ballard?" he said.

"Not at all," Ballard said. "I'm just telling you the facts, sir. If he goes, I go."

"Understood. But let's take things one step at a time. Let's see how this thing goes and then we can decide the future."

"Yes, sir."

40

THE LAPD PRESS conference was carried live on KCAL's 4 p.m. newscast. Bosch watched from his home and had to sit and marvel at how the chief of police managed to tell the story of Ted Rawls with such command authority and yet leave out so many salient details of the story. He spun a tale of a serial killer being identified through DNA by members of the newly re-formed cold case squad and then killing himself as members of the unit closed in. Not mentioned was the fact that the killer was a member of the unit that was closing in on him, or that he had been placed on it by Councilman Jake Pearlman, his long-time friend. Rawls was simply described as a man who made a living from a chain of small businesses. No names of the Open-Unsolved Unit investigators were mentioned, and Renée Ballard, who stood behind the chief at the podium, was not called upon to speak. The chief finished his five-minute reading of a prepared statement by lavishing praise on the unit and Ballard, its lead detective. The upshot of the whole thing was that another serial killer was taken out of play thanks to the hard work and dedication of the OU team as well as the foresight of the administrators who had reconstituted the previously shuttered unit.

Apparently feeling confident in his spinning of half-truths, the chief said he would take a few questions. That was when things didn't go so well for him. The first question was a softball about why he had decided to reboot the cold case unit. But the second question was a curveball that tailed right into the strike zone.

"My sources tell me that the investigator who exchanged fire with Rawls before he killed himself was none other than Harry Bosch. Bosch was involved in numerous shootings before he retired from the department. Now he's back, and my question is, were you consulted, and did you approve of Bosch being added to the team?"

The woman who had asked the question was unseen because the camera was trained on the podium and the chief of police. But Bosch thought he recognized her slight Caribbean accent.

The chief tried to deflect.

"As I said in my statement, there are components of the investigation that are continuing. One of those components is the officer-involved shooting, and I am not going to comment on what is an ongoing investigation and personnel matter. That would not be fair at this time. Suffice it to say, our internal investigation will be fully and independently reviewed by the District Attorney's Office, as is our protocol with all officer-involved shootings."

As the chief raised his arm to point to another reporter, the original questioner loudly fired a follow-up at him.

"In court documents regarding prior shootings by Harry Bosch, he was described as a 'gunslinger.' Did that weigh in the decision to put him on this unit?"

The word *gunslinger* made the chief blink.

"Uh, I am unfamiliar with that," he said. "As I just said, I am making no comment at this time regarding the officer-involved shooting. And that's all I have time for today."

He quickly turned from the podium and headed across the plaza to the safety of the PAB. Questions shouted after him were neither answered nor acknowledged. Ballard and a tight grouping of media relations people followed in his wake. Bosch had watched Ballard as she turned to follow the chief. He could see dread clearly drawn on her face.

After the press conference, the broadcast switched to a live report from the scene of the Rawls shooting. A female reporter introduced recorded interviews with residents in the normally quiet neighborhood. It was strictly filler, but in her wrap-up the reporter mentioned that Councilman Pearlman had scheduled a 5 p.m. press conference to discuss the case and his personal connection to it.

At 5 p.m. Bosch switched from KCAL, which went to non-news programming, to the start of a news hour on KNBC. The anchor immediately cued up Councilman Pearlman's live appearance on the granite steps of City Hall behind a podium adorned with the city's seal.

In a brief address, Pearlman praised the work of the Open-Unsolved Unit, noting that his office had played the key role in reinstating it. He also said that the identification of Rawls as the killer of his sister and Laura Wilson did not bring his family closure, but finally knowing the truth was enough to hopefully bandage the wounds of the past.

He, too, left out many key facts, namely that he and his chief of staff had placed Rawls on the very unit that unmasked him as the killer. He also failed to mention that Rawls had likely chosen Laura Wilson as a victim while knocking on doors in support of Pearlman's first bid for office in 2005.

The councilman ended his short statement by saying that he would be taking no questions and asking that his and his family's privacy be respected. Bosch cynically viewed this last part as a means of avoiding inquiries that could result in political damage.

Bosch turned off the screen and sat there thinking about how the truth was always manipulated by those in power. It bothered him to know things that shouldn't be kept secret.

He thought about the look of dread he saw on Ballard's face and wondered if she had been forced in some way to stand next to the chief and be part of the manipulation. He wished she had at least called him to give him a heads-up.

It was then that he realized Ballard might have done so but he wouldn't have known, because his phone was either in direct police custody or still somewhere in his Cherokee after being jarred from his hand when Rawls sent his car into the tailspin. The Cherokee was presumably in a police impound yard.

Bosch got up and went to the kitchen. He used his house phone to call his cell phone number and check for messages. He had two. The first was a heads-up call from Ballard that came in at 2 p.m. and outlined the timing of the two press conferences. The second was a message left just ten minutes earlier from Juanita Wilson in Chicago. She asked him to call her back. Bosch grabbed a pen and Post-it out of a kitchen drawer and wrote her number down.

The landline was a cordless phone. He took it out to the back deck of the house to make the call.

"Mrs. Wilson?"

"Detective Bosch, I'm sorry to disturb you. Thank you for calling me back so quickly."

"You're not disturbing me. Did Detective Ballard call you?"

"She did. She told me what happened, that the man who killed my Laura is dead."

"Yes, he killed himself when we were closing in on him. I'm sorry. I wanted...we wanted to take him alive so he could be punished."

"Don't be sorry. I believe he is being punished. He's in Hell."

"Yes, ma'am."

"Call me Juanita."

"Juanita."

"I called because I want to thank you for what you did. Detective Ballard told me. I hope you're okay and will heal quickly."

"I'm fine, Juanita."

"And I want to thank you for the answers. I told you I was holding on for answers."

"I understand."

"Thanks to you and Detective Ballard, I can let go now...and I can join Laura and my husband."

Bosch wasn't sure what to say. He knew that almost everybody believed in something, holding a hope that there wasn't just an empty void at the end.

"I understand," he said.

He looked out across the Cahuenga Pass to his sideways view of the Hollywood sign. He felt the inadequacy of his response to her.

"I'll let you go now," Juanita said. "Once again, thank you, Detective Bosch."

"Harry."

"Thank you, Harry. Goodbye."

"Goodbye, Juanita."

Bosch clutched the phone in his hand as he thought about Juanita waiting years for answers and then not even getting the full truth of things. A deep font of anger started to well up inside him.

Bosch limped back inside the house and used his laptop to search for a phone number. He called it and asked by name for the reporter whose voice he had heard at the LAPD press conference. As he waited for the transfer, he went back out to the deck. He was staring out across the pass when the voice with a slight Caribbean accent came into his ear.

"Keisha Russell, how can I help you?"

"You called me a gunslinger on live television."

"Harry Bosch. It's been a while."

He remembered how she said his name. It sounded to him like she was taking a bite out of a crisp apple.

"I thought you were in D.C., covering politics."

"I got tired of the winters. Plus, I almost got killed at the Capitol last year. Decided it was time to come home to my first love, covering crime."

"I thought covering politics was covering crime."

"Funny. And funny that you called me. I wanted to call you but couldn't find anybody around here who would share your number. Did you call just to complain, or is there something you want to say?"

Bosch gave one last thought to holding back, but quickly the images he carried from the case—Sarah Pearlman, Laura Wilson, and even Juanita Wilson—crowded such consideration out.

"You're being used," he said. "You were smarter than that last time you were on the beat."

"Really?" Russell said. "Used by who?"

"The source who told you I was the shooter. They told you about me but not the rest of the story. They're more concerned with getting rid of me than getting the whole truth out."

"Is this conversation on the record?"

"Not yet."

"Then I'm going to have to go. I'm on deadline. If you want to meet after I file, then I'd definitely be up for that. It's been a long time. Maybe we get a drink and you can school me on who's who in the zoo."

It was an old LAPD expression, a caution that was just as useful when answering a code 3 radio call—lights and siren authorized—as when delving into the abyss of department politics. Step one was assessment: determining who's who in the zoo.

"Maybe after things shake out a little bit," Bosch said. "If I'm still here."

"I wouldn't bet against it," Russell said. "You may or may not be a gunslinger, but you're definitely a survivor. Anything you think I really need to know before I file this story?"

"Right now, you only have half the story."

"Then tell me the half I don't have."

"It's not my place."

"What if I lay off the gunslinger stuff and keep it on point with what happened Sunday? I do you that favor, what do you do for me?"

"Where did that come from?"

"'Gunslinger'? I had to dig deep. That was a Honey Chandler

quote from a motion she filed back in the nineties. Remember her? The actual quote was 'Bosch is a gunslinger who shoots first and asks questions later.' She also called you a cowboy in the motion. I love that and I'm definitely going to use it in my story."

Bosch caught a flash memory of the civil rights lawyer before she was murdered by someone trying to impress him. Honey Chandler had been Bosch's nemesis, and he didn't doubt that she would have labeled him a gunslinger in one of her documents or even in open court, but he had respected her in the end.

He dropped his gaze down to the freeway at the bottom of the pass. It was in full rush-hour inertia.

"Yes," he said. "I remember Chandler. Like I remember you being a reporter who always wanted to get it first but still get it right."

"That's a low blow, Harry. It's always blame the messenger. But I'm asking you to help me get it right. If you don't want to, then who is to blame?"

Bosch hesitated for only a moment before speaking.

"There was a fox in the henhouse, Keisha."

That was followed by a long silence before Russell responded.

"What does that mean?" she asked.

"You didn't get this from me," Bosch said. "Confirm it somewhere else. Rawls was the fox."

"You're talking in riddles. What henhouse are we talking about?"

"Rawls was a volunteer for the unit. He was working on the Pearlman and Wilson cases. Right there with us."

"The Open-Unsolved Unit—are you fucking kidding me?"

"I wish."

"And they're trying to hide that to avoid the embarrassment."

"You wanted to know who's who in the zoo."

"So, let me get this straight. Renée Ballard put a serial killer on her own cold case team."

"No. It wasn't her call. He wasn't her choice."

"Then who?"

"You should maybe call Nelson Hastings at the councilman's office and ask him that question."

Bosch could hear Russell's muffled laugh even though it was apparent she had put her hand over the phone. Then she came back clear.

"This is just too fucking good," she said.

"Remember, confirm it on your own," Bosch said. "Not from me."

"Don't worry, Harry. I will. You trust me? You used to."

"That was a long time ago. I'll know if I can trust you when I read the paper tomorrow."

"You'll see it online at ten."

"I don't subscribe."

"Then wait till tomorrow. But let's get that drink soon."

"You do this right, and drinks are on me."

"That's a deal. And I gotta go. Deadline's in an hour, and thanks to you, I still have a lot of work to do."

"Happy hunting."

Bosch disconnected and looked down into the pass again. Nothing was moving. The city's arteries were clogged.

41

BALLARD WANTED TO be the first one in to work, but as she entered the archive room, she heard the rhythmic mechanical sounds of a multipage job being printed in the copy room. She looked in and found Bosch sliding documents over the three rings of a binder as more were being printed.

"Harry, what are you doing here?"

He looked at her for a long moment before answering.

"Uh, I work here. Unless I'm fired and they didn't tell me."

"No, I meant, I thought you'd take some time. To heal up."

"Two days was enough. I'm fine. I'm good."

"Last time I saw you, that knee looked kind of wobbly."

"I bought one of those compression sleeves at CVS. It works pretty good. But you should see the mark it leaves on my leg."

Ballard stepped all the way in and looked at the binder. He was obviously putting together a murder book.

"So what's this?" she asked.

"I'm copying the files I don't have on the Gallagher Family case," he said. "I'm going to start back on it."

"I thought we were clear on copying files, and yet here you are."

Bosch said nothing as he put a stack of documents back on the rings of one of the original murder books. Ballard put the box she was carrying down on a counter next to the binder Bosch was stacking.

"Talk to me, Harry. What's going on?"

"Look, I haven't been in the department for a long time, but I still know how to read the tea leaves. They're going to tell you to get rid of me. And that's fine. I don't want to cause you any more problems than I already have. But when I go, who's going to work this?"

He pointed to the case's seven binders on the counter.

"So I figure I'll take it with me," he said. "And I'll keep working it. I'll call you when I find McShane."

"Harry, I'm not going to bullshit you and tell you everything is copacetic," Ballard said. "But I told them, if you go, I go. I said that directly to the chief."

Bosch nodded.

"I appreciate that," he said. "I really do. But you shouldn't have done it. It won't stop them from doing what they want."

"We'll see," Ballard said.

"We will, and probably pretty soon."

"What was in the *Times* this morning doesn't help. Did you read it?"

"I don't read the *Times*."

"They got a lot that wasn't said during the chief's press conference."

"It's what they do."

"This Keisha Russell, the reporter—do you know her?"

"Uh, yeah, but last I heard, she went to the Washington bureau. That was, like, I don't know, a long time ago. Years. I'm surprised she's still around."

"Yeah, well, she is, and she's in L.A. now, and she laid the whole thing out. Rawls being in the unit, and that the councilman's office put him there. That's why I'm in early—because Nelson Hastings called me at six this morning."

"I bet he was hot. Is that the box from Rawls's car?"

"He was hot and he still is. And don't change the subject. Whoever fed Russell that story really put me in deep shit."

The copy machine finished its job and the room was silent.

"I'm sorry to hear that," Bosch finally said. "There was nobody named in the story?"

"'Sources said'—that was it for attribution," Ballard said. "And Nelson thinks I'm one of those sources. I mean, she did call me. Three times, in fact. But I never talked to her, didn't even return the calls to say, how'd you get my number and no fucking comment. Nothing like being blamed for something you didn't do."

"I know how that is. I'm sorry. But maybe it's good that it's out there and the public knows. Don't you think?"

"Not if they shutter the unit again. What Pearlman gives, he can also take away. And why not? His sister's case is solved. He already got what he wants out of it."

"You really think they'd shut the thing down because of Rawls?"

"You and I have both seen worse decisions made. That's why you can forget about Gallagher for now."

"What do you mean?"

Ballard picked up the box again and turned toward the door.

"Rawls is still priority one," she said. "If we connect him to other cases and start clearing them, then maybe they won't cut us. And if they try, maybe somebody will leak *that* to

Keisha Russell. Then they'll look bad and have to back the fuck off."

Ballard walked out of the room, leaving Bosch there. She had no doubt that he was behind the story in the *Times*. When she didn't recognize the name of the reporter that Hastings yelled over the phone at 6 a.m., she did a search on the *Times* website of Russell's prior stories and saw that in the nineties she covered the cop shop. Several of her stories were about cases worked by a detective named Harry Bosch. She was annoyed with Bosch. Not so much for what he did—she had to acknowledge that getting the full story out there was something the department should have done in the first place. She just wished he had come to her first and they had planned it together. On top of that, she wished he had owned up to his part in the story. It showed that he did not trust her as much as she had thought.

She took the box to the interview room. It was more than an hour before the other investigators started to trickle into their stations in the pod. By then, Ballard was at hers and Bosch was at his, keeping his head down, even though Ballard knew he was there. Colleen Hatteras was the first of the others to report for work, and she immediately started peppering Ballard and Bosch with questions about Rawls, the shooting, and other aspects of the case. She, too, mentioned the *Times* story, but her questions mostly came because this was the first time she had seen Ballard and Bosch since the shootout on Sunday. Bosch had been off and Ballard had borrowed a desk at PAB and worked from there Monday and Tuesday so that she could be easily reached by the FID investigators as well as by the media relations people and command staff.

"Colleen, hold on a second," Ballard said. "I don't want to

have to answer the same questions four times as the others come in. So let's wait for everybody to get here and then I'll tell everyone what I know and what I want everybody to be working on this week. Okay?"

"Okay," Hatteras said. "I get it. But I just want to go on the record and say, I got a bad vibe from Ted Rawls. I didn't want to say anything before, because he was a colleague. But I felt it when he was here—a super dark aura. I have to admit, I thought it might be coming from Harry, but now I know. It was definitely Ted."

"Thank god," Bosch said. "Such a relief to know my aura isn't super dark."

Ballard heard Bosch say it but couldn't see him because of the privacy wall. She leaned down over her desk so Hatteras wouldn't be able to see her smiling at the rejoinder. Then she got serious.

"Um, you know something, Colleen?" she said. "I'm going to have to write up an after-action report on Rawls and this whole thing. So, I don't want you to stop with the IGG stuff. Keep working it and see if you can further establish genealogical links. If we can show the value of that in this case, I think it will go a long way with command staff."

"On it, boss," Hatteras said. "And now that we know the family tree has Rawls on the L.A. branch, I can start working it back the other way."

"That's good, Colleen. Let me know when you have it all together."

"Roger that."

Ballard rolled her eyes. Those two words were becoming her biggest pet peeve.

By eight thirty, Masser, Laffont, and Aghzafi were all in place at the pod and Ballard stood up so everyone could see her.

"Okay, guys, listen up," she began. "First off, I appreciate you all coming in on short notice because I need the whole team on this. We are not finished with what is now known as the Ted Rawls case. When he took his own life Sunday—in fact, one reason he probably did so—there was a box in the trunk of his car. We recovered it and it contains personal items that may have come from other victims. I'm talking about jewelry, hair-brushes, makeup compacts, little statuettes and knickknacks— all kinds of things."

"Souvenirs," Hatteras said, stating the obvious.

"Yes, souvenirs," Ballard said. "And I want all of us to see what we can do to possibly connect these items to other victims. All we know for sure is that he killed Sarah Pearlman in '94 and Laura Wilson in '05. That's a big gap. And it's a big gap between '05 and Sunday, when Rawls, thanks to Harry Bosch, was put out of commission."

"Hear! Hear!" Masser said.

He stood up and raised a hand over the privacy wall, offering Bosch a high five. Bosch obliged, though it appeared to Ballard to be a reluctant and half-hearted effort.

"I've spread these items out on the table in the interview room," Ballard continued. "I want us to go in there, look them over, maybe pick a piece or two, and go to work. I know it is a long shot, but let's see if we can possibly match some of this property to some cases."

She pointed to the archive shelves where all the unsolved cases were kept.

"We all know that there are lots of families out there waiting for answers," Ballard said. "You all might have a different view, but I would focus on those years between Pearlman and Wilson. We know Rawls got sick after Wilson—he got a kidney transplant—and it may have put him out of the killing business. But I think he was probably active during the years between those two kills. I've invited Councilman Pearlman to come here to look at the items in case he can identify something belonging to his sister, but I don't know if he'll take me up on that. Meantime, I bagged everything individually yesterday after the lab took swabs and looked for prints. What you have on the table are items that yielded no forensic follow-up. Any questions?"

Laffont raised his hand like he was a student in a classroom.

"Tom?" Ballard said.

"What about his home and office?" Laffont asked. "Anything there?"

"Good question," Ballard said. "Detectives from RHD spent almost all day Monday searching his house, office, and a storage unit he rented. They found nothing of evidentiary value. Most of you probably know he was married and had a young daughter, and it looks like he kept that part of his life separate. Needless to say, they remain in complete shock about all of this. It looks like Rawls kept his souvenirs in his office in Santa Monica and that was why he was there Sunday—to grab them and go. There was also a packed suitcase in the car. He was about to split."

"Any idea where he was going?" Aghzafi asked.

"Not at the moment," Ballard said. "There was nothing on his phone, in his pockets, or in the car indicating where he was going. His passport was in his pocket, so possibly Mexico or Canada. We think he was just trying to get out of Dodge after he realized that we were onto him."

Ballard looked at everyone, expecting more questions.

"If that's it, let's get to it," she said. "The elephant in the room is that Rawls was one of us, and the optics on that are not good. So let's get on this and see if we can improve those optics by closing more cases. Let's show them our value."

Ballard sat back down while the others stood up to go to the interview room. All except Bosch. He waited till the others had filed into the room to look at the souvenirs, then spoke to Ballard from the other side of the wall.

"Keisha Russell was the one who called me a gunslinger at the press conference," he said. "So I called her on it. I didn't know she was back in town and back on the cop shop, and then I hear her voice calling me a gunslinger, just to get a rise out of the chief. And then…I let it slip. I said we had a fox in the henhouse because I knew from that press conference what they were going to do. They were going to just sweep that shit under the rug like they always do and…I didn't think it out, Renée. I should've known it would come down on you, and I fucked up. I'm sorry."

Ballard nodded slightly. Not because Bosch had confirmed what she already knew, but because he had come clean with her and admitted it. The trust she thought was broken was now restored.

"It's okay, Harry," she said. "Just go in there and find something that closes a case for us."

"You got it, boss," he said.

She smiled.

42

BOSCH STOOD UP and looked over the privacy wall at Ballard. She was working on her computer, her fingers moving at an amazing speed as she typed, but he couldn't see the screen to know what she was doing. She spoke without taking her eyes off her work, whatever it was.

"Did you find something in there to run with?" she asked.

"No, not yet," Bosch said. "The others are still in there. I'll check it out later, see what's left. I was thinking about taking a drive up to Santa Monica first."

"I just heard you on the phone asking about some kind of hauling schedule. Is it that?"

"Yeah. There's something that's been bothering me about what Rawls was doing Sunday."

Ballard now looked up at him from her screen.

"What?" she asked.

"All right, just hear me out on this," Bosch said. "On Sunday, when I drove by the alley and saw his car behind the shop, the trunk was open and he was nowhere to be seen."

"Yeah, he was inside his office, gathering his souvenirs."

"Right, we think he was doing that. And you said that after

291

the shootout, the box of souvenirs was found in the trunk of his car and there was also a suitcase there."

"Yeah, on the back seat."

"Okay, so why'd he open the trunk before going inside the shop?"

Ballard shrugged.

"Because he knew he was bringing out the box," she said.

"But would you open the trunk before you went inside?" Bosch said. "Or would you wait till you were coming out with the box? I mean, it wasn't this big box he'd need two hands to carry."

"I don't know, Harry. I think you're overthinking things."

"Maybe. But when I saw you with the box today, it hit me. That box could have easily fit in the back with the suitcase or on the passenger seat next to him. Why'd he put it in the trunk?"

"Does it matter? It's one of those things we're never going to be able to nail down and know. A known unknown. Every case has them."

"Yeah, but what if the trunk was open because he was taking things out? What if he was getting rid of stuff? Evidence, other souvenirs. He took it all from his house or his storage unit, wherever he had it, put it in the trunk, then drove to the shop, where the back alley was lined with dumpsters behind the businesses. Maybe I didn't see him in the alley because my view was blocked by the dumpsters."

"The hauling schedule. Have those dumpsters been emptied this week?"

"Not till tomorrow."

"So you're going to go dumpster diving."

"It's going to bother me if I don't."

"Let me finish this email and I'll go with you. I don't think you should be climbing into dumpsters with those ribs and that knee. And I have CSOs in my car."

Bosch knew she meant crime scene overalls. Most detectives kept work boots and overalls in their trunk for working messy crime scenes.

"My ribs and the knee are fine," he said. "But we're going to need a step stool or a ladder—no matter who goes in."

"Go check with building maintenance to see what we can borrow," Ballard said. "I'll send this email and meet you at my car."

"On it."

43

THEY WERE SEARCHING the fourth of five dumpsters in
the alley behind Montana Shoppes & Suites. They had started at
the west end of the alley and worked their way east. Nothing
relating to Rawls or the case had been found in the first three
searches. Ballard, wearing rubber boots and navy blue overalls,
was standing waist-deep in a green dumpster located behind a
women's apparel shop. It meant the refuse was largely innocu-
ous and dry. The first dumpster they searched had been filled
with coffee grounds and other garbage from the breakfast café
that anchored the west end of the plaza.

Each dumpster search required the excavation of three days'
worth of refuse, since they were looking for something that
Rawls might have dumped on Sunday.

"There's nothing here," Ballard said.

She was using the long handle from a push broom to poke
around in the bottom layer of the dumpster. Bosch had borrowed
it from the maintenance department along with a stepladder.

"All right, then come on out of there," Bosch said.

He held his hand up to her. She took off a work glove,
grabbed his hand, hoisted her hips onto the steel rim, and swung
her legs over to the ladder. Bosch helped her down.

"The things I do for you, Harry," she said.

"Hey, I didn't ask you to come out here," Bosch said. "If it makes you feel better, I'll do the last one."

"No, you'll get your clothes all dirty. I'm just giving you a hard time because we haven't found shit out here and these CSOs are hotter than hell."

Once she was off the ladder, Bosch started throwing the bags of trash and other refuse they had removed back into the bin.

Ballard moved on to the final dumpster, carrying the step-ladder with her. She put her glove back on, then flipped the heavy plastic cover back and started excavating the top layer of bags and boxes. The east side of the property was anchored by a large home decor store. It sold smaller furnishings like lamps, artwork, and candles. The trash here was similar to the last dumpster's in that it wasn't wet, didn't smell particularly bad, and was easy to excavate. It had largely been deposited in shipping boxes stuffed with form-fitted foam packaging and Bubble Wrap. There were also broken pieces of wooden shipping crates.

Bosch joined her and they quickly emptied the top half of the dumpster, dropping everything they pulled out onto the alley's asphalt.

"I can't believe nobody's come out of one of these places yet to ask what the hell we're doing," Ballard said.

"Maybe my pal, the angry homeowner on Seventeenth Street, will come over," Bosch said.

"Who?"

"Some guy who lives in the neighborhood back here. I posted up in his driveway Sunday when I was waiting for Rawls to make a move. He came out and went full Mrs. Kravitz on me."

"Mrs. Kravitz?"

"The busybody neighbor on that old sixties show *Bewitched*. You never watched the reruns when you were a kid?"

"Before my time, I guess."

"Jeez, I'm old."

Once they had removed the first layer of debris, Ballard climbed the ladder, put her gloved hands on the rim of the dumpster for support, expertly swung her legs over the edge, and dropped into the bin.

"You're getting good at that," Bosch said. "The Olympics are coming to town in a few years. You're the Simone Biles of homicide."

"You're a funny guy, Harry," Ballard said. "This is just another useful skill I'll hopefully never need again."

She started handing boxes over the rim to Bosch, who found places for them on the ground.

She eventually found space for her feet on the floor of the bin and was better able to brace herself to lift the heavier debris. She focused on an open crate in the corner. It held a sculpture of a woman and child that had a one-inch-wide crack running through the plaster. She attempted to lift it but realized it would be too heavy to raise over the rim to Bosch. She instead lifted it slightly and swung it to her left to reposition it. When she turned back to the corner, she saw a crushed cardboard box that had been beneath the sculpture crate.

"Harry," she said. "Take a look."

She heard his feet clunk on the steps of the ladder, and then he was leaning over the rim.

"Be careful with that knee," she said.

She pointed to the crushed box in the corner.

"Same size box as the one in the BMW trunk," she said.

She took off her gloves and tucked them under an arm. She then pulled her phone out of a zippered pocket in her overalls and opened the camera. She took three photos from three different angles by leaning one way and then the other. Then she opened the video camera and handed the phone to Bosch.

"I'm going to open it," she said. "You run video."

"Got it," Bosch said.

Ballard put her gloves back on and squatted down next to the crushed box while Bosch hit the record button on the phone.

Other than having its dimensions—16 x 16 x 6—stamped on its side, it was an unmarked cardboard box that appeared to be a match for the one recovered from Rawls's BMW that Ballard had carried into the homicide archives that morning. It was unsealed, but the top had been crushed, and this forced Ballard to rip its flaps to get it open. Inside, at the top, was a folded piece of clothing. Ballard leaned back on her heels to make sure Bosch got a clear view with the video.

"It looks like a nightgown," she said. "Let's get it out of here before we start looking through it. You can kill the video."

Bosch did so and handed the phone back to Ballard. She then stood up with the box and handed it over the lip to Bosch.

"I'm going to make sure there's nothing else in here," she said.

Bosch took the box over to Ballard's city car and put it down on the hood.

Ballard spent the next five minutes moving debris around in the dumpster so she could determine that nothing else had been deposited by Rawls. After climbing back over the rim and down the ladder, she helped Bosch throw the debris they had removed back into the bin.

She stripped off her work gloves and put them in the back pockets of her overalls. She then pulled a pair of latex gloves from a front pocket and put them on as she walked to her car. She could tell when she had handed the box out of the dumpster to Bosch that there was something heavy beneath the clothing folded on top.

Bosch followed her to the car.

"You want to go through it here or wait?" he asked.

"I want to take a quick look," she said. "See what we've got."

She handed her phone back to Bosch so he could record her further examination of the box's contents. She lifted the item of clothing out and confirmed it was a white flannel long-sleeved nightgown with an embroidered fringe at the collar and cuffs. There was no label inside the neckline and there were no other identifiers. It appeared to be clean. No blood or other stains on it.

Ballard shifted position so she could look down into the box.

"Harry, get this," she said.

Bosch moved in next to Ballard and focused the camera on the box. At the bottom was a pair of pink slippers that looked like stuffed bunnies with the nose at the point of the big toe. Beneath these Ballard could see part of a wooden handle. Holding the nightgown up with one hand, she reached in with the other and pulled out the bunny slippers. At the bottom of the box was a stainless-steel hammer with a polished wood handle.

They both stared down at it for a long moment without speaking.

"Murder weapon?" Bosch said.

"What I was thinking," Ballard said. "Maybe. Now we just need to find the case."

She did not touch the hammer because she knew the handle

might hold fingerprints and its steel head and claw could hold DNA. She carefully put the slippers down on top of the hammer in their original position, then with both hands held the nightgown up by its shoulders and folded it lengthwise. When she did this, the right sleeve swung against her and she felt the heft of something more solid than an embroidered cuff.

She ran a hand down the length of the sleeve and closed it around something caught inside the cuff. She worked her fingers inside the cuff and pulled out a bracelet. It was a thick, braided metal band with one charm attached, a painter's palette with six tiny dots of color along the rim and the word *GO* engraved at center.

"ID bracelet," Ballard said. "It probably belonged to a boyfriend and was too big for her wrist. It must have slipped off when she took off the nightgown."

"Or when someone else took it off her," Bosch said.

"There's that. Do you think it's *go* or *G-O*?"

"Is that the engraving? It's too small for me to make out."

"Yes, *G-O*. I wonder what it means."

"You'll know that when you connect a case to it."

Ballard nodded and looked down the alley toward the back door of the DGP store.

"So he parks down there, carries a box up here to the farthest trash bin, and then dumps it," she said. "But then he leaves the second box with his other souvenirs in the BMW and drives off. Does that make sense?"

"No," Bosch said. "But I've been thinking about that."

"And?"

"Come over here."

Bosch walked away from the car and headed toward the end

of the alley twenty feet away. Ballard put the nightgown back in the box and placed the bracelet on top of it. She then caught up to Bosch. When they got to the end, he pointed diagonally across 17th Street to a 1950s ranch that was the first residential house behind the Montana shopping district.

"That's the driveway I backed into after I saw Rawls's car in the alley," he said. "His car was pointed east, so I thought that when he left, he would come out this way and I'd see him and then follow."

"That's where Mrs. Kravitz confronted you?" Ballard asked.

"Yeah. I was looking this way at the alley when the guy came up alongside me, banged his fist on the roof of my car, and started giving me what for. It was a distraction and I took my eyes off the alley to deal with it. He was kind of loud because he was king of the castle and didn't want me there. So I was think-ing...maybe Rawls took the one box down to the dumpster and then he heard the dustup out in the street."

"He checks it out, sees it's you, and figures he's gotta get the hell out of here."

"Right, so he runs back to his car, turns it around in the alley, and takes off. But he's still got the other box in the trunk. I pull out of the driveway, cruise by the alley up here, and that's when I see him, when he's pulling out down at the other end."

They walked back to Bosch's car in silence. Ballard guessed that they were both rethinking the scenario they had just spun, looking for holes in the logic of it.

"It feels like something is off," Bosch finally said. "Something missing. Why would he use the dumpsters behind his busi-ness? It wasn't smart. There had to be another reason for him coming here."

"There was," Ballard said. "I didn't tell you this, but RHD interviewed the guy who was working in the shop Sunday. He told them that Rawls came in the back door, said hello, and then went right to the safe in the back room that's used for keeping backup cash for all the shops. The employee said Rawls took all the money. We know from what was in Rawls's pockets that it was nine hundred dollars."

"His go money."

"Right. But the story he told his employee was that he needed the cash to put down on a car he was buying. So he took what was in the safe and then left by the back door."

"That works. He goes there to get the cash and dump the boxes of souvenirs. He pulls up, pops the trunk, but goes into the store first to get the money. That's when I drive by and see the trunk open but no sign of Rawls. Then I go around the block and post up in that driveway. Rawls comes out of his store and takes the first box up the alley to the last dumpster, distancing it from his store just in case. But after he dumps it, he hears the guy yelling at me. Rawls checks it out, sees me, and hauls ass back to his car."

"He makes a U-turn in the alley so you won't see him leave and goes out the other end. It works, but we'll never know for sure. Was he going to put the second box in a different dumpster? Why didn't he carry both boxes to the dumpster at once? We could spin our wheels on this forever."

"One of the known unknowns," Bosch said.

"Exactly."

"So now what?"

Ballard pointed to the box sitting on the city car's front hood.

"I want to take this back to Ahmanson and go to work on that bracelet," she said. "And I'll get the hammer to forensics."

"I had a hammer case once. It was the murder weapon, and we recovered it from the L.A. River in a spot where there was actual water in the channel. It had been in there for something like thirty-six hours and looked clean as a whistle. But they still found blood in the wood where it connected to the steel head. The victim's blood. We made the case."

"So maybe we'll get lucky with this one and connect it to a victim. Let's go back."

She picked up the box and headed to the trunk.

"When we get back to Ahmanson, I'm going to go," Bosch said.

Ballard popped the trunk and put the box in. She closed it and moved to the driver's-side door. She looked at Bosch over the roof of the car.

"Go where?" she asked.

"Sheila Walsh has percolated long enough," Bosch said. "It's time I go see her."

"What about Rawls?"

"I figure you've got Rawls covered. You've got everybody else working it."

"You're going to see Walsh by yourself?"

"Yeah, like before. Better that way."

Bosch opened his door and got in the car. Ballard did the same.

"What if her son is there?"

"Not a problem. He's scared of me."

"Probably with good reason."

44

BOSCH HAD RENTED a car on Tuesday, picking it up at Midway after meeting his daughter for lunch at a vegetarian restaurant on Sunset. He had earlier made an inquiry about his own car at the police garage but was told detectives from the Force Investigation Division had not released it yet. The helpful garage attendant also told him that the car was inoperable because the frame had been bent during the accident that preceded the shooting with Rawls. Despite his claim to Ballard that the old Cherokee was invincible, Bosch now knew that he had most likely driven it for the last time.

He pulled up in the rental in front of Sheila Walsh's house. If she was on the watch for him, she wouldn't recognize the car. He sat for a minute collecting his thoughts and deciding how he was going to play this. It had been almost a week since Walsh had called him and angrily told him to stay away from her and her son. Bosch needed to put her in a mindset that told her he would not be going away until she broke and revealed whatever secret she knew about Finbar McShane.

He got out and walked up the stone path to the front door. He knocked sharply, the kind of rap that would hopefully startle anyone inside. Nothing happened. He reached into the pocket of his jacket and brought out the paper-clipped packet of documents to have them ready.

Raising his fist to hammer on the door again, he heard Sheila Walsh's voice from the other side.

"Go away. You're not coming in."

"Mrs. Walsh…Sheila, open the door. I have a search warrant here."

"I don't care. Go somewhere else with your damn search warrant."

"Doesn't work that way. If you don't open the door, I'm going to kick it in."

"Sure, an old man like you. Go ahead and try. I've got the dead bolt on."

"I've been kicking in doors for forty years, Sheila. It's not about strength. It's about the placement of the pressure. One of the first things they teach you. You hit the right spot and the lock itself breaks the jamb. It will then cost you three or four hundred dollars to fix it—and you have to figure out a way to secure your house till you get somebody out to do it. Nobody ever thinks about that. They don't show that part on the TV shows."

A long moment of silence went by.

Bosch stepped back as he would have if he were going to kick the door in. There was a peephole and he believed she was watching him.

"Stand back," he said. "I don't want to hurt you."

At the moment he would have raised his leg and reared back to kick, Walsh's voice came through again.

"Okay, okay! Don't kick my door in."

He waited and heard the locks turn. The door finally opened and Sheila Walsh stood there, pure hatred in her eyes.

"Smart decision," Bosch said.

"What do you want?" Walsh asked.

"To be honest, I would rather just talk to you than have to search your house. That would take the rest of the day, when we probably could clear this up with a simple conversation."

She didn't move.

"A conversation about what?" she asked.

"Do you want to do this out here in front of your neighbors?" Bosch asked. "Or can we sit down inside?"

She stepped back and let him in. Bosch had not lied to her. He did, in fact, have a search warrant, but it was a copy of a warrant from another case and signed years earlier by a judge who was long retired now.

"In here," Walsh said.

She led him to the dining area instead of the kitchen this time. An open laptop and paperwork were spread on the table. On the wall to the left of it, several unfolded pamphlets and flyers were taped to the sky-blue paint. Bosch saw maps of what looked like the Caribbean and the Gulf of Mexico as well as photos of cruise ships, floor plans of state rooms, and schematics for entire decks. The dining room was the headquarters of her online travel agency.

"Before I say another word, I want to hear you say you will leave my son alone," she said. "He's been through enough and he has nothing to do with this."

"I can't make that promise," Bosch said. "Four people are dead, Sheila. A whole family. And I'm going to find the man who did it. If I have to use your son to get there, I will. It's as simple as that. But it's you who controls this. You cooperate, and there will be no need for me to put pressure on your son or tell his employers about his involvement in this."

"That isn't right. He isn't involved!"

"You think it was right that the whole Gallagher family was buried in a hole out in the desert?"

"Of course not. But I had nothing to do with it! You don't think I feel the horror of that? I do. I think about it every single day."

"What did Finbar want?"

Her head rocked back in surprise at Bosch's directness.

"What are you talking about?" she asked.

"Come on, Sheila," Bosch said. "You know what I'm talking about. Your son was the one who broke in and stole from you. You got lucky when they found McShane's print and you could lay it on him. But it was your son, not him. McShane was here at some point before the break-in and I want to know why."

"You're crazy. You won't let this go, and this is harassment. I could file a complaint against you."

"You could. But if you think this is harassment, you haven't seen anything yet. I'm never going to stop coming here. Not until you tell me what you know."

She shook her head and then put her elbows on the table and her face in her hands.

"Oh my god, what am I going to do?" she said. "You won't fucking stop."

Bosch pulled the paper clip off the documents he had brought. They were folded lengthwise. He thumbed off the last page and slid it across the table to her.

"Open your eyes, Sheila, and take a look at that," Bosch said. "I think it will help you do the right thing here."

She dropped her hands to the table.

"The right thing?" she protested. "What are you talking about?"

"Just look at it," Bosch said.

She pinned the paper to the table with her thumbs and leaned over it to read. Soon she started shaking her head.

"Help me," she said. "What is this?"

"It's a copy of a page from the California penal code," Bosch said. "P-C thirty-two—it deals with the crime of aiding and abetting murder."

"What?"

It was a shriek more than a question.

"Oh my god," she followed. "What are you—"

"Look at the last line," Bosch said. "Read it."

"I read it. I don't know what it means. I don't know what you want."

"It's the statute of limitations. Three years for aiding and abetting a homicide. What that tells you is that you're in the clear, Sheila. No matter what you did, you can't be touched now."

"You think I had something to do with killing them? Those beautiful children? Are you out of your fucking mind? Get out! Get out of my house!"

She pointed toward the door as she rose from her seat.

"Sit back down, Sheila," Bosch said calmly. "I'm not going anywhere."

She didn't move. She held her arm out raised, her finger pointing toward the door.

"I said *sit down!*" Bosch yelled.

His voice scared her. She dropped back into her seat, her eyes wide with panic.

"Listen to me," Bosch said, his voice returning to an even tone. "I checked you out eight years ago. Once I figured out the date the Gallaghers disappeared, I confirmed you were on a boat in Cozumel. I got photos, verified witness accounts, credit-card statements, everything. I know that McShane waited until you were gone to do it so there would be no chance of a witness, nobody to call the police. But you know something, Sheila. You know something and now is the time to tell it. You're in the clear legally. So it's time to clear your conscience as well. Talk to me, Sheila. You do that, and I leave you—and your son—alone. I'll be out of your life forever."

She put her elbows back on the table, gripped her hands in front of her face, and looked down at the photocopy. Soon Bosch saw tears drip onto the paper.

"Time to do the right thing," Bosch said. "Think about those beautiful children and tell me. What was McShane doing here?"

She worked her fingers against themselves and then looked up over her knuckles at Bosch. For the first time, he saw that they were haunted by something. Something she had been carrying inside.

"He was here," she said. "He came to see me."

Bosch nodded. It was a thank-you. It was now time to draw out the whole story.

"When?" he asked.

"Promise me," Walsh said. "You will leave my son alone."

"I already told you. You tell me about McShane, and I will leave you and your son alone. That is a promise."

Walsh nodded but took a long moment to settle herself and compose the story.

"He came because he wanted money," she finally said. "He said he had lost all of his in a bad investment. He threatened me. I gave him what he wanted, and he went away."

"Threatened you how?"

"I promise you I didn't know about Stephen and his family. What happened to them, I mean. But in that year that they were gone—before anyone knew—I figured out what Fin was doing to the business."

"The bust-out?"

"What's that?"

"Selling equipment and ordering more to be sold as well. Eventually the business collapses. But before that happened, McShane took off."

"Whatever it's called, I knew what he was doing. I worked at Shamrock from the beginning and knew how to read the books. At that time, we didn't know what had happened to Stephen, but I could see the business wasn't going to make it. I had my son to think about. So...I told Fin I wanted my cut."

"And what was your cut?"

"I knew what he was bringing in, because I had seen the purchase orders and I made some calls to our customers to find out what he was selling things for. I told him I knew what he was up to and that I had added it all up and wanted half. Four hundred thousand or he'd go to jail. He gave it to me."

Bosch said nothing, hoping his silence would keep her talking.

"But then...they were found," she said. "Up there in the Mojave. And Fin had disappeared. I knew how it would look.

Like I had been part of it. I couldn't tell you what I knew. I couldn't tell anybody, because I looked guilty."

Bosch nodded as part of the story fell together after so many years. He thought about Sheila mentioning the arc of the moral universe when he'd been here last. He wondered if she knew then that the arc was bending toward her.

"You said he came back here for money," Bosch said. "How much did you give him?"

"All four hundred thousand," Sheila said. "Every cent. I never touched it. I couldn't after I knew what he did."

"When exactly did this visit occur? How long before the burglary you reported?"

"A few weeks. Maybe a month."

"You said a few minutes ago that he threatened you. Exactly how did he threaten you?"

"He said to give him the money, or my son would get a hot shot, and the next time I'd see him, he'd be on a slab at the coroner's office. He said he'd then tip the police about the money and I would be arrested. I didn't know about any statute of limits or whatever it's called. But my son—back then, he needed me. I couldn't let that happen."

Bosch nodded and stayed silent.

"But he didn't have to threaten me," Walsh said. "Or my son. I didn't want the money. Not after Mojave."

Bosch nodded again but this time he spoke.

"Why did you call the police after the burglary?" he asked. "You knew your son did it."

"I didn't!" she said. "I had no idea. You think I would call the police on my own son? I didn't know until Jonathan told me. When he found out I had called the police, he told me and said I had to protect him. When they called and asked about McShane and his prints, I knew how to do it. Just say it was McShane."

"Where is he, Sheila?"

"My son? You know where—"

"No, McShane. Where is he?"

"I don't know. How would I know?"

"Are you saying you had four hundred thousand dollars in cash under your mattress and you just gave it to him and he left? There had to have been some kind of transfer."

"It was in Bitcoin. That was how he gave it to me, and that was how I kept it. I transferred it back to him on my laptop right here. And that was when he picked up my paperweight. While he was watching me and showing me how to do it."

Bosch knew that tracing such a transfer would be almost impossible and would never lead to a physical location.

"What business did he invest in that he lost his half?" he asked. "He had to have told you something."

"He said, 'Never invest in a bar,'" Sheila said. "I remember that. That was all."

"What was the name of the bar?"

"He didn't say."

"Where was it?"

"Again, he didn't say. And I wasn't really interested in asking. I just wanted him to leave."

Bosch knew that tracing a bankrupt bar with no name and no location six years or more after the fact would be like trying to trace Bitcoin. Impossible. He now had the fuller story but was no closer to Finbar McShane. He looked down at the old search warrant on the table and started to paper-clip it back together.

"He did say one thing that might help you," Sheila said.

Bosch's eyes came up to hers.

"But I want assurances that none of this can ever come back on me or my son," she said. "And Jonathan can never know what I did."

She was crying again, this time not trying to hide it with her hands. Bosch nodded.

"The arc of the moral universe bends toward justice, Sheila," he said. "What did McShane say that can help me?"

She nodded and used her hands to dry the tears on her cheeks.

"He looked at my pamphlets up on the wall there and said, 'There's only one place in the world where you can see the sunset at dawn.'"

Bosch looked up at the wall but couldn't make the connection.

"I don't get it," he said. "What does it mean?"

"There's a ship called the *Dawn*," she said. "Part of the Norwegian line. It moors in Tampa, Florida, and every week it sails down to Key West, stops for a day, and then navigates out to the Bahamas before turning around and coming back. It's a popular itinerary. I've sold many trips on that boat and made a lot of commissions. I knew exactly what he meant when he said it, because I'd heard that line before. It's part of the sales pitch. They get great sunsets in Key West. Especially from the deck of the *Dawn*."

Bosch looked up at the pamphlets taped to the wall and saw the *Norwegian Dawn*.

Sheila reached over to one of the stacks of folded pamphlets she had at the side of the table, chose one, and handed it to Bosch.

"Here," she said. "Take it."

"Thank you," Bosch said.

Bosch looked at the pamphlet and opened it. It showed happy people in bathing suits frolicking in the ship's pool or in colorful boat clothes strolling on the deck. There was even a photo of people lined up at the deck rail and watching a sunset. Key West, Bosch thought. He knew now where he was going to look for Finbar McShane.

45

BALLARD CRANKED THE shelves just wide enough apart for her to slip in and move down to the 2002 cases. She ran her finger along the case numbers on the spines of the murder books and then pulled the binder she was looking for.

When she got back to her workstation, Colleen Hatteras was standing there waiting for her.

"What's up, Colleen?"

"Not much. I was wondering if you need any help with what you're doing."

She gestured toward the box on Ballard's desk. It was the one recovered from the dumpster in the alley behind Ted Rawls's business in Santa Monica.

"I think I've got it," Ballard said. "There's not really an IGG angle on this yet."

"I could make calls if you want me to," Hatteras said.

"There's no call to make yet. This is the seventh of seven possible cases. The first six didn't match up—in my opinion."

"What exactly are you looking for?"

"A case that matches a missing white nightgown, bunny slippers, and a bracelet. There is also probably going to be blunt force trauma as a cause of death."

Ballard sat down and opened the murder book she had just retrieved. She then flipped over the table of contents to the initial incident report.

"You want me to back-read?" Hatteras said. "I'm not really doing much. The IGG stuff on Rawls has dried up. I'm just waiting on responses. I could go back to what I was working on before, but I feel bad dropping off Rawls when there are so many unanswered questions."

"What about the souvenirs? Aren't you working on those?"

"I was, but I hit a wall. I found no connects to open cases."

Ballard knew that if she didn't give Hatteras something to do, she would probably hover over her all day.

"Tell you what," she said. "While I go through this last case, why don't you take this and see what you can find out."

As she spoke, Ballard reached into the cardboard box and retrieved the bracelet that had been found in the sleeve of the nightgown. She had since encased it in a plastic evidence bag. She handed it to Hatteras.

"All right," Hatteras said. "What are you looking for?"

"Anything and everything," Ballard said. "Who made the bracelet? Where was it sold? There are initials on the charm. At least, I think they're initials. I would love to know who did the engraving and whose initials they are. I already ran it through digitized property reports and got no hits. So what's left is, we try to find out where it came from. I know it's a long shot, but give it a try, okay?"

"You got it."

"Thanks."

Hatteras went away like a dog with a bone, even though Ballard believed it would be a failed mission. But it would be worth it in terms of covering all bases and not having Hatteras constantly interrupting her.

She read the initial summary of the 2002 case she had just retrieved from the archives. The victim's name was Belinda King. She was only twenty years old when she was murdered. Her naked body was found on the floor of the bathroom of her apartment in the Oakwood section of Venice. She was a student at nearby Santa Monica Community College, studying creative writing. Ballard remembered that Rawls had gone to Santa Monica CC, and it would likely have been just a few years before Belinda King. But that might be no more than a coincidence.

Belinda King matched almost all the parameters Ballard had entered in her search of digital records. She had gleaned these from the items found in the box from the dumpster and the known elements of Ted Rawls's kill patterns. Ballard believed she was looking for a victim who was young, female, and attacked at night in her home by an unknown intruder who left no DNA. The victim would also have been found naked—considering that Rawls had taken her nightgown—and cause of death was likely blunt force trauma, if not specifically attributed to blows from a hammer. The victim may have also had a boyfriend or fiancé who had given her a charm bracelet. The final box Ballard had to check on the search protocol was that the case had to be open and unsolved.

The search brought back seven hits and the King case was the seventh book Ballard had pulled. The first six were not completely dismissed, but they didn't feel right to Ballard for various reasons. She was hoping the seventh case would be a conclusive hit, but as she moved on from the written summary to the crime scene photos, she quickly dismissed it as a possible Ted Rawls kill. The victim was found nude and had been beaten to death, but Ballard judged that she was too heavy in the torso to have worn the nightgown comfortably. Additionally, the circumstances of the case led investigators to believe she knew her killer and may have engaged in consensual sex with him before he turned violent. There were no indications of sexual assault.

Disappointed, Ballard leaned back in her chair. She flipped the murder book closed and put it on top of the stack of books from the other cases she had reviewed. She decided she would not return them to the shelves in the archive. She'd have Harry Bosch, with his long experience as a homicide detective, review the cases to confirm or deny her conclusions about each one.

She put the frustrations of a wasted day aside and decided to take one more run through the department's digitized crime data, this time removing one of the descriptor filters to see if it brought up more matching cases.

The descriptor she dropped was the requirement that matching cases be unsolved. She checked the "All Cases" box, and the new search returned nine more case extracts with matching similarities. Because the Ahmanson archive contained only murder books from unsolved cases, Ballard stayed on the database and reviewed the digital case extracts, ready to write down any victims' names and case numbers she thought might require a fuller look. This more exacting review would require her to go to the original investigators to pull murder books from closed case files and conduct interviews.

She moved through the nine extracts quickly and didn't write down a single case citation in her notebook. Though all were similar in methodology to the murders of Sarah Pearlman and Laura Wilson, they were all closed by conviction following a jury verdict, or in two of the cases, a guilty plea. Ballard knew that any of these could have had a wrongful conviction or even a false confession, but with the abbreviated extracts alone, it was impossible for her to see anything suspicious about the cases. In extract form, they were all cut-and-dried case summaries and mug shots. Nothing else.

Ballard logged off the database and sighed, frustrated with the knowledge that she had been spinning her wheels all day.

She felt the need for Harry Bosch's supportive words. She knew that she could complain to him about wasting her time and he would come back with wisdom and encouragement. He would remind her that there were always more dead ends in a homicide investigation than there were leads that panned out. To him, that was a basic equation of the job. He had once told her it was like baseball. The best hitters failed more than half the time. It was the same chasing leads in homicide work.

She pulled her phone and called Bosch, but it went straight to voice mail.

"Harry, it's me. Call me back when you get a chance. I need to talk to you about how fucked up today has been. Bye."

She stood up and put the phone in her pocket. She saw Hatteras hunched over her desk in the next station in the pod.

"Colleen," she said, "I'm going to take a walk to clear my head and then get a coffee from upstairs. You want anything?"

"No, I'm fine," Hatteras said. "You knew this was a locket, right?"

Ballard had already started walking away from the pod when she heard the question. She turned on her heel and moved back toward Hatteras.

"What?" she asked.

"The charm," Hatteras said. "It has a hinge. It opens and there's a little photo inside."

Ballard leaned over Hatteras's shoulder and saw that the painter's palette charm did indeed have a hinge that allowed it to be opened like a tiny book. There was a face shot photo of a young man with jet-black hair and a struggling mustache above a wide smile.

"You shouldn't have taken that out of the evidence bag," she said.

"I had to," Hatteras said. "I wouldn't have gotten it open if it was still in the plastic."

"I know, but I hadn't had it processed for prints and DNA."

"I'm so sorry. I thought you said everything had been run through forensics."

"But not that. We just recovered it today."

Hatteras dropped the bracelet on her desk as if it were red hot.

"It doesn't matter now," Ballard said. "You've handled it."

Ballard was staring at the small photo. She leaned down to see it closer. The young man looked familiar to her but she couldn't quite place him.

"Do you by any chance have a magnifying glass, Colleen?"

"No, but Harry does. I saw him using it the other day."

Ballard went around the pod to Bosch's station. There was a small magnifying glass on top of a stack of printouts. She grabbed it and returned to Hatteras's desk.

"Let me look at it," she said.

Hatteras got up and Ballard sat down. She used the glass to magnify the image in the open locket.

"That's got to be G-O," Hatteras said. "Don't you think?"

Ballard was silent. The young man in the photo she was looking at was clearly Latino, with brown skin, dark eyes, and a full head of swept-back black hair. She now identified the familiarity. She realized she had seen a version of that face just minutes before.

"I think I know this guy," she said.

She got up and went back to her station, handing Hatteras the magnifying glass as she passed.

"You know him?" Hatteras asked.

"I think I just saw him," Ballard said.

She sat down and quickly rebooted the department's crime data bank on her screen. She pulled up the last search and quickly scanned through the case extracts she had just finished reviewing. With each one, she went immediately to the mug shot of the defendant convicted in the murder. The seventh extract contained the mug shot of a man convicted of killing his girlfriend in 2009.

"Let me see the locket and the magnifier," she said.

"Can I touch it?" Hatteras asked.

"You already have. Bring it to me."

Hatteras brought both items to her. Ballard used the magnifier again to look closely at the face in the locket photo and then turned back to the computer to make the comparison.

She was sure she was looking at different photos of the same young man. In one shot he was smiling, in the other, looking grim. She stood up and signaled Hatteras to switch into her seat. She held out the magnifying glass.

"Colleen, look at the mug shot on the screen and compare it

to the photo in the locket," Ballard said. "Tell me it's not the same guy."

Hatteras went back and forth from computer screen to locket three times before rendering a verdict.

"They're the same," she said. "Definitely."

"Okay, let me get to the computer," Ballard said.

Hatteras jumped up and Ballard quickly took her seat back. She clicked off the photo on the screen and pulled up the details of the convicted killer. His name was Jorge Ochoa, he was thirty-six years old, and he was serving a life sentence for murdering his girlfriend, Olga Reyes.

"Jorge Ochoa," Ballard said. "He could have Americanized it. Used the name George."

"G-O," Hatteras said. "I think you're right."

Ballard scribbled down the case number and the names of the victim and suspect. The extract also contained the location of the crime on Riverside Drive in Valley Village. It was a North Hollywood Division case.

The extract had no crime scene photos, and details were limited. The victim's cause of death was listed as blunt force trauma but that was a wide catchall classification. Ballard needed the murder book from the case to confirm that it was connected to the items found in the discarded box.

"Colleen, I'm going up to the Valley to pull this case," Ballard said. "I won't be coming back today."

"Can I go with you?" Hatteras said. "I feel like I had some-thing to do with this—whatever it is."

"You did have something to do with it. You did good work. But this is field work and your job is the IGG work. I'll see you tomorrow if you're coming in. I'll update you then."

"I'll be here."

"Okay, good. And great work, Colleen. Thank you."

Ballard quickly loaded her laptop and files into her backpack, grabbed her Van Heusen jacket off the back of her chair, and moved toward the exit, leaving Hatteras watching her go.

When she got to the parking lot, Ballard pulled her phone and called Harry Bosch again. She was once more greeted with his outgoing greeting telling all callers to leave a message.

"Harry, me again. Where are you? I think I know who the white nightgown belonged to. Call me back as soon as you get this."

She put the phone away and jumped into her car.

46

THE DRIVE FROM Miami to Key West was four hours on the Overseas Highway. Along the way, it was mostly mom-and-pop motels, restaurants, sandal factories, and kitschy T-shirt and souvenir shops, all punctuated by long bridges across startling turquoise water on which the sun was reflected in diamonds. Bosch had arrived late to Miami the night before, picked up a rental car, and gotten to Key Largo before he pulled into the parking lot of a motel with a glowing neon VACANCY sign and shut things down for the night.

Now it was morning, and his plan was to hit Key West by noon and start looking for Finbar McShane. His starting point would be the Key West Police Department. He had made no advance call and had no appointment. He liked the idea of coming in blind.

Just past Marathon, a backup behind an accident on the Seven Mile Bridge added almost an hour to the drive. It was after 1 p.m. when he pulled into the KWPD parking lot. When Bosch got out of the rental, his injured knee was stiff and throbbing from the long drive. He had not taken any pain medication because he wanted to stay alert while driving, but now he popped the trunk, unzipped the duffel bag he had packed in L.A., and popped two tabs of Advil. He hoped the Advil would be strong enough to reduce the pain soon.

The police department was painted in orange and pink pastels. Its front desk was actually an exterior window behind which an officer sat at a counter. Bosch waited in the sun, second in line behind a man asking how to report the theft of a bicycle. Bosch could feel the humidity coating his skin. The air even felt heavy in his lungs.

Finally it was his turn and Bosch limped up to the window, holding his badge out. There was a speaker and microphone set in the glass.

"Hello," he said. "I work with the Los Angeles Police Department cold case squad. I'm here on a case and wanted to see if I could speak to somebody in missing persons."

The glass was tinted almost as dark as a limousine's rear windows. Bosch could barely make out the outline of someone sitting on the other side but could not tell whether he was talking to a man or woman.

A male voice came through the speaker.

"A missing persons cold case?" he asked.

"Uh, no," Bosch said. "But I think a missing persons detective will be able to help me locate the individual I tracked here."

"And your name?"

"Harry Bosch."

"Did that badge say retired?"

"It did. I work as a volunteer investigator. I previously worked cold cases when I was in the department. They asked me to come back after I retired."

"Okay, let me call back there. If you wouldn't mind, step back from the window so others can come forward."

"No problem."

Bosch stepped away from the window and posted up on its left side. He turned, looked around, and saw that there was nobody else waiting to come forward.

Five minutes went by slowly. He leaned against the wall next to the window to take weight off his knee. The pills he had ingested had yet to reduce the pain.

No one else approached the window, and the man behind it offered Bosch no information. Bosch could feel his shirt starting to stick with perspiration to his back. He took off his sport coat and held it over his arm.

Finally, there was the metal clack of a heavy door opening, and Bosch saw a man in a guayabera shirt step out but hold the door open. The shirt barely disguised that the man had a gun and badge on his belt.

"LAPD?" he said.

"That's me," Bosch said.

"Come on back."

"Thank you."

He held out his hand as Bosch approached the door.

"Kent Osborne."

Bosch shook his hand.

"Harry Bosch," he said. "Thanks for your time."

"Gotta make time for the LAPD," Osborne said. "That's the big time."

Bosch smiled uneasily. There had been a slightly sarcastic tone in Osborne's voice.

Osborne led Bosch to a detective bureau, where he counted desks for sixteen detectives. There were no signs hanging from the ceiling denoting crime sections. Half the desks had men or women sitting behind them, and most of them had eyes on Bosch as he came in.

Osborne's desk was the last in the first row. He pulled a chair from an empty desk and rolled it over in front of his.

"Have a seat. Are you hurt? You're limping."

"I was in an accident Sunday. Messed up my knee."

"Looks like you messed up your ear, too."

"Yeah."

Both men sat down. Osborne checked something on the screen of his desktop computer and then looked at Bosch.

"So, what can I do for you, LAPD?" he asked.

"I don't know if the guy behind the window explained anything, but I work cold case homicides," Bosch said. "I'm working a quadruple case—four members of a family murdered with a nail gun and then buried in the desert."

"That's gotta hurt."

Bosch did not acknowledge the poor attempt at gallows humor.

"The case is almost nine years old," he said. "We recently reopened it and there's a person of interest. We have a solid witness that puts him here, but that was at least six years ago."

Osborne frowned.

"Six years in Key West is a long time," he said. "This town turns over quick. People come and go. Why'd you ask for a missing persons dick?"

Bosch had not heard the term applied to a detective in a long time, and possibly never in the real world.

"Because of the crime in L.A.," he said. "This guy played a long game. Took a job, worked his way up over the years until he was a valued employee, then killed the owner and his family and looted the business in a classic bust-out scheme. My guess is he came here to do it all again."

"As far as I know, we got no families murdered here, LAPD."

"My witness back in L.A. said he invested in a bar in Key West and then the bar went belly-up. I think if he's here, he's moved on to something else."

"And the missing persons part?"

"Do you have a case involving a prominent person—like a business owner—who's gone missing?"

Osborne leaned back in his chair and swiveled it back and forth as he considered the question.

"Nothing like that, that I know of. Our cases are mostly about bored teenagers going up to Miami, tourists getting so shit-faced at Sloppy Joe's they can't find their way back to the motel. Can't think of a prominent citizen going missing."

"What about a bar going under six or seven years ago?"

Osborne let out a laugh.

"There isn't a shortage of those," he said.

"Nothing comes to mind?" Bosch pressed. "I'm talking something substantial. My guy put four hundred thousand into it and lost it."

"Tell you what, the guy you should talk to is Tommy over at the Chart Room."

"The Chart Room. That's a bar?"

"At the Pier House."

"The Pier House?"

"You don't know shit, do you, LAPD? It's a hotel at the end of Duval. I think you gotta stay there to get into the Chart Room these days. Place was a dive back in the day. Now they keep the riffraff out."

"And Tommy?"

"He's been slinging booze there forty years plus. And he knows the local bar trade better than anybody in this building."

Bosch nodded. He then raised his sport coat up with one hand, reached into a pocket, and pulled out a document he had copied from the Gallagher Family murder book. He handed it to Osborne, who unfolded it. It was a BOLO flyer. At the top it had a California driver's license photo of Finbar McShane. Below it were four smaller copies of the photo that had been altered by a police artist to show four possible new looks that McShane could have adopted after fleeing. In the altered photos, McShane alternately had a full beard, a goatee, long hair, or a shaved head. Bosch had put out the BOLO on McShane shortly after originally being assigned the case. That made the photos almost eight years old and of questionable value. But it was all he had to offer.

"This your guy, huh?" Osborne said.

"Yeah," Bosch said. "Recognize him? Seen him around?"

"Can't say I have. How old is that BOLO?"

"About eight years. He'd be forty-four now."

"That's a long time ago. They couldn't come up with new stuff?"

"They're working on it. How would you feel about showing that at roll call? See if any of your street people have seen him."

"I guess I could do that. It's a long shot, though."

"I would appreciate it anyway."

Osborne grabbed a Post-it pad and put it down in front of Bosch.

"Write your cell number down, and I'll call you if I come up with anything."

"I don't have a phone. I lost it and need to buy one today. I can also call you tomorrow from the hotel."

Osborne made a face as if to ask, who doesn't have a cell phone?

"What hotel?" he asked instead.

"I'm going to see if they have a room at the Pier House, I guess."

"LAPD must have a nice hotel allowance. That place'll run you at least five hundred a night this time of year."

Bosch nodded.

"Thanks for your help," he said. "And the roll call."

"Not a problem," Osborne said. "You sure you're okay, LAPD?"

"Yeah. Why?"

"I don't know. You seem kind of shaky there."

"It's the humidity. Not used to it."

"Yeah, we get that a lot 'round here."

Back in the parking lot, Bosch took a moment before getting back in the rental to look up at the sky. A row of cumulus clouds was moving over the island. Bosch felt that the light was different here, not as soft as in California. There was a bright harshness to it.

He got in the car and thought about Osborne, wondering if he could trust him. He wasn't sure. He started the engine and pulled out.

47

BALLARD HELD HER badge cupped in one hand while she knocked on the door with the other. It wasn't long before a short woman with the same coloring and features as Jorge Ochoa answered the door.

"Mrs. Ochoa?" Ballard asked.

"*Sí,*" the woman said.

Ballard immediately wished she had gotten a Spanish-speaking officer to go with her. She could step away and call North Hollywood Division to see if one was available but instead pressed on. She held up her badge.

"*La policía. Habla inglés?*"

The woman frowned but then turned away from the door and yelled in rapid-fire Spanish back into the house. The only word Ballard identified was *policía*. The woman then turned back to Ballard and nodded as though she had just fixed the problem. After an awkward and silent minute, a young man appeared behind the woman at the door, his dark hair disheveled from sleep. He was almost a carbon copy of what Jorge Ochoa looked like in the mug shots she had reviewed when reading the murder book.

"What?" he said.

He was clearly annoyed with the early wake-up, even though it was almost noon. Ballard quickly assessed the VB tattoos on his arms and read him as a member of the Vineland Boyz street gang. She knew that a gangster's day typically started in the p.m. hours. This was early.

"You're Oscar, right?" Ballard said. "I want to talk to your mother about your brother."

"My brother's gone," Oscar said. "And we don't talk to cops. *Adiós, puta.*"

He started to close the door but Ballard reached her hand out and stopped it.

"You call somebody who wants to help your brother a whore?"

"Help him? Shit. You coulda helped him when he said he didn't do it. But no, you people just threw away the key."

"I want to show something to your mother. It might be what gets Jorge out of prison. If you want me to leave, I'll leave. But next time you visit your brother, you tell him I was here and you sent me away."

Oscar didn't move or speak. Then his mother spoke to him in a whisper. Ballard knew enough Spanish to know she had asked her son what the woman wanted. Mrs. Ochoa had heard Jorge's name mentioned.

Oscar didn't answer her. He turned back to Ballard and made room for her to enter.

"Show her," he said.

Ballard stepped in. She had spent the night before reviewing the murder book she had pulled at North Hollywood station. Her first effort in the morning was to attempt to track down the family of Olga Reyes. But it appeared that her family had left Los Angeles after her murder, and Ballard had not yet been able to locate them. The closest she came was a neighbor who said she thought the family had gone to Texas.

That left the Jorge Ochoa side of the equation, and here she was at his mother's cookie-cutter house in a post–World War II tract in Sunland.

Ballard was led to a small, modestly furnished living room, where she immediately saw signs that she was on the right track. Several framed paintings and sketches that had the look of prison art hung on the walls. All were on butcher paper and signed in pencil.

"Did Jorge want to be an artist?" she asked.

"He *is* an artist," Oscar said. "Show her what you got and then go."

Ballard was annoyed with herself for not thinking through her question.

"Okay," she said. "Tell your mother I am going to show her a photo of a piece of jewelry and I want to know if she's ever seen it before."

While Oscar made the translation, Ballard swung her backpack off her shoulder and opened it on the floor. She removed a file folder containing an 8 x 10 color photo of the bracelet with the artist's palette charm, which she had printed at home that morning. She gave the file to Oscar to give to his mother. She wanted him invested in this as well.

Oscar opened the file and looked at the photo with his mother. Ballard watched the woman for a reaction and saw the recognition in her eyes.

"She's seen it before," Ballard said quickly.

Oscar and his mother exchanged words and Oscar translated.

"She said it was my brother's. He gave it to Olga because they were in love. Where did you find it?"

Ballard knew the question had come from him.

"I can't tell you right now," Ballard said. "But I think your brother is going to get out of prison with it."

"How?"

"I think I can prove that somebody else killed Olga."

Suddenly Oscar's tough shell cracked and Ballard saw hope and fear in his eyes. He then turned away and translated for his mother.

"*Dios mío,*" she said. "*Dios mío.*"

She reached out and grabbed Ballard's hand.

"Please," she said.

Oscar's hard shell slipped back into place.

"You better not be fucking with us," he said.

"I'm not," Ballard said. "Ask your mother if she knows where Jorge got the bracelet."

The exchange in Spanish was quick.

"She doesn't know," Oscar said.

"What about the charm?" Ballard asked.

The next exchange didn't need to be translated. The woman shook her head. Ballard looked at Oscar.

"What about you?" Ballard asked.

"What do you mean?" Oscar asked.

"Was your brother in Vineland Boyz?"

"No, but you people at the trial sure tried to make it look that way."

"What I'm getting at is, where do Vineland Boyz get their chains?"

Oscar didn't answer, his hesitation rooted in the gang rule

about talking about the gang to the police. It could get him killed.

"Do you know what *provenance* means?" Ballard asked. "Besides having your mother identify the bracelet as your brother's, I may need to establish where Jorge got it. Then I would have two confirmations when I go to the District Attorney's Office."

"He was not a gangster," Oscar said. "He was an artist."

Ballard knew from the review of the case file that the prosecution presented photos of street art attributed to Jorge Ochoa and used it to suggest gang affiliation. It was an underhanded way of tilting a jury's view of him.

"I'll leave you my card," Ballard said. "If you think of anything, maybe a local store where Jorge might have gotten the bracelet, call me."

"I don't talk to the *policía,*" Oscar said.

"Even if it might help your brother prove he didn't kill Olga?"

Oscar was silent on that question. Ballard looked at his mother. "*Gracias, señora,*" she said. "*Estaré en contacto.*"

As soon as she was back in her car, Ballard pulled her phone and called Harry Bosch. Adrenaline had started coursing through her veins the moment Jorge Ochoa's mother recognized the bracelet. Ballard needed to tell someone about the twist the case was now taking and Bosch was her first choice.

But the call once again went directly to message.

"Harry, it's me again. Where the hell are you? Things are happening fast and I need you on Rawls. I've connected another case to him, and get this, somebody's in prison for a murder Rawls committed. I'm sure of it. I need you to call me back as soon as you get this."

She disconnected and sighed in frustration. But soon her

annoyance with Bosch turned to concern. He was old and not in the best health. Besides inflicting the obvious injuries, the crash on Sunday had seemed to take something out of him.

Ballard opened up her contacts list on her phone and called Bosch's daughter. He had previously mentioned that Maddie was working a mid-watch shift, so she figured she should be neither asleep nor at work.

Maddie Bosch answered promptly.

"Maddie, it's Renée Ballard."

"Hey, what's up?"

"Uh, have you talked to your dad lately? We're supposed to be working on something and I can't seem to reach him."

"Well, I saw him Tuesday when we had lunch and then I dropped him off to pick up a rental car. But I haven't talked to him since then. What's—"

"I'm sure everything is fine, but I really need to talk to him. Do you mind doing something for me? He once told me that you let him track your phone and you track his. Is it still that way?"

"Yes. So you want me to see where he's at?"

"That would help, if you don't mind. I really need him on a case I'm working."

"Hold on."

Ballard waited while Maddie used her phone to check her father's location by tracking his cell phone.

"Um…okay, I have him at the OPG lot at West Bureau. No, wait, that's old. His phone must be off or the battery's dead. That's from Sunday night, and it's the last location I have."

Ballard put two and two together. The official police garage would have been where they took Bosch's car after the Rawls incident Sunday.

"It's in his car," she said. "He was talking to me when his car got hit by Rawls, and the phone went flying. His phone must still be in the car and the battery probably died Sunday night."

"So then where is he?" Maddie asked, starting to sound worried.

The middle ground between concern and panic had entered Ballard's thinking.

"I don't know," Ballard said. "Does he still have a landline at the house?"

"He does," Maddie said. "Let me call it, and either he or I will call you right back."

They disconnected and Ballard sat in the car and waited, knowing that her next move would be dictated by who called her back.

When the call came in a minute later, it was from Maddie.

"He didn't answer. I left a message but now I'm worried."

"When do you go in today?"

"I'm actually off."

"Do you have a key to Harry's house? I think we should check it out."

"I have a key. When?"

"I'm up in the Valley. I could get there in about thirty minutes tops."

"Okay, it will take me the same. I'll meet you there."

"Okay. If you get there first, maybe you should wait for me before going in."

"We'll see."

"Well, I'm on my way."

They disconnected and Ballard started the car. Her tires squealed on the asphalt as she pulled out. She wanted to get to Bosch's house before his daughter did.

48

BOSCH SAT ON the bed with his bad leg up. He had a bag of ice on his knee and it seemed to ease the discomfort the second dose of Advil hadn't yet reached. He was in his room at the Pier House and studying the tourist map of Old Town that he had received from the front desk clerk when he checked in. Clearly marked on it were the sunset viewing spots and the wharves where the cruise ships docked. He planned to check these out in his needle-in-a-haystack search for Finbar McShane.

His room had a small balcony and a view of the turquoise water. His eyes were drawn to it because he was so used to the coldly forbidding blue-black water of the Pacific. He now saw a large catamaran cruising slowly by, seemingly every inch of deck space occupied by a passenger. Painted along the side of the hull was a phone number for reserving a spot on a sunset cruise.

Before coming to his room, he had used a resort map, also given to him at check-in, to locate the Chart Room, and learned it did not open until five. He planned to be there then, with the hope of talking to the bartender before the place got crowded.

He had an hour to wait, so he decided to use the time walking through Old Town and showing around the BOLO flyer with the many possible faces of Finbar McShane on it. He got up and put the bag of ice in the bathroom sink. The ice and the painkiller had combined to make the knee feel usable—for a while.

He left the room and the hotel and started making his way up Duval Street, stopping at Sloppy Joe's and other bars and asking bartenders if they recognized the man in the photos.

He got no takers. But he did get the idea that most of the bartenders and waitresses he showed the flyer to had fled from something themselves before landing in Key West. A bad life, a bad relationship, a bad crime—it didn't matter, but it made people hesitant to finger a fellow traveler on the runaway trail. Bosch didn't mention to any of those he spoke to that the man on the flyer was the only suspect in the killing of a whole family. He didn't want to upset their romanticized version of running away from the past.

He got back to the Pier House by five and went directly to the Chart Room, which was tucked into a first-floor hallway in the main wing of the hotel. A man with gray hair pulled back into a ponytail was unlocking the door when he got there.

He entered and Bosch followed him in. The bar was small, about the size of a hotel room, because that was clearly what it had once been. There was a six-stool bar on the left side and there were a few small tables and sitting spots on the right. It looked to Bosch like the place would be over capacity with just twenty people.

Bosch took the first stool and waited for the man with the ponytail to come around behind the bar. It was all dark wood, with lights under the three tiers of liquor bottles, creating an amber glow. There were many photos pinned on the walls, almost all of them yellowed by time. There were no windows with a view of the water. This was a place for worshipping alcohol, not the setting sun.

"That looks like it hurts," the bartender said.

He pointed at Bosch's ear.

"It's not bad," Bosch said.

"Fishhook?" the bartender asked.

"I wish."

"Bullet, then."

"How do you know that?"

"I know fishhooks from Key West. Bullets from Vietnam."

"Right. Who were you with over there?"

"Marines One-Nine."

"The walking dead."

Bosch knew about the walking dead. The First Battalion, 9 Marines took more casualties than any other unit during the war, hence the name they came to be known by.

"What about you?" the bartender asked.

"Army," Bosch said. "First Infantry, engineer battalion."

"The tunnels."

"Yeah."

The bartender nodded. He knew about the tunnels.

"You in the hotel?" he asked.

"Room two-oh-two," Bosch said.

"Don't look much like a tourist."

"I guess I gotta get some shorts and sandals and maybe a Hawaiian shirt."

"That'll help."

"Are you Tommy?"

The bartender stopped his busy work behind the bar getting ready for the night and looked directly at Bosch.

"Do I know you?" he asked.

"No, first time in Key West," Bosch said. "Over at the police station, I was told that you were the man I needed to talk to."

"About what?"

"The bar trade in Key West. I'm trying to locate a bar that closed down six, maybe seven years ago."

"What was it called?"

"That's the thing. I don't have a name."

"Seems kind of fuzzy. You a cop?"

"Used to be. Now I'm just trying to find a guy who came here from L.A., invested in a bar, and then lost it all. My name's Harry, by the way."

He offered his hand across the bar top. Tommy wiped his hand on a bar towel and shook it.

"How long you been here, Tommy?" Bosch asked.

"Put it this way: longer than anybody else," Tommy said. "This guy you're looking for—he's got a name, right?"

"He does, but I don't think he's using it here. Finbar McShane. He's Irish."

Bosch studied his eyes to see if there was any flare of recognition. There was.

"The Irish Galleon," Tommy said.

"What's that?" Bosch asked.

"That's the bar. Two Irish guys opened it about eight years ago. Well, one guy did and then the other guy came over and they were partners. Like we needed another Irish pub in Key West. Fixed it up outside so it looked like a Spanish galleon, you know? The place lasted a couple years and then it got shuttered. They lost their asses, left a shitload of creditors that never got paid."

Bosch knew there would be records of ownership with state and local agencies monitoring alcohol licensing, maybe a bankruptcy filing as well. Getting the name of the bar was a good lead.

"Did you know them—the partners?" he asked.

"No, they were outsiders, not locals," Tommy said.

"What about their names?"

"Nah, not sure I ever knew the names of those guys."

"Who would?"

"That's a good question. Let me think. You going to drink or just ask questions?"

"Bourbon."

"I've got Michter's, Colonel Taylor, and a little bit of Blanton's left."

"Blanton's, neat."

"That's good, because I'm still waiting on my ice."

Tommy used the hand towel to polish a rock glass and then poured a generous shot of Blanton's. He put the glass down in front of Bosch. It looked like there was enough left in the round bottle for one more shot.

"Slainte," he said.

"Cheers," Bosch said.

A man entered the bar, carrying a large stainless-steel bucket full of ice. He hoisted it over the bar and Tommy took it and poured it into a bin. He handed the bucket back.

"Thanks, Rico."

Tommy looked at Bosch and pointed to the ice bin.

"I'm good," Bosch said.

Tommy held up a finger like he wanted to pause everything while he considered a new idea.

"I think I know somebody," he said. "You're going to take care of me for this, right?"

"I am," Bosch said.

He watched as Tommy pulled a corded phone out from under the counter, dialed a number, and waited. Bosch then heard Tommy's side of a brief conversation.

"Hey, remember the Irish Galleon? What happened with those two guys?"

Bosch wanted to take the phone and ask the questions, but he knew that was probably a quick way to end the call and Tommy's cooperation.

"Oh, right, yeah, I think I heard something about that," Tommy said. "What were their names?"

Bosch nodded. It was turning out he didn't need to coach Tommy.

"And where did Davy go?" Tommy asked.

The call ended a few seconds later, and Tommy looked at Bosch but didn't report what he had just heard. Bosch got the message and reached into his pocket. He had hit an ATM for four hundred dollars at the airport before takeoff the day before. The money had come in denominations of fifties and twenties. He now peeled four fifties off the fold of cash and put them down on the bar.

"The original owner was Dan Cassidy," Tommy said. "But he left the island after they closed the bar down."

"Where did he go?" Bosch asked.

"My guy didn't know. His friend from Ireland that he took on as a partner was Davy Byrne, but everybody thought that was bullshit."

"What do you mean?"

"It was an alias, clear as day. Davy Byrne's was the name of a pub in *Ulysses,* the Joyce novel about Dublin. Supposedly it's a real place over there, still in business after a hundred years. So people around here thought he was like an IRA guy or something who came here and changed his name because he was too hot to handle back there."

Bosch didn't say that the Troubles were largely in Northern Ireland, not Dublin.

"Did your guy say whether he ever met him?" he asked instead. "Think he could pick him out in a photo?"

"He didn't say but I doubt he ever did meet him," Tommy said. "He's got the Bud distributorship for all of Monroe County. So he knows what's going on in every bar in the Keys, but he hasn't driven a delivery route himself in years. He did say these guys stiffed him for a couple grand's worth of beer when they shut it down."

"You have a cell phone?"

"Sure."

"Can you take a photo of this and shoot it to your friend anyway? You never know."

Bosch unfolded the BOLO flyer on the bar top. Tommy looked at it for a long moment. Then he slid it down the bar until it was directly under one of the pendant lights, took a cell phone out of a pocket, and took a photo of the flyer. He handed the flyer back to Bosch.

"Los Angeles Police Department," he said. "I thought you weren't a cop anymore."

"I'm not," Bosch said. "That's old. From a case I had when I was still carrying the badge."

"He's like the one that got away or something? The white whale, 'Call me Ishmael,' and all of that?"

"*Moby-Dick,* right?"

"Yep. First line of the book."

Bosch nodded. He had never read the book but he knew who wrote it and that Moby Dick was the original white whale. Between the references to Joyce and Melville, he got the idea that he might be talking to the most well-read bartender in Key West. Tommy seemed to know that was what he was thinking.

"When it's slow in here, I read," he said. "So, what did he do? Your white whale."

"He killed a family of four," Bosch said.

"Shit."

"With a nail gun. The girl was nine and the boy thirteen. Then he buried them in a hole in the desert."

"Oh, man."

Tommy put his hand down on the fifties and slid them back across the bar top toward Bosch.

"I can't take your money. Not for something like that."

"You're helping me here."

"I'm sure no one's paying you to chase this guy down."

Bosch nodded. He understood. He then asked the most important question.

"Did your friend the beer distributor say whether Davy Byrne is still on the island?"

"He said, last he heard, Davy was working on the old charter docks. But that was a few years back when he heard that."

"Where are the old charter docks?"

"Right below the Palm Avenue Causeway. You got a car?"

"I do."

Tommy pointed toward the back of the bar.

"Easiest way is to take Front Street out of Old Town and get on Eaton," he said. "Eaton becomes Palm Avenue. You go over the bridge and there's the marina. You can't miss it."

"How many boats are we talking about out there?" Bosch asked.

"There's a lot. My buddy didn't know which boat this guy was supposedly working."

"Okay."

"And if I were you, I'd go now. This part of town is going to start filling up for sunset. Traffic will be a bitch and you'll never get out of here."

Bosch lifted his glass and took the first and last sip from it. The bourbon was sweet on his tongue but fire in his throat. He realized he probably should have ordered something that would have gone down easier, like a port or a cabernet.

"Thanks for your help, Tommy," he said. "Semper fi."

"Semper fi," Tommy said, apparently accepting the Marine salutation from a non-Marine. "Those tunnels, man…What a fucked-up place."

Bosch nodded.

"What a fucked-up world," he said.

"It's an angry world," Tommy said. "People do things you'd never expect."

Bosch took two of the fifties off the bar top and put them in his pocket. He slid the other two back toward Tommy.

"Finish off the Blanton's for me," he said.

"Glad to," Tommy said.

On his way out, Bosch held the door for a couple in shorts, sandals, and Hawaiian shirts on their way in.

49

BALLARD WAS LEANING against her car in front of Bosch's house, thinking about the last conversation they'd had. Bosch had said he was going to do the follow-up interview with Sheila Walsh about the Gallagher case. He had hoped she would trade protecting her son for revealing what she knew about Finbar McShane. Ballard decided that if she didn't find Bosch by the end of the day, then she would locate Sheila Walsh and pay her a visit as well.

Maddie Bosch's car came around the bend and she pulled into the empty carport. Ballard met her at the front door.

"I knocked," Ballard said. "No answer."

"Then I hope he's not in there," Maddie said.

"Why don't you let me do a quick circuit before you come in?"

"I'm a big girl, Renée."

"Just wanted to make the offer."

"I get it. Thank you."

Maddie took a set of keys out of her pocket and unlocked the door. Without hesitation, she pushed it open and entered ahead of Ballard.

"Dad?"

There was no answer. Ballard stepped into the living room and looked around to see if anything seemed out of place. She checked Bosch's stereo and saw that the record on the turntable was the King Curtis album he had been playing when she picked him up the week before. She guessed that his joining the cold case squad had fully consumed him to the point where he hadn't had time to listen his music.

"Dad, you here?"

Nothing.

"I'll check the back," Maddie said.

She disappeared down the hallway while Ballard went into the kitchen to check the sink and trash can for any signs of life. Both were clean and empty. Ballard went back to the living room and stepped into the dining room, where two neat stacks of documents sat on the table. She moved around behind it and leaned over to read what Bosch was last working on here. She could hear Maddie's steps on the wood floor and knew she was continuing to move about—a sign that her father was not back there.

Soon Maddie emerged from the bedroom wing of the house.

"He's not here," she said.

"The kitchen is clean and the trash can is empty," Ballard said. "Like he didn't want to leave anything that would stink up the house while he traveled."

"But where would he go?"

"That's the question. Do you know what sort of suitcase he has?"

"Oh, yeah. He has one suitcase. It's old and beat up, with wheels that barely turn anymore."

"Why don't you see if it's here."

"I'll check his closet."

Maddie went back down the hallway and Ballard leafed through one of the two stacks on the table. They were documents from the Gallagher Family case.

Ballard noticed that the table had a drawer, most likely to hold silverware or napkins if it was used as an eating table instead of a worktable. She reached down and slid it open. It contained mostly utensils from to-go meals as well as some pens, paper clips, and Post-it pads. There were also several loose pills in the drawer and an envelope with *Maddie* written on it. Curious, she lifted out the envelope and saw that it was sealed. She then picked up one of the pills. It was light blue and disk-shaped. There was no brand stamp or other identification other than the number 30 imprinted on it. She guessed that this meant the pill was a 30-milligram dose.

She heard Maddie's steps coming back down the hallway. Without giving it much thought, Ballard palmed the pill and closed the drawer as Maddie came into the room.

"The suitcase is there," Maddie said. "But he also has this duffel bag that he uses for short trips. That's gone. He went somewhere without telling me."

"Has that happened before?" Ballard asked.

"Well, not that I know of. He called me last week when he was just going to Chicago for one night. But who knows— he could have made lots of trips without telling me. There's no way for me to know."

"Right."

"But now I don't feel good about us being in here invading his privacy. I think we need to leave."

"Sure. I have an appointment downtown I've got to get to."

Maddie pulled her keys and stepped back so Ballard could go out first before she locked the door. Once she was outside, Ballard turned back to Maddie.

"I'm sorry if I overreacted, Maddie. It's just that we were in the middle of a case and, with him getting banged up Sunday, I was a little worried about him sort of disappearing without a word. But I'm sure he'll turn up."

Maddie nodded.

"Sure," she said, but she seemed unconvinced.

"How did he seem when you saw him Tuesday for lunch?" Ballard asked.

"Uh, okay. Normal. I mean, he was still sore from the crash, his knee was hurting him, but he was Dad. He was talking about wanting to get back to work on a case. The usual stuff for him."

"And nothing from him since that lunch?"

"No. Should I be worried, Renée?"

"I don't really know. Last we talked, he was going to see a witness that he had spoken to before but who was not going to like seeing him. And that was it."

"Maybe we have to go see that witness."

"We?"

"I'm off today. But I'm a cop and he's my father. Who was the witness?"

"Wait a minute. Let's not jump the gun here. Maybe he—"

"Who's jumping the gun? You said he went to see a witness— in a murder investigation, I assume. And no one has heard from him since. What's wrong with this picture?"

"Okay, look, I have to go downtown for a meeting at the D.A.'s office. Let me do that, and then I'll run down a location on the witness. If your dad doesn't show up by then, we'll go see her tonight."

Maddie said nothing and Ballard could tell she was frustrated by the delay.

"What you should do," Ballard said, "is go back inside and write a note to your dad that says he needs to call you as soon as he gets home. Just in case he's just out of pocket without a phone and we're worrying over nothing. Will you do that?"

"Yes," Maddie said sullenly.

"Okay, then I'm going to go, and let's keep each other in the loop. You okay?"

"I'm okay."

"Good. I'm sure everything's fine. I'll talk to you later."

They went their separate ways, Ballard to her car and Maddie back into the house.

Ballard drove down the hill and jumped on the Hollywood Freeway. She headed south to downtown.

Checking the time on the dashboard, she saw that she could just make it to the SID lab before her appointment at the District Attorney's office. She wanted to find out what the pills she had found loose in Bosch's worktable drawer were and what he would be taking them for. She knew she was committing a breach of Bosch's privacy that was far beyond what his own daughter had objected to earlier. But there was something going on with Bosch and she needed to find out what it was.

50

THE PARKING AT Charter Boat Row was wide open. All the action for the day was complete and most of the boats had been buttoned up for the night. Bosch walked along the seawall, reading the names of the boats and the signs showing contact information and charter availability. The boats ranged from thirty-foot open fishers to deep-sea cruisers with multiple decks, cabins, and lookout towers.

Near the end of the row, a man was using a hose to spray the decking of a large cruiser with an open salon and room for a large fishing party. It was low tide, so the boat and the man were below Bosch and the seawall. Eventually the man looked up and saw Bosch. He wore a salt-crusted baseball cap that said DECK DOCTOR on it. He pointed to the faucet where the hose he was using was attached.

"Hey, pal, can you turn the water off for me?" he called up.

Bosch walked over and turned off the hose.

"You get back in late?" Bosch asked casually. "Everybody else is gone."

"I don't go out," the man said. "I just clean boats."

"Got it. Deck Doctor. Do you clean Davy Byrne's boat?"

The man shook his head.

"Uh, he doesn't have a boat," he said. "The *CJ* is Henry Jordan's."

"The *CJ*," Bosch said. "Which one is that?"

"About nine or ten down. You walked right by it. *Calamity Jane.*"

"Oh, right, I saw it."

"Davy might act with the tourists like he owns it, but Henry kept a majority ownership. I know that for a fact."

"So Davy's just an investor?"

"More like an employee. But you'd have to ask Henry about that when he gets back."

"Back from where?"

"No idea. Can you hand me down the charge line?"

Bosch looked around and saw a thick yellow electric cord coiled and left on a hook attached to a steel girder. The girders supported the corrugated shade structure that ran the length of the boat row. One end of the cord was attached to a high-voltage plug. He unhooked the coil, fed some of it out, and then tossed the rest down to the Deck Doctor. The man walked the other end over to an electric attachment port beneath the gunwale and plugged it in. Bosch assumed it would recharge the boat's batteries and other electric devices.

"So," Bosch said. "How long has Henry been gone?"

"Almost a year, I guess," the Deck Doctor said. "He supposedly took Byrne's money and said, 'See ya.' He and the wife took off on a trip around the world and left Davy to run the boat, live on the floater, everything. A sweet deal, you ask me, but that's none of my business."

"What's a floater?"

"Houseboat. On the other side of the causeway, there's the marina on Garrison Bight. That's where all the floaters are, including Henry's. A lot of the guys with boats here live over there, get to walk to work."

Bosch nodded.

"Sweet," he said. "You don't know which one is Henry's floater, do you?"

"You mean the address? No," the Deck Doctor said. "But his is the one with the smiley-face pirate on the roof."

Bosch wasn't sure what that meant but didn't ask for clarification.

"You'll know it when you see it," the Deck Doctor said. "You some kind of cop or something?"

"Or something," Bosch said. "How long have you been doing this, working on the boats?"

"The quick answer is all my life. But if you mean here on the charters, I've had my cleaning business about eight years."

"How long has Davy Byrne been around?"

"Here? He definitely showed up after me. Maybe six years ago. I remember because old Henry was looking for a partner, and I was trying to scrape the cash together. But then Davy Byrne came along and beat me to it. To this day, I don't know how. He supposedly lost his ass on that pub he ran before he showed up here."

"I heard about that."

"Yeah, he couldn't run a bar right, then he shows up here and thinks he knows all about charters and catching fish."

Bosch nodded. He now had a solid grasp on the Deck Doctor's sour grapes.

"So, you said Henry's been gone almost a year?" Bosch asked.

"I don't know, at least eight or nine months," the Deck Doctor said. "Supposedly they're hitting all seven continents. But that's according to Davy Byrne."

"Listen, thanks for your help. Can you do me a favor? If you see Davy, don't mention me."

"Don't worry. I don't talk to that guy."

Bosch walked back down the row to his car. He saw that the sun was riding low in the sky. It would be sunset soon. He had planned to be at the Mallory docks, Key West's sunset mecca, for the island's signature moment, but he was juiced by the idea that he might know where Finbar McShane was. There would be another sunset tomorrow. If he was still here to see it.

The parking lane was one-way. It took him on a swing under the causeway and then out at the entrance to another marina. He saw boat ramps and, beyond them, the houseboats grouped together on the water like a floating village. Most of them had smaller runabouts with outboards attached to back-door docks and decks. The houseboats were painted in pastels, two-story structures sitting on barges and lashed together to create a community.

From Bosch's angle of view he counted eight houses extending out into Garrison Bight. The second-to-last house had a sloping gray roof with a large yellow smiley face painted on it. It had a black eye patch and a red bandanna with a skull-and-crossbones pattern. The siding of the house was a matching yellow, and a small outboard boat was tied up to its back porch.

The parking lot in front of the floaters was crowded. Bosch had to park in the next lot down and walk back. His knee was beginning to hurt again but he had left the bottle of Advil in the hotel room. By the time he got to the ramp down to the floaters, he was limping.

There was no security gate on the gangway leading down to the floaters. Bosch held the railing and carefully stepped down the steep ramp until he was on the wide and level concrete pier that connected all of the houseboats.

He casually walked down the pier like a tourist marveling at this floating neighborhood. He spent equal time checking out each residence on either side of the pier as he moved. When he came to the yellow house that was second from the end, he saw that the sliding door on a second-floor balcony was open with a screen pulled closed across it. He could hear music coming from inside—a reggae beat, but it wasn't a song he could identify.

Bosch used his injury to his advantage here. He stopped and leaned against a light pole at the end of the pier. He raised his left leg, bringing his foot up and down as if working out a stiff joint. And he studied the yellow floater. He saw that the decking extended down the right side of the house, offering a narrow access to the back deck and the skiff tied up to it. He also noted the double locks on the front door.

Satisfied with the intel he had gathered, Bosch headed back to the gangway. He had seen enough. He believed that the man he had been chasing for many years was inside the yellow house. He needed to go back to his hotel room. He needed to take more Advil and work out the plan for when he would come back under the cover of night.

51

BALLARD HAD BEEN ten minutes late to her four o'clock appointment with Vickie Blodget, the prosecutor assigned to handle cases from the unit. Ballard had always had an easy and open relationship with Blodget, but she was off her game in giving the case overview, leaving out details and delivering them out of order. She had been in a fog since leaving the lab. The Olga Reyes case had been pushed out of her brain by Ballard's need to find Harry Bosch.

"Let me make sure I understand the chain on this," Blodget said. "Bosch saw Rawls put the box in the dumpster, but then you waited three days to go retrieve it? Why?"

"No, no, that's not what I meant, and I'm sorry if I'm confusing you," Ballard said. "Bosch did not see him dump the box. It just came to him later that Rawls might have been in the process of dumping evidence when he saw Bosch and decided to make a run for it. So, in other words, he dumped the box, saw Bosch, then ran back to his car and took off."

"But why did you wait three days to go back? See, that's a problem. If he didn't see Rawls dump the box, we're going to have a difficult time linking it."

"Well, who else could it be? The dumpster is literally sixty feet from the back door of a serial killer's business. Bosch got banged up pretty good in what happened Sunday. He fucked up his knee and ribs in the crash, not to mention a bullet whizzing by his head and clipping his ear. It took him a couple days to put two and two together, and then we went dumpster diving."

Blodget nodded as she wrote a short note on a legal pad.

"Well, that's the thing," she said. "Those three days. It could have been anybody who dumped the box. As you know, the shootout with Rawls hit the media in a very big way. Somebody could have seen the story and then gone down there to dump the box, hoping it would be found and linked to Rawls."

The fog was burning away. Ballard stared at Blodget incredulously.

"You've got to be kidding me," she said. "What is going on here? This kid's been in prison for thirteen years. I mean, he's not even a kid anymore. He shouldn't be there."

"Are you a hundred percent sure about that?" Blodget asked.

"Yes, I am. Jorge Ochoa is innocent."

"It was a DNA match."

"Yeah, and she was his girlfriend. That was his defense: they had sex that night, he went home, and the killer came next. And now we know that's what happened. It was Rawls, not Ochoa. The murder weapon was in the box. You have the autopsy report right there in front of you. Blunt force trauma, circular impacts to the skull, one inch in diameter. Those were hammer blows, Vickie. It's obvious."

"I know all of that, Renée. That's not the point. We need linkage to Rawls. Were there any prints on the box? Anything that directly ties it or its contents to him?"

"No, I had it processed. No prints, no fibers, no DNA from Rawls. But remember, he was getting rid of the box. He would have made sure it was clean and not traceable to him. The only flaw in the plan was that we were onto him and Bosch was watching. He didn't count on that until he saw Bosch and tried to flee."

"There are just too many holes in it. I can't take it across the street. Not yet. I need you to get more evidence."

Blodget's office was in the Hall of Justice, which was directly across Temple Street from the downtown criminal courthouse, where the elected D.A.'s office was located on the sixteenth floor.

"You said Bosch got into an argument with a resident there," Blodget said. "Did you talk to this man? Did he see Rawls dump the box?"

"I doubt he had an angle on it," Ballard said. "But no, we haven't talked to him. I didn't think it was necessary when the rest is so obvious."

"And nothing in property or evidence storage from the case?"

"No. After Ochoa lost his last appeal, there was an evidence disposal order from the court. There is nothing but what you have right there. No crime scene to go back to, no witnesses to show photos of Rawls to. Just the box."

Blodget nodded and wrote something down.

"Then there's nothing I can do at the moment," she said. "I'm sorry, Renée."

"This is because of the recall, isn't it?" Ballard said.

The district attorney was facing a recall election because his liberal policies of making it more difficult to send offenders to prison had resulted in a surge in crime stats across Los Angeles County. New directives from the sixteenth floor, which did not require bail for most crimes, prevented prosecutors from adding penalty enhancements for use of guns in the commission of crimes, and deferred prosecution for misdemeanors and even some violent felonies, had created a revolving-door justice system. The media routinely reported on suspects freshly released from jail without bail or without being charged and then committing exactly the same types of crimes—sometimes within hours.

Though the D.A. attempted to blame this on the Covid pandemic and the need to lessen crowding in jails during the crisis, he had lost the support of the law enforcement agencies in the county as well as a significant percentage of the populace. A well-funded recall campaign was underway. A story about the D.A.'s Office putting an innocent man in prison—even though it was long before the current D.A. was elected—was not going to help him keep his job.

"Look, I'm not going to deny the reality of what is happening across the street," Blodget said. "But I know how this will go. I go over there with this case as it is, and they'll kill it and Ochoa never gets free."

"So you're telling me to wait until after the recall," Ballard said. "Make Jorge Ochoa wait up there in Corcoran for another six months for something he didn't do, never mind all the years he's already spent there."

"What I'm telling you is that if I take it across the street right now and it gets rejected, then good luck taking it a second time, no matter who is in the corner office on sixteen."

Ballard nodded and held her tongue. She knew Blodget was not her enemy. The situation was what it was. And she needed to keep Blodget on her side because there would be future cases with issues that would come in wobbling. She would need Blodget then.

Ballard also knew this was not the only place she could take the case. There was an alternate way to free Jorge Ochoa if she wanted to risk it.

"Okay," she said. "Thanks for hearing me out. But I'll be back with this one when the time and evidence is right."

"I hope you do bring it to me, Renée," Blodget said.

Ballard got up to leave.

As she left the Major Crimes Unit, her cheeks grew hot with humiliation as she thought about the meeting earlier that day at the house where Jorge Ochoa grew up. The distrust that Jorge's brother had voiced about the police and the justice system had just been validated. Ballard had promised to stay in touch with Jorge's mother and brother, but now she had no idea how she would ever be able to face them again.

Waiting for the elevator, Ballard checked her phone and saw she had no signal. This was not surprising. The Major Crimes Unit was located in the former jail at the top of the Hall of Justice. Though renovated into offices years earlier, the floors and walls were still concrete and reinforced with steel to prevent escape. The structure was notorious for knocking out cell service. It wasn't until Ballard stepped out of the elevator on the ground floor that her texts and voice mail messages came through. There were several from Maddie Bosch.

Call me.

Need to talk ASAP.

Where are you?

There were also two voice mails but Ballard didn't bother to listen to them, deciding to quickly call back instead as she headed down Spring Street to the PAB. Maddie picked up the call right away and spoke as if they were already in mid-conversation.

"This is weird. After I went back into the house to write my dad a note, I found this envelope in a drawer with my name on it. So I opened it, and it was this long letter to me about how good a person I am and how I'm strong and what a good cop I'll be. Like stuff he wanted me to know after he's gone, you know?"

Ballard knew exactly what the note was meant for but didn't want to make Maddie any more upset than she was.

"Well, Maddie," she said. "Maybe it was just something he—"

"And then I fucking missed a call from him," Maddie interjected. "I was so stressed about this note I found and I couldn't get you, so I went and I worked out at the station, and he called while I was in the shower afterward."

"Did he leave a message?"

"Yes. He said he was in Key West and he was fine. But it was kind of weird."

"What do you mean? How was it weird?"

"Well, not like him. He was saying he was fine and he was working a case and that he loved me very much. He just didn't sound right. He said I was the best thing that ever happened in his life. And then with the note I found…I don't know. I'm really worried."

"Do you have the number he called from on your phone?"

"Yes, I called it back as soon as I heard the message. It's a hotel in Key West, and I asked for Harry Bosch's room and they put me through. But he didn't answer. I've called three times and he doesn't answer."

"What's the hotel?"

"It's called the Pier House."

"Okay, I'm on it, Maddie. I'll call you back as soon as I know something."

"And listen, there's one more thing that adds to the weirdness of what's going on with him."

"What?"

"I was looking for paper to write a note on and I opened a drawer in his worktable. That's where I found the note to me. But there were also some loose pills in there. And the unit I'm on now, we've backed up enough narco operations for me to know counterfeit fentanyl when I see it. I don't know where he got it or why, but he has fucking fentanyl in that drawer."

It was a confirmation of the information Ballard had gotten earlier at the lab.

"Okay, Maddie, try to stay calm," Ballard said. "There's gotta be an explanation for that. And he'll tell us once we find him. So let's just calm down until we get to that point."

"Okay, I'll try," Maddie said. "But please find him. And let me know what I can do to help. I mean it."

"I understand. And I will."

Ballard disconnected, then immediately did an internet search on her phone for the Key West Police Department. She called the main number, identified herself, and asked for the commanding officer on duty. She told a lieutenant named Burke that she needed an emergency welfare check on a guest at the Pier House. She gave him Bosch's details and asked for a callback as soon as he was checked on.

Not knowing how long it would take the KWPD to react, Ballard next called the Pier House and talked to the man in charge of the hotel's security. She explained the situation and asked him to go to Bosch's room for a welfare check. He in turn explained that their policy did not allow them to force entry into a possibly occupied guest room without the police being present.

"Well, they're on their way," Ballard said.

She disconnected and felt useless waiting on word from people three thousand miles away. She opened a search window on her phone and tried to figure out how fast she could get to Key West. Fifteen minutes later, she had just reserved a rental car to go with the red-eye flight to Miami that she had booked when a call came in with a 786 area code.

"It's Bob Burke, KWPD."

"Did you check his room?"

"We did, but it was empty. Bosch is not there and there's no indication of anything amiss. Two shirts on hangers in the closet, a toothbrush, a duffel bag. His wallet is in a drawer next to the bed. One of my guys asked around, and the bartender in the Chart Room said Bosch was in there earlier and had an expensive shot of bourbon. I don't know if it helps, but the bartender said he was asking about an Irish guy named Davy Byrne. That ring any bells?"

Ballard hesitated. It sounded like Bosch might have located Finbar McShane, or at least the alias he was using.

"Uh, the name isn't right," she said. "But he was tracking a suspect in a cold case we're working out here. The suspect's Irish."

"Well, maybe he found him," Burke said. "But there's no

sign of foul play in his room. I'll do some digging around here, check with our dayside people to see if they know anything about this."

"Please do, and call me as soon as you know something. I'm flying out tonight and will be on the ground in Miami at dawn."

"You got it. And, oh, I nearly forgot this. There was one other thing with the room. There was an envelope on the desk. It was sealed and addressed to someone named Renée. Does that mean—"

"Yes, that's me. Why would he have a note there for me? I'm in L.A."

"That I don't know. Maybe he knew you'd be flying out."

That suggestion gave Ballard pause. Was Bosch manipulating her from three thousand miles away?

"None of this is adding up," she said. "Another thing is, why would he go out without his wallet? It doesn't make sense."

"It was in a drawer. Maybe he forgot it. Maybe he didn't want to risk losing it."

Neither possibility seemed plausible to Ballard. Her anxiety about Bosch was growing.

"Could you go back in and open the envelope addressed to me?" she asked.

"Uh, no, we're not going to do that without being able to show cause," Burke said. "Right now, we have no crime and no evidence of a crime. We can't go beyond the welfare check we already conducted. I'm sure I don't need to school you on the Fourth Amendment and unlawful search and seizure."

"You don't, Lieutenant. It's just that—"

"I'll get back to you if I learn anything from our dayside team. Okay, Detective?"

"Okay. Thank you."

Ballard disconnected and checked the time. Her red-eye was scheduled to take off in four hours. That left enough time for her to track down Sheila Walsh and find out what had sent Bosch to Key West.

52

BOSCH SAT IN the parking lot at Garrison Bight and watched the floating houses in darkness. The full moon above cast a line of undulating yellow reflection on the water, like a pathway to the house with the smiley-face pirate on the roof. He watched the lights inside the houses go out one by one. The house where Davy Byrne lived was the last to go dark.

Bosch watched and waited for another hour, the bourbon from hours earlier still backing up like fire in his throat. He contemplated his plan and the risks involved, knowing that one way or another, there would be justice before dawn for Stephen Gallagher, his wife, and his young son and daughter.

Finally, at 3 a.m., he got out of his car and walked toward the gangway leading down to the floating homes. He was wearing clothes as dark as the sky. His hands were gloved and he carried a screwdriver he had bought at the CVS across Front Street from the Pier House.

The gangway was slick with moisture caused by the night's dropping temperature. He gripped the handrail and moved down it slowly and carefully, mindful that any misstep would set off a flare of pain in his knee. He was managing it at the moment with a fresh dose of painkillers.

Once he was on the concrete pier, he expected to be exposed by motion-sensitive lights on the houses, but no light flashed on. He suspected that the gentle movement of the floating homes would be a constant trigger and that had led to the banishment of such basic security measures.

When he got to the second house from the end, he crossed the gangway onto the foredeck without hesitation. He stopped there and waited and listened, attempting to determine if his arrival had been noticed.

Nothing happened, and he moved to the side deck that led to the rear of the house. He had brought the screwdriver so he could pop the sliding door on the rear deck and gain entrance, but when he got to the back, he saw that the slider had been left open a foot and that a screen door was the only thing between him and entrance to the house.

The screen door was locked, but he used the screwdriver to easily poke a hole through the screening. Then his fingers tore it wide enough to fit his hand through. He reached in, unlocked the door, and then carefully and quietly slid it open.

He slipped into the home. Stepping out of moonlight, he found complete darkness inside. He waited a few moments for his eyes to adjust. He saw a large flat-screen TV attached to a wall and a couch set against the wall opposite, a low table in front of it. Beyond the room where he stood was a dining room and a pass-through window to a kitchen. The glow from a digital clock on a microwave told him it was now 3:10.

On the right he saw the form of a set of stairs leading to the second level. He took a step toward the stairs but stopped when he heard a voice from behind.

"Don't fucking move."

Bosch froze. A light came on behind him. He raised his hands to shoulder height and slowly turned. He dropped the screwdriver down his sleeve as he did so.

A man sat on a stuffed chair in the corner next to the sliding door. Bosch had entered and walked right by him in the dark. The man was holding a gun pointed at Bosch's chest.

It was Finbar McShane. Bosch easily recognized him from the photos on the BOLO sheet in his back pocket. He had a full beard now that had gone to gray and a shaved scalp that was darkly tanned from days on the open water on the *Calamity Jane*. He had obviously been waiting in the dark for Bosch.

"Who are you?" he asked.

"Doesn't matter who I am," Bosch said. "Who told you I was coming?"

Bosch hoped it hadn't been Tommy, the bartender at the Chart Room.

"Nobody had to tell me," McShane said. "I saw you out there today, trying to look like a tourist in your cop clothes. I know tourists and I know cops."

"I'm not a cop. Not anymore."

"What the fuck does that mean?"

"It means this is over. There are others and they know I'm here. They'll follow. You're done…McShane."

The use of his real name put a momentary alarm in his eyes, but then it was quickly gone, replaced by the confidence of knowing he had the gun and the upper hand.

"Turn around. All the way around."

Bosch was wearing black jeans and a maroon dress shirt. He hadn't planned on working under cover of night when he had packed for the trip. He turned, keeping his hands up, showing he had no weapon. He came all the way around and they were looking at each other again.

"Let's see your ankles," McShane said.

Bosch nodded. McShane was playing it smart, not coming close to Bosch, in case he was hiding a weapon. Bosch reached down and pulled the legs of his pants up, careful to keep the screwdriver from falling out of his sleeve. He showed that he wore no ankle holster.

"No weapon," McShane said. "You came to kill me and you didn't bring a weapon?"

"I didn't come to kill you," Bosch said.

"Then what? Why are you here?"

"I want to hear you say it."

"Say what, motherfucker? Stop talking in riddles."

"That you killed the Gallagher family."

"Jesus Christ...you're from L.A. Well, you came a long way for nothing, old man. To end up at the end of an anchor chain in forty feet of water."

"Is that what happened to Henry Jordan and his wife? You wrapped them in chains, put them in the water? How about Dan Cassidy? Is he down there, too?"

Now Bosch saw a momentary look of surprise on McShane's face.

"Like I said, there are people who know all about you," Bosch said. "And they're coming right behind me. This time you don't get away."

"Really? You think?"

"I know. So you have a choice. Tell me about the Gallaghers and we go back to L.A. Or you make your move here and try to run."

McShane laughed.

"Boy, I guess that's what you call a no-brainer," he said.

"I doubt you'll get much further than Marathon," Bosch said.

"Yeah? Well, you got some balls, old man, I'll give you that. But I also got news for you, I'm not going back. And what makes you think I'd even try to drive out of here?"

"Because before I came here, I visited your boat. *Calamity Jane*? It's not going anywhere with water in its fuel tanks."

"You'd better be bluffing, you fuck."

"I guess you could take a plane, but that's so easily tracked. The Overseas Highway is your only real choice and that's a long drive. They'll pick you up before you get to the mainland."

"You've got it all figured out, don't you?"

Bosch didn't answer. He just stared at the gun, ready for it, ready for the end. McShane stood up, keeping it aimed at his heart.

"So you're wearing a wire, then? Sent in here to get me to confess? Open your fuckin' shirt."

Bosch lowered his right hand and started unbuttoning his shirt.

"No, no wire," he said, opening his shirt. "Just you and me. I want to hear you say it. Then do what you have to do."

McShane took a step closer.

"I'll give you what you want, old man. I'll tell you. But they will be the last words you ever hear."

"Were they asleep?"

"What?"

"Emma and Stephen Junior. The kids. Were they asleep when you killed them? Or did they know what was coming?"

"Would that make it better for you? If they were asleep, if they didn't know."

"Were they?"

"No, they were on their knees. And they knew what was coming. Just like their parents. What do you think of that?"

McShane's eyes were bright with the memory, and in his dark pupils Bosch saw an emptiness that was void of all humanity. A deep rage welled up in him as he flashed on photos he had once carried of Emma and Stephen Jr. A primal scream for justice came from the darkest folds of his heart.

McShane seemed to sense what was coming and lurched toward Bosch, raising the barrel of the gun toward his face.

"Turn around. Get up against the fucking wall."

Bosch was ready for it. He dropped his hands and dipped his shoulders to the right as if about to turn as instructed. But then he took a half step back to his left, dropping the screwdriver out of his sleeve and into his hand.

As McShane came in close, Bosch shot his right hand out to grab the gun and deflect its aim upward. At the same moment, he brought his left arm up and drove the screwdriver into McShane's ribs.

McShane's body tensed with the impact and he groaned. Still holding him close, Bosch pulled the screwdriver back and then savagely drove it in a second time, this thrust delivered at a new and upward angle. He threw his full weight into McShane and rode him four feet back and crashing into the wall.

He pinned him there, holding the hand with the gun up and

keeping pressure on the screwdriver. He felt McShane's sticky and warm blood on the hand that gripped the tool.

Leaning into McShane, Bosch was close enough now to feel his last, desperate breaths on his face. He had not killed a man so close since the tunnels of fifty years before. He held McShane's eyes as he felt the tension and strength in his body weaken and start to ebb away with his life.

McShane's grip on the gun weakened and finally released. The weapon bounced off Bosch's shoulder and clattered to the floor. Then McShane started to slide down the wall, his eyes holding a surprised look in them.

Bosch let him go and he dropped into a sitting position, propped against the wall, still pierced by the screwdriver. His blood soon flowed down his body and to the floor.

Bosch kicked the gun across the floor, stepped back, and watched McShane bleed out, his eyes losing their focus and finally staring blankly at nothing at all.

53

THE RED-EYE LANDED at Miami International at 6 a.m. and Ballard was on the road to Key West within an hour, a large coffee in the cup holder of her rental car. Her biggest concern at the moment was staying alert during the four-hour drive and keeping the rental between the lines on the Overseas Highway. The plane from L.A. had been full and she had booked one of the last seats. She'd been assigned a middle seat in economy and ended up bookended by two men who had no trouble falling asleep and snoring for the whole flight.

She, in turn, didn't sleep a wink. Instead, she thought about Harry Bosch and what he might be doing so far from home.

Halfway down the archipelago to her destination, she moved out of range from the Miami radio stations and ended up listening to a Florida Keys weather station, which repeated the same news every fifteen minutes. An unusual pre–hurricane season storm had formed off the coast of Africa and was heading toward the Caribbean. The anchor at the weather station in Marathon said they were watching this development closely.

She was less than ten miles from Key West and about to call the KWPD, when her phone buzzed. It was a call from L.A., where it was not yet 8 a.m. She took the call.

"This is Renée Ballard."

"Mick Haller. You left me a message last night."

"Yes, I did."

"Sounds like you're driving. Can you talk?"

"I can talk. I'm a detective with the LAPD. I've worked with Harry Bosch."

"My brother from another mother. I know who you are, Ballard. Is this about Harry? Is he all right?"

She didn't want to get into the possibility that Bosch was not all right.

"It's about a case I think you should take on," she said.

"A little unusual to get a referral from the police," Haller said. "But go ahead, talk to me."

"Let me start by saying this is a nonreferral referral. You can't say I tipped you to the case."

"I understand."

"I need to hear you say it."

"It's a nonreferral referral. If I move forward with whatever it is you're about to tell me, your involvement ends with this call and I will not reveal it to anyone. Good?"

"Good."

"Then talk to me. I have to get ready for court."

"Olga Reyes. LAPD case number zero-nine-dash-zero-four-one-eight. You should write it down. She was murdered in 2009. Her boyfriend, Jorge Ochoa, was wrongfully accused and convicted of murder."

"A habeas case. You know how hard a habeas case is?"

"But you've gotten innocent men out. Harry told me."

"Yeah, once in a blue moon."

"This is a blue moon, then. Ochoa is innocent, and the LAPD

and the D.A.'s Office know it. They're sitting on it because of the recall election."

There was silence on the other end.

"Are you still there?" Ballard asked.

"I'm here," Haller said. "Go on."

"I run the Open-Unsolved Unit. You heard about the Ted Rawls case?"

"Of course. I also heard it was Harry who was on one side of that gun fight. I've left him five messages this week, but he hasn't called me back."

"He probably didn't get them. His phone is still in evidence. Anyway, Ochoa was convicted of killing his girl-friend. It was a slam dunk DNA case. Only he didn't kill her. Rawls did."

"So the shorthand is, you found evidence linking Rawls to Olga Reyes and the D.A.'s sitting on it."

"You're good."

"Good and pissed off. This guy Jorge is where now?"

"Corcoran."

"Okay, what do I subpoena? Who do I subpoena?"

"You subpoena me and all evidence related to the Olga Reyes case. I gave you the number. We found items missing from the Reyes crime scene in a dumpster behind Rawls's business office. He had just dumped it when he saw that Harry was watching him. The rest you know from the news."

Haller made a slight whistling sound, then spoke.

"What's the evidence?"

"Her nightgown and a bracelet Jorge gave her. I went to see his mother and she confirmed the bracelet."

"That's how I get into this. I go see the mother, sign her up,

375

and take it from there. Nobody will ever know the tip came from you."

"I appreciate that. Also, we have the murder weapon, a hammer. Rawls kept it all. You can match the hammer to the autopsy report."

"You're putting this on a silver platter for me. You got the mother's name and address handy?"

"As soon as I'm off the road, I'll send them to you."

"Okay, then. I think I'm good to go."

"Thank you for doing this."

"A pleasure, Detective Ballard. You'll be hearing from me, and if I get this into court and put you on the stand, you may regret this phone call."

"I'm not worried about that. If you treat me as a hostile witness, it will be good cover. But you'll also be calling Harry Bosch. He worked this with me."

"I guess we'll cross that bridge when we come to it."

After disconnecting, Ballard called the KWPD to arrange for an officer to meet her at the Pier House so she could have the door to Bosch's room opened by security. She wanted to read the note he had sealed and addressed to her. She believed it would give her insight into where Bosch was and what he was up to.

When she got to the Pier House fifteen minutes later, there was already a KWPD car in the parking lot. Ballard parked next to it and entered the lobby and found two uniformed officers waiting for her with the resort's head of security. She showed her badge and credentials, and the resort security man, Munoz, said he had a key card to Bosch's room ready to go. They all walked out a rear door of the lobby and onto a pathway through a maze of lush tropical trees and plants, around a pool, and toward a building containing four floors of rooms.

They squeezed into a small elevator, because the security man said it was closer than the stairs to room 202.

At the door of the room, the security man knocked and leaned his head toward the doorjamb to listen.

"Resort security," he called out. "Mr. Bosch? Security."

He waited a few seconds and then knocked again. He pulled a key card from his pocket to unlock the door.

"Security," he said. "We are opening the door."

54

BOSCH WAS SO deeply asleep that the first knock on the door barely penetrated his dream about the tunnels. He was moving endlessly through a dark and tight space with no beginning and no end.

On the second knock, he opened his eyes. He was on a bed in a strange room. It was dark, the curtains drawn, save for the light from the bathroom. He heard the click from the room's door. He sat up.

"Don't shoot!" he called out. "Don't shoot!"

They opened the door, came in, and walked down the entrance hallway and into the room.

He saw it was Ballard, along with a man in a suit and two uniformed officers.

"Harry," she said. "Are you all right?"

"Renée," he said. "What are you—you came."

She didn't answer him. She turned to the men behind her and held her hands up in a stay-back gesture.

"He's fine," she said. "False alarm. Everything's okay. You can all—"

"Are you sure, ma'am?" the suit said. "He looks confused."

"You woke me up," Bosch said. "Yeah, I'm confused."

He checked his hands and clothes for blood but all were clean. He had fallen asleep in his clothes. His hair was still slightly damp from the shower after the long night's cleanup.

The older of the two officers pushed past Ballard and entered the bedroom. He turned on the lamp on the bedside table and looked at Bosch, who was now sitting on the side of the bed. Bosch's feet were bare and he was wearing a clean long-sleeved shirt and pants. He had not packed anything to sleep in.

"Sir, are you all right?" the officer asked.

"I'm fine," Bosch said. "I'm just not used to people coming into my room in the middle of the night."

"Sir, it's almost noon. Have you ingested any drugs or alcohol?"

"No, nothing. I'm fine. I'm just…tired. I stayed up too late."

"Would you like medical attention?"

"No, I don't want medical attention."

"Are you planning to harm yourself or others?"

Bosch forced a laugh and shook his head.

"Are you kidding? No, I have no plans to 'harm' anyone, including myself."

"Okay, sir, we're going to leave you with your colleague. Is that okay?"

"That's okay. That would make me happy."

"Okay, sir, you have a good day."

"Thank you. I'm sorry for the callout. I'm just a deep sleeper, I guess."

The officer turned and headed to the door, followed by his partner. He had a radio mike on his shoulder. He turned his mouth toward it and reported to dispatch that they were clearing this scene without incident. The man in the suit followed the officers out.

"Thanks, guys," Ballard called after them. "Sorry for the false alarm."

Bosch heard the door shut. He waited for Ballard to speak first.

"Harry, what the fuck?"

"What? What are you doing here?"

"Like them, making sure you're okay."

"You flew across the country to make sure I was okay?"

"I think you wanted me to. The Sheila Walsh interview. The call to Maddie. You were leaving bread crumbs."

"If you say so."

"I do."

Bosch stood up and looked around for his socks and shoes. They were on the floor by a chair in the corner. He walked over, sat down, and started putting them on.

"You found McShane, didn't you?"

Bosch didn't answer. He concentrated on the task of tying his shoelaces. He then stood up and pulled the curtain open. He squinted at the harsh sunlight reflecting like cut diamonds off the water and into his eyes.

"Where's the note you left for me?" Ballard asked.

Bosch looked back at her. She was still standing by the door from the entry hall, like she didn't want to come all the way into his room.

"What note?" he said.

"This wasn't the first wellness check on you, Harry. They came in last night. You were gone but your wallet was in the drawer, and there was an envelope with my name on it on the desk. Bread crumbs."

"I don't know what you're talking about."

"Sure you do."

"There's no note, Renée."

She was silent and Bosch knew that she had figured out everything.

"Then I guess that means you did find him. What happened?"

Bosch looked back out at the water.

"Let's just say the case is closed," he said. "And leave it at that."

"Harry," Ballard said. "What did you do?"

"It's closed. That's all you need to know. Sometimes..."

"Sometimes what?"

"Sometimes you do the wrong thing for the right reason. And this was that time and this was that case."

"Oh, Harry..."

Bosch read her disappointment and anguish all in the way she said his name. He still couldn't turn to face her.

"Would it help you to know I had no choice?" he asked.

"No, not really," Ballard said. "Whatever happened, however it happened, you put it in play."

Bosch nodded. He knew that was true.

"Can we just talk about something else?" he said.

"Like what?" Ballard said. "Like about your little blue pills?"

"What are you talking about?"

"The knockoff fentanyl I found in the drawer at your house. That your daughter also found."

Bosch turned away from the view and looked at her.

"You were in my house?"

"You were missing in action. I was worried. So was Maddie. She found the pills and the note you left for her."

"Shit, that's been in there for a long time. Months."

"Well, she read it and is understandably upset. Add in the pills, and it's a goodbye note. What's going on with you, Harry?"

"I'll talk to Maddie. She wasn't supposed to find that note for at least a few months."

"What does that mean?"

Bosch moved over and sat down on the end of the bed.

"Your empath, Colleen? She was right."

"What are you talking about?"

"About the dark aura she thought at first was coming from me."

"Tell me what that means."

"I told you about that case I had, where I found the missing cesium."

"Yes."

"Yeah, well, it's come back around. The pills they were giving me only delayed things. It's in the marrow now."

There was a long pause before Ballard reacted.

"I'm sorry, Harry. Are they still treating you?"

"I've had some radiation, yeah."

"What is the prognosis? How long before—"

"I haven't asked, because I don't want to know. I keep those pills in the drawer for when it's time for the end of watch."

"Harry, you can't do that. Maddie doesn't know any of this?"

"No, and I didn't want her to."

Bosch looked up and over his shoulder at her.

"Okay," Ballard said. "But you need to tell her. In fact, we need to call her right now to tell her I found you and you're okay."

"We can call her but she doesn't need to know about this other stuff," Bosch said. "She's starting her life and she shouldn't have to worry about me."

"This really fucking sucks."

"It is what it is. I take those pills out of the drawer every morning. Then I put them back at the end of the day. When it's the right time, I won't."

"You can't do that, Harry."

"If I don't, it's going to get messy. I don't want that. I want Maddie to have the house and a life without any ghosts."

"But that's exactly what you'll be leaving her. A ghost."

"I really don't want to talk about this anymore, Renée. I'll talk to Maddie when I get back to L.A. Right now, I need to make a call."

"A call to who?"

"Stephen Gallagher's sister in Ireland."

"What will you tell her?"

"Not much. Just that justice is done, and I'll leave it at that. I think they're five hours ahead of us over there. I don't want to wait too long. It should be daylight for her when I call."

"Then what?"

"Then I'm going to drive back to Miami and try to catch a plane home."

"Will you at least text your daughter and tell her you're okay?"

"I don't have a phone. Why don't you text her and say I'll talk to her tomorrow. I have to think of what to say."

"All right, Harry. I'll do that."

"Thank you. What about you? You just got here. You want to go back with me?"

Ballard looked past him and out at the water.

"I was thinking of sticking around for sunset," she said. "They're supposed to be awesome here."

Bosch nodded.

"That's what I hear," he said.

"Tell me one thing," Ballard said. "Off the record or whatever way you want to."

"I'll try."

"Did you come here to kill him?"

Bosch was silent for a long time before he answered.

"No," he finally said. "That wasn't the plan at all."

EPILOGUE

BY PRIOR AGREEMENT, Ballard drove because Bosch didn't want to put the miles on his rental. She picked him up at six and they were at the spot off the Old Spanish Trail before eight, thanks to her use of the car's code 3 lights and a steady ninety-mile-per-hour pace.

Bosch got out with the wooden box that carried the ashes of the Gallagher family. Years before, Siobhan Gallagher had asked Bosch to scatter the ashes of her brother and his family because it didn't seem right to send them back to her in Ireland, the place Stephen had left so long ago. Bosch said he would do it, but he had waited, deciding not to carry out the final task until he had closed the case and brought justice for the family.

Now was the time.

They walked through the brush to the place where the four rock sculptures stood near the mesquite tree. None of the towers had crumbled since Bosch's last visit. They stood solidly balanced at four different heights: father, mother, son, and daughter.

Ballard and Bosch had not spoken much during the drive. It had been that way since Key West. But when he had told her of his plan to go to the desert to scatter the ashes, she had immediately asked if she could join him. And now they were there, at the hallowed ground where she knew Bosch had drawn the fire and the drive to take the case to its end—to a place where he had done the wrong thing for the right reason.

They stood in front of the rocks, Bosch holding the box with two hands. A dry wind was coming down out of the north, gently moving the petals on the flowers at their feet. Ballard started with an easy question.

"How'd things go with Maddie?"

Bosch seemed to consider an answer for a while before speaking.

"We talked and she now knows what's going on with me. She's not happy that I kept it from her, but I think she understands why I did. She said she wanted to move back home to take care of me but I said no. She's got her own life to live. I just hope I don't become a distraction that makes her lose focus on the job."

Ballard nodded.

"She's a good cop," she said. "I think she'll be fine."

Bosch offered nothing else. Ballard squatted and picked one of the small white flowers. Holding the stem between her thumb and forefinger, she spun it like a pinwheel.

"Why did McShane pick this spot?" she asked. "Was it random?"

"Probably," Bosch said. "But we'll never know. One of the known unknowns, I guess."

"I thought maybe he would have told you."

Bosch turned his eyes from the rocks to look down at her.

"No, he didn't," he said.

"That's too bad," Ballard said. "Did he own up to any of it?"

She stood up next to him and he nodded.

"Yeah. All of it. He told me he did it."

"Under duress?"

Bosch scoffed.

"He had the gun, not me."

Ballard understood now how it had gone down.

"You know what I think? I think you went there to trade yourself for that confession. You left your bread crumbs and were willing to sacrifice yourself if it meant someone would be able to follow and take him to ground. That we'd get him for you, if not for everything before. But then something happened...and you changed your mind."

Bosch maintained a silent vigil for almost a minute. Then he nodded toward the two shortest towers of rock.

"They were awake and...aware...when he killed them. Those two kids. It was the question I always carried, and that haunted me more than him getting away with it."

He stopped there, but Ballard said nothing.

"It's an angry world," Bosch said. "People do things you'd never expect. That they'd never expect themselves."

Ballard nodded.

"I get it."

"No. I hope you never get it."

Silence followed. Ballard looked around, checking the distant ridgeline and the salt flats and then bringing her eyes back to the flowers at her feet.

"It's so easy to forget that there's great beauty in the desert," she said.

Bosch nodded.

"And these flowers, they're amazing," Ballard said.

"Desert star," Bosch said. "I know a guy, says they're a sign of god in this fucked-up world. That they're relentless and resilient against the heat and the cold, against everything that wants to stop them."

Ballard nodded.

"Like you," Bosch added.

Ballard looked at him. He said nothing else. It took her a moment to find her voice.

"Thank you, Harry," she said. "For telling me the truth."

They stood silently for a long moment before he spoke again.

"You know I'm not coming back to the unit, right?"

"Yes, I know."

He opened the top of the wooden box and stepped closer to the rock sculptures. He reached in and took a handful of the gray dust. He held his hand out and let it fall through his fingers. He did it three more times and then he turned the box over and let the rest pour out, a gust of wind taking much of it away and across the land.

"Ashes to ashes," he said. "Isn't that what they say?"

He then closed the box, turned, and started walking back to the car.

"I'm ready," he said.

Ballard followed.

They got in the car and drove off, back to the city.

ACKNOWLEDGMENTS

The author wishes to thank many for their help and contributions to this novel. They include Asya Muchnick, Emad Akhtar, Bill Massey, Pamela Marshall, Mitzi Roberts, Rick Jackson, Tim Marcia, David Lambkin, Dennis Wojciechowski, Jane Davis, Heather Rizzo, Henrik Bastin, Linda Connelly, Paul Connelly, Terrill Lee Lankford, Shannon Byrne, and William Ahmanson. Any factual shortcuts or mistakes in the politics, procedures, forensics, nephrology, geography, botany, and investigative genetic genealogy are strictly the fault of the author.

ABOUT THE AUTHOR

MICHAEL CONNELLY is the author of thirty-six previous novels, including #1 *New York Times* bestsellers *The Dark Hours* and *The Law of Innocence*. His books, which include the Harry Bosch series, the Lincoln Lawyer series, and the Renée Ballard series, have sold more than eighty million copies worldwide. Connelly is a former newspaper reporter who has won numerous awards for his journalism and his novels. He is the executive producer of three television series: *Bosch, Bosch: Legacy,* and *The Lincoln Lawyer.* He spends his time in California and Florida.